Also available from
ROSEMARY ROGERS
and MIRA Books

SURRENDER TO LOVE
AN HONORABLE MAN
WICKED LOVING LIES
A RECKLESS ENCOUNTER
SWEET SAVAGE LOVE
SAVAGE DESIRE

ROSEMARY
Return to Me
ROGERS

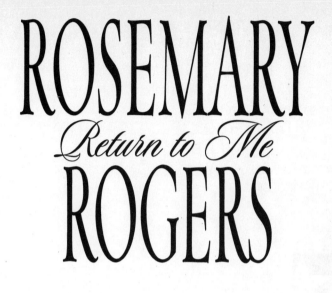

MIRA®

ISBN 0-7394-3871-9

RETURN TO ME

Printed in U.S.A.

To my readers,
old and new,
with thanks.

1

Washington, D.C.
June, 1865

The summer night was warm and humid, reminding Cameron of her home in Mississippi, as her stylish horse-drawn carriage slowed to a halt on the brick-paved drive in front of the Rowe-James Hotel in Washington, D.C. She gathered the skirts of her blue-and-white Pekins silk evening gown and grasped the white-gloved hand offered by a red-liveried footman, allowing him to assist her onto the lamp-lit walk. The slight breeze from the Potomac ruffled the mass of rich red curls that fell down her back, revealing cascading diamond-and-sapphire earrings sparkling to her bare shoulders.

Cameron's heartbeat quickened. The elegant Rowe-James Hotel held only happy memories for her. It was here that her husband had first proposed marriage almost four years and what now seemed a lifetime ago. Here, on their wedding night, they'd danced in their luxurious suite, drunk champagne and made love until the dawn cast a golden light on their silken pillows.

Approaching the columned doorway, she glanced up at

the black bunting that garlanded the entry, a stark reminder that only two months had passed since President Lincoln's assassination. The fragile country was still in mourning, in shock, as of yet unable to accept that their beloved leader, who had freed the slaves, saved the Union and vowed to heal the young nation's wounds, had been so foully murdered.

"Good evening, Mrs. Logan." A uniformed doorman swung open the imposing brass doors.

"Good evening." She offered a kind smile as she swept into the magnificent Greek-columned lobby, a vast, high chamber bustling with men in dark frock coats and women in elegant evening attire.

"Mrs. Logan!" A distinguished gentleman with a plump, dark-haired lady on his arm, bowed. "So glad to see you. I hear Captain Logan is back in Washington."

"He is indeed, Senator." Cameron smiled, but did not linger in conversation.

"Mrs. Logan, good to have you with us." The formally dressed maître d' bowed, then escorted her through the dining room. "Your usual table?"

She nodded, lifting her dark lashes and smiling graciously. "The captain will be joining me as soon as his business is complete. I expect him any moment."

The maître d' beamed as he escorted her through a labyrinth of white-linen covered, candle-lit tables. The elegant dining room hummed with the sound of hushed voices in polite dinner conversation underscored by the discreet notes of a grand piano.

"Your favorite table, Mrs. Logan, perfect for a homecoming." Mr. Douglas pulled the damask-upholstered chair from the table near the window. The dark blue velvet drapes had been drawn back. Cameron could see the sparkling gaslights of the city all the way to the distant curve of the Potomac River in the distance, where ships sat in anchor, their lanterns glowing against the encroaching darkness.

"Thank you, Mr. Douglas. The captain will be pleased."

"Something to refresh you while you wait?"

She plucked off her elbow-length, white silk gloves and laid them on the table beside her beaded reticule. "Champagne."

"Of course. Albert!" He snapped his fingers at the nearest waiter. "Champagne for Mrs. Logan. A bottle of Moët & Chandon's best *cuvée* from Captain Logan's private wine closet."

"Look at her," Alma Meriwether whispered from behind the cover of her fan. "Flirting shamelessly with the maître d'. My, but she thinks she's everything and a cup of tea, doesn't she?"

"Who is she?" breathed her niece. Noreen Meriwether had only arrived in the nation's capital a week earlier and this was her first night to see and be seen in such a public arena. She was so excited that she could barely draw breath.

"Oh, my dear heavens! You've so much to learn." Aunt Alma worked her heavy jowls, using her fan to shield her conversation from those around her. "*That,* my dear, is Mrs. Jackson Logan, wife of *Captain* Logan."

Noreen blinked and then gulped. She may have led a sheltered life in her father's Methodist home, but not so sheltered that she had not heard of the dashing war hero, rumored to be the most successful spy in all the Union army during the war. "*The* famous Captain Logan?" She spoke in a hushed voice, as if she kneeled before the altar of God.

"Some might say infamous," her aunt replied.

Mr. Meriwether tipped his menu and stared at his wife

through oval spectacles. "Mrs. Meriwether, lower your voice before someone hears you."

"It wouldn't be any news they don't already know," she half whispered, reaching for her niece's gloved hand on the linen-covered table. "My sweet, Mrs. Logan isn't just Captain Logan's wife, she is the daughter of the deceased Senator Campbell from Mississippi." She leaned closer to Noreen, fluttering her carved ivory fan. "*They say* that the senator's sudden death was no accident at all, but that he was murdered by his own son."

Noreen's eyes bulged. "Murdered by his own son?"

"Oh, you don't know what this young man was like," Aunt Alma continued, flustered with excitement.

"You knew him?"

"Goodness, of course not. But *they say* he was a sexual deviant, my dear sweet child."

Noreen gulped once. Twice. She didn't know who *they* were, nor did she have any earthly idea what a sexual deviant was, but just the implication made her want to fall to her knees in prayer for the damned soul.

"*They say* that Grant Campbell, that woman's brother—" she nodded toward Mrs. Logan "—tried to sell his sister's virtue on an auction block in Baton Rouge, just after the war began."

Light-headed, Noreen reached for her own fan. One never heard such lewd tales in her hometown of Dover, Delaware. Such sinfulness simply did not exist. She wanted to turn away, to cover her ears to her aunt's scandalous gossip, for she knew it, too, was sinful, but she simply could not help herself. "Heavens, his own sister…an auction block? Whatever…" She panted, suddenly feeling overheated. The lace collar of her new blue taffeta evening gown rubbed against her throat and she tugged at it.

"You don't know the half of it," her aunt murmured,

pulling Noreen's hand from her collar. "The sister in question is a n-e-g-r-a." Aunt Alma lowered her lashes as if to apologize for having to make that confession, even by spelling it out. "As black as tar."

"Mrs. Meriwether!"

Noreen had never seen her uncle's face so red. When her aunt glanced up, Uncle Ralph knowingly eyed the black waiter discreetly setting the next table.

Aunt Alma gave her husband a wave of dismissal, as if the servant's presence meant nothing to her. "I jest not," she told Noreen from behind her fan.

"No!" Noreen whispered. Her pale blue eyes widened, then narrowed as she glanced at the ivory-skinned, auburn-haired young woman seated at the windows. The young woman appeared too beautiful to her to be real. The sister of a negra woman? "But how—"

"Her father consorted with his slaves, of course." Aunt Alma rolled her eyes heavenward. "You know these Southerners."

Noreen nodded slowly as if she understood perfectly. She didn't. She didn't know any Southerners; she had no idea what her aunt meant, but she didn't dare ask. Her gaze slipped past her uncle's shoulder to the gloriously beautiful Mrs. Logan again.

"At some point, the senator had legally claimed this so-called n-e-g-r-a *daughter*," Aunt Alma went on, catching Noreen's arm, forcing her to peer into her aunt's face. "And he left her a king's ransom in precious emeralds and diamonds!"

For some reason, that bit of gossip shocked Noreen more than anything else her aunt had said. Perhaps because her own father saw such little worth in his daughters. "A daughter born out of wedlock to a slave woman made rich by her white father? That cannot possibly be true," Noreen breathed, knowing she damned her own self by participating in such hearsay, but unable to help herself. "How do you know?"

"Well!" her aunt huffed. "My sister heard that bit of news only last month. The girl was living in New York City for the duration of the war. With family friends, they say. Since she was born a slave and still considered a n-e-g-r-a, it wasn't safe for her to live in Baltimore. You had to be above the Mason-Dixon line, you know. The sister ordered a broach to be made for Mrs. Logan at Tiffany's in New York. My sister Mabel's jeweler at Tiffany's told her that it was one of the most perfect emeralds he had ever seen. You simply can't fathom the cost."

"Heavens," Noreen said, almost tongue-tied. Her gaze strayed to Mrs. Logan again, looking at her in a new light.

"And what of the rumors of the captain's philandering?" came a female whisper from the table beside them. "You mustn't forget the Marie LeLaurie scandal. They say she's a spy, too, and that she worked *closely* with the captain. He and Mrs. Logan have been wed four years, but he's been on *secret missions* all that time. I hear they haven't laid eyes upon each other in more than a year."

"Oh, my, you are absolutely right, Mrs. Connor." Aunt Alma leaned back in her chair to speak to an overly plump woman in a satin gown with thinning hair held beneath a mop of a lace bonnet who could have been her twin. "Mrs. Connor, Mr. Meriwether's niece, Miss Noreen Meriwether," she introduced. "Noreen, Mrs. Connor, a *dear* old friend."

Noreen cut her eyes to the woman at the table behind them and gave a quick nod, unsure of proper etiquette under the circumstances. "Pleased to meet you, ma'am," she muttered. She looked back at her aunt, fascinated by the whole shocking tale. She had never imagined a trip to her aunt and uncle's would be so exciting.

"But what of Mrs. Logan?" Noreen dared. "Surely she cannot be held responsible for—"

"Horses," Aunt Meriwether interrupted.

"Horses?" Noreen breathed.

"She—" Mrs. Connor cleared her throat "—breeds them."

"No!"

"Yes," the woman behind them hissed. "Arabians. She stables them in a farm outside of Baltimore and actually conducts business with male buyers. And she rides astride, through Baltimore, *unescorted,*" she added quickly, as if her first statement was not scandalous enough.

Noreen covered her mouth with her gloved hand. "Oh, my!"

"And what of that jaunt to Europe last year with her sister, the n-e-g-r-a." Aunt Alma spelled the word out yet again. "The newspapers touted them the toast of Paris!"

"Mrs. Meriwether," Uncle Ralph groaned.

"Unescorted," Aunt Alma whispered.

"Shocking," Mrs. Connor reflected.

"Shocking," Aunt Alma echoed. "I don't know how she shows her—"

"Mrs. Meriwether," Uncle Ralph whispered loudly, slapping his menu on the table.

Mrs. Connor snapped around in her chair as if a puppeteer had yanked her strings and she pretended to fuss with her napkin.

Noreen clasped her hands in her lap and stared straight ahead across the table at her uncle, mortified. If he sent her home for her ill behavior, her father might well put her out of the house.

"I believe that will be enough stinging gossip for one

evening, Mrs. Meriwether.'' Uncle Ralph leaned as far forward across the table as his rounded middle would allow him. ''You should not be filling my impressionable niece's head full of such malarkey.''

''But Mr. Meriwether—'' Aunt Alma drew herself up indignantly. ''It's all true.''

''I don't care if it's true or not, you old biddy.''

''Oh.'' Aunt Alma sucked in a breath of air but did not exhale.

''Mrs. Logan's husband is a war hero and they both deserve our undying respect.'' His mouth turned up in a half smile. ''Besides, she's too damned lovely to deserve such an attack on her character. Now place your orders, ladies, or I will escort you home without your supper.''

Cameron was so anxious to see Jackson that her stomach tumbled beneath her tight corset, although sipping the chilled champagne seemed to be calming her. Her husband had returned to Baltimore for a stolen night whenever he could, but it had been too long since they'd truly been together, and she missed him more than she'd thought possible. She wanted him home so that she would have a companion, a friend, a partner. She had high hopes for this marriage that seemed to be just beginning tonight.

Knowing Jackson always appreciated the latest fashion, Cameron had carefully chosen her attire this evening, a blue-and-white silk evening gown that bared her pale shoulders and décolleté. And though current mode considered it risqué, she wore her rich auburn hair trailing down her back in a coiffure of simple yet elegant curls. Jackson had always loved her hair. It was her hair, he said, that first caught his eye the summer she was seventeen when he first visited Elmwood, her father's plantation. Her auburn hair and her amber eyes.

"Pardon me, madam, for disturbing you, but I believe the maître d' has made an error."

Cameron glanced over the rim of her crystal etched champagne glass to see a dashing gentleman in an azure blue coat standing beside the table. He was well over six feet tall, lithe and muscular, with a head of dark hair pulled back in a neat queue and tied with a black silken cord. The hair was completely out of fashion and yet, on him, seemed ideal. It made him appear enigmatic, even dangerous. Men like this could easily lead a lonely woman such as herself astray.

She lifted her lashes, taking in his arrogant stance and swaggering grin. Not only was he was strikingly handsome, but he obviously knew it.

"An error? What sort of error, sir?"

"Well…" He glanced out the window and then back at her.

"I believe Mr. Douglas has inadvertently given you my table."

She smiled, setting down her champagne flute. "Sir, I believe it's you who are in error, as this is *my* table. It has always been my table whenever I happen to come to Washington."

He sighed, slightly bored. "No. This is my table. It's the only one *I* ever sit at when *I* have business in Washington."

She leaned back, amused by the repartee with the insolent rogue. Unlike most women of her age and class, she rarely sought the companionship of other women, finding them dull and frivolous. Her father had always said she should have been born a man; perhaps he was right.

"And what are we to do, sir? As you can see—" she opened her arms, narrowing her eyes "—I'm already seated and there are rules which govern possession of such public properties."

"Well, as I see it, we've no choice, madam, but to share the table." He pulled out the chair across from her and sat down before she could utter a word in protest.

"Sir, you cannot sit there. I await my husband." Cameron's amber eyes lit with shock and annoyance.

He shrugged extraordinarily broad shoulders. "His loss. He should not have left such a stunning woman unescorted and unprotected from gentlemen of such dubious reputations as myself. Waiter." He motioned to the table. "Another champagne flute, if you would."

"Sir, I did not invite you to partake of my champagne." Cameron leaned forward to look him in those gray eyes. "I should have the maître d' called to see you escorted out of here for your insolence."

When waiter brought the flute, the handsome intruder arrogantly poured himself a healthy portion, sitting back casually in his chair to sample it. "Now, now, you wouldn't cause a scene and disturb all of these fine ladies and gentlemen, would you?"

Cameron glanced surreptitiously at the tables surrounding them. From the glances and the occasional outright stares, she could see that people had noticed her handsome visitor. "Sir, again, I must ask you to leave. You will cause a scandal. My reputation will be destroyed."

His dark gray eyes sparkled with a brazenness few men could manage successfully. He managed it exceedingly well. He downed the last of the imported French champagne and smiled enigmatically. "One request, then, before I go. One dance."

"I said nothing of dancing," she protested as his fingers closed over her wrist. In spite of her resentful tugging, they were as inexorable as steel manacles.

"Come now, just one dance."

Cameron struggled in earnest as he pulled her from her chair and slipped his arm around her small waist.

The lone piano player began to play a haunting waltz as the rogue ushered her toward the open floor.

"Humor me," the intruder whispered, his breath warm and entrancing in her ear.

"I don't want to dance," Cameron murmured. Now that she was on her feet, she was feeling the champagne. Or was it he who set her off balance, making her feel slightly tipsy? "No one else is dancing. The music is completely unsuitable—"

He clasped her hand and put his other hand firmly on her waist, entrapping her.

"You looked so beautiful sitting there alone at the table beneath the windows, so solitary, so vulnerable and yet so courageous. I'd put you up against a band of renegade Confederate soldiers any day of the week." He caught one red curl, wrapped it around his finger and inhaled the scent. "God, you smell good."

Cameron felt dizzy and utterly consumed by the man who held her in his arms. The scent of his masculinity, the feel of his arms around her, was what she dreamed of alone in her bed at night. She had never viewed herself as one of those weak-kneed females who could be overcome by a man in a single glance, by a single silly compliment. But she was overwhelmed by this man.

"I have a key in my pocket to a suite right here in the hotel," he murmured huskily, brushing his lips across her rice-powdered cheek.

The dance floor seemed to spin around her as they waltzed, the candlelight glittering like constellations of stars. "Sir, I couldn't. They're all watching. The table. Dinner."

He dragged his hot mouth across her cheek, making it difficult for her to think clearly. "We can eat later."

"I've left my reticule." This last protest was weak, barely audible.

"I'll buy you another and fill it with gold coins."

Cameron could hear the murmur of voices around them rising above the piano music. She'd be the gossip of the town yet again, and she'd not yet recovered from the last bout brought on when she had mounted a bucking Arabian that had thrown one of her trainers. It wasn't appropriate for a lady of her status to straddle a horse, they said. It wasn't *seemly.*

Cameron's face began to burn. Now everyone was staring at them. He practically dragged her down the length of the dining room, past all the couples who were just sitting down to dinner, past the dowagers with their fluttering fans and raised eyebrows, and the waiters with their discreetly shuttered faces. Out into the marble lobby and up the lushly carpeted grand staircase he led her, turning to look at her only once to inquire if she'd rather be carried up the staircase.

He halted halfway down the long corridor and pushed her up against the hand-painted wallpaper, holding her hands to her sides as he covered her mouth with his.

When he at last tore his mouth from hers, she couldn't speak. Couldn't think. Suddenly nothing mattered but his touch as images of bare flesh to bare flesh flashed in her mind.

He grabbed her by the arm and hurried down the corridor toward the double doors at the far end.

"Please," she managed to say, breathlessly. "So many saw. I'll not be received in any home in—"

"As if you've ever cared about what anyone thought." He halted beside the doors of the Potomac Suite and again pinned her against the wall. As he took her mouth, he brought one hand up to cup her breast.

Her breast tingled, then seemed to bloom at his touch, suddenly aching with desire.

As his kiss deepened, she parted her lips, savoring the taste of him and the champagne he had consumed. She moaned aloud as his hand brushed the swell of her breast and his thumb slipped beneath the low-cut bodice of blue silk to stroke her nipple.

"Someone will see us," she groaned as she tried to push him away.

Still pinning her against the wall, he put an arm above her head and gazed into her eyes. "And what will they see, my love? A man who passionately desires his wife?"

Now she laughed wantonly and threw her arms around him. He drew her tightly against his hard, muscular frame, pressing her pelvis to his, and stroked her hair.

"I missed you," she whispered, surprised as emotion welled in her throat and she found she was suddenly near to tears. "I've missed you so much, Jackson. And it seems as if it's been worse since I knew you were coming home. I thought tonight would never come."

He drew back and gently wiped her single tear with his thumb. "Well, I'm home now and, God willing, I'm not ever going to leave you again." He brushed his lips against hers.

Cameron returned his gentle, husbandly kiss, but the moment she felt his lips against hers, the fire within her began to flame again. She melted into his arms, parting her lips, needing the taste of him more greatly than she needed the air to breathe.

With one hand, he held her in his arm to keep her from

falling. With the other hand, he turned the brass key in the lock. Pushing the paneled mahogany door with his booted foot, Jackson swept Cameron into his arms and carried her over the threshold.

2

The luxurious hotel suite glowed with candlelight. The rich, dark silk bed linens had been drawn back enticingly, and a bottle of champagne and two crystal flutes rested beside the bed. A silver tray of cheeses, fruits and breads was nestled amid lavish bouquets of roses.

"You conceited rogue." Cameron tipped back her head, gazing at him through slanted amber eyes, and laughed. "You had this all planned."

"Guilty as charged." Jackson lowered his mouth to her throat and pressed a slow kiss to her throbbing pulse. "I've thought of nothing but this for weeks."

Cameron lifted her head and encircled his neck with her arms, meeting his mouth, her tongue flicking out to brush his. "And what if I had refused you? That was all quite embarrassing in the dining room. It would have served you right if I had gone home without you."

He grinned wickedly, still holding her in his arms. "Had you left me, I'm quite sure I could have found another woman from that room to take your place."

"More unfounded arrogance," she purred, running her hand over his fine, blue coat lapel. "Now, close the door, else we'll surely have an audience."

He kicked the door shut with his boot and let her slide through his arms until her new kid slippers, dyed blue to match her gown, met the floor.

"You haven't been eating," she whispered, kissing his cheek, his chin and then his mouth again. "You're thin."

"Not from lack of food—" he pressed her hand to his beating heart "—but lack of love."

She laughed, hearing the huskiness of her desire for him in her throat. "But I have always loved you, Jackson, loved you since that day you rode up my father's elm-lined drive the summer I was barely seventeen."

"That's not the kind of love I meant." He reached beneath her gown to slide his hand over her silk-covered calf and then higher. "And you well know it."

Cameron giggled and pushed his hand away. "You are incorrigible."

"Just the way you like me." He grabbed her shoulders and spun her around. His fingers found the endless length of tiny pearled buttons of her new gown and he began to loosen them, one at a time. As he worked them free, he buried his face in her hair and inhaled the scent of her.

Cameron leaned back against Jackson, her husband until death did part them, and lavished in the warmth and strength of his arms and the teasing of his fingertips on her bare back. She arched her spine and pressed her buttocks to his groin. He was already eager for her; she could feel him hard and hot, even through the layers of silk and wool clothing.

"Oh, do hurry, Jackson," she whispered, blood suddenly pounding in her temples. She ached for him from the tips of her toes to her tingling scalp.

"Hurry, my love?" he crooned in her ear.

"Yes." She breathed in short gasps. "This is all taking too long."

"Well, we certainly can't have that." He grasped the delicate material of the gown and tore it open. The fabric split with a great ripping sound as buttons shot about.

"Jackson! My gown."

"I'll buy you another gown. A dozen. You see, I'm in a hurry as well. I cannot wait another moment longer for you." He spun her around in his arms, tearing the costly silk off her shoulders.

Their lips met in another dance as he pushed the ruined gown over her waist and to the floor. He yanked at the strings and ribbons of her undergarments. In moments she was standing naked but for her slippers and stockings, surrounded by mountains of silk and starched crinolines.

"Can't we put out some of the candles?" she asked, the uncertainty apparent in her wavering voice.

"I want the light so I can see you," Jackson whispered, chasing her uncertainties into the darkness again, at least for the time being. "All of you."

He kissed her shoulder, her collarbone and then dragged his mouth lower. Cameron looped her arms around his neck, closed her eyes and felt herself sway in her heeled slippers as he cupped her breast and brought his lips to her puckered nipple.

"Jackson," she half laughed, half moaned. "I'm going to fall."

"I'll catch you." He tightened the pressure of his arm on her back and cradled her in his arms, sucking her nipple, laving it with the heat of his wet tongue.

"Jackson, please, can't we go to the bed?"

He smiled a smile that could have brought any woman to her knees in surrender. "I thought you would never ask."

"Arrogant scoundrel," she accused as he took her by the

hand and led her to the four-postered, silk-draped bed. "You never change, do you?"

"You'd have me no other way." He caught her around the waist, kissed her until she was breathless again and then pushed her back onto the bed.

"This is unfair," she murmured languidly. "Take off your clothes and come to bed, husband."

"You're not quite naked," he said lasciviously as he lifted her foot and slowly slipped off her shoe. Next, he grasped her French silk stocking and slowly, seductively rolled it down.

Cameron's breath caught in her throat as his fingertips brushed her thigh, her knee, her calf. Every inch of her skin seemed to pulse with need for him.

Jackson threw her stocking over his head and it fluttered to the floor like an abandoned battlefield pennant. She opened her eyes to meet and hold his gaze as he slipped off her other shoe and the last stocking.

She trembled like a willow leaf in a rising wind as gusts of emotions shook her to the core.

"Take them off," Cameron breathed, looking up at Jackson. She gave his chest a playful push with her bare foot. "Take off your clothes. All of them."

"Yes, ma'am." He saluted as if she were General Grant. His gray-eyed gaze lingered over her, and she watched as he removed his coat, his waistcoat, his cravat and shirt. He kicked off his boots and shed his stockings. She nibbled on her lower lip, her breath increasing as she watched his fingers find the clasp of his trousers. An iniquitous smile crossed her face as he sprang forth from the rich fabric, tumescent and glorious in his maleness.

Cameron knew she should be ashamed of herself, ashamed of her wicked desire for this man. But she couldn't help herself and pressed the length of her pale body to

Jackson's, molding bare flesh to bare flesh as he slid into bed beside her. She met his mouth and parted her lips to accept his tongue and slid her hand down over his taut belly, then lower.

Jackson groaned and pushed her hand away. "You are impatient, wife."

She laughed huskily as he rolled her onto her back and rested on his side against her. "I've waited a long time, husband, for what is rightfully mine as your wedded wife. I will not be put off."

"And I will not be put off. Have no fear of that." He licked the tip of his forefinger and began to draw a line between her breasts. "I, however, have learned the virtue of patience, something you, my dear, know nothing about."

Gooseflesh rose on her skin, though she was not cold. He drew his line lower. Licked his finger again and moved his hand even lower.

Cameron closed her eyes and lifted her hips instinctively as his finger came to the apex of her thighs. "Jackson," she whispered.

"Cameron, my sweet Cameron. I cannot tell you what it meant to me all these months, these years, knowing you were here waiting for me." He palmed his hand over the mound of short, red curls and she moaned in delight.

"Love me, Jackson," she begged.

"Always." He lifted up on the bed and pressed his mouth to the hollow of her belly. She gave no protest as his hot tongue drew a path lower.

Cameron's first climax came quickly...hard. Jackson knew her, knew her body, better than she knew herself. He played her like a fine instrument, knowing just which strings to pluck.

"Oh!" Cameron cried, clutching Jackson's broad shoulders as wave after wave of pleasure washed over her.

Jackson stilled and rested his head on her belly. She stroked his freshly washed dark hair.

"Would you like to lay upon me?" she whispered when she had again caught her breath. "I could show you a trick I know."

"And where did you learn this trick, madame?" He slid up in the bed and lay beside her, his hand resting casually on her bare hip.

She drew her finger down the center of his chest, over the patch of springy, dark hair. "Oh, this wicked man taught me."

"Wicked, was he?"

She leaned down and caught his nipple between her teeth. Jackson groaned.

"Wicked, indeed," she whispered. "A sly stranger who took my virtue from me out of wedlock and used me for his own sinful pleasures."

"And did you enjoy those sinful pleasures?"

She brushed her hand over his muscular stomach. "Oh, very much, sir."

He threw back his head and laughed, his rich voice echoing off the painted ceiling above.

Cameron closed her hand over the smooth skin of his warm, stiff member, and his laughter died away until it was a groan.

"You said you had a trick?"

"Several," she purred. "He was an excellent instructor."

Jackson brushed his mouth against her cheek and pushed her hand away. "Enough, woman." He rolled over to straddle her and leaned close to gaze into her eyes. "Or the fun will end before either of us would like it to."

She laughed and lifted her head to meet his mouth again.

As they kissed, she felt his hardness against her damp, hot skin and she parted her thighs.

Jackson took her quickly, with one long, sweet thrust. Cameron cried out in surprise...in relief.

"Is this what you had in mind, my love?" Jackson pinned her wrists to the bed, loomed over her and lifted to stroke.

"Precisely," she gasped as she closed her eyes and pursed her lips.

Jackson lowered his body and then rose over her again. She writhed beneath him. Lifted to meet his thrust and lifted again.

Ripples of molten delight quickly became waves. They washed over Cameron again and again. She tried to hold back, to make the moment last, but she couldn't. She dug her fingernails into Jackson's bare shoulders as every muscle in her body seemed to contract at once. She cried out, calling his name, arching her back. She heard him groan in her ear, and they lifted and met one final time before falling back in the bed, panting for breath.

Cameron held tightly to Jackson as the peak of ecstasy became waves and the waves became ripples again. When she could find her voice, she hugged him and whispered, "Welcome home, Jackson."

He slid onto his side and drew her against him. "I'm glad to be home." He smoothed her cheek with the back of his hand, rough and callused, toughened by the years of the war.

"Ah, Cameron, I have great plans for us, for you and me and the family I hope we will have."

She gazed into his eyes and then lowered her lashes, her heart beating. Why was she feeling so vulnerable again? "I should tell you about...about family," she said, unable to meet his gaze.

He caught her chin and lifted it, forcing her to look into his eyes.

"What do you mean?" Jackson asked pointedly.

"You're going to be a papa."

When he didn't immediately respond, Cameron felt a sudden panic in her chest. Her lower lip trembled. "You're not pleased."

His face lit up and he grabbed her, pulling her against him and crushing her in his arms. "No, no, Cam, that's not it at all. I...I'm just shocked."

"Shocked? Did you think me too old at twenty-seven to get with child?"

"Of course not." He laughed and brushed the dark hair off his forehead, then hugged her again. "It's just that we have been together so infrequently."

"We've apparently been together enough." She began to relax again. "Don't you remember that night we shared in New York a month ago? I was visiting Taye and you came in through the window. You're lucky I didn't put a hole in your chest with my derringer, thinking you an intruder."

"But it was barely a night—I left before dawn."

"Barely a night is all it takes," she teased.

"Oh, Cameron. A baby!" His dark brows knitted. "But are you sure? Only a month—"

She smiled. "I'm sure. Women know these things."

"You and I are going to be parents," he whispered as he kissed her forehead. "Oh, Cameron, wait until I tell you my plans. Wait until you see the land I've bought us on the Chesapeake Bay."

"Land? Whatever do you mean?" The smile fell from Cameron's face as quickly as it had brightened it.

He reached out to stroke her cheek but she pulled back. "Land to build a home, of course. I know you don't like the city life. I knew you would want to move onto acreage once the war was over and it was safe again.''

''And you bought land without consulting me?''

''It's a plantation on the shores of the Chesapeake Bay, Cam. There's a beautiful brick plantation house on the edge of the shore and a lawn that rolls right to the water's edge. The house will have to be expanded, of course. Redecorated. But I know you're going to love it.''

Cameron sat up, her hand sliding to her still-flat belly. ''But I want my baby to be born in Mississippi.''

''That's impossible.''

She drew herself up on her knees to face him. ''It is not, as you say, impossible. Mississippi is my home. I only came to Baltimore because you insisted I wait out the war here. I never agreed to live here forever.''

''Cam, please, calm down.''

He reached out for her, but she pushed his hand away. ''I am calm,'' she said from between clenched teeth. ''And I'm calmly telling you that I want this baby born in my home of Mississippi.''

''But *this* is my home, our home. And in time it can become yours, too, Cam. Ours and our children's.''

''I want to go back to Mississippi, Jackson.''

''I understand, but you can't, sweetheart.''

''Why not?'' she demanded, feeling her lower lip tremble. ''Damn you, Jackson, you never change. You've been with me an hour and you're already thinking you know what is best for me, thinking you can order me about. Why can't I go home?''

''You've seen the newspapers, Mathew Brady's godawful photographs, but even they don't tell the whole story. Mississippi is in ruins, sweetheart. The entire damned South is in ruins.''

Cameron's heart contracted in pain, and this time when

Jackson reached for her, she allowed him to take her into his arms.

"I cannot express to you the devastation of the land below the Mason-Dixon," he said quietly. "It is beyond comprehension. The burned fields, the salted wells...the lifeless spirits of the survivors, bands of people, black and white, just wandering.

"And where would you have this baby, anyway?" he asked, smoothing her hair with one hand, speaking softly. "In a burned field? In an abandoned house?"

"Oh, Jackson," she murmured as she fought her tears.

"I know. I know. Let's not talk about this anymore. Not now." He lay back, drawing the coverlet over them, and pulled her closer. "There will be tomorrow and the next day and the next to talk about our future."

"All right," she whispered. "But this discussion isn't over. I'm no longer a seventeen-year-old child to be manipulated by the men in my life. *Any of them.*"

He lifted his head to take her mouth hungrily. "No, you are no child, wife. That's clear."

She chuckled in her throat and lay back on the bed, feeling the strength of his desire on her bare leg again.

3

The following day, Jackson and Cameron made their journey from Washington, D.C., to Baltimore in their coach.

"We're home, Mrs. Logan." Jackson smiled, brushing a light kiss across her lips as the coach turned onto a wide, tree-shaded avenue, lined with imposing brick mansions, most three stories high. Halfway down the avenue, the coach pulled into a circular drive leading up to the imposing front entrance. A uniformed butler opened the door and hurried down the curved brick staircase to greet the couple.

"Captain Logan. Mrs. Logan. Welcome home."

The former owner of the mansion, a relative of the governor of Maryland, had hired a noted European architect with a taste for classical antiquity to transform the interior of the square redbrick Georgian into a showplace of Greek Doric extravagance.

Although Cameron was fond of walking in the walled, formal French garden at the back of the enormous house, she found the huge, ornately carved marble fireplaces drafty and the dozens of cupids and goddesses that peered down at her from every niche and corner tiresome. The three-story, fourteen-room house, with its imported French wall coverings, Venetian crystal chandeliers and black-and-white Italian marble-tiled entrance hall, might be the height of fashion, she often conceded, but she much preferred the comfortable simplicity of her beloved Elmwood.

In the first days after Jackson's return, the household was in turmoil as everyone settled into the new routine of having the master home again after four years. The hours, the days, slipped by so quickly that Cameron barely had time to catch her breath. Jackson spent his days at the docks, inspecting the ships he had acquired during the war and reacquainting himself with the thriving shipping empire he had inherited from his father.

His trusted friend and manager, Mr. Lonsford, had worked for Jackson's father before him. He had worked for the Logans since he was a boy and had done exceedingly well for the family shipping empire during the war. Despite the hardships to the county's economy, Cameron observed wryly, it seemed that her husband was now far wealthier than he had been before.

Each morning, after sharing breakfast in bed with Cameron, Jackson left and often did not return home until it was time to go to the theater or to a dinner party. With Cameron occupied with the household and her herd of Arabian horses, she and Jackson barely had time to be alone together, and when they were alone, their unchecked passions took precedence over serious conversations.

Dawn had barely tinged the eastern sky one morning as Cameron watched Jackson pull on black riding trousers, followed by tall black leather boots. He told her he had an important appointment in Washington today, but he would reveal no more to her.

"More tedious war business," he explained, lightly brushing off her inquiries.

"I don't understand, Jackson. The war is over. How can

you possibly have more business with the War Department?''

Wrapped in a silky dressing gown, Cameron rested on a pile of pillows in the middle of the silk-draped rosewood bed and sipped a cup of warm chocolate. ''Why are you so secretive? I'm your wife, not the enemy. And why can't you tell me what you're doing for President Johnson...or Secretary Seward? All this 'war business' takes up too much of your time! How can you be a spy if there is no war?'' she asked, growing agitated by the moment. ''Damn it, there aren't any enemies to spy on!''

He eyed her disapprovingly as he stood before the tall, gilded Italian mirror and knotted his cravat. ''I prefer not use that word.''

''It's what you were. What you still are, apparently,'' she accused.

He glanced at their closed door. ''Cameron, we have a staff of over thirty men and women in this household. Do you really think this is something we should be shouting from the rooftops?''

''I'm not shouting, for God's sake. But if you think the staff doesn't know you were a spy—if you think anyone in Baltimore or Washington doesn't know you were a spy— you are sadly mistaken.''

''I don't have time to argue with you. Not this morning.'' He jerked the knot from his cravat and started again. ''I'm going to be late for the first train.''

She set the delicate porcelain teacup down on a bedside table and rose to her knees on the bed. ''And you're going to be gone until late tonight, I suppose.''

''I'm afraid I will.'' He swiped an unruly strand of hair off his forehead.

She glanced away. ''Damn it, Jackson,'' she muttered.

"I know, sweetheart." Dressed, he came to her, leaned over and planted a husbandly kiss on her mouth.

She frowned. "You're avoiding me. You're avoiding everything here except your damned shipping business."

"I'm not. I still have obligations to the country. I have a great deal on my mind right now." Jackson walked to a chiffarobe, opened it and pulled out a black felt hat, one of many he owned. "Saturday, the week after next, we're hosting a ball for our returning Union Army officers. The guest list will be small, approximately three hundred. Can you manage?"

So he was just going to change the subject. Again.

She climbed out of bed, her white silk dressing robe fluttering behind her. "Just three hundred? Can I manage?" She walked barefoot across the polished hardwood to the porcelain washbowl, poured fresh water into it and splashed her face. She had to bite back the string of retorts that played on the end of her tongue.

She kept her gaze focused on the tiny blue flowers painted across the water pitcher, allowing only a hint of sarcasm to tinge her voice. "Certainly I can manage. A ball in two weeks' time for 150 men and their wives? It's what we Southern woman were bred to do."

"I knew it." He came up behind her, rested his hands on her waist and kissed the back of her head. "That was what I told Ulysses." He released her. "Supper tonight, late? Just the two of us?"

She turned around, but he was already halfway out the door. "Jackson, my sister is coming today. I hoped you might be here to dine with us." She reached for a linen towel beside the washbowl and patted her face dry. "I reminded you twice this week that she was coming today."

"That's right. You did." He placed his hat on his head. "So you'll be staying home today. Good. Maybe you can rest a little."

"Whatever do you mean, *rest?* I'm going out to the farm as I go every day."

He lingered in the doorway. "I'm just concerned you're becoming overly tired. Surely your stable manager can handle the horses for one day without you."

"But I can stay here and *rest* preparing for a party for three hundred? I don't think so, Jackson."

He sighed. "I just want to be sure you're getting enough rest for the baby's sake—and yours, of course."

"Of course," she said tartly.

"Well, don't stay long and give Taye a kiss for me when she arrives. I'll try not to be too late."

And then he was gone.

In frustration, Cameron threw the towel at the open door, then slammed it shut with her bare foot. Pacing their bed-chamber, hot tears of anger flowed down her cheeks. This was not how she had imagined Jackson's homecoming, how she had imagined their first days together would be. She had thought this would be such a happy time. A time to celebrate the coming of the baby and make plans for their life together, a time to grow close and reacquaint themselves with each other. She dashed the tears away, feeling more alone than she had in the darkest days of the war when she had no idea where in the South Jackson was, or if he was dead or alive.

She picked up a silver-handled hairbrush from her dressing table and then slammed it down. "Rest," she grumbled, walking to her chiffarobe to find fresh underthings. "The next thing I know you'll want me to take carriage rides in the park and start knitting booties!"

"Secretary Seward, good to see you again. Please, sir, don't get up." Jackson crossed the dark-paneled White House office to greet the Secretary of State who had begun to rise from behind his enormous desk, but slowly eased back into his chair.

William Seward had been injured the same night President Lincoln was assassinated in the plot to kill the top three men in the succession of the United States government. John Wilkes Booth's associate, Lewis Payne, broke into the Secretary of State's bedroom and stabbed him repeatedly with a bowie knife. Seward's recovery had been slow, but he was said to be improving daily. He had agreed to continue as Secretary of State under President Andrew Johnson and was handling what work he could until he made a full recovery.

"Since when have I become Secretary Seward again, Jackson? Please."

Jackson laughed as he gripped the older man's hand, which seemed as strong as before his brush with death. He tried not to stare at the angry gash across one cheek that would disfigure the man the rest of his life. "Good point, Will. I'm glad to see you're on the mend."

"Hell, it's been two months. About time I dragged my sorry self here. I promised my wife just a few hours, though." A smile flickered on his ragged face.

"Women. I understand." Jackson nodded and then chuckled. "Truthfully I don't understand them a bit, and it's getting worse." He thought back to his conversation with Cameron that morning. She could sure as hell be difficult. She seemed to have no understanding of all he had been through these last four years while she was settled comfortably in his mansion in Baltimore. Had she no understanding of his loyalty to his country? He couldn't turn his back on his friends in congress, the senate and the White House. Not now, when the politics of the nation were in such turmoil. If Booth and his comrades' goals had been to assassinate the nation's leaders to set the government in turmoil, they had certainly accomplished that. But the Union would prevail. Of that, Jackson was certain.

He returned his attention to the Secretary of State. "How is your son? I understand he was also injured the night you were attacked."

"He's doing well. Thank you for asking."

"You've done a hell of a job getting through this, Will. I'm not sure if I was in your place that I could have dealt with it as you have."

"President Johnson has great plans for his Reconstruction of the South. This is not a time to wallow in self-pity," Seward said humbly as he indicated a chair in front of his desk. "Now please sit down. I can't tell you how pleased I was when one of my staff members passed on your message concerning this mission. I'm glad you've stepped on board."

"As I have told you before, sir, I am always willing to serve as my government sees fit."

Jackson's gaze moved to one of the walls of Seward's dark-paneled office. There was a map of the entire North American continent with lines hand-drawn. He noted that the Russian territory, Alaska, had been marked. Jackson had heard rumors that Seward thought the purchase of that frozen wasteland from the Russians might be advantageous to the United States. Rumor also had it that Seward's mind had been affected by the stabbing. Why else, people said, would he even consider so outrageous a prospect?

"Excellent," Seward said. "I told the president we could count on you. We're searching for a band of outlaws, Jackson." He pushed a stack of papers across the broad walnut desk toward Jackson. "They call themselves Thompson's Raiders."

Jackson began to scan the reports. "Under the command of Captain Josiah Thompson, 16th Mississippi."

"Of course, we don't even know if Josiah Thompson is still alive. There are witnesses who saw him shot and he's on the missing in action list. It was thought he died at Gettysburg, but it's certainly possible that he escaped wounded, held up somewhere to recover—"

"And didn't quite make it to Appomattox for the surrender," Jackson offered dryly.

"Precisely. As the report indicates—" Seward pointed to the document "—we know very little except that there's been enough talk to be concerned. We don't even have a positive location. These ghost men seemed to be skirting back and forth between Tennessee, Mississippi and Alabama. But if Thompson has half as many men behind him as we hear, he could be a genuine threat."

"We've got a lot of angry, unemployed Southerners who would like nothing better than to shoot up congress."

"Or assassinate our new president," Seward said pointedly.

Jackson glanced over the top of the report, meeting the Secretary of State's gaze. "I'll look into this, sir, and get a full report to you as soon as possible."

"Excellent. Of course, I don't have to tell you that this information is sensitive. We don't need rumors of this kind of thing spreading. It's bad for the country right now, bad for reconstruction. We need to be fighting for reconciliation. Giving credence to dissenters will only fracture the country further. The war is over and we must move on."

Jackson slid out of his chair. "I'll see what I can find out around Washington, then I'll meander on south, stop and visit some friends here and there in the areas where Thompson's reported to have been. I'll put my ear to the ground and try to distinguish truth from gossip."

Seward grinned. "I knew you were the man for the job.

And I hear that Cherokee is headed this way from California. Think he would assist you?''

"Falcon Cortés, yes."

"Excellent. And Mrs. Marie LeLaurie has also agreed to assist you. She is presently here in the city. She says she can meet with you tonight."

Jackson hesitated. Marie? He had heard she was in the city, but he hadn't seen her since his return home.

Seward glanced at Jackson and cleared his throat before speaking. "I, um, I've heard the rumors, of course, but I assumed—"

"False. They are all false, sir."

"She can meet with you this evening and turn over what information she's brought with her from New Orleans." The Secretary of State slid another piece of paper across his polished desk, this one with the name of a small, intimate restaurant in Washington on it and the time Marie would meet him.

Jackson grabbed up the paper and added it to those tucked under his arm. Damn! If he had to meet Marie tonight, he would have to telegram Cameron that he would not be able to make it home until the early hours of the morning. Considering her mood, he knew she'd be angry, but he had to take this mission. It was obvious that the Secretary of State saw these Thompson's Raiders as a serious threat.

"Thank you, sir," Jackson said.

Seward rose from his chair slower than he had when Jackson had entered the room. He thrust out his hand. "No, Captain Logan, thank you."

4

"She here, miss. The carriage just pulled up."

Cameron looked up from her desk to see one of the servants, Addy, standing in the doorway of the west parlor Cameron had turned into an office. Cameron gave a small sound of delight and quickly tucked the letter she'd been writing into a leather folder. She'd been responding to an interested party's bid for one of her prime Arabian studs, but that correspondence could wait until tomorrow. Even her beloved horses came second to the joy Cameron felt in welcoming her dear sister.

"Hurry, miss," Addy said. "Miss Taye, she truly here."

Cameron wiped her ink pen and tucked it safely into a drawer, then rose swiftly from her chair. "Oh, goodness. Taye, at last. I thought she'd never get here!"

Taye, who was six years younger, had been Cameron's constant companion while they were growing up in Mississippi. She was the daughter of Elmwood plantation's housekeeper. But Sukey, a freed slave, had been so much more than a housekeeper. After the death of Cameron's mother when she was seven, Sukey had become Cameron's surrogate mother. And it was not until four years ago, after the death of her father, that Cameron and Taye discovered they had been raised as sisters because they *were* sisters. Cameron's father, Senator David Campbell, was also Taye's father.

Cameron licked her fingertips and tried to smooth a wayward red curl. "Hopeless," she muttered and then hurried off for the front hall.

"Cameron!" Taye burst in the door in a gay cloud of pink silk and taffeta. Taye was a picture of beauty, as she had always been. With rich, honey-colored skin, dark, silky hair and shocking pale blue eyes, she was a striking young woman.

Cameron threw out her arms and hugged her tightly. "I can't believe you're here at last," Cameron cried. "Let me get a look at you." She took Taye's hand and spun her around as if she were her dance partner.

Taye turned gracefully on heeled slippers, tilting her head just so to show off her new straw-and-pink tulle traveling bonnet. As she spun on the black-and-white marble-tiled floor, she tapped her parasol.

"Heavens, you're beautiful and you've traveled hundreds of miles." Cameron smoothed her hair self-consciously. "And look at me, a wreck, and I've not left the house today."

Taye linked her arm through Cameron's and leaned closer. "So is what you suspected true?"

Cameron nodded excitedly.

"Oh, Cam. I'm so happy for you and Jackson." Her blue eyes danced with pleasure. "And how are you feeling?"

"Fit as a fiddle, of course." She led Taye down the hall. "Addy, could you send someone to the garden with refreshments?"

"I will, Missy Cameron. I surely will. Cook's made those raisin scones you like so well."

The two women walked down the long hallway and out

onto the rear summer porch of the mansion, then Cameron led Taye across the lawn to a small table in the shade of an ancient oak tree.

"This garden is lovely." Taye smiled when she heard the soft splash of water. In the nearby fountain, twin marble cherubs holding pitchers poured an unending stream of water into a circular pool below them.

"Yes, it is, isn't it?" Cameron answered. "This garden is really the only thing I love about the house."

"It is impressive and rather..." Taye searched for the right word. "Rather..."

"Overdone," Cameron said. They both laughed. "You know me, I always was hopeless at Greek."

Taye's eyes sparkled with warmth. "And how is he? Handsome as ever?"

"He's fine." She made a face. "Though how I would know that, I'm not certain. He barely blows through here on his way from one business engagement to another."

Cameron watched Taye remove her bonnet and gloves with graceful, ladylike movements. She couldn't help noticing that her sister moved with a refined air of confidence she hadn't shown in her younger years.

During the war years, Taye had lived with Campbell family friends in New York City. Because her mother had been a slave and Taye was considered a Negro, even though her father was white, it hadn't been safe for her to live south of the Mason-Dixon line. Cameron had visited Taye regularly and certainly noticed small differences in her sister's demeanor, but in her mind, Taye was still seventeen, doting on her, always in her shadow. Cameron had the suspicion that this elegant young woman before her would walk in no one's shadow now.

"Jackson is just never home," Cameron confessed. "We

barely see each other except in bed, and then talk is the last thing that interests him.''

Taye giggled, but her cheeks didn't color as they once would have at the mention of sexual relations. ''And you're complaining about *that?* Most wives would give their eye-teeth for such a handsome, attentive husband.'' She soft-ened. ''Especially now, when so many good men have died.''

''No, of course I'm not complaining that he still desires me.'' Cameron struggled to explain. ''It's just that so much time has passed since we married. I do love Jackson and he certainly loves me, but I somehow thought things would be—'' She hesitated. ''I don't know...*different.*''

''Give him time.'' Taye reached across the table to squeeze Cameron's hand. ''Give yourself time.''

A serving girl dressed from head to toe in white walked out into the grass carrying a tray of fresh lemonade, the promised scones and tiny iced sponge cakes.

''Thank you, Martha,'' Cameron said. ''I'll serve. You can go back to what you were doing.''

Martha grinned, dipped a curtsy and retreated into the house.

Cameron stood to pour Taye's lemonade.

''Oh, goodness,'' Taye said, coming to her feet and tak-ing the blown-glass pitcher out of her sister's hands. ''Sit down and let me do that.''

''I don't need to be catered to.'' Cameron sat down hard in her chair. ''For heaven's sake, it's a baby I'm carrying, not a disease.''

''Of course.'' Taye began to pour the lemonade. ''It's just that I want to do this for you, Cam. I know I can never repay you and Jackson for all you've done for me, but at least give me these small satisfactions.''

Cameron took a linen napkin from the silver tray and

reached for one of the sweets on the plate. Though she was not even far enough along in her pregnancy to show, she found herself constantly hungry. At this rate, she'd be the size of a heifer before the child saw the light of day.

"Have you heard from Thomas?" Cameron licked white sugar icing from her fingertips.

Taye passed her a glass of lemonade and took her seat again. "Yes, I received a letter just before I left New York. He'll be here within the week."

Cameron slanted her eyes mischievously. "And how soon after he arrives will we be hearing wedding bells?"

Thomas Burl had been Senator Campbell's attorney. He had been sweet on Taye in the months before the war fell upon the South, and before she escaped safely to New York, he had made his feelings known to her. They had promised to marry at the end of the war, if their feelings remained the same, and had kept in regular contact over the years. Though Thomas was quiet and reserved, he had a good heart and he loved Taye—and she loved him.

Taye's lovely, sun-kissed skin pinkened in pleased embarrassment. "I've barely seen him in the last year. Perhaps his intentions have changed."

Cameron sipped her lemonade and laughed. "And perhaps he's grown hair on that balding head of his, too." She glanced sideways at her sister. "Of course he intends to marry you. I have a feeling that's precisely why he asked Jackson if he could come here to stay for a while. He wants to court you, but he has no relatives nearby to live with."

"I'm thankful Jackson will have us."

"You're my sister, Taye. Of course he'll have you. Or there will be hell to pay from me." Cameron took another sip from her glass. "Anyway, I'm so glad to have you here. Jackson announced this morning that we'll be having a ball for three hundred in less than two weeks."

Taye's bright blue eyes widened. "Three hundred? My goodness!"

"It's a welcome home ball for Union officers. Apparently Jackson and Mr. Ulysses S. Grant are well acquainted."

"Well then, I arrived just in time, didn't I? Leave everything to me. Baltimore and our newly returned officers will have a ball the likes of which they have never seen before." She cut her blue eyes to Cameron. "Mississippi style."

"There you are, Jackson." Marie LeLaurie rose from her chair in a cozy corner of the intimate restaurant and presented her cheek. She was dressed stylishly, as always, in a rich red silk gown that transformed her thick wealth of stunning black hair and creamy olive skin from merely lovely to exquisite.

"Marie." Jackson glanced around to be sure he saw no one he knew before joining her. He kissed her smooth cheek that smelled of a French cologne he knew she had specially blended for her in Paris.

"You're late," she chastised. "I was afraid you weren't coming."

He took the seat across from her.

"Wine?"

He shook his head.

"But it's an excellent burgundy." She pursed her red-stained lips, lips he had once brushed his own against, and pouted. "I know you like burgundy. Should I order something else?"

"No. No, this will be fine." He watched as she poured the wine. "Marie, I cannot stay long. My wife—"

"She will be jealous?" Marie teased, coquettishly.

"What I was going to say is that my wife is expecting

our first child, and I would like to get back to Baltimore tonight, however late.''

''A papa!'' She laughed and tipped her wine glass to his in toast. Her voice was as rich as the wine she drank. ''Congratulations. You will be a good father, I think, Jackson.''

''Seward says you have information for me.'' He glanced up from the table again.

In the restaurant, there was only one other couple dining and they were elderly; they paid no mind to the man and woman who could well have been on an assignation…or meeting to pass on secret information vital to the government. Marie had picked the perfect place to meet, and in truth, she made the perfect spy. She was beautiful and she was brilliant, yet always unthreatening. Men naturally trusted her, believing no woman so lovely could possibly betray them.

''Jackson, Jackson,'' she chastised. ''You are always all work and no play.'' She made a clicking sound between her even white teeth. ''You really should enjoy life more, as I do.'' She tossed her head, and her long, dark hair sailed as if on a windswept beach. ''Life is too short,'' she whispered with those mesmerizing red lips.

He leaned back in his chair, mentally trying to distance himself from Marie. He had Cameron to think about. His child. He loved Cameron, loved her desperately. And he loved their unborn baby. He'd not let his attraction to Marie allow him to make a mistake that could cost him his marriage. He had already made that mistake once and vowed it would never happen again.

''I haven't much time, Marie. Just tell me what you know.'' He glanced at the elderly couple again. All he needed was for a gossiping dowager who knew Cameron from the Women's League to see him here alone with Marie. ''We really shouldn't be seen in public together, anyway. I know too many people here in Washington and too many know me.''

She lifted the glass of ruby wine to her ruby lips. ''Then the next time I will be sure we meet in a place that is more *private*,'' she purred.

Several nights later, Jackson walked up behind Cameron where she was standing in front of the gilded mirror in their bedchamber. He placed his splayed hands on her hips, leaning over and grazing her bare shoulder with his lips. ''You look tired,'' he murmured. ''Are you certain you're up to this?''

Cameron trembled at his sensual caress. They'd begun making love before they were married, during the first days of the war when Cameron's whole life was crumbling at her feet. Her father was dead; her despicable brother, Grant, was selling off the family plantation piece by piece and trying to marry her off. Physical lovemaking with Jackson had always been good, but since his return, it had been even better. His touch, his heated glances, set her aflame, so much so it troubled her that Jackson should have such control over her body. Over her emotions. All she had to do was bring up a subject he deemed unpleasant, and he immediately began to woo her with scorching kisses and damnable roguish charm. She knew what her husband was doing, and yet, he had only to stroke her with hard, lean fingers and whisper sweet, wicked words into her ear and she tumbled helplessly into his trap every time.

Cameron studied Jackson's reflection in the mirror as he remained bent over her, watching her. He was as handsome as ever, as dashing as ever. While some men had returned from the war mere shadows of themselves, Jackson had thrived in the turmoil and danger of the last four years. If anything, despite the tiny lines on his forehead, he was even

more devilishly attractive than he had been in his younger
years. He was what any Southern woman would have considered a great *catch*—staggeringly wealthy and highly respected. Now there was even talk of him running for a
political office. He was everything a woman could hope for
in a man.

But was it all too good to be true? When they had first
married and Cameron came to live in Baltimore, there had
been whispers that their marriage would never last. That
the handsome captain was not a man meant to be tied down
to a single woman. Her gaze flickered to his as he waited
for her reply.

Had they been right?

The very thought put her on edge, turning her nerves
raw. "Roxy was down with colic," she said.

The blooded Arabian mare had been a gift from her father for her twenty-second birthday. Her brother had sold
the horse, but Jackson managed to locate the mare and have
her shipped to Baltimore. "She's better now, but it was a
long day." Cameron plucked at the hair that framed her
face.

Taye had been in earlier to help her dress and create her
elaborate coiffure for the evening. Tonight they were dining
in celebration of Thomas Burl's arrival.

"I thought you weren't going to go to the barn every
day." Jackson kissed her neck, still watching her in the
mirror.

She shrank at his touch, moving away from the mirror.
"I never said I wasn't going every day," she protested.
Walking to a rosewood table, she opened a black lacquered
box from the Orient and removed a pair of pearl earrings.
"*You* said that. I had to go today. Didn't you hear me?
Roxy was ill. She could have died."

His gray eyes were instantly stormy. "Look, Cameron,

I understand how important those damned horses were to you when I was gone. But I'm home now. You don't need to spend every waking moment at that farm. It's really not appropriate. Why have the herd at all? God knows we don't need the money.''

"Why have the herd at all?" she challenged. "Maybe because it's the only tangible thing I have left of my home. Of my father.''

He sighed. "All right, so keep the horses. But you're really not needed at the farm every day. I want you here, in our home. You're my wife and this is where you belong now.''

"So you can come and go as you please? And what would you have me do?'' She pushed the second earring into her earlobe and whirled around to face him. "Sit around all day and wait for you to come home from the shipyards or one of your secret meetings in Washington? What about the day Taye arrived? I waited for you that night and you didn't come home. Not until three in the morning.''

"I sent you a telegram. I ended up having to hire a coach. I explained—''

"You didn't *explain* anything. You only said you would be late.''

He groaned impatiently. "I have a great deal of business to take care of. Four years is a long time to be gone, Cam. Even with Josiah to look after—''

"That night had nothing to do with your business,'' she snapped. "So don't tell me that it did. You were in Washington. Again.''

He paused, then spoke. "Just because the fighting is over, that doesn't mean the war is over. The South is literally smoldering. I still have a duty to fulfill.''

She lowered her hands to her hips. "And exactly when

will that duty be fulfilled? The soldiers who survived are home with their wives and children.'' She stared at him pointedly. "When are you coming home, Jackson? When will the war be over for us?"

"When it's over," he answered stiffly. "When my service is no longer required by my country."

"And what am I supposed to do in the meantime? Simply *breed?*"

"There are plenty of household matters for you to manage here." He gestured. "The ball for instance. Surely there's a great deal of preparation."

"Surely there is, for a ball *you* planned without first asking me," she snapped. "Just like the dinner parties you plan without asking me. The men you bring home for supper without warning. The household staff you hire and fire without so much as a glance my way."

"Cameron—"

"And now that Taye is here, your little plan is complete. I'm of no use to anyone. Taye has come in and taken over planning the ball, with your blessing apparently. All I've had to do was choose the color of the table linens and point to which midnight buffet I prefer. Jackson, she even ordered a gown for me!"

"I'm sure she's only trying to be helpful. Taye is a very capable young woman."

"Of course she is. But so I am. I just don't like being treated this way. By you or Taye. It's as if everyone suddenly thinks I'm made of spun sugar with the brains of a mouse. What am I supposed to do all day if I can't go see my horses, and Taye is running the household?"

He shrugged. "How should I know what gentlewomen occupy themselves with? Can't you take up needlepoint or—"

"Don't you dare talk to me about such nonsense. Don't

you dare!'' Cameron found herself fighting tears of fury. ''I despise sewing. I cannot bear being treated as if I were an ornament. Am I supposed to sit here in this museum of a house with nothing to do but walk from room to room and wish I was home?''

Jackson jerked his black frock coat off the back of a chair and scowled at her. ''You are *home* now.''

''My home is in Mississippi,'' she said softly, not knowing if she wanted to cry or break something over his head.

He paused as he slid his long arms into the sleeves of the new coat. When he spoke again, his tone had softened. ''No, not anymore.''

Tears welled in her eyes. Why was she crying all the time? She had cried more since Jackson came home than she had the whole time he'd been gone. ''You said we would talk about this.''

''And we will.'' He draped his arm over her shoulder. ''But not tonight. Our guests are waiting.''

Cameron glanced up at Jackson. She didn't want to allow him to manipulate her like this, but she didn't want to constantly fight with him, either. She wanted to have a nice evening with Taye and Thomas and the few close friends they had made over the last years who had been invited tonight.

She tipped her head back to allow Jackson to brush his sensual lips against her mouth. ''I'll bow to you this time, husband, but I'm warning you, I'm not about to take up needlepoint. And you've not heard the end of this. You can't just sweet-talk me every time the conversation gets uncomfortable for you.''

''I can try.'' He gave her that boyish grin of his, nodded and then opened their bedchamber door. ''Mrs. Logan.''

She curtsied, thinking, God, I do love him, but will life with him always be this difficult?

And then they walked down the grand staircase arm and arm to greet their guests.

The simple eight-course evening meal, featuring roasted squab, lamb cutlets, pearled onion potatoes and fresh squash soufflé, served with three wines, was exquisite. After the small party of a dozen of Baltimore's finest ladies and gentlemen had dined, they moved to the elegant parlor. Traditionally, the ladies and gentlemen would separate at this point, but Cameron told her guests that the war had divided her and her husband for four years and no walls would divide them now.

In the parlor, brandy and champagne were served beneath the watchful eye of a pantheon of plaster gods and goddesses, as Taye entertained them on the grand piano with a selection of classical music.

Cameron left her chair beside Mrs. Rhettish, where they had been discussing her mother's gout, and moved to the darkened window where Thomas stood watching Taye as she played a charming piece from a young French composer, Jules Massenet. Last year on their trip to Paris, Cameron and Taye had heard the young man play, and Taye had become enamored of his sound and composition.

"Have you asked her yet?" Cameron whispered.

Thomas Burl's face flushed. He was a tall, thin man with long gangly legs and arms that had once made Cameron think he looked like a stork. He had sandy blond hair that was thinning rapidly and he wore wire-frame glasses perched on the end of his thin nose. Her father had once actually considered Thomas a possible suitor for Cameron, but then Jackson had come into her life.

Even though Thomas was too sedate for her taste, she loved him like a brother. Thomas had worked closely with the senator for years, often in Mississippi and Washington, D.C.

"Mrs. Logan." Thomas's face was now beet red. "You embarrass me. I've barely been here twenty-four hours."

"Since when am I Mrs. Logan? It's Cameron, remember?" she chastised. "You've been here twenty-four hours and you've still not asked Taye to marry you? You'd better make haste." She nodded to the elderly, bearded gentleman speaking with Jackson. "Mr. Gorman is mad for her. His third wife passed recently, and I understand he is looking for number four. He would be an excellent prospect for our dear Taye, but I'm quite certain you are her first choice."

Thomas glowed with pleasure, glancing at Taye, then at his highly polished shoes. "You don't think I would be forward to ask her tonight?"

"I think you should take her walking in the garden after our guests depart. I think you should ask her to marry you, and I think you should kiss her soundly—on the lips."

"Oh, my," he breathed, looking quickly to Taye. "I'm not certain I can—"

"Kiss?" Cameron demanded under her breath. She laughed and Taye looked their way, then back at the keyboard.

Cameron leaned in to her father's friend. "Well, you'd best figure it out, Mr. Burl." Realizing she had shocked him beyond words, she smiled. "Have no fear. She'll like it." She squeezed his arm. "And so will you. Now if you'll excuse me, I think Jackson is trying to catch my attention." She dipped a polite curtsy.

Thomas bowed stiffly.

As Cameron glided past the piano toward Jackson, she winked at Taye.

* * *

"Did you enjoy yourself this evening?" Jackson asked as he loosened the strings of Cameron's lace-and-satin stays. Jackson refused to allow Cameron's personal maid into the bedchamber, insisting it was his job to dress and undress the mistress of the household now that he was home.

Cameron held on to the bedpost, exhaling with relief as he eased the constriction of the undergarment, wondering how much longer she'd be able to wear the boned stays before she would have to set them aside for her pregnancy. "It was very nice. I love Mrs. Rhettish. A woman after my own heart. Did you know that she ran her husband's mercantile store on Broad Street while he was off in the war, and now that he's returned, he's working for her?"

Jackson laughed. "I have news for you, Cam. Knowing Violet Rhettish, she ran Carl's business, and Carl, well before the war." He handed her the stays. "It's no wonder the man was disappointed when the war was over. He was actually forced to come home to her."

She hit him across the stomach with the stays and he grabbed her around the waist and lifted her onto the bed. She fell back on the soft feather tick and he buried his face between her breasts.

"Jackson, I'm trying to undress."

"And I'm merely trying to assist, madame." He grinned, standing up to release her.

Cameron slid off the bed and padded barefoot to the window. She drew back the heavy velvet drape slightly and peered into the lantern-lit garden. "Do you think Thomas will get up the nerve to ask Taye to marry him?" Below, she could just make out the pair, sitting on a small stone bench beneath a rose arbor.

"I'm certain he will. He told me he's already making plans to reopen his law office. He has only to decide in which city."

Cameron watched Taye and Thomas, almost wishing she could hear what they were saying. "He should open his office in the North, of course, where Taye will be safe and accepted."

Jackson removed his silk cravat and then his starched white shirt to bare his muscular chest. "Perhaps. But Mississippi is in desperate need of educated men like Thomas, and he does have his father's offices in Jackson. There's the family plantation, too, or what's left of it."

Still holding back the drape, Cameron lifted an eyebrow, turning to her husband. "Oh, so Taye should go home to Mississippi, and I shouldn't?"

Jackson walked stark naked, and glorious in his manhood, across the wood floor and grabbed her by the hand. "Will you come away from that window, woman, and come to bed?"

She let the drapes fall.

"Give them a little privacy," he said, wrapping her in one arm. "And us as well."

He slid his hand beneath her chemise to cup her breast, and she let her eyes drift shut. The man infuriated her, and yet, when he touched her like this, she was all but melted sugar in his mouth.

"Again you change the subject," she accused. "And you forget, I'm still angry with you from earlier."

"Give me a moment and then tell me if you're still angry." He covered her mouth with his, thrusting his tongue, and when he drew away, she was limp in his arms.

"Cheater," she managed to say finally.

"No." He gazed into her face, capturing her as he always did with the breadth and depth of his gray eyes. "But this *is* cheating."

Jackson rested his hands on her hips and slowly slid to his knees. Cameron gasped as he lifted the hem of her chemise and kissed the inside of her knee. It was just a tiny, fleeting kiss, little more than a brush of a butterfly's wings, yet it set her flesh on fire.

Cameron swayed on her feet as his fingertips brushed the tender flesh of her inner thigh.

"Jackson…"

Lifting the linen skirt higher, he thrust his head beneath the fabric and pressed his warm mouth between her legs, finding her already hot and wet for him.

She couldn't fight him. She couldn't win.

"The bed…" she groaned as his tongue flicked out, delved. Cameron ran her fingers through his silky, dark hair as a ripple, a wave, of wicked pleasure washed over her. Then another and another as he stroked her with his tongue, plied her with his probing fingers.

"Jackson, please…" Cameron gripped Jackson's shoulders to steady herself as she struggled to find her voice. To stop him. But the waves of pleasure were already building and she pressed her hands to his shoulders, gripping them to keep from tumbling to the floor. His fingers found the soft, moist folds of her flesh and she surrendered to him yet again.

"Are you certain this is what you want?" Taye asked softly, gazing into Thomas's brown eyes.

He could barely hold her gaze. He kept looking away from her, his gaze flickering from her to objects in the dark garden. "Of course I'm certain. It's what I've lived for all these years," he said, his voice earnest.

Taye reached out and stroked Thomas's shaven cheek. "You understand it would be difficult. My skin is pale, but we could not hide my heritage if anyone chose to condemn you for who I am, for who I was born."

"Y-you were born a Campbell," he stammered. "The

daughter of David Campbell, one of the greatest senators of our time.''

"*And* the daughter of a house slave,'' she reminded him. "Half of my family came from the Highlands of Scotland, but half came from the jungles of Africa.''

He stared hard at the pink roses that vined beyond her shoulder and then forced himself to look at her. ''I want you to be my wife, Taye Campbell. W-will you do me the honor?''

She smiled. ''As long as you understand that I would not hold you to anything we said in the heat of the moment, years ago. The war had just begun, we were all in a fret—''

He shook his head. ''I...I love you, Taye. I have always loved you. And I want to marry you. I want you to have my children, God willing.''

Taye smiled. This was the moment she had been dreaming of since the war began. When Thomas had first declared his love for her on the back stair of Elmwood's plantation house the night Fort Sumter was fired upon, she had been so frightened that she had denied her attraction to him. She had run from him. But Thomas had not given up on her; he had pursued her with a quiet determination that she couldn't help but love. All through the war he had written to her and come to New York City to see her when he could. They had talked of marriage and a family, and now it would all come true.

She gazed into Thomas's warm, dark eyes. ''Then yes. I'll marry you, Thomas Burl.''

''Th-thank you,'' he stammered, his eyes wide.

Taye rested her hands on his shoulders and kissed him squarely on the lips.

''My. Oh, my,'' Thomas muttered, flustered when she pulled away.

She laughed and took his hand. ''You had better get used

to that,'' she teased. ''If you're going to marry me, Thomas,
I want to be kissed. Often.''

''Would you care to go for a stroll in the garden before
you retire?'' He bobbed off the bench as if it had been set
aflame.

She laughed, her voice light and musical on the night
air. ''I would love to go for a walk.'' She stood and slipped
her arm through his and then walked down the path into
the darkness, and into her future with Thomas Burl, Es-
quire.

5

"'Scuse me, Miss Cameron, Miss Taye." Addy stepped into the doorway of Cameron's office where the two women had been taking their afternoon tea.

"There's a gal to see ya, Miss Cameron." The young servant sounded tentative. "I tole her she got to go 'round back where the other negras enters the house, but she won't budge off the front steps. She right out there where everyone walkin' by can see her, actin' all uppity, like she *belong*."

Puzzled, Cameron patted her lips with her linen napkin. "Who is she? Someone we know?"

"Someone lookin' for work, most likely. She's same as every Southern negra girl, I s'pose. Masta set us free and we got nowhere to go. No way to feed our little 'uns." Addy rested a fist on her waist. "This girl, she say her name is Naomi and that—"

"Naomi?" Cameron flew out of her chair, looking to Taye. "Could it possibly be?"

Taye rose in a far more ladylike fashion, but was equally excited. "I don't know. We never heard from her after we parted on the docks that day we found Jackson here in Baltimore."

Naomi had been a house slave at Elmwood and had been known as a voodoo priestess. When Grant had sold Elmwood's slaves after their father died, Naomi managed to escape. She'd traveled with Cameron to rescue Taye in Baton Rouge and eventually had made the long trip north from Mississippi on the Underground Railroad with the sisters. The three women had formed an unbreakable bond during those weeks and months. When last Cameron had seen her, in September of 1861, Naomi was headed north to Philadelphia to be reunited with other family members who had journeyed safely out of the South.

Cameron flew out of the office, clutching fistfuls of her sprigged green day gown. She threw open the massive front door to see their Naomi standing on the marble steps, dressed in bright blues and yellows with a turban around her head, beaming like a Methodist preacher with his first convert.

"Heavenly Father," Cameron swore, thanking Him at the same time. She opened her arms and Naomi stepped into them, smelling of cloves, sandalwood and home. "Naomi," she breathed, fighting tears again. "Is it really you?"

"Flesh and bone," she answered, with a husky laugh. "No spirits here."

Cameron released her and stepped back to make room for Taye.

"I was afraid I would never see you again," Taye murmured, hugging Naomi tightly.

"And isn't that nothin' but nonsense? I told you we'd meet again. That night we was all walkin' through the field and ole Harriet Tubman was leading us north, I seen it in the stars."

Taye stepped back, releasing Naomi.

"Well, don't just stand there, come in." Cameron waved her into the exotic front hall with its marble floor and oriental painted wallpaper where long-legged storks with golden feathers looked down on them.

"Just come right in the front door and let the neighbors talk." Cameron laughed, seeing the shocked look on Addy's face. "You can join us for tea and cake, Naomi."

"Well, Miss Cameron, I'd be pleased to come in, but there's a little somethin' holdin' me back." Naomi pointed to a crude buckboard in the circular drive.

Cameron stepped outside to get a closer look at the buckboard and the black man who sat on the bench calmly holding the leather reins. Here was a huge, handsome, young man dressed in soft brown breeches with a pale blue workman's shirt. His hands were clean and he was wearing brown leather boots.

"That there's my husband, Noah," Naomi said proudly. "And that little bundle tucked beside him is our little babe, Ngosi. Born almost three months ago."

"You're married, with a baby?" Cameron smiled, so pleased Naomi had found happiness after all the tragedy of her early days. In the Elmwood household, Naomi had been the slave woman who "serviced" white male guests, and she had been abused sexually by Grant. Cameron had been appalled by it all, but had been unable to fight years of Southern tradition in a household run by men. Slave traders had killed Naomi's lover, with whom she had attempted to escape north. Seeing that Naomi had found a man to love again made Cameron's heart swell.

"Well, what is he doing in the wagon?" Cameron exclaimed. "Come in, come in."

"Now, Miss Cameron. I got to get some things clear here before I step foot in this big ole city house and eat that cake of yours. My Noah and me, we had a nice cabin in New Jersey. My Noah, he was a free man before the war. Got a trade. He builds with his hands, fine furniture. We was happy as crows at a pig butcherin', but one morning I got up and I throwed my bones and the spirits tole me ya needed me.'' Naomi studied Cameron with black eyes that seemed to see through to her very soul. ''Ya need me, Miss Cameron?'' Her voice was silky smooth, like the dark silt of the river that had flowed through Elmwood plantation.

The hairs on the nape of Cameron's neck prickled, and she gave a little laugh to cover her discomfort. She had always been a little fearful of Naomi's voodoo practices, as were all the whites in Elmwood and in the surrounding county. Cameron didn't even know if she believed in voodoo, but she knew the slaves she had grown up with did, and so she had been raised with a healthy respect for the religion they had brought with them on the slave ships. ''I…I don't know that I need you,'' Cameron said, flustered. ''But I'm certainly glad to see you and to have you and your family stay as long as you like as my guests.''

''You feverish, Miss Cameron? I'm not talkin' about bein' your guest,'' Naomi scoffed. ''I'm talkin' 'bout comin' here to work for you. Run your house, whatever you be needin'. My Noah can get work anywhere in the city, good as he is with his hands and a slab of wood.''

Cameron glanced at Taye and then back at Naomi. ''Our housekeeper just announced this morning that she would be leaving us for retirement. Would you consider—''

Naomi thrust out her hand and laid it on Cameron's abdomen, taking her completely by surprise. ''How far ya gone with this chile, Miss Cameron?''

''Only a little more than a month…''

Naomi didn't smile. ''Ya be needin' me, all right.'' She looked over her shoulder. ''We're stayin'. Take the wagon 'round back, Noah, and get that baby out of there. I'll be with ya shortly, soon as I have some of that cake with my girls.''

* * *

A few days later, Cameron returned home from the farm where she stabled her horses. Plucking off her gloves, she walked slowly up the grand staircase, surprised as she turned on the landing to hear the rhythmic sound of a saw.

Cameron whipped off her hat and dropped her gloves into it as she reached the second story, walking down the long hallway, past her own bedchamber, toward the sound. As she walked, the gilt-framed portraits of Jackson's ancestors that lined the walls seemed to stare disapprovingly down at her. Placing her riding bonnet on a small table, she took a deep breath and realized she felt like a stranger in this hall, in this house. It just wasn't home, and the longer she was away from Mississippi, the more homesick she became. It wasn't her pregnancy that was making her feel tired, it was her unhappiness.

At the end of the hall, Cameron stepped into a small bedchamber used for storing furniture. She looked from two carpenters in leather aprons to a hole that had been cut in the wall to the next bedchamber.

"What do you think you're doing?"

One of the men yanked an old hat off his head and plucked at his bristly, orange beard. "Well, putting in the doorway 'tween the two rooms, ma'am."

She looked through the hole that had been cut in the wall. She could see the small four-poster bed, the gauzy summer draperies pulled shut over the windows on the far wall. There was also a French chest of drawers that had been covered to prevent damage from the dust.

"Why are you cutting a doorway?"

"'Cause I was tole to, that's why, ma'am."

"Told by whom?" she demanded.

"The captain, ma'am. We're ship builders, me and Bernie, but he sent us to his house to put this doorway in."

Cameron turned and stormed out of the room, back downstairs and into the kitchen where she knew she would find Jackson's personal servant. Alfred served as butler, secretary and whatever else Jackson needed when he was here at home. When Jackson was gone, which was most of the time, Alfred parked in the massive kitchen and helped himself to many a slice of pie from the looks of his expanding waistline.

"Alfred?" Cameron called as she walked into the kitchen.

"Yes, ma'am." Alfred leaped off the stool on the far side of the work counter, struggling to swallow a mouthful of apple tart.

"Where is the captain this afternoon?"

Alfred swallowed hard and his Adam's apple bobbed beneath his starched white cravat. In Jackson's household all servants, black or white, butler to lowly stable boy, dressed well. He provided their clothing and demanded they always look clean and neat.

Cameron dropped her riding bonnet on her head and thrust her hands into her gloves.

"He's at the docks, I believe, ma'am. At the warehouse. Is there something I can do for you?"

She wasn't dressed properly to ride astride, but she was too angry to take the time to go upstairs and redress. "Please let Taye know, when she returns, that I will be home shortly for tea." She cut through the kitchen, headed for the back door. "I don't think this will take long."

In the rear yard, she called to a young stable boy and ordered Roxy to be saddled. In ten minutes time, she was astride.

"Don't ya want me to go with you, Mrs. Jackson?" the stable manager asked. "The captain will be hoppin' mad with me if I let you go out of here on that horse, unescorted.''

"I told you, Joe, I ride alone. I'll make it clear to the *captain* that I ordered you to stay here.''

Joe stepped back, passing her reins up to her. "Well, you be careful, ma'am. Them docks can be dangerous.''

"Not as dangerous as I am right now.'' She smiled, softening her tone, knowing she couldn't be angry with the workmen upstairs, or Jackson's servant, or the stable master. But she could be angry with Jackson. Damned angry. "Thank you, Joe. I'll be careful. I promise.''

Cameron was just urging Roxy out the rear drive when Taye pulled up in a carriage driven by Thomas. "Have a good time?'' Cameron asked, adjusting her boots in her stirrups.

"Lovely,'' Taye said. But her tone was forced. Cameron could see in Taye's blue eyes that something was wrong, but she could also see that this wasn't the time to bring it up.

"Where are you going?'' Taye waited until Thomas dismounted and came around the carriage to help her down. He tipped his hat toward Cameron before lifting his hand to Taye's.

"Down to the docks to see Jackson. He and I have something to discuss,'' she said tartly.

"Well, come down and I'll go with you. We can take the carriage. You shouldn't—''

"I'm too damned mad for the carriage.'' Cameron sank her heel into Roxy's flank, and the sensitive Arabian bolted. "I won't be long,'' she called over her shoulder.

Cameron wove her way slowly down the crowded streets, passing wagons loaded with goods, carriages of women and a funeral procession. She saw old men, graying and hunched over, and young lads, working as if they were men, but there were so few between the ages of twenty and forty. The toll of the war, she thought grimly.

Cameron smelled the harbor long before she reached it. The pungent scent of the salty Atlantic, mingled with the stench of fish and unwashed bodies, assaulted her nostrils.

Just as her boots hit the wooden planked dock in front of the Logan warehouse, Josiah Lonsford, Jackson's business manager, came hurrying out to meet her.

"Mrs. Logan, you should not be here unescorted."

"It's good to see you, too, Josiah." She smiled. In the four years that Jackson had been gone, she and Josiah Lonsford had become good friends. Not only had he kept her abreast of the financial health of her husband's business, but they had often shared a meal in her home, and Josiah had been willing to offer advice as she had imagined her father would have, had he still been alive.

He lowered his voice so that the others who bustled around them wouldn't hear. "Does Jackson know you're here?" he asked quietly. "I cannot imagine he would approve of you riding alone at the docks."

"Speak of the devil!" She pulled impatiently at the fingers of her gloves, one at a time. "Have you, by chance, seen my dear husband?" The ride over had calmed her, but she could feel her anger building again. She took a deep breath of the stinging salt air.

"He's inside. I'll walk you in." Josiah passed Roxy's reins to a lad in a torn, striped sailor's shirt. "Stay here with the horse and keep her safe." He offered Cameron his arm, which she took.

"He's upstairs in the office," Josiah said. "I'll walk you up."

"That won't be necessary." Cameron patted his arm. "But thank you, Josiah. It was good to see you. You must come for supper one night. I've missed our talks." She grasped her petticoats and started up the crude wooden staircase that led to the second floor and Jackson's office.

Josiah stood at the bottom of the stairs and watched her go, shaking his head. He seemed to sense there was about to be an angry outburst, but he held his tongue. That was another reason she liked him.

Cameron entered the office without a knock or announcement, not caring how busy Jackson was. His business would have to wait. She threw open the door and walked into the unpainted, utilitarian office to see Jackson and three gentlemen sitting around a table playing cards.

"I'd like to speak with you for a moment, if I could, husband," she said sweetly, her ire building.

The three men—she didn't know any of them—immediately rose in their chairs, offering awkward greetings. They left cards and drinks on the table, while scooping their money into their hands as they backed away.

"We should go anyway, Jackson," a bold one said.

"Aye, we should be going. We'll talk later."

Jackson remained in his chair, booted foot propped on the table, cigar protruding from his mouth, the smoke circling his head as it drifted away.

"Nice game of cards?" she asked, not knowing if it was the stench of the cigar smoke making her sick to her stomach or her anger.

He shrugged. He had removed his suit coat and it hung carelessly over the back of his chair. His cravat hung loosely and untied around his neck. "I was winning."

"I thought you were working here today."

He lazily inhaled on the cigar one last time and then ground it out in a dish on the edge of the table. His foot and the boyish grin remained where they were. "I *was* working."

She lifted a feathered eyebrow. "Looks to me like you

were gambling. Smoking.'' She glanced at the half-empty
bottle of good Jamaican rum. "And drinking.''

"You don't understand my business." He lowered his
foot at last and came out of the chair. "These men like to
mix business with pleasure. I was simply being a good
businessman, sweet.''

He tried to rest his arm on her shoulder but she pushed
it away. "Damn you, Jackson! Don't you *sweet* me. Why
are there men in our home, as we speak, cutting a hole
between one bedchamber and another?''

He looked at her as if she had asked why there was a
Japanese garden in the parlor. "To build the nursery. I
thought the governess should have her own room connected
to the nursery. I put them in rooms at the end of the hallway
so that you wouldn't be disturbed by late-night crying.''

"A nursery?" she seethed. She had suspected, of course,
but to hear him actually say it only baited her further.
"You're building a nursery, and you never consulted me?''

"Not building a nursery, my sweet, just adding a con-
necting door to rooms already there.''

"Don't quibble words with me! You know what I mean.
I am the one having the baby." She threw her gloves down
on a folded hand of cards. "*I* should have been consulted.''

He looked almost hurt. "It never occurred to me that
you didn't want a nursery.''

She stared at him. He still didn't understand. "Jackson,
it's not about whether or not I want a nursery, it's that you
didn't ask me. You never ask me anything before making
decisions that affect me, that affect us." She took a breath.
"What if I don't care if the baby wakes me? What if I want
the baby next to us at night?''

"I don't understand what all the fuss is about." He
raised his hands, as if in surrender. "So make a different

room a nursery. Make them all nurseries. I don't care,'' he barked at her.

She took a breath and quieted. "Just ask me before you make decisions like this, all right?"

He glanced away from her. "I've never been one to consult others. It's not how I work. Too many people depended on me for protection. To protect their secrets. No one cared if I consulted them so long as they came out alive." He snapped his head around to look her in the eye. "Do you have any idea how that makes a man feel? How hard it is to know every step you take could get the man behind you killed?"

Cameron took a deep breath and felt her anger wane. She wanted to cry; she could feel the burn of the tears behind her eyelids. Now it was frustration that bubbled up inside her. Jackson said so little about his role in the war, so little about what he had actually done and even less about how he felt.

Now she wanted to say she was sorry. She just didn't know how. He was right. This was a trivial matter. There was no need for her to become this angry, to embarrass him in front of potential business clients.

Cameron just stood there with her hands at her sides. She was never good at apologies.

At last he looked up from the nail he stared at on the planked floor. "Cameron, I—"

"You don't have to say it." She took a step toward him; he met her halfway. "I'm the one who should be apologizing," she whispered.

"Ah, Cam." He rested his chin on her head, enclosing her in his arms. "I was so worried when I realized I was finally going home. I mean, I was happy to be coming to you. But what if I'm not a good husband? You've had such a tragic life. What if I make you even more unhappy?"

She closed her eyes against tears as she lifted her chin. His mouth came down on hers, firm and possessive, and when he drew back she was breathless, shaky.

"You could never make me unhappy as long as you kiss me like that," she breathed.

His eyes clouded with desire, and he leaned over to take her mouth again.

She pressed her hand to his chest, wrapping a finger around his cravat. "Jackson, we couldn't," she whispered, feeling naughty. "Not right here in your office. Someone might come."

He wrapped her in his arms and backed her slowly against the wall, never taking his gray-eyed gaze from her. "Then that would be half the fun of it, wouldn't it?" he teased.

"Jackson, we mustn't," she giggled, parting her lips. But she already knew that she would.

6

"We shouldn't be doin' this," Noah protested gruffly.

Naomi laughed, pushing the door of their room shut. The sleeping chamber was just a tiny loft room over the kitchen, but it would be warm in the winter and was cool today because of its very own window. The walls were white-washed, with plenty of wooden pegs to hang clothes, and the smooth plank floor didn't creak. But the best part of the little room was the enormous rope bed Miss Cameron had given them as a belated wedding gift. It was the biggest bed Naomi had ever slept in in her life. It had to be as big as Miss Cameron's.

"What do ya mean we shouldn't be doin' this?" Naomi purred. "You forget ya married me?"

He laughed, but turned his face away when she tried to kiss him. "Ya know what I mean, sweet molasses. It's the broad light of day." He lifted his handsome chin toward the open window.

"That's the way I like it," she whispered, brushing her lips over his dark beard stubble. "Daylight, so I can see my man." She pressed another kiss to the open V of his blue tick work shirt and at the same time brought her hand up beneath the pouch of his trousers. "My *big* man."

Noah groaned and closed his eyes. "Ain't you got work to do, miss keeper of this big ole fine and fancy city house?"

She kissed his chest again and then flicked out her tongue to taste his salty, dark skin. "None that won't wait."

"The baby."

Naomi glanced over her shoulder at her son sleeping contentedly in the sturdy cradle Noah had built with his own capable hands. "Sleepin' like one," she cooed.

"Lordy, you gonna be the death of me, woman," Noah grumbled good-heartedly as he wrapped his arms around her narrow waist and covered her mouth with his.

With one good kiss, Noah lifted Naomi off her feet and carried her to their new bed. She had covered it with a quilt her mother had made her. It was a quilt the color of yellow sunshine and happiness—what her mother had said she deserved.

Naomi threw her head back on her goose down pillow and laughed, her voice seeming to echo off the white-washed walls. "Come to me, lover."

"Someone gonna hear ya," Noah warned, yanking his shirt over his head.

Naomi reached out to stroke the corded muscles of his chest and then lower to his ridged stomach. Far in the back of her mind, she remembered the first man she had ever loved. Not the first man she had ever stripped naked for; they were too many to count. But Manu, Manu had been her first love. He had been a slave at a neighboring plantation, and for two years they were lovers. They met in the swamp beneath an old cypress tree, and there Manu spread his mantle for her and gave her his love. He had made her feel as if someone cared about her, but the most important thing he did was give her hope.

In the summer of '61, the slavers killed Manu while trying to capture him on the banks of the Pearl River, not far from Elmwood. She didn't blame him a bit for running, letting them shoot him in the back. She didn't fault him because she knew that once a man tastes freedom, the weight of iron shackles are too heavy for a soul to bear.

Naomi focused her gaze on the man above her as he lifted her skirts and fumbled with the tie of his breeches. She gently brushed his hand aside, and without taking her gaze from his, she loosened the fabric, letting him spring hot and stiff into her waiting hand.

"I love ya, Noah Freeman," she whispered.

"Love you," he groaned.

Noah was a simple man of simple words, but it was all she needed to hear. Their dark-eyed gazes still locked, she parted her thighs and welcomed him in, hot and pulsing. Letting her eyes drift shut, she encircled his shoulders with her thin arms and thanked the gods she had this new life.

"Taye, we shouldn't." Thomas stiffened at her touch.

Taye rolled her eyes, refusing to step back. They were alone in the library, the pocketed panel doors closed. She had called him here under the ruse of wanting his recommendation on reading material. But she had really invited him here so that they could be alone for a few minutes.

Oh, yes, they had spent the entire morning together shopping on a busy street in Baltimore. She had made several purchases for herself and Cameron, and Thomas had followed diligently behind, collecting parcels and returning them to the carriage. But he had never said anything more personal all morning than, "Yes, I believe blue is an excellent color for new napkins."

Taye remained in front of Thomas, blocking his escape through the closed door. She reached out and brushed the sleeve of his dark brown coat. "We're going to wed," she murmured. "I think you've a right to kiss me on occasion."

His eyes darted to and fro and he refused to meet her probing gaze. A dark red blotch of embarrassment rose from his starched cravat upward over his face.

"But here," he protested. "Such a public place. Anyone could come in. Your reputation, dear."

She almost laughed. At seventeen years old she had been taken by her half brother Grant to Baton Rouge to be sold into prostitution. She had come inches from having her virginity auctioned in a whorehouse parlor, saved just in the nick of time by Jackson and Cameron. If that incident had not ruined her reputation, surely a kiss from her fiancé wouldn't, either. But she held her tongue, knowing Thomas didn't like her to speak of those bygone days.

Taye caught his hand in hers. It was larger, but not a great deal so. He still had small, rough calluses from his work on Jackson's ships during the war, and she wondered what those hands would feel like on her bare skin.

An attorney by trade, Thomas had been a jack-of-all-trades for the last four years, serving the beloved Captain Logan in any way he could.

She squeezed his hand in hers. She knew he was shy, but they had to start somewhere, didn't they? "Thomas, no one will see. Just a chaste kiss." She lifted her chin to look at him provocatively through her lashes. "Or maybe a not-so-chaste kiss?"

His Adam's apple bobbed. "Taye, please. There is a time and place for everything, and this is neither the time nor the place to…to display one's affection."

She released his hand with a sigh. Heavens, she couldn't make him kiss her, could she?

She stepped away. She would retreat for now, but she would not surrender. She would not give up on her desire—

not just to be loved, but to feel as if she were *in love.* "So what do you recommend I read next?" she asked blandly. "Alexis de Tocqueville's essays on democracy or the new Victor Hugo?"

"Jackson," Cameron said, her voice husky with desire. "Good heavens! Not on the gaming table."

He laughed as he pushed the cards and brandy glasses to the floor with one sweep of his hand and seated her firmly on the edge of the table. "And why not?" He grinned wickedly as he untied her bonnet and tossed it to the floor. "I do, after all, want to be considerate of your condition. What kind of man do you think I am? Do you think I would take my wife standing at the door?"

She lowered her gaze as he opened his trousers. His erect member sprang from the fabric, stiff and shocking in its enormity, and she found her breath catching in her throat. "Of course not, my love," she teased, her voice raspy with desire. "What would ever make me think you would be so *base?*"

With one hand, he threaded his fingers through her hair, not caring if he ruined her coiffure. With his other hand, he reached beneath her layers of skirt and petticoats to the place that was already soft and damp for him. Their mouths met hungrily. His fingers stroked the blossoming folds and she groaned, suddenly feeling as urgent as he.

"We have to hurry. Someone's going to come."

"Us," he whispered in her ear.

She could feel her face grow heated with a mixture of desire and embarrassment. He always treated her with respect in public, but in private, he sometimes spoke to her as if she were his whore. Worse, she behaved so. It frustrated her that she liked his crude words. She was ordinarily a woman in such great control of herself, of her body and her emotions. What was it about Jackson that always sent her spinning out of control?

"Now," she groaned in his ear. She slid to the edge of the card table and grabbed his bare hips, guiding him into her.

She gasped as he entered, moaned as he filled her in a way no one else could.

Jackson closed his eyes and held her tightly, rocking back and forth. Balanced precariously on the edge of the table, she was helpless to do anything but cling to him and let him guide her in the motion.

As he stroked her, pushing further toward the edge of fulfillment, the walls of the small office faded, the sounds in the warehouse below drifted away. There was nothing in her world but the two of them, the touch and feel of Jackson's skin and the sound of his ragged breathing.

Cameron was shocked by how quickly she reached climax. How hot she had been for Jackson, how needy. How could she be so angry with him one moment and want him so badly the next?

Jackson grunted and then leaned forward to rest his chin on her forehead. Panting, she lowered her legs and pushed down her skirts.

He kissed her temple gently. "Now where were we, darling? What were you saying?"

She laughed and pushed him back, but he would not budge. "You're a wicked, corrupt man and you have corrupted me. Coercing me to do such a thing in broad daylight on your card table!" She smoothed her skirts. "It's a good thing the senator is dead because he would be mortified to see how immoral his daughter has become."

Jackson laughed heartily. "You forget that your father and I were good friends and that I knew him well. Perhaps better than you in some ways, my sweet." He brushed her love-bruised lips with his fingertip. "I think Senator David Campbell would be proud to know you've allowed yourself to love the way you have."

"Whatever do you mean by that?"

He reached down to fasten his breeches. "Only that your father had a great capacity to love, and he found great happiness in that love, that's all."

"You mean Sukey," she said tentatively. It was not until after her father's death that she discovered he had had more than just a sexual relationship with their housekeeper. Apparently, when he died, they had been in love for more than twenty-five years.

The door rattled and swung open, startling Cameron. She slid forward off the table and Jackson stepped back. Her gaze darted to the scattered cards and glasses and her bonnet tossed carelessly to the floor. It couldn't be retrieved at this point without drawing greater attention to it.

She tried not to look too flustered as the man dressed in short breeches and a striped sailor's shirt pulled off his knit hat. "Ma'am." He nodded to her and turned his attention to Jackson. If he saw the mess on the floor, he gave no indication. "They be ready to see ya on the *Miss Virginy,* if you're ready, Captain Logan."

Jackson smiled as if he had not nearly been caught with his pants around his ankles. "Thank you, Charlie. I'll be down directly, just as soon as I have completed my *business* with Mrs. Logan."

His tone could easily have been interpreted twofold.

Cameron stiffened. "We're *quite* finished, sir."

Jackson flashed the sailor a grin. "We're *quite* done, apparently. I'll be down in a moment."

The sailor nodded, backed out of the office and closed the door.

"Heavens," Cameron groaned, snatching her bonnet off the floor. "If that man had walked in a moment before—"

"But he didn't," Jackson interrupted cheerfully. "Now let me walk you down to the carriage."

"I can find my way," she said sweetly.

He took her elbow. "I'm going down."

Outside the warehouse, Jackson saw Roxy and turned to Cameron, instantly angry. "You rode here? Alone?"

She eyed him, bristling. "I've been riding horseback since I came off my mammy's apron strings." She strode toward her mount. "I'm perfectly capable of riding this horse fewer than two miles down a city street."

"That's not the point." He grabbed her elbow, lowering his voice to a dangerous level. When Jackson was really angry, he got deadly quiet.

Her own anger rose. "You cannot order me about, Jackson. In case you didn't realize it, slavery has been outlawed in these United States."

"It's not safe for you to be riding like this, carrying our child," he countered.

"That's nonsense. The baby is no bigger than a pea. I'm not going to hurt myself, and I'm not going to hurt this child. Give me a leg up," she ordered the boy holding Roxy's reins.

The boy looked to Jackson for approval.

He threw up one hand. "Why the hell not? If you don't help her mount, she'll be climbing on barrels to get up herself."

The boy cupped his hands and Cameron managed to reach the saddle. Her mount had been rather unladylike, with more than a small showing of her pale blue petticoats, but she landed safely astride the saddle and took the reins from the boy.

"I'll see you tonight," she called over her shoulder to

Jackson. "Don't forget our dinner party for the senators and their wives."

She didn't wait for a response. Instead, she sank her heels into Roxy's flanks and took off at a canter.

"Damn, I just don't know what to do with her, Taye," Jackson confessed. Leaning on the balcony railing, he took a sip of his brandy and stared out into the darkened garden. They had stepped out for a breath of fresh air while the wife of the senator from Maryland entertained them with a truly earsplitting rendition of a popular tune.

"I knew you'd be angry that she had rode Roxy to the docks, but there wasn't any way I could stop her. You know how determined she can be."

He smiled, thinking of the long days he and Cameron had spent together in the summer of 1861. First in Baton Rouge, then on his ship, then on the road from Biloxi to Jackson. She had been so determined to get back to Elmwood that she'd nearly walked across the state of Mississippi. It was that fortitude of hers, which so angered him now, that he had truly admired in her then. It was just one more reason he would love her until death parted them... and likely beyond that.

"I don't expect you to be her caretaker, Taye." He glanced at her. She was dressed in a lovely pale blue satin and white-striped silk gown and the hue matched her eyes almost exactly. "You did that long enough in Mississippi."

She smiled kindly. "I do it because I love her. And because, no matter what she says, I know she needs someone to look after her." She stood beside him and leaned on the rail, then to his surprise, she took the brandy from his hand and stole a sip. "The senator's death hit her harder than she would like us all to believe. Grant's, too."

"And what of you?" He watched her in the darkness. "David was your father, too."

She handed him back his brandy snifter. "It's different. I always loved him because he was so good to my mother and me, but I didn't realize he was my father while he was still living. I don't think the feelings can be the same. Do you?"

Jackson groaned and finished off the brandy. "I doubt I'm the person to ask. I seem quite capable in the dark with a band of Confederate soldiers on my tail, but I can't even handle my own wife."

She laughed. "No one *handles* Cameron Campbell Logan."

"You've got that right," he said miserably. "I fear I've done nothing right in her eyes since I came home." He glanced at her and then into the dark garden again, uncomfortable with his thoughts, but needing to voice them. Marie's image appeared in his head and he pushed it away. He had made the right decision with her; he knew that. But seeing her again, having to work with her, made him question his choices. "Has Cameron said anything to you, Taye, about—" He paused. "I don't know. Regrets?"

She turned her head to stare at him. The lamplight behind them illuminated her honey skin, making her even prettier than by daylight. "Regrets? About you?"

He nodded.

"Are you mad?"

He laughed. The Taye he had known before would never have said such a thing. In those days she had been afraid of him, nearly jumping out of her skin every time he spoke to her.

"You're worrying too much." She patted his hand. "She loves you the way only Cameron can love. Wildly, passionately, sometimes out of control." There was almost envy in her voice. "The two of you belong together and you know it. It's just going to take some time to adjust to married life."

"Adjust?" he grumbled. "We've been married four years."

"Legally, yes, but you've never *lived* together. Two bulls as stubborn as the two of you, give it some time."

"I just thought that once we were together, things would settle down. Especially now with the baby coming."

She stood up, tightening the white lace shawl around her shoulders. "You forget that she was an independent woman these last four years. She had no father or husband to look after her, to make decisions for her."

"I would never have married her and left her here if I had thought she couldn't take care of herself."

"Of course you wouldn't have." She smiled. "But now that you've come home, Captain, you cannot expect her to set aside her independence and be your little wife." Taye smiled with a wisdom far beyond her years. "That's not the kind of woman you really want anyway, is it?"

He picked up his snifter, thinking he might need a refill. "I don't know," he said dismally.

She smiled kindly. "I'm going inside. It's getting cool."

"I'll be in just as soon as the senator's wife ceases that caterwauling."

She laughed again and disappeared into the house in a flounce of pale blue silk and the air of a true lady.

7

Cameron looked in on Taye, who was meeting with the head cook to go over the menu for the upcoming ball, then set out on horseback to Mrs. Cartwright's hat shop. One of the young houseboys rode behind her to carry her purchase back to the house. It would have made more sense for her to take the carriage this morning, but the fact that she knew Jackson preferred it made her choose to ride.

At the hattery on a busy street on the south side of town, amid a row of quaint little boutiques catering to ladies and gentlemen of quality, Cameron dismounted and tossed her reins to the uniformed boy standing outside the shop. She smoothed her riding skirt sewn of a soft, butter yellow sueded leather, and entered the tiny shop. The room was filled with rows of hats, some imported from Europe, others made in New York. Two staid, rigidly corseted female clerks, both clad in identical black taffeta day dresses and black lace caps, glided soundlessly between the displays of bonnets and the lengths of laces, ribbons, feathers and rosettes one could choose from to adorn a new hat. This morning, the shop was also filled with chattering women.

Seeing that Mrs. Cartwright, the proprietress, was occupied with a customer, Cameron stepped down one of the aisles to look at the grosgrain ribbons. She was hoping to find a dove gray to match a hat she had at home.

"Did you hear he's back in town? My neighbor, Mrs. Ports, saw him just yesterday, the handsome devil," came a female voice from the other side of a shelf stacked high with wooden spindles of ribbon.

"I heard," came a whisper in a conspiratory tone. "Everyone who is anyone is talking about him."

Cameron couldn't see the two women who were gossiping, but their voices carried well.

"He's been home less than a month and they say he's already philandering. And of course they say *she's* back in Washington, as well."

"*She?*"

"That Marie LeLaurie. She's staying at The Grand."

"The one he's been carrying on with? No!"

"Yes! All that black hair—God knows it cannot be natural," the woman hissed. "And it's even worse than that."

"Heavens. I'm shocked," breathed her companion. "Do tell."

"Well, one of my parlor maids has a cousin who has a friend who is a laundress in their home. You know how these negras are inbred," she added briskly. "Well, they say the missus is expecting."

"It cannot possibly be true! There hasn't been a word breathed at my Tuesday tea at The Grand."

"Well, the laundress would certainly know."

Cameron grabbed a spindle of gray ribbon she thought would possibly match her hat, shaking her head. She despised gossips. The poor woman they were speaking of didn't deserve to be talked about so.

"I'll have to look into that, then. My husband plays cards with a gentleman who does business with him in the harbor."

Cameron started to walk toward the front counter, then froze, a shiver running through her. A man who had recently come to town, who had a pregnant wife, who carried on business at the docks? Cameron reached out to steady herself with one hand, the gray ribbon clutched tightly in her other hand.

"Perhaps something has been said about his wife's condition."

"Oh, I think not. Captain Logan would know better than to make such a public announcement."

The spool of thread hit the wooden floor with a loud clap and rolled down the aisle.

"I mean, how far could she possibly be gone? He's..."

Cameron grabbed a shelf to support herself for a moment, feeling light-headed and dizzy.

The gossips were talking about Jackson. Talking about her.

Suddenly the air was stifling and she feared she might faint.

Holding on to the shelves for support, she made her way down the aisle toward the door. As she gripped the doorknob, the proprietress called out to her.

"Mrs. Logan! I'm sorry. I can help you in just a moment. It's only that Mrs. Henry—"

"It's all right," Cameron managed to say as she opened the door. "I...I'm in a hurry today. I'll come back another day."

"What's wrong?" Taye asked, reaching across the tiny game table, her blue eyes wide with concern.

Cameron shook her head, setting her cards aside. She and Taye had settled in the parlor after a supper alone to play cards, but her head wasn't in the game. "Nothing."

"Don't tell me that. You've been moping around the

house for days. Saturday night is the ball. All of our war heroes will be here. Ulysses Grant will dance in your ballroom! You simply cannot receive your guests with such a sour puss.''

Cameron stared at her hands clasped in her lap. Two days had passed since she heard the women gossiping. She tried to push their words out of her mind, but she simply couldn't. She tried to convince herself that Jackson would never cheat on her. He loved her. And when would he have time to cheat on her? He worked morning to night in his office at the docks, unless he was in Washington. And Jackson was certainly not frolicking in the Secretary of State's office with a woman!

But what if it was true? Her lower lip trembled.

"You have to tell me," Taye said simply.

Cameron glanced up at her sister. "Do you think Jackson would cheat on me with another woman?"

Taye laughed aloud. "Absolutely not."

Cameron glanced away, tears of relief stinging her eyes.

"Why ever do you ask such a ludicrous thing?" Taye clasped Cameron's hand in hers, forcing her to look at her again.

"I heard these women the other day…talking," Cameron said haltingly. "About Jackson. They said—" She faltered. "They said everyone was talking about how he was cheating on me."

"It's not true."

"I know it's not." Filled with self-doubt, Cameron twisted her emerald-and-diamond wedding ring around and around her finger. "But they also said they heard I was pregnant, which *is* true."

"Who were they?" Taye demanded angrily. "Because I would not hesitate to pay a call on them and confront them myself."

Cameron shook her head. "I don't know who they were. I couldn't see them. It doesn't matter anyway." She looked up. "I know it's just vicious gossip but—" The look in Taye's eyes made her halt in midsentence, her stomach falling as a lump rose in her throat. "You know something."

Taye shook her head emphatically. "I don't."

"Taye, you were never a good liar." Cameron rose from her chair, her hands shaking. "They said the woman was here in town. If you know anything about—"

"Cameron, listen to me." Taye rose, clasping both her sister's hands. "Jackson is not cheating on you. He wouldn't. It's only that..."

"What?"

Taye sighed. "I did hear some of the same gossip last week. I was at the market with the cook."

"And you didn't tell me?" Cameron yanked her hands away and walked to the window draped in heavy ivory brocade. "How could you not tell me?"

Taye walked up behind her and grabbed Cameron's shoulder, forcing her to look at her. "I didn't tell you because it was two housemaids speaking out of place. I didn't tell you because the way to halt gossip is to stop repeating it. I didn't tell you because it isn't true."

"Well, it better not be." Cameron turned and sailed out of the room. "Because if it is, I swear by all that's holy, I'll kill him!"

Taye took the stairs to Jackson's warehouse office one at a time, plucking off her calfskin gloves finger by finger.

"Come in," Jackson called at her knock, sounding preoccupied. "Door's open."

She strolled in to find him seated at his desk, piles of paper everywhere. It was a man's room, spare, utilitarian, with plain oak furniture battered by use. No rugs covered the bare plank floors and the single window was badly in need of washing.

"Taye." He rose from the desk, obviously surprised by her unannounced visit. "Cameron's all right, isn't she? The baby?"

"She's fine." Taye closed the door behind her. "I came because I wanted to talk to you, alone. It will only take a moment. Thomas is waiting downstairs for me in the carriage."

"Talk to me about what? You really shouldn't come down here, Taye. There are all sorts of seedy—"

"Jackson, sit down and shush." Taye was shocked by her own abruptness.

Even more shocking was that Jackson sat down.

She studied his handsome, roguish face, carefully watching for any unspoken response. "There's been gossip going around town, and I want to make sure there's no truth to it."

The muscles in his jaw seemed to tighten, but perhaps it was just her imagination.

"What kind of gossip?"

"People are saying you are having an affair with another woman."

He stood up abruptly, pushing the heels of his hands down on the desk. "That is preposterous. I am not—"

"*I* heard it the other day, and now I learn that Cameron has also heard it," she told him sternly.

"Someone told my wife that I was cheating on her?" He ground out his words angrily.

"No. She overheard it in the hat shop a couple of days ago."

"Days ago? Why the hell didn't she ask me about it then?"

"I don't know. Probably because she didn't believe them."

"She didn't believe them," he said, "because it isn't true. Cameron knows I love her. I would never do anything to jeopardize our marriage."

"I should hope not."

"I'll go home now." He reached for his coat thrown over an old chair marked with splashes of green paint.

"No. Then she'll know I came here, and there will be a big fuss about me putting my nose where it doesn't belong. I just wanted to make sure it wasn't true, because I told her it wasn't."

He dropped his coat on the chair again and ran his fingers through his long hair. "Of course it isn't."

She watched him, so wanting to believe him. She did believe him. But she had learned a little of men in the last few years, and she knew they were very different than women in ways of the heart. "The word is—" she drew out her words carefully "—that this woman you are having an affair with is staying at The Grand in Washington."

He turned away from her almost violently and reached for a bottle of scotch on a bookshelf against the unpainted wall. "I said I wasn't having an affair, Taye!"

She nodded crisply. "Excellent." She began to pull on her gloves. "I just wanted to be sure. Because if you are, if you hurt my sister that way, she won't get the chance to kill you."

He brought his glass to his lips, his gaze meeting hers.

Taye lifted her chin a notch. "She won't have to, because I'll do it first. See you at supper. Don't be late. We've an impromptu concert prepared, which I'm certain you will enjoy."

Jackson watched Taye walk out the door and then slung back the glass, downing the shot of scotch in one swallow.

He flinched as the smooth bite of the liquor went down his throat to burn in his stomach. "Son of a bitch," he whispered. Then he grabbed his coat and strode out the door. "Jeremy," he barked. "Get me my horse. I need to get on the next train to Washington."

Ordinarily Jackson would have been more careful, not entering The Grand Hotel from the front doors where footmen greeted him by name and senators and congressman rushed to shake his hand. Ordinarily he would not have strode through the Greek columned lobby, up the stairs directly to Marie's room. Ordinarily he was not this angry.

He slammed his fist against the door he knew was hers. "Open up."

"Who is it?" Marie called in a voice as sweet as honey.

"You know who it is," he retorted.

The door opened almost immediately and Marie greeted him wearing a red silk dressing robe that left little to the imagination. Her slender feet were bare, her rich, ebony hair unbound and loose around her shoulders. "Jackson, dearest," she purred. "Had I known you were coming—"

"What the hell do you think you're doing?" He walked in and slammed the walnut paneled door behind him.

"What—"

"You heard me. I said, what the hell are you doing?" He clenched his fists at his sides. "I'll tell you what you're doing! You've been spreading rumors all over town that you and I are having an affair. Rumors that have gotten to my wife, as you had hoped. You devious bitch."

"Jackson." She thrust out her plump lower lip, not in the least offended by his name calling. "I'm hurt that you would even suggest—"

"Don't start with that, Marie." He grabbed a handful of

her gown and it fell open, revealing her large pale breasts with their dark areoles and protruding nipples.

Marie looked down at her nakedness and then up at him, her dark eyes glazing over with passion. "Jackson," she whispered.

Realizing he had not yet let go of her gown, he loosened his fingers and watched the red silk fall from his hand. The alluring scent of her musky perfume filled his nostrils, his mind. "No, Marie," he heard himself say.

She pressed her nearly naked body to his. "Just once more?" she breathed, closing her eyes, tipping her chin upward to be kissed. "I've missed you so."

Jackson took her by the shoulders and pushed her back, not roughly, but hard enough to make her take a step to keep from falling.

"You loved me once." Her eyes flew open. "You told me so. Why can't you love me again, if only for a few moments?"

He pressed his lips together and looked away, feeling his heart pounding in his chest. What she said was true and he couldn't deny it.

Jackson *had* loved Marie once. A lifetime ago, after he'd left Cameron that summer she was a girl of seventeen, he'd returned to the life he had known before. Trying to forget that fire-haired, tawny-eyed Southern temptress, he'd worked hard for his father in their shipping business. He drank, he gambled, he enjoyed the ladies. Marie was one of them, but she had been special from the first night he'd met her.

At the time, she'd been married to an older man, already an invalid by the time Jackson spotted her in a gambling hall in Atlanta. Their torrid affair had lasted more than four years, and for a short time he had fantasized about marrying her when her husband died. But then another man caught

Marie's eye and she strayed. That was when Jackson realized he could never be happy with Marie; her definition of *love* and *commitment* did not match his. Shortly thereafter, he returned to Elmwood and fell in love all over again with Senator David Campbell's daughter. And then the war began.

Jackson forced himself to focus his gaze on Marie again, and he could see that her feelings were hurt. Damn, he didn't want to hurt her. He only wanted to stop her before she ruined his marriage, before he hurt Cameron. Marie was a manipulative woman. That was why she made such a good spy and that was how she had lured him into her web again, if only for a very short time.

"I have to get home to my wife. Just keep your mouth shut. You understand?"

She rushed to the door, not bothering to cover her luscious body with the red silk. "Wait, we have business to discuss. I've received information. We need to go to New Orleans and speak with a man who has talked to Thompson himself."

"I'm not going to New Orleans, Marie." He put his hand on the doorknob, in a hurry now to get out of the room. It wasn't that he was tempted by her beautiful breasts or her exquisite nipples. Rather, he felt a recurring shame for what he'd done more than a year ago. What he had done to Cameron.

"You have to go, Jackson." She covered his hand with hers on the knob. "Seward is counting on us. I spoke with him this morning. President Johnson is counting on *you,* Jackson."

"I said I have to go." He yanked open the door.

"Go then," she called after him, sweetly. "We'll talk at your homecoming ball."

"Don't you dare come, Marie," he called over his shoulder. He couldn't breathe. He needed air. "It's not safe."

"Don't be silly," she laughed. "What can I tell the congressman? You know, I wouldn't miss it for the world, dear. Wait until you see my gown."

Jackson rushed down the stairs and through the lobby, and only when he was on the brick sidewalk outside the hotel did he at last take a breath.

The tantalizing scent of Marie's perfume lingered in his nostrils.

Cameron heard Jackson enter the bedchamber behind where she sat at her mirrored dressing table, but she didn't turn around as she unfastened one of her earbobs. It was after midnight and their dinner guests had just departed. "You were late again tonight."

"I told you I was sorry. The train from Washington was running late."

"I thought you were at the warehouse today." She glanced at his reflection beside hers in the gilded mirror embellished with golden cherubs.

He leaned over to kiss the back of her neck behind the loose chignon of curls she had tied up with purple ribbons to match her gown. "Something came up."

Cameron rose, avoiding his touch. "Jackson, I want to ask you something."

He had gone to his chiffarobe to put away his dinner jacket. "Taye is a truly gifted pianist. I thought the concert tonight was excellent—"

"I said I want to ask you something."

"Thomas, however, is not as nimble at the keyboard as he might think." Jackson's fingers found his cravat and he began to release the knot.

"Jackson—"

"Damn it, no," he snapped suddenly, spinning around to face her.

She stared at him, her hands falling to her sides. Tonight she wore a Sicilian bodiced gown of deep purple, with a lavender crinoline beneath it. The new fabric rustled beneath her nervous fingertips. "No what?" she asked stiffly. "You haven't even heard my question yet."

"I already know your question and the answer is no, I am not having an affair with another woman." He jerked off his cravat and threw it to the floor.

"How did you know—" She stopped and then started again. "Did Taye—"

"It doesn't matter, Cam." His fingers flew over the buttons of his white shirt. "What matters is that you shouldn't listen to what old, dried-up biddies say in hat shops." He slipped out of the shirt, letting it fall to the polished floor beside his cravat. "You shouldn't listen to malicious gossip. What you should do is ask your husband."

"There you go again." She gestured angrily.

"There I go again *what?*"

"Telling me what I should and should not do! I am not a soldier, Jackson, and I am not in your army. You will not control me!"

"What are you talking about? You asked me if I was having an affair. I'm not. How could I possibly have time for an affair? I barely have time to wipe my—" He grunted and turned away.

Cameron just stood there staring at him, her anger bubbling up inside her until she thought she couldn't control it.

Jackson stood in front of the door for a moment in silence, then turned back to her. "I think we need to talk about this tomorrow."

"I don't want to talk about it tomorrow. I want to talk

about it tonight. Now. I cannot live this way, Jackson. You cannot come back after four years and take over my life.''

''I think we should talk when we've both had a good night's sleep.'' He walked to the bed and began to pull back the damask linens.

''I don't think so,'' she said softly.

''I know you don't think so, but—''

''I mean,'' she interrupted, ''that I don't think you'll be sleeping here tonight.''

''What?'' He spun around.

''You heard me.'' She opened the door and called for her personal maid waiting down the hall. She did not close the door when she stepped back. ''You need to sleep elsewhere, Jackson. I'll have Addy prepare a bedchamber down the hall for you.''

''I don't want to sleep down the hall!''

She stared at him with those cat's eyes of hers. ''You want everything your way. You want to order me about. You want me to just ignore gossip concerning you. Concerning me. Well, that's not the way I want things. If you don't want to do things my way, then you can sleep elsewhere. I don't want you in my bed now, not now. Not until...until this has been settled between us.'' She folded her arms over her chest.

''Cameron—'' He started to speak then halted. ''Fine,'' he snapped.

He grabbed an armful of clothes, his boots and his gun in a holster and brushed past her.

Cameron just stood there watching him. She refused to cry, refused to surrender to the cold despair that threatened to suffocate her...to drown everything that she held dear.

8

"God above, Taye, can't you tighten it just a little more?" Cameron groaned, leaning on the broad, painted window frame in her bedchamber.

Tonight Cameron and Jackson were throwing a ball for the Union's victorious officers and their wives, and to Cameron's way of thinking, it couldn't have come at a worse time. After sending Jackson packing from her bedchamber three nights ago, they had barely spoken. Jackson left early, for God knew where, and he stayed late. Cameron knew they couldn't go on like this indefinitely, but she felt he needed to come to her, to apologize for his behavior. Then she'd be ready to talk.

Tonight would not be the night, though. Carriages had already begun to arrive, and Cameron would be expected downstairs shortly to stand at her husband's side, smile at his guests, murmur greetings and pretend nothing was wrong.

"Cameron, you're still thin as a fence rail," Taye declared, tying her sister's stays precisely where they were. "If I tighten it any further, your entrails will spill out, and won't that be a fetching sight on the ballroom floor?"

Cameron had to laugh at Taye's illustration. "All right."

She threw up her arms, settling them over her layers of gored petticoats and her bell-shaped crinoline. "Fine. I'm already married. What difference does it make if I'm as broad as a barn?"

Taye lifted Cameron's ball gown from the bed and carried it to her. It was just like the days in Elmwood when their father had thrown the best parties in all of Mississippi. Cameron had loved dancing and dining and seeing and being seen at those balls, but now she realized that half the pleasure had been in preparing for the great events, with Taye at her side.

"Now you're just being silly," Taye chastised. Carefully, she raised the leaf green ball gown of satin broche with festooned lace flounce en tablier and lowered it over Cameron's head.

Cameron held her arms high and allowed her sister to settle the lovely new dress over her petticoats. Once the gown was on, Taye walked in a circle around her, flouncing the satin. Cameron tugged at the short, puffed sleeves.

"You're still as slim as you were at eighteen. You're always the loveliest woman in any room and your husband adores you."

Cameron gave a very unladylike snort. "Adores me as a mantelpiece. Something to dress up and show off when his friends come to town and then send me back to my chamber when the evening is done." She waggled her finger. "If he adored me, you think he'd stand to be sleeping down the hall? If he adored me, don't you think he would at least sit down and *discuss* with me our going home to Mississippi?"

Taye stood before her, adjusting the off-the-shoulder pointed bodice of the gown. "I know you don't want to hear this, but maybe this one time he knows what's best. Thomas says that the city of Jackson was badly damaged in the war. Many of the plantation homes were burned to the ground. The soil has been left untilled so long that meadows are growing where fields once were." She lifted her dark lashes to meet her sister's gaze. "I'm not certain there would be anything for you to go home to."

"So you're taking his side?" The minute the words came out of Cameron's mouth, she wanted to bite them back. She didn't want to argue with Taye, not when she and Jackson weren't getting along. "I'm sorry. I suppose I'm just still a little irritated with you for going to his office and talking to him about that gossip."

"I'm not taking his side at all." Taye remained unruffled, ignoring Cameron's comment about her little jaunt to the docks. She guessed that while Jackson may have admitted to his wife that Taye had been there, he did not divulge exactly what had been said.

"I'm telling you what Thomas told me," Taye continued. "He's been south to see to his father's law offices. He says they are in great need of repair. Vagabonds were actually living there. It would take a lot of work before he could even set up his practice."

Cameron's lower lip trembled. "So that's where you intend to go, after you're wed? *Home?*" Her voice quavered with the last word.

"I don't know where we're going yet," Taye said gently. Her tone lightened. "Besides, it's too early to talk of such plans. It's completely inappropriate. We're not even officially engaged yet. We've yet to make the announcement."

"Well, as soon as that matter is taken care of, we're going to make the engagement official." Cameron reached out and squeezed Taye's hand. "And I'm going to throw you the biggest engagement ball Baltimore has ever seen."

Taye beamed. "It's what I've always dreamed of."

"And that's why you shall have it." Cameron walked to

the full-length mirror to take in her reflection. She reached out her arm and pulled Taye beside her. Taye had picked a charming blue-and-yellow gown with a shockingly low bodice and short, billowed tulle sleeves.

The two women didn't look much like sisters. Cameron was half a hand taller than Taye and was more greatly endowed with womanly curves. Cameron's hair was a deep auburn—her paternal grandmother's Highland hair—and her eyes were a honeyed amber. Taye had locks the color of a silken crow's wing and exquisite pale blue eyes, so unusual for a mulatto. And her skin was a honey-bronze sun-kissed color, her complexion perfect. She had their father's nose. Cameron could see it now, though she had not noticed it before. Perhaps because she had been afraid to...

"We should go downstairs," Taye suggested softly.

Their gazes met in the mirror.

"I'm glad you're here," Cameron said softly. It was difficult for her to articulate her feelings sometimes, but she needed Taye to know how greatly she cared for her. "I wish that we could never be separated again."

Taye laughed and kissed Cameron's cheek, then smoothed it to be sure she had left no telltale lip pomade. "You're so serious tonight, too serious for a ball. Let's go, *cherie*. I want to dance and sip champagne."

Cameron turned to Taye, her sister's laughter contagious. "Is this the same girl that I had to coerce into putting on one of my ball gowns and coming down to *watch* others dance only a few short years ago?"

Taye's blue eyes sparkled with fond memories. "And then your dashing Jackson asked me to dance—"

"And you shocked everyone in the county," Cameron recalled proudly. "Don't you remember? Grant stomped right up to you on Papa's ballroom floor and accused Jackson of dancing with one of his servants."

Taye pressed her lips together at the mention of Grant, and Cameron reached out to touch her arm. "I'm sorry. Tonight is supposed to be a happy night. I shouldn't have mentioned him."

Again, Taye's blue-eyed gaze met Cameron's. "But we do need to talk about him. About what happened at Elmwood that night," she finished softly.

"Another time," Cameron said softly.

"Yes," Taye agreed as Cameron offered her hand and the two left the bedchamber together. "But we must talk of it, sometime."

"We will, just not tonight." Side by side, arm in arm, the two walked gracefully down the grand staircase to greet their arriving guests.

Every room in the town house was filled to capacity with men dressed in handsome blue officer's uniforms and ladies in their finest ball gowns. The war was over and there was no longer a need to pinch pennies or wear last year's gown. The fabric colors seemed even brighter than they had been before the war: blues, yellows, greens, peaches. The women were like a great bouquet of spring wildflowers blooming amid the classical Greek urns, glittering chandeliers and marble pillars. The halls and chambers of the house were filled with the sounds that came only from victory at war. There was gay laughter, manly boasting and a few shed tears.

And the music... While Cameron had been annoyed that Jackson had secured musicians without consulting her, she had to admit he had hired the finest in all of Baltimore. Every room was filled with the sweet resonant sounds of violins and the echo of a grand piano from the ballroom. In one secluded room a young woman, dressed in a Grecian white gown to match the cavorting nymphs pictured in the shockingly expensive, hand-painted Italian wallpaper, strummed a harp.

Cameron and Taye separated in the receiving hall and Cameron made her way from room to room, greeting what appeared to be all of Baltimore and Washington society. She smiled at her husband's guests, laughed at their jests and called again and again for more champagne, more canapés, and tried not to think of her own tribulations. The war had been long and costly, and Baltimore society was ready to take a fresh breath of air and enjoy the finer amenities life had to offer. And tonight Captain Jackson Logan was providing them.

An hour or more after Cameron descended the stairs, she breezed through one of the parlors and caught a glimpse of Jackson. He was dressed handsomely in a dark blue frock coat, slender trousers and a starched white shirt and cravat. His hair was tied back neatly in one of her own navy satin ribbons which was so Jackson-like that she wanted to laugh. What man on earth would dare wear a woman's ribbon in his hair in public but Captain Logan?

And was the ribbon a flag of truce? She had to wonder.

He was standing near the window with a group of gentlemen, one talking heatedly. In the midst of the men in uniform, he stood out like a majestic peregrine among pigeons. As she glided through the room, she could feel her husband's gaze on her. Hungry. It was the first he had looked at her that way in days.

She felt as if she were standing naked in the middle of the room…and that both thrilled and angered her. She was thrilled to still feel such passion for her husband, but angered because it meant he held a control over her that she did not care to acknowledge.

Cameron had told Jackson she would not sleep with him until matters between them had been settled. But she had not realized how much she would be punishing herself...how many hours she would lie awake, straining to hear the sound of his footsteps in the hall or the squeak of her bedchamber door. She could have sworn her hunger for him had grown since she'd discovered that she was with child.

She glanced up and, against her will, flashed him a suggestive smile. She didn't care if it was utterly inappropriate in public; at this moment it felt to her as if it was just the two them in the room. Besides, this was their home, and she *was* married, wasn't she? Didn't a woman have a right to flirt with her own husband? Especially when all the other women in the house seemed to think they could flirt with him?

Jackson took a step as if coming to speak to her and her heart leaped in her breast. She did miss him so in her bed. Thinking about him coming to her after the party, imagining that they might slip away to be together amid the gathering, caused her nipples to grow taut and slick moisture to gather in the most intimate parts of her body.

Then reality washed over her like cold rain, and her resolve stiffened as she glided out of the room. She was not going to make this easy for him. If he wanted her, he would have to apologize first.

Jackson watched Cameron hasten from the room to avoid him and he stopped short. He wanted to go after her, to sit and talk with her and try to work out their differences, but she was making it so damned hard.

"There you are, Jackson."

Before he turned, he knew who it was. That silky voice, that scent. "Marie," he said softly, turning to face her.

"Surprise." She held up her hands. "What do you think of my new gown? It's all the rage in Europe."

She looked like a Greek goddess in a filmy white empire waist garment with yards of folded fabric that fell from beneath her breasts in a cloud of sheer silk. She looked so remarkable that she could have been one of the sculptured marble goddesses in the house, come to life. Jackson frowned and spoke beneath his breath. "I asked you not to come."

She smiled regally. "I couldn't very well tell the congressman I couldn't attend with him, now, could I? Besides, I have more information. We leave for New Orleans tomorrow."

He walked to a table that had been set up for gentlemen to help themselves to various brandies. He passed over the brandy for scotch. If anyone pointed Marie out to Cameron, they were liable to have a catfight right in the middle of the ballroom floor. He needed to get Marie out of here before too many people saw her. "You need to leave here at once. If it's absolutely necessary, I can meet with you in the morning."

"Leave? Whatever will I tell the congressman?"

He kept his rigid back to her. "I don't give a damn what you tell him."

"My, we are testy tonight. The gentleman who came to do my hair this afternoon intimated that Captain Logan is no longer welcome in his wife's bedchamber. I set it aside as gossip, but now I see there is some truth—"

"Marie," Jackson said sharply, turning to face her.

She pressed her ruby lips together. "You're serious. You want me to go."

He nodded.

She paused, studying his face. She was so lovely, she could take a man's ability to breathe from him. Certainly his ability to reason.

"All right, Jackson," she murmured, reaching a gloved

hand to stroke his cheek. "But we do need to talk. Send me a message in the morning. Early. I'll meet you wherever you like."

Jackson nodded, not trusting himself to speak. He drained his glass as she turned and glided out of the room.

Cameron swept into the hall from the library, bound for the kitchen, when she caught sight of Jackson, still in the parlor, out of the corner of her eye.

That woman! Smiling flirtatiously up at Jackson. Her gloved hand stroking his cheek. Who was she? She had to be the wife or the daughter of one of the many honored guests. But how dare she flirt so openly with her host while Cameron, his wife, was present? How dare he! A shaft of anger cut through her.

Hearing her name frantically called, Cameron turned to a matronly woman who was waving her lace fan, trying to catch Cameron's attention.

Cameron vaguely recognized her, but couldn't place the face at first. Then suddenly it all came tumbling back. Home at Elmwood, dancing in the ballroom. This woman had begged a dance from Cameron's father. A widow, she had been chasing the senator like a bear after honey for months.

"Mrs. Fitzhugh!" Cameron walked over and hugged the rotund woman with genuine delight. "It's so good to see you." She leaned back to gaze into the older woman's round face. "The last time I saw you was at Papa's farewell ball the night Fort Sumter was fired upon. What are you doing here?"

"Why, I've married," she gushed. "Mr. Martin works in the war department. A very essential post." She lowered her lashes. "Of course, I'm not at liberty to say what he does."

"So it's Mrs. Martin now," Cameron said kindly, her gaze straying to the older woman's dark, highly arched eyebrows. "How long have you been in Washington?"

"Not long, not at all." Mrs. Martin's slack-jawed face grew rosy with pride. "We've just set up housekeeping not far from the White House."

Cameron reached for her hand that protruded from lace half gloves. "How long since you've been in Jackson, Mississippi?"

"Why, only a few months. My father died and I had matters to settle there."

"I'm so sorry to hear that." Cameron peered into the older woman's light brown eyes. "Did...did you happen to pass Elmwood in your travels?" Cameron didn't know why she asked. She didn't know what she expected Mrs. Martin to say or why she would want to hear a first-person account of the burned ruins of her home, but she couldn't help herself.

"As a matter of fact, I did." Mrs. Martin fluttered her carved ivory fan, excited by the attention she was receiving from the hostess of the ball. "A few windows broken, and the grass is high, of course, but she really looked rather fine, considering what—" She clutched her fan to her chest. "Considering what we have all been through."

"I'm...I'm sorry. You must be mistaken," Cameron managed, her heart beating far faster than it had a moment before. "Elmwood burned in the summer of '61. I saw the smoke myself, smelled the burning wood as we ran for our lives."

"No, no, I'm quite certain, dear. Elmwood still stands. Most of the outbuildings are gone, of course, burned to the ground, as you say. Those lovely stables of yours, gone. But the manor house still stands, I assure you."

Cameron felt light-headed, and for a moment feared she might faint.

"Are you all right, my dear?" Mrs. Martin clasped Cameron's hand. "Should I call for a servant? Have you need to lie down?"

Cameron willed the room to cease spinning. She took a great breath of air that now seemed stifling in the house, and then another.

Elmwood was standing? Why hadn't Jackson told her? He had been there with her the day they'd fled the plantation with Taye and the slave girls. He'd seen the soldiers and then the smoke, too. They'd hidden all day in the crumbling mill ruin, hidden from Confederate soldiers who were burning everything they couldn't use to prevent the Union from using it.

And Jackson had been to Elmwood during the war! The bastard had brought her the portrait of her, Grant and Taye, painted when they were young, saying the canvas had somehow survived.

The bastard. The liar. He didn't want her to know her home still stood. He didn't want her to go home to Elmwood.

"If you'll excuse me, Mrs. Martin. Duty calls."

The elderly woman swept a curtsy and Cameron hurried off in the direction she had last seen Jackson.

Taye slipped out of the parlor and down the hall, holding back her tears of frustration. As she hurried, the music from the ballroom faded.

She and Thomas had shared a glass of champagne and danced several waltzes, but he had made no attempt to get her alone, or to even speak alone with her. He didn't seem to want to get to know her better, and yet, when she tried to talk to him about it, he didn't understand what she meant.

He was hurt, thinking she thought he was neglecting her in public. That wasn't it at all; he was the perfect gentleman in front of everyone. But she wanted intimacy. She wanted passion. Was it too much to ask for that, when they were not yet wed?

Taye walked down the hall, her yellow-and-blue gown rustling with each step. With the money her father had left her in the form of a pouch of jewels, she was now a wealthy woman. Because she had invested the money well, she was quite independent; she didn't have to marry at all. But she wanted to marry. She wanted to have children. She wanted a passionate life with a man she loved, a life like the one her sister had. Was that too much to ask for?

At the end of the hall, Taye slipped out a side door and followed a brick walk around the house to the garden. The moment she stepped into the open, she hugged herself in the surprising chill of the June evening.

She turned and looked back at the imposing brick house, and considered returning for a shawl. But as she stared at the twinkling lights that spilled from every window, as she listened to the hum of voices and the music of the violins, she knew she couldn't go back inside. Not now.

She would take a walk, get a breath of fresh air, and then she would go back inside to stand at Thomas's side and try to be the woman he wanted her to be.

The large, English-style garden, with winding brick paths, hidden benches and vined arbors, was really quite breathtaking in the daylight and just a little spooky at night.

A quarter moon lay low in the sky, and when Taye glanced overhead, she could see the pinpricks of thousands of stars. Staring up at the sky, she followed a little path that she thought led to the fountain with the stone angel, one of her favorite pieces in the garden.

Taye turned the corner around a boxwood hedge and

walked into something solid and warm on the path. Startled, she drew back. "Oh, goodness, I'm sorry," she said, flustered.

The handsome man, dressed in a black coat and black trousers, looked at her but did not speak.

She took a step back, feeling a shiver of fear, and turned to go, but then she felt his warm hand on her bare arm.

"Do not retreat so fast." He had a strange accent, one she could not place. His voice was warm and liquid, like molten iron. "I mean no harm to you."

"You're here for the ball," she said shakily. Every bit of instinct she possessed told her to run.

"I am not one much for such large gatherings," he said, slowly letting his hand fall.

She looked up, and in the moon's glow she saw almond-shaped black eyes, black hair pulled back to trail down his back and a long, distinct nose. The stranger's skin was close to the color of her own, yet she knew instantly that he was not mulatto. European, perhaps? Yes, that was it. He must be a native of one of the Mediterranean countries, which would account for his complexion. Yet his accent was definitely not Italian, and not Greek, either.

"I...I just came out for a breath of fresh air," she stammered, attempting to regain her composure. "I am Taye Campbell." She didn't offer her hand. She kept her fingers clasped together at her waist to hide their trembling.

"I know who you are."

There was something about the timbre of his deep voice that mesmerized her. "You do? Have we been introduced? You must forgive me," she said. "I've met so many this evening. Captain Logan has many friends."

"We have not been introduced. But I have been watching you all night."

"You have?" She swallowed, that ripple of fear present again.

"You are very different from your sister."

She felt her cheeks grow warm. "We had the same father, but not the same mother," she explained stiffly.

"That isn't what I meant."

Taye nibbled on her lower lip. The man was standing too close for propriety. She could smell his hair, his skin that seemed to have a copper red hue. He smelled fresh, like the woods.

"I...I should go."

"Don't." His arm circled her, catching her and pulling her close.

Taye opened her mouth to cry out, and the mysterious man shocked her by covering it with his own.

9

Taye lifted her arms to push the stranger away, but he was too strong for her. His mouth was hot and hard against her lips and she couldn't move, could not breathe. His warmth and the scent of his maleness enveloped her.

Against her will, her lips parted.

He pulled her even closer, wrapping his arms around her. His tongue entered her mouth, wet and warm and tasting of good brandy.

Her mind screamed no, yet a part of her body was saying yes. Her mouth slacked. She stopped fighting him. The taste of him and the feel of his body molding to hers overcame her.

She had never tasted, never felt anything so astonishing. Her skin leaped in reply.

Shocked by her own reaction, Taye jerked back suddenly and he released her. She struck him hard in the face with her palm. "You ought to be ashamed of yourself," she accused heatedly. "I'll have you know I'm an engaged woman!"

A smile played on his sensuous lips. "You do not kiss like a woman engaged to another man."

Taye lifted her skirts, turned and ran back down the path she had come.

Thankfully, she found her way out of the garden immediately. She ran in the back door, through the kitchen and up the servants' staircase, not intending to stop until she reached the sanctity of her bedchamber.

Her breath came in great gulps. How dare he kiss her? He had not even introduced himself. She didn't even know his name!

Unconsciously, her fingertips brushed her swollen lips as waves of heat washed through her. She swallowed against the constriction in her throat and tried to pretend that his lingering scent didn't cling to her skin and gown.

She was shocked by own behavior. A part of her had taken pleasure in the exhilaration. A part of her had enjoyed the passion of his kiss.

She was mortified by her response to the man's mouth on hers.

Taye hurried down the hall to her room and slammed the door behind her, trembling. Here she would be safe from that detestable man, but would she be safe from herself?

Cameron found Jackson surrounded by a group of army officers. Where was that beautiful, white-gowned woman? She pushed through the circle without so much as a *pardon me* and lifted her chin to meet her husband's charming gaze eye to eye. "May I speak with you privately, Captain Logan?" she asked icily.

"Why, certainly, madam. Gentlemen, if you will pardon us?" Jackson smiled as he offered his arm to escort her from the room.

She spun on her heels, her petticoats a swirl of green

satin broche, and walked out of the parlor and down the hall.

"Won't here do?" Jackson asked as they passed a servant carrying a tray of champagne glasses on his shoulder.

"I think not," she snapped over her shoulder, dodging the champagne. "I want to go somewhere where I can shout."

He exhaled loudly. "Cameron, General Grant is expected—"

"It cannot wait," she intoned from between clenched teeth, walking down a back hallway and out a door that led to the courtyard.

"It's cool out," he said as they walked into the open, away from the protection of the redbrick walls of the house. "I should get you something for your shoulders."

"I don't want a wrap."

"Cameron—"

She spun around. The bricked courtyard was illuminated by a dozen burning torches and was filled with carriages and horses. It was empty of humans, however, save for the stable hands near the barn doors.

Cameron caught and held Jackson's gray-eyed gaze. "Elmwood is still standing," she said quietly.

"What?" He blinked as if he had expected her to say something else.

"Mrs. Martin." She threw up a hand. "She was once Mrs. Fitzhugh. You remember her from Jackson? Always twittering and batting her lashes at my father? She was at that last ball at Elmwood, the night the South fired on Fort Sumter."

"You brought me out here to tell me who Mrs. Fitzhugh is?"

"Who she is doesn't matter, Jackson. What matters is that Mrs. Martin says she passed by Elmwood only a few weeks ago.'' Her voice caught in her throat. ''And she tells me Elmwood still stands. She tells me that my home did not burn to the ground that night the soldiers came and we fled for our lives.''

''Cam.'' Jackson reached out to take her arm.

She drew back as if she had been burned. Her eyes filled with tears and she tried to brush them away with her hands.

''Damn you, I feel so betrayed, betrayed by the one person I love most in the world. First there was...was that nasty gossip this week, and now this. How could you?'' she whispered raggedly, choking back sobs. ''You know what Elmwood meant...means to me.''

He frowned, looked down at his highly polished boots, then at her again. ''Exactly what did Mrs. Fitzhugh say?''

''Martin,'' she corrected.

''Whoever the hell she is!''

''She said Elmwood still stands. My home isn't destroyed. What more is there to say?'' Cameron beseeched with open arms.

''Did she tell you that the kitchen addition on the back of the house is gone? Did she tell you that many of the windows are shattered?'' He took a step closer, becoming more callous with each word he spoke. ''Did she tell you that soldiers took shelter in your father's office and burned his rare books and antique furniture for fuel? That horses were stabled in the west parlor? How about the pigeons roosting in the upper bedchambers and bats in the chimneys? Did she mention that in her *report?*''

''This isn't about Mrs. Martin! This is about you.'' She poked her finger at him. ''You lied to me.''

''I didn't lie. I just allowed you to believe what you already thought to be true because the house was in such ruin. Because you couldn't go home anyway.''

Cameron's lower lip trembled. She didn't care about the

kitchen or the windows or the pigeons or even her father's books. All she cared about was that Elmwood was still there. It was still standing, and she *could* go home to it. Home to her father's memory. And no one could stop her.

Jackson glanced away, his body stiff, his jaw tight with anger. "This is neither the time nor the place to talk—"

"When is the time?"

"Not now."

A cold tingling sensation pricked the nape of her neck. Hadn't she said almost the same thing to Taye earlier when her sister had wanted to talk about what had happened the night Grant died? For a moment, she felt almost light-headed.

"Not while we are entertaining guests," Jackson finished, snapping her back to the present. She opened her mouth to speak, then clamped it shut. She would not fall for his game again. She had been trying for weeks to get Jackson to talk about Elmwood, to talk about at least considering going home. If he had been unwilling in the last three weeks, what made her think he would change his mind now?

"Fine," she heard herself say flatly.

"Cameron, don't be like this." Tiny lines formed around his mouth and eyes. "Listen to me. I didn't do this to hurt you. You have to believe that. My only intention was to protect you." She refused to meet his gaze.

"You have no idea what the South looks like. The desolation is beyond imagination. Typhoid. Cholera. Consumption. It's not a healthy atmosphere for a woman in your condition."

"I'm not a frail blossom, Jackson. I'm strong. Our baby is strong."

"You are not immune to disease. And that aside, Mississippi is not the place you knew. The people are not the people you—''

''It's clear to me that you think you know what's best for me. That you think I'm incapable of using judgment concerning my own life…concerning our life.''

''Damn you, woman! It's not like that.''

''No? Isn't it?'' She shrugged. ''I should return to my duties as hostess. That, perhaps, I am capable of performing—with my limited intelligence. If you'll excuse me.'' Suddenly she was cold and near to shivering. She brushed past him abruptly, hugging herself for warmth.

She lifted her skirts and hurried for the door that led into the house, determined not to let him know how badly he had hurt her.

''Cameron—''

Instead of joining her guests, Cameron ran up the servants' back staircase and retreated to her bedchamber.

''Damn that busybody Mrs. Fitzhugh,'' Jackson seethed, considering going after Cameron. But he knew there would be no talking to her now. Not tonight. He'd have to wait until she calmed down, until she would listen to reason.

As he glanced at the door that had swung shut behind his wife, he reached inside his coat and drew out a French cigar. Damn, he'd made a mess of this, of his entire homecoming, it seemed.

What had ever made him think he was going to be able to do this? To be a husband? A father? What could possibly have made him think he could succeed as either? Had he been such a love-struck starry-eyed fool?

And that beautiful, spoiled, high-strung girl he'd taken as his bride, could she ever be content in the role of lady, wife and mother?

Jackson walked across the brick pavement toward the

stable where several young men had slipped out to smoke. "Can I bother you for a light?" he asked grimly.

One of the boys hurried to offer a sulfur match. Jackson stood in the front of the stable and drew on his rich, pungent cigar. He exhaled slowly and watched the curl of smoke drift into the darkness. He knew he should return to his guests, at least speak to General Grant, whose arrival had just been announced, but his quarrel with Cameron had left a bad taste in his mouth. So had Marie's bold appearance in his home. He would have to rein her in or tell Seward he could no longer work with her.

He dropped the cigar to the bricks and ground it out with his boot, realizing he hadn't really wanted it in the first place. One of the stable boys scooped it up to dispose of it, and Jackson nodded in thanks.

Jackson gazed up at the massive redbrick house that had once been his father's, and movement to the left caught his eye. He spotted the figure of a man at the end of the garden path, and squinted in the dim torchlight to see if it was who he thought it was.

"Cortés?" he called into the darkness.

The raven-haired man stepped into the torchlight. "Jackson." He offered his hand and the men shook, then embraced. It was not Jackson's way with other men, but it was Falcon's.

"It's good to see you, my friend." When Jackson was with Falcon Cortés, he found himself speaking in the same measured cadence. There was something simple and direct about Falcon's speech patterns, and Jackson admired the man for that directness. "I didn't think you would come. I know how you feel about public gatherings."

Jackson had met Falcon Cortés in New Orleans in the winter of '62. Falcon had worked for the Union Army as a spy on occasion, and he and Jackson had gotten into several precarious skirmishes, the kind that bind men for a lifetime. Jackson figured he owed the Indian for saving his life at least twice, maybe three times, and he had done the same for Falcon. Though there was a great deal of discrimination against men like Falcon Cortés, born of a Cherokee mother and a Mexican father, Jackson didn't care what color the man's skin was. He had seen the man's heart, and for that heart, he would love Falcon like the brother he never had for the rest of his days.

Falcon stepped back and lifted one broad shoulder. "It was good of you to invite me." He spoke perfect English, but there was a lilt to his voice that Jackson only ever heard among the Indians. "To not come would be a dishonor to your name."

Jackson chuckled. "I don't know about that, old friend, but I'm glad you came. You're staying the night, aren't you?"

Falcon nodded.

Jackson indicated the garden. "Taking a little walk?"

"Do you know you have a nest of baby rabbits near the back gate?"

"I did not."

"And a beautiful woman near the statue of the angel."

Jackson grinned. Falcon liked the ladies as well as any hot-blooded male, but Jackson had never known him to have a relationship that lasted more than a few days. Most, only one night. In the months he had worked closely with Marie LeLaurie and Jackson, it was obvious he did not approve of their relationship.

"You found baby rabbits *and* a woman in my garden? Sounds like you had a successful evening." Jackson crossed his arms over his chest, thankful for the excuse to remain outside a few moments longer. Hopefully, by the time he entered the house, Marie would be gone and Cameron would have calmed down a little. "So who was the fortunate young lady, might I ask?"

"She has skin the color of peach honey and eyes of blue topaz," Falcon said in a poetic voice. "She is called Taye, I have been told."

Jackson lifted a brow. "Taye is it?" He chuckled. "My sister-in-law. She is indeed beautiful. She is also taken by another man."

"I am not so sure of that," Falcon said with a sense of mystery in his voice.

Jackson studied the Indian carefully, but his friend gave no further explanation, and he knew him well enough to know he would not. "Well, my friend, I should return to my guests. I've been out here long enough."

Falcon looked to the great house where sounds of music and laughter wafted from the open windows. "I wondered why you were here and not within the walls of your lodge."

"Little spat with my wife."

"Ah. Hair of fire, tongue of fire."

Jackson chuckled. "You've got that one right." He slid his hands into his trouser pockets. "She's been a little temperamental the last few weeks. She is expecting our first child."

Falcon nodded. "You must be very proud."

"Scared shitless, if you want to know the truth." There was an easy pause between them. That was something else Jackson admired in Falcon. He was comfortable in silence in a way most white men were not.

At last, Jackson gave a wave. "Come in. Let's share a glass of firewater, and I'll introduce you to General Grant. It's about time you met the man you've been working for."

Jackson walked down the hallway, boots in his hand so that he would not disturb his guests staying the night. The last carriage had pulled out around three in the morning, and he had sent the servants all to bed. The ball had been an astounding success, and the cleaning could be dealt with tomorrow. The entire household staff had worked flaw-lessly tonight, and he guessed they wanted just what he wanted, a soft pillow beneath their heads.

Jackson halted at the bedchamber he shared with Cam-eron. He had decided on his way upstairs that he needed to at least tell her good-night. He knew he'd probably end up down the hall again, but he wanted to put forward that small gesture. After their argument, he'd seen her only once, dancing with General Grant.

Jackson laid his hand on the doorknob, then thought again. Instead of just walking in, he knocked. "Cameron?"

He heard movement and the door jerked open. "What do you want?" she challenged.

She was dressed in a pale yellow dressing gown, her hair pulled back girlishly in a ribbon, her eyes tear-swollen.

Jackson immediately grew defensive. "I just came up-stairs to—"

"You're not sleeping here, if that's what you think!"

His jaw tightened. "Please, Cam…the guests—"

"Don't you tell me what to do! I'll shout if I want!"

"Fine," he said turning away. "Good night."

"Don't come back, either," she called after him, "be-cause the door will be locked."

"Have no fear," he muttered, turning to leave, his boots in his hand.

"What?"

Jackson knew he just needed to walk away. He was tired to the bone and he worried about this whole Thompson's Raiders assignment. His last bits of information had been rather disturbing, and he would have to meet with Marie tomorrow whether he wanted to or not. He had to find out what she knew.

Just walk away, he told himself. But he couldn't. He turned around to face her. "I said you can have no fear. I won't be knocking on your door again any time soon, Cam. You highly overrate your attraction to me."

"Good!" she shouted. "Because I don't want you near me! Do you understand?"

He chuckled, but he was far from amused. "You won't have to worry about me tapping on your door, dear wife," he said sarcastically. "Because I'm leaving tomorrow."

He didn't wait for her to ask for where. He'd had no intentions whatsoever of going with Marie, but now that he had spoken the words, his mind was made up. "I'm going to New Orleans. I don't know for how long. Maybe your disposition will be improved by the time I get back."

"And maybe it won't!" she yelled, slamming the door. "Son of a bitch," Cameron muttered under her breath as she turned the key on the door and wiped at the hot tears that ran down her cheeks. Fine, he could go to New Orleans. He could abandon her like he always did. But she wouldn't be here when he got back.

Jackson stomped down the hall, his boots still in his hand, but he didn't go to the bedchamber he'd been relegated to. He was too angry to sleep. Instead, he headed back down the grand staircase, in the dark, for a drink. Maybe a good scotch would settle him. Right now, all he wanted to do was hit something. Hit someone.

He was surprised to see lamplight coming from under the door of his study. He opened the door and walked in, and was pleasantly surprised to see Falcon Cortés.

Falcon turned from the open window that looked out into the dark garden. "I thought you had said good-night."

Jackson shrugged and sat down on the edge of a leather chair. He dropped his boots on the floor. "No bed to go to," he grumbled.

Falcon chuckled. "Locked out?"

"Of course not." Jackson kicked one boot with his stocking foot. "Yes. Locked out, if you must know. I suspect everyone in a one-hundred-mile radius already knows." He rose, walked to his desk and reached for a bottle of scotch. "Of course, I could get in, if I wanted to. This was my damned house to begin with, before I got the clever idea to marry the little chit."

"Of course," Falcon said stoically.

"But who wants to climb into that den?"

"A she-bear can be dangerous," Falcon agreed. "Sometimes she is better left alone. Bait her, and she may take your head."

Jackson adjusted the front panel of his flannel trousers. "Or worse." He raised the bottle. Just having Falcon here lightened his spirits. "Drink?"

Falcon nodded.

Jackson poured them both a shot and they swallowed in silence. He refilled the glasses.

Falcon eyed him. He must have known that Jackson had had quite a bit to drink before he went upstairs. It was that kind of look.

Jackson pushed the shot glass toward his friend and tipped the other glass to his mouth. The second one went down smoother than the first, and Jackson began to relax. Damn it, he was the man of the house. Cameron was his wife. She was bid by law, before God, to do as he said, wasn't she?

"Cameron wants to go home to Mississippi," Jackson explained to Falcon. "She wants to have the baby there."

"There has been much devastation in the South."

"That's wh...what I tried to tell her." He heard his words slur slightly. "She says she wants to go home to the house she was born in, but..." His words drifted out the open window.

Falcon listened calmly, nursing his second shot.

Jackson poured himself another. "Well, I'm just going to tell her that it's out of the question." He nodded, liking the sound and volume of his own words. "In the morning I'm going to tell her that she will stay here where she's safe, and that will be the end of it. She will not be going to Elmwood." He slammed a fist down on his desk in emphasis. "Then I'll head to New Orleans, see if Marie's lead takes us anywhere. And then I'll come home. If I let Cameron stew for a week or two, she'll be ready to listen to reason."

Falcon only nodded thoughtfully.

"So that's it." Jackson reached for the scotch bottle again, then let go. He turned to Falcon. "You want to go to New Orleans?"

Falcon studied him with those intense black eyes. "With Marie?"

Jackson nodded.

"And you think this is wise, considering your past?"

"Listen, friend." Jackson clamped his hand on Falcon's back. "I don't want to be lectured by you on this subject. Whatever Marie and I once had is done. This is strictly business. We go. We put our ears to the ground, and I come home to my shrewish wife." He managed a chuckle.

Falcon stared at the floor for a moment and then glanced up. "I told you when I came that I am here for as long as you have use for me." He opened his broad bronze hands. "So it is to New Orleans we go."

10

Early the following morning, Taye opened the door to Cameron's bedchamber to find her packing trunks.

Jackson had left at first light, without speaking to his wife, according to the servants.

"What do you think you're doing?" Taye asked, knowing full well what Cameron was doing. She closed the door for privacy.

"I'm going home to Elmwood," she said haughtily. "I want you to come with me, if only for a few weeks, but I'll understand if you want to remain here with Thomas."

"My hesitation doesn't concern Thomas." Taye retrieved a frilly white crinoline from the floor and tossed it on the bed. The truth was, she realized, the idea of getting away from here, away from Thomas, appealed to her right now. She needed time to think, time to get her head straightened out. Thank heavens that arrogant man had left this morning with Jackson, before she came down for breakfast. She wasn't certain she could have faced him with Thomas in the same room, not when her lips were still burning with his kiss.

"It's not safe to go alone. Two women unescorted—

there's no saying what could happen," Taye lectured. "Not if what Thomas and Jackson told me is true of the South."

"Nonsense. They were just trying to frighten us. We'll be perfectly safe. We'll be taking the train." Cameron lifted a carpetbag to carry it to the door, but Taye waylaid her and took it from her. "There will be others aboard," Cameron continued obstinately. "Besides, I've packed my pistol." She patted the deep pocket of her traveling gown, sewn in for just this purpose.

"We're just going to go without telling Jackson?" Taye asked.

"And just how would I tell him?" Cameron spun around angrily. "He's gone, Taye." Her voice caught in her throat and came out as a sob. "He's gone. Gone and I don't know when he'll be back."

"There, there," Taye soothed, wrapping her arms around her sister. "It will be all right. He's just stomped off angry. He'll be back."

Cameron held tightly to Taye, her tears dampening both their gowns. "But what if he's gone with that horrible woman?" She sniffed. "What if he *isn't* coming back?"

"I'm telling you that I know Jackson, and I know you." Taye smoothed Cameron's glossy red hair tied back in a knitted snood. "This will all blow over."

"You think so?" Cameron shuddered and then took a step back, accepting the handkerchief Taye pressed in her hand.

"I do. But I also believe you would be better to wait here for Jackson, rather than having him come home to an empty house." Taye shook her head, imagining the thunder. "If he has to chase you all the way to Mississippi after he's just returned from New Orleans, he's going to be angry, Cam."

Cameron wiped her eyes. "Well, he can just be angry.

And if he wants me back as his wife, truly wants me back, he'll have to come to me on my terms, won't he?''

"Thank you for seeing me on a Sunday, sir.'' Jackson offered his hand to Secretary of State Seward across the wide expanse of his desk. "I apologize for the inconvenience, but the information Mrs. LeLaurie has related demands immediate action.''

Seward shook his hand. "No apology necessary. Your message got me out of a long afternoon of listening to another of the Vicar Wicket's long, dull sermons.''

"I would like to introduce Falcon Cortés, Mr. Secretary. As I have told you before, Mr. Cortés was instrumental in several vital—''

"Mr. Cortés's exploits are well known in Washington's higher circles. This country owes him…owes both of you a greater debt than we can ever repay. Your devotion to the Union and the repeated acts of courage which the two of you—''

"Simply doing our duty, sir,'' Jackson said. "And we were lucky.'' He smiled at Falcon. "Although I've rarely seen anyone with such total disregard for his own personal safety.''

Falcon frowned. "As you say, we were lucky. Many brave men were not so fortunate.''

"He will be accompanying Mrs. LeLaurie and me to New Orleans,'' Jackson continued.

Falcon stepped up to the desk and nodded respectfully before shaking Seward's hand. "It is good to meet you, Mr. Secretary.''

"Good to meet you, at last, Cortés.'' Seward pumped his hand. "Jackson has been singing your praises for years.''

"Jackson is free with his words.''

Seward gestured, stiffly. "Please, gentlemen, sit.''

"We can't, sir." Jackson raised his head. "We've left Mrs. LeLaurie making arrangements at Union Station. But you sit, please. I know your physicians would not approve of you even being here. First the carriage accident that laid you up, then the assassination attempt."

Seward chuckled, his hollowed face filling out a bit. "Not the least to say, my wife." He lowered himself slowly into his chair; it was obvious his injuries from the attempted assassination had not yet entirely healed.

"Jackson, you understand how important it is that this man and his cohorts be stopped as soon as possible. President Johnson doesn't need any more damned distractions. He has many opponents to his Reconstruction plan for the South, and tempers flare regularly on the Senate and House floors." Seward absently brushed the bright red scar across his cheek that would be a permanent reminder of the attack made on him. "There are many who are saying that Andrew Johnson, self-educated tailor-turned-politician, should never have become president after the assassination. They say Lincoln had only asked him to run on his Union ticket in '64 to placate Southerners still left in Washington. Many radical Republicans see our Tennessee-born president as a confederate and the enemy, despite his words and deeds. Thompson's Raiders must be stopped! Now, tell me what you know and what your plans are, where you'll be going. I'll arrange for safe houses, should you need them, and also cash. Have you need of additional weapons?"

Jackson shook his head, offering a wry grin. "We're all armed, of course, even Mrs. LeLaurie, but we prefer to use our wits rather than firepower when possible. We'll bring these men to you, sir. Alive."

"I know you will, Jackson. That's why I was so adamant that you help us out, at least this one last time." Seward opened his arms. "After this, it's up to you."

Jackson nodded, backing toward the door. "We'll see, sir. Thank you for receiving us."

"Godspeed, Jackson, Cortés."

"Thank you, Mr. Secretary," Jackson and Falcon responded.

Outside the office, Jackson closed the heavily paneled door behind them.

"You sure you want to do this, friend?" Falcon said.

Jackson scowled, walking away. "Don't ask me again. Right now I can't wait to get the hell out of this town."

"Cameron, are you sure this is what you want to do?" Taye asked as the women left the bedchamber. "You're certain you don't want to at least wait a day? Jackson may have second thoughts and—"

"I'm leaving today." With a carpetbag in one hand, she closed her bedchamber door, then picked up her other bag. "I hope I've brought what I need, but I didn't want to bring trunks. I'd rather not make any more fuss than necessary. I'd just as soon get out of here as quickly as possible with as few of the servants knowing as possible. I can have my things sent to me later."

Taye followed her down the hall, weighted down by two heavy canvas traveling bags.

Cameron halted at the top of the rear servants' staircase and listened. She heard trays clinking, orders being given for servants leaving the kitchen, but there was no one on the stairs. "We may just be able to slip out the back this way."

Taye balanced carpetbags in each hand. She had changed into a simple traveling gown, like her sister's, a practical sunbonnet and sturdy boots. "I still cannot believe you're really going to do this," she murmured. "I cannot believe *I'm* going to do this."

"Do you want to say goodbye to Thomas?"

Taye shook her head. "That won't be necessary."

Cameron found her tone of voice odd. "Did you two have an argument?"

"Of course not. Now let's go, if we're going." Taye probed Cameron's shoulder.

"You *didn't* fight with Thomas?" Cameron turned to face Taye.

Taye pressed her lips together and shook her head.

Cameron could tell by the look on her sister's face that something had happened, but what, she didn't know. It felt strange that Taye would not immediately tell her; once, they had shared everything. But Cameron would not press Taye now. There would be time on the train to talk.

At the bottom of the narrow stairs, Cameron halted and peered around the corner into the kitchen, where one of the cooks was arguing with another over the burned edges of a pan of biscuits. She stepped into the hall and shot past the kitchen door, Taye's hurried footsteps soft behind her.

Cameron placed her hand on the white glass doorknob and drew a deep breath. In another moment they would be safely out of the house.

"Miss Cameron! Jus' where you two think yer goin'?"

Cameron spun around. "None of your business, Naomi," she said crisply. "Go about your duties."

Naomi strode down the hall toward them, wiping her dark hands on her pristine apron. "Where you think the two if you is goin' with yer bags in yer hands and yer ridin' boots on your feet? Hmm? Sneakin' out of here like a thief takin' a loaf of bread." The head housekeeper shook her head as if disgusted.

"Naomi, we don't have time for this," Cameron whispered harshly. "When my husband returns and asks where we've gone, you'll have nothing to say if you don't know."

Naomi whipped off her apron, still shaking her head. The gesture reminded Cameron of the days at Elmwood when Sukey had been head housekeeper and had caught her and Taye up to no good. It was the same disappointed look, the same stern voice. Cameron had to struggle not to feel twelve years old again.

"You goin' home, ain't you, Miss Cameron?" Naomi shook the apron at her.

Cameron stared stubbornly.

"I know the captain done left in a huff this morning, but that ain't no reason to be takin' off like this."

Still, Cameron would not answer Naomi.

"I jest knew it was a matter of time before ya took off." Naomi harrumphed and headed for the kitchen. "Now you wait right here 'til I speak with my Noah and grab up that baby of mine. You two ain't goin' nowhere without Naomi."

Taye looked from Cameron to Naomi, her lips pressed together.

"That's really not necessary," Cameron said in her best mistress tone. "Taye and I are quite capable of—"

Naomi stepped up to Cameron, her dark face in Cameron's face. "Either you wait for me, missy, or I'm chasin' down the captain, clear to New Orleans if I have to, and I'm telling him jest what yer up to."

"You wouldn't," Cameron demanded.

Naomi stood her ground, arms crossed stubbornly over her chest.

For a moment the two women, once mistress and slave, now something far more, stared each other down.

Cameron broke eye contact first. "I suppose it wouldn't hurt to have someone with us," she said begrudgingly.

"I 'spose not." Naomi's dark eyes seemed to spark.

"Now you go out to the stable and get them little lazy negra boys to harness a carriage. I'll be out directly."

Naomi watched the two women slip out the back door and shook her head in disappointment. She had seen this coming, Cameron and the captain arguing, the gossip all over town. Still, Cameron didn't belong traipsing off to Mississippi, especially considering what the bones had told her. And if Cameron didn't have the sense to know that running away wasn't going to solve any problems, at least Taye should have. That girl was getting more like Cameron every day. Just as stubborn and headstrong. Just as foolish.

But Naomi knew she would go with Cameron whether it was bad for her marriage or not. The bones didn't send you to save a marriage. Naomi was here because Cameron needed her and because, in the coming months, Naomi knew that her friend would be tried near to breaking. And she knew that she was here to catch Miss Cameron when she fell.

Naomi climbed the narrow stairs that led to the tiny rooms above the kitchen where she found her Noah seated at a small table. Baby Ngosi slept in the cradle beside the bed, his thumb comfortably plugged into his mouth.

Noah had a lit candle on the desk and was gripping a book Cameron had loaned him from the captain's extensive library. It was a primer meant for children, but Noah acted as if it were made of gold.

Naomi had no desire to learn to read—it was an aspect of the white man's life she wanted no part of—but it was important to Noah. He wanted to be able to teach their son to read when Ngosi was old enough because he insisted that letters and ciphers would be the only way the African free man could make his way in this new world that President Lincoln had created.

Noah was too wrapped up in the white man's life to her

way of thinking. He didn't even call their son by his proper African name, Ngosi, *blessing* in the old talk. No, Noah had to call the boy Nathan, as if giving him a white name would make folks forget the color of his skin. Foolishness, she thought. A boy needed to be brought up prideful of his own people, to remember that he had the blood of African warriors and kings pumping strong in his veins.

"I have to go to Mississippi," Naomi said, fingering the gris-gris bag she wore around her neck, carefully kept hidden beneath her dress. She walked to a wood trunk under the window and drew out a sailcloth bag. She stuffed a clean petticoat into it and began to gather the things a voodoo priestess would not travel without—her leather bag of throwing bones that had been her grandmother's, candles of various colors, incense and several paper envelopes of powders and herbs. She talked as she packed, fearful that if she gave Taye and Cameron too much time, they might do something foolish like try to leave without her. They were smart women, both of them, but to Naomi's thinking, sometimes neither had enough sense to find an egg in a henhouse.

"Now I'll be taken little Ngosi with me 'cause he still needin' his mama's milk, but—"

"Goin' to Mississippi?" Noah barked, turning on the three-legged stool he sat perched on. "Like hell you are!"

Naomi went right on packing. "I don' know how long I'll be gone. I 'spect the captain'll be right along after us, soon as he's done with his business in N'Arlins, so I may be back within the month."

Noah rose off the stool. "You hear me, woman. I said you're not goin' to Mississippi alone—"

"I'm not goin' alone. I'm goin' with Miss Cameron and Miss Taye."

"And yer sure as hell not takin' my boy there!"

Naomi never slowed down. "You go right on to work every day in the city like yer 'sposed to. I'll tell Addy to make you a pail for yer midday."

Noah grabbed the sack from Naomi's hand. "You listenin' to me, woman? I said no wife of mine is goin' to no Mississippi. These is dangerous times. They lynchin' darky girls like you down there."

She frowned and snatched back her bag. "You been listenin' to those fools down to Bayou's again, ain't ya?" Bayou's was a blacksmith's shop that also served as a saloon and catered to the free black men of the city. Located down near the harbor, it was a rough place that Naomi didn't think her husband had any business going to. But like his name said, Noah Freeman was free to be a fool like the rest of them.

"Miss Cameron needs me" was all she said. "I have to go."

"The captain know Missus Logan was takin' off the minute he left?" Noah demanded.

"No. And if you send word to him—" Naomi brought her finger beneath her husband's nose, not caring that he was a full head taller than she and outweighed her by more than two stone. "I'll put a curse on that big ole stick of yours so that it won't rise for a month!"

He took a step back. "You sure Miss Cameron and Miss Taye gonna be safe? I hear it ain't safe for decent women there, white or black." He paused. "I could go with ya."

She shook her head. "Yer a good man to offer, but this is somethin' I got to do alone. Don't worry yer head. Between my bones and Miss Cameron's pistol I know she got in her pocket, I think we'll be safe enough." She lifted up on her toes and puckered her lips. "Now give Naomi a kiss and hand me that bundle of boy. My ladies are waitin' for me. I think we got a train to catch."

Noah lifted the sleeping child and lowered him into the muslin sling Naomi had tied across her chest. As Ngosi settled against her breast and snuggled into the warm fabric, Naomi reached up and stroked her husband's beard-stubbled chin, not wanting to see the tears forming in his eyes. "I won't be gone long, lover. You keep that bed of ours warm for me."

11

Cameron, Taye and Naomi took the train from Baltimore, heading south toward Richmond. There they would spend the night and try to locate a train that would take them closer to Jackson, Mississippi. However, no railroad employees seemed able to tell them exactly how they would accomplish that or what train they would need to take. Despite the uncertainty, Cameron was determined to keep going.

So many train tracks had been purposely destroyed by Union soldiers. It would take months, years to restore train service as it had been before the war. Until then, passengers would have to make do.

It was not until the train was south of Washington, D.C., and into Virginia that the scenery began to change and evidence of the war surrounded them. Cameron knew the battles sites by heart—Manassas, Fredericksburg, Chancellorsville, Petersburg, Wilderness, Cedar Creek. But now those places weren't just marks on a map or black ink in the newspaper. The battlefields in the ravaged land around them were real.

The women fell into silence in the mostly empty passenger car, staring out through the sooty train windows as the countryside passed in an almost surreal way. No one spoke; there was nothing to say that could express the aching heartbreak they were feeling.

A house and outbuildings just south of Washington had been burned to the ground. Cameron had certainly seen houses ravaged by fire before, but what she had not seen was a burned house with four white wooden crosses in the front yard. The tiny farmstead had become a cemetery.

She felt tears burn the backs of her eyelids as she wondered whose graves those were. Did they belong to the family who had lived in the house and died of hunger or been killed by renegade soldiers? Or had men died fighting on this front lawn and been buried by their comrades, their loved ones never to see their graves? Which was more tragic? she wondered.

As the train chugged south, Cameron began to realize that while the fields in Eastern Maryland were planted and thriving, the fields in Virginia that had not been burned had been left to grow fallow because there were no seeds to plant, no healthy men to work the soil. In many places, roads had grown into weedy paths. Front yards that had once been manicured by scythe or sheep were growing into tangled meadows. And evidence of fire was everywhere. Brush fires had burned fields, woods and homes. Towering shade trees and orchards had been hacked down along the roadside to serve for firewood for cold, hungry soldiers. The countryside was black and empty.

And the graves. The graves were the hardest to bear. They were everywhere. In the churchyards. On private properties. Even occasionally by the roadside with nothing to mark a man's passing but a crudely constructed wooden cross. Who would mourn these lost men? Who would tend their graves?

When the war had come four years ago, Cameron had

understood intellectually why it had to be fought. Her father, though a Southern senator and planter, had been a staunch supporter of the antislavery movement. She understood that to set men and women free, it might come to war. But never, in her wildest dreams, had she ever considered the price Americans, Northerners and Southerners, would pay for the conflict.

By the time the women reached Richmond that evening, Cameron was exhausted, mentally as well as physically. She barely remembered the carriage ride to one of the few hotels accepting guests and was thankful for the darkness that shielded her eyes from the horrors the city had experienced.

"Is this the best you can offer us?" Cameron had demanded of the driver as he stopped the sagging coach in front of a wooden two-story building with a broken front door and a rusty tin stovepipe protruding from a boarded-up front window. "Are you sure this place is respectable?"

"Richmond House has mattresses on their beds, private rooms for respectable women and a roof that don't leak unless it's rainin' cats and dogs." He pointed with the tip of his carriage whip. "Don't look like much, but they got a covered well and a dining room. Lessin' you and yer girls fixin' to sleep on the tracks, you'd best take whatever beds they got. Richmond's streets ain't no place for decent folks after dark."

"Let's go back to the station," Taye said. "I've got a bad feeling about this place."

"Ain't no other," the driver warned. "Most places won't take women travelin' without their husbands."

"It will be fine," Cameron said. "So long as we can get a hot bath, clean sheets and something to eat. I don't know about you, but I'm starving."

The interior of Richmond House was little better than

the outside. The only room available was a narrow cub-byhole in the back, wedged under a slanting tin roof. The floor was bare, the blankets on the bed thin and patched and the wallpaper water stained. The hotel stank of mold, grease and cooking onions. Refusing to eat in the dining room without Taye and Naomi, who were not welcome in the ''public'' room, Cameron asked to have their meal brought up to the room. There, they ate a cold supper of ham, cabbage and water, and fell into an exhausted sleep.

Sometime in the middle of the night, Cameron began to feel ill. She got up, drank some water from a pitcher provided by their host, and used the necessary pot. She prayed she was not getting ill, but was just tired and unfamiliar with the simple food they had consumed. By morning, she felt even worse, but she was determined to get to Elmwood as quickly as she could. There, everything would be clearer, not so dismal. She just had to get there.

''Cam? Are you all right?'' Taye, who was repacking one of their carpet bags to leave for the train station, turned to her sister.

Cameron stood near the bed and pressed her hand to her abdomen. The squalid room seemed to be spinning around her. She was sick to her stomach again, but there was also cramping. Lower in her belly. Suddenly she was afraid that there was something wrong with the baby, and an over-whelming fear gripped her as tears filled her eyes. All she could think of was Jackson. She wanted Jackson.

''Cameron?'' Taye repeated.

But Cameron could barely hear her. Taye's voice seemed to come from far away.

''Naomi,'' Taye said in that distant voice. ''I think there's something wrong with Cameron.''

''No. No, I'm fine,'' she mumbled. She looked down to be sure her dress was not stained with blood. No blood.

Just indigestion. The baby was fine. But her head was pounding and her tongue felt thick and fuzzy in her mouth. "Just...just a little tired is all," she heard herself say. "Didn't...didn't sleep well last night."

Cameron saw Taye come toward her. Then the room spun viciously and her sister seemed to whirl out of sight. Another cramp racked Cameron's body and she doubled over. At the same time, the dirty floor seemed to come up from under her and she felt her knees buckle. Her head must have hit the bedstead as she fell because there was a sudden blossom of pain in her head.

Then blessed darkness.

Cameron stirred, unsure of where she was, who she was with. She felt as if she were floating, but there was pain in her head and an even greater pain in the pit of her stomach. She moaned and someone pressed something damp and cool to her burning head.

"It's been nearly a week. She's not any better."

Was that Taye?

"She be all right," came another familiar voice. "It was jest that bad water, I tell ya. We boil the water, she get better once it moves through her belly and out."

"I don't understand how it can be the water. You drank it. I drank it. I think we need to find a doctor," Taye said.

Yes, it had to be Taye. And the other woman? Cameron knew her liquidy voice. It was Naomi.

"Ya git her a doctor and she'll be worse off!" Naomi scoffed. "She the only one got sick 'cause her body was weak to start with! I jest thank Noah's Lord this boy chil' of mine was drinking my milk and not that water, else he might be sick, too. A mama's teats got a way of filterin' out the bad spirits."

"I just can't believe there's nothing we can do but sit

here and wait for her to get better,'' Taye protested, adjusting the cool cloth on Cameron's head.

Cameron wanted to speak up. She wanted to tell Taye that she didn't want to be here. Here was Richmond. She remembered now. But she wasn't supposed to be in Richmond. She wanted to go to Elmwood. She knew she wouldn't be sick if she could just get to Elmwood. If she could just tell Taye and Naomi.

But Cameron couldn't find any words. Her mouth wouldn't obey. The women went on talking as if she were not there.

''''Sides, we ain't doin' nuthin'. I tole you, we boil water. Every bit that goes in her mouth. The heat kills the bad spirits. We got to keep givin' it to her. Wash out the bad with the good.''

''I only wish I knew how to find Jackson. He'll be so upset with us when he realizes we left Baltimore and Cameron got sick in Richmond.''

''Ain't no way to get him. Ya said so yerself. He gone to Lez-i-ana. He'll be back soon enough. He'll find his wife gone and he'll come after her. Sure as rain.''

Cameron felt Taye adjust the cloth on her forehead again. It felt so good that it made her want to sleep. Just sleep.

''I hope she lives long enough for Jackson to find us'' was the last thing Cameron heard before she fell asleep.

''Place your bets, gentlemen,'' a man in a crisp white shirt and red silk vest called.

Jackson carelessly threw down several bills for his next wager, then scooped up the ivory dice and tossed them.

The crowd that had gathered around the gaming table on the riverboat *Saint Louis* clapped and exclaimed with excitement as Jackson won again. Men and women he didn't know called him by name. Some offered to buy him drinks.

A woman offered herself to him in a husky whisper in his ear.

The swinging oil lamps that hung from the ceiling cast bright light over the room. Whiskey flowed freely and there were ladies of the evening roaming the gaming tables to keep patrons happy. The light, the women and the noise were all meant to keep a man on his feet, spending money, but they only made Jackson wish he were anywhere but here.

Jackson sighed with boredom. In the years before the war he'd enjoyed gambling immensely and had been considered a high-stakes patron of great acclaim in most of the gambling houses throughout the South. He'd gone days without sleeping or eating to play endless games of poker or craps and never felt so alive. But the pastime no longer interested him.

They were a week into their trip, and Jackson was growing impatient. He had still not obtained any information on Thompson and his raiders. Tonight, he had hoped to be contacted on the gambling floor, but it was well after midnight. For whatever reason, his anonymous contact would not be showing his face tonight. Jackson even wondered now if there *was* an anonymous contact. He wouldn't put it past Marie to make up the whole story to get him here alone with her.

Jackson sighed irritably. His father had always told him that a woman was nothing but a thorn in a man's side, and he was beginning to think the old man had been right. Couldn't live with them, couldn't live without them.

Jackson glanced up from the gaming table to survey the crowd of well-dressed, wealthy gamblers. If his contact had been among them, wouldn't he have made himself known by now? He just wanted to turn in for the night, go to sleep and escape into blessed oblivion where he didn't have to pretend. And where he didn't have to think about the spirited, copper-haired beauty who was his life.

Jackson rolled the dice. He'd been mistaken in thinking that putting hundreds of miles between them would somehow ease his anger...or the pain of her rejection.

A part of him wanted to turn around and head for Baltimore, to make what had gone wrong in his marriage right again. But a bigger part of him was stubborn. Cameron had caused all the discontent between them. She wasn't satisfied with her role as wife; he had been perfectly content. She deserved to sit and stew at home.

"Bets again, gentlemen," the man in the red vest announced.

Jackson took a portion of his last winnings and tossed them out without counting the bills, glancing up to see Marie approach the gaming table holding shots of whiskey in each hand. Tonight she was dressed in a pink silk gown that complemented her olive skin and ebony hair, making her even lovelier than she appeared by daylight. And those ruby lips—a man just couldn't take his eyes off those lips and the promises they seemed to whisper, even when she was silent.

"There you are, Jackson," Marie purred, sidling up beside him as she pressed a glass into his hand. She tipped her chin for a kiss and he leaned over her, gaining full view of her tantalizing breasts, a whiff of her intoxicating perfume. His mouth brushed her red lips and she sighed coquettishly.

"Are you winning?" Marie looked up at him through a veil of black lashes as she sipped her whiskey.

"I always win." He reached for the dice, but she scooped them up.

"Give them here, sweet," he said, trying not to sound

impatient. Eyes were watching. Ears were listening. He had to be careful to be who he wished to appear.

Marie tossed back her head of glossy black curls piled high in an elaborate coiffure and kissed each ink-dyed ivory die. "For luck."

He accepted the dice she dropped into his hand and threw them. He won again.

Marie set down her glass and clapped her hands together before scooping up the money in handfuls. "I told you my kiss was good luck."

Jackson looked down at her. "I think I've had my fill. I'm going to turn in."

"Excellent idea," she purred.

"Add Captain Logan's winnings to his account," Marie ordered as she glided away on Jackson's arm. "He's grown bored with your little games."

They left the bright white lights of the gambling hall and walked outside along the deck toward the passenger cabins. The warm, pungent breeze swept off the dark waters of the Mississippi and reminded Jackson of his days sailing the ocean when he was a young man working for his father in the family shipping business. Those were simpler days.

"We wait one more night," Jackson said under his breath. "If your contact does not come—"

"He'll be here. I told you. He said he had to be careful. We pull into another port tomorrow morning. That must be where he is boarding."

"One more night," Jackson repeated, "and then we disembark." He halted at her cabin door.

"Do you want to come in for a drink?" She ran her hand up his arm, and even through the fabric of his evening coat he could feel the heat of her desire for him. It irked him that Marie could obviously crave him, while Cameron, his own wife, didn't want him in her bed.

But he would not go inside. It was a bad idea. Marie was too tempting and he was in too foul a mood. "Good night, Marie."

She smiled and smoothed his cheek with her hand. He let her, telling himself it was all for appearance's sake. Everyone knew of Jackson's fame from the war, so it was easier to pretend to be himself than another. He had boarded the *Saint Louis* with Marie on the pretense of traveling to New Orleans on business. He assumed that everyone would naturally presume he was traveling with his mistress; it was the perfect deception. He had told the purser that in order to "keep up appearances," he and Mrs. LeLaurie would require separate cabins.

"Good night," she murmured submissively, slipping soundlessly into her room.

Jackson found Falcon waiting by his cabin door, staring out into the darkness. "Anything?" Falcon asked.

"No. I'm going to bed. If we're not contacted by tomorrow night, I told Marie we're calling it a bust and going home."

Falcon nodded. There was room enough for Falcon to share the cabin with Jackson, but each night he slept on a bedroll on the deck, insisting he preferred sleeping beneath the stars. "I will see you in the morning then, friend."

Jackson nodded and entered his cabin. It was spacious for a riverboat and decorated in heavy oak wainscoting and plush draperies and bed linens. He stripped off his clothes, letting them fall on the floor of the dark cabin and walked naked across the oriental carpet, tacked on the floor, to the bed built into the wall. Moonlight streamed through the open porthole, casting a band of light over the bed to the door.

Jackson lay down on the feather tick across the smooth linen sheets and tucked his arm beneath his head. He stared at the dark-paneled ceiling and listened to the creak and groan of the wood as the boat eased down the Mississippi. He was tired, but he knew it would be a long time before he slept. Images of Cameron and Marie danced in his head, often one superimposed over the other. He heard their voices, so different, other times hauntingly familiar. Marie was easy to be with, so pliable. And Cameron, she was so often so...difficult. But he didn't love Marie anymore. He loved Cameron. Didn't he?

Jackson had not been in bed ten minutes when he heard a sound outside his door. He froze, listening. Someone was standing there. Right at his door. Listening. Someone who did not belong there.

In one quick motion he drew a pistol from beneath the mattress, and by the time the door eased open, he was on his knees on the bed, weapon drawn.

"Sweet Jesus, Jackson. What a crass way to greet a woman."

She closed the door behind her as he lowered his pistol. His entire body trembled, but his hands did not shake.

"Damn it, Marie, I could have shot you," he grumbled as he tucked the loaded pistol back under the bed.

She stepped into the path of moonlight that streamed through the porthole, and he drew in his breath. She was stark naked.

Against his will, his body responded and there was no way to hide it. "How the hell did you get down the passageway like that?" he snapped.

She rested her hands on her rounded hips. She was shapelier than Cameron. Her breasts and hips were larger, her waist somehow smaller. She had let down her hair and it fell in black waves over her shoulders and down her back. She had the perfect mistress's body.

"When did you get to be so dull, Jackson?" she purred.

"Is that what marriage has done for you?" She glided closer. "Made you a dull boy?"

Jackson swallowed hard, then licked his lips, trying to think about something other than the dark patch of hair between her thighs. He ran a quick mathematics equation in his mind. Mentally counted the beams overhead. Made an inventory of his shoes in the trunk at the foot of the bed. Slowly, the tightening in his groin eased a little.

"Jackson," Marie breathed.

And just like that, with one word from her, he sprang upright and hard again.

It would be just one night, he thought. Just one. Cameron had thrown him out of her bedchamber. She had denied him his husbandly carnal privileges. Didn't he have the right to seek solace in another woman's embrace? And such a willing embrace it was.

Jackson leaped off the bed and snatched up the sheet. When she stepped into his open arms, he covered her naked body, taking care not to touch her bare skin. "What the hell are you doing in here like this, Marie?"

She replied by pressing her mouth to his, warm and pliant. There was something about the familiarity of her taste and the fact that she wanted him. Marie *wanted* him.

Jackson's resolve crumbled as he crushed her mouth with his. The sheet fell away and he gripped her bare, soft buttocks feverishly with both hands.

Marie moaned, pressing her hips to his, tantalizing him.

Jackson grabbed one pendulant breast and lowered his head to take her dark, thick nipple in his mouth. He sucked hungrily, not caring if he hurt her.

Marie clung to him, making little panting sounds. "Take me," she moaned, reaching down to grasp his engorged member. "Please, Jackson, take me now before I die for want of you."

Jackson grabbed a hank of her black hair and jerked her head backward, covering her mouth with his again. Just this one time. No one would know, he told himself. He deserved her.

Then he opened his eyes and saw amber eyes, not black. *Cameron.* It was her eyes looking into his.

He had loved Cameron from the moment he had met her. It was a deep, ferocious love, a different love than what he had ever felt for Marie or could ever feel for her.

This…this was just physical. This was about lust and anger and pain of rejection. He knew that.

With every ounce of strength he possessed, Jackson grasped Marie by her shoulders and pushed her back. "No, Marie." He clenched his fists as his sides, still fighting the desire that throbbed inside like a wound that would not heal.

"I don't understand." She sounded genuinely hurt and he felt his chest tighten in response.

"What don't you understand? I said I'm not interested."

"But Jackson, you kissed me tonight at the tables." Her red lips pouted. She sounded so forlorn. "You kissed me here. I thought—"

"Don't confuse the game we play with reality, Marie. You know better. Out there—" he pointed "—it was all part of the game."

"And here?" she whispered.

"I'm sorry." He took another step back. The tightness in his groin was beginning to ease. His mind was gaining control of his body once again. Marie was as lovely as a dark angel, the scent of her skin, heavenly. But he could not allow himself to falter. Not again.

"But I miss you. I need you. Don't you still desire me?" she questioned in a husky, sensuous voice.

He gestured stiffly, his words stiffer. "I'm a married man now."

She drew closer. "You were a married man that night outside of Atlanta, too."

Jackson turned away from Marie, her naked body still silhouetted lusciously in the golden moonlight. "I told you that was a mistake."

She stepped closer, ran a hand down his bare back, over his buttocks. "But it wasn't a mistake. It was the best—"

"Marie! Damn you!" He clasped both of her arms and pushed her away from him. "That was a mistake." He looked away, unable to face her...to face himself. "I was lonely. I was scared. I—"

"You could never be scared of anything, Jackson. That's why I'll always love you," she whispered.

"Well, you mustn't." He made himself look into those dark eyes that he feared might yet cast him under a spell. "You mustn't because I love another now." He wanted to tell her she had had her chance years ago, but he didn't. He didn't want to talk about their past. He just wanted her out of his cabin. "I love my wife. I love Cameron and I don't love you."

"You bastard," she stormed, taking a step toward him.

There was a soft tap on the door and Jackson's gaze flickered to the wood paneling.

"Jackson?"

"Come in," he called gruffly.

Marie made a barely audible sound of derision under her breath as she wrapped the sheet tighter around her nakedness. She didn't like Falcon any more than he liked her.

The Cherokee appeared in the doorway, cast in shadow. "I heard voices," he said. "I wanted to be certain you did not need me."

Jackson smiled in the darkness. Falcon was clever; he

would give his friend that. "Marie was just leaving. Would you walk her back to her cabin and be certain she gets inside safely?"

Falcon held the door open, giving Marie no choice but to walk out the door as graciously as possible, given the circumstances.

"One more day," Jackson called quietly after her. "And then I'm going the hell home."

At Jackson's insistence, they disembarked the riverboat in Baton Rouge two days later. Marie's contact had never appeared and Jackson was in a foul mood, feeling that she had wasted his time.

"I don't understand why you don't want to stay a day or two," Marie said from beneath the lace of her pale yellow parasol as they crossed the rotting dock where the riverboat had moored. "You always loved Baton Rouge." She slid her hand over his shoulder. "Baton Rouge always loved you, Jackson."

Ignoring her, he glanced over at Falcon. "As soon as the bags are unloaded, we'll go to the station. God only knows how long we'll have to wait to catch a train north. Tracks are still out all over the South."

Falcon nodded his dark head, his gaze darting about as a crowd of vendors elbowed between the sweating lines of black men unloading the ships to envelop the disembarking passengers. Crowds made the Cherokee uncomfortable.

A dirty woman with a huge goiter on her neck pleaded for travelers to buy her fresh milk. A young boy in a straw hat hawked a tin of sweets. Behind them, a coffee-colored dwarf with a shaven head was doing a brisk business in steamed crawfish. The humid air hung thick with the scents of rotting fish, tar and stagnant water. The stench assaulted Jackson, battering his senses as much as the cacophony of

whistle blasts, cursing, creaking cart wheels, braying mules
and the off-key serenading of a band of musicians who
obviously believed that volume could overcome a lack of
talent and sobriety.

"Sir, a few pennies for a man in thirst?" A bearded,
one-armed soldier garbed in the tattered gray rags of what
had once been a Confederate uniform thrust his face into
Jackson's, startling him.

Marie gave a squeal of disgust, drawing back for fear
the filthy man might touch her.

"Step aside," Falcon grunted, trying to put himself between Jackson and the soldier.

Jackson thrust his hand inside his coat for loose coins,
unable to keep himself from pulling back as the stench of
the man's body assaulted his nostrils. "You'd do better to
buy yourself a meal and a bar of soap than a shot of whiskey."

"Captain Logan," the soldier whispered, bringing his
face even closer. "I've got a message for you." He spoke
like an educated man.

Jackson's gaze flitted to Falcon, silently telling him to
drop back. Then he looked back at the soldier and drew
out a suede coin purse from his coat, knowing anyone could
be watching them. "Have you no pride in yourself, man?"
he chided.

"I cannot believe you are going to give him money,"
Marie protested, shaking out the hem of her yellow lawn
gown. "Beggars will never learn to find honest work if we
continue to give them handouts."

"What is it?" Jackson whispered to the soldier, taking
his time to remove the coins from the bag. "And why
should I believe a word you say?"

"For the sake of 'Puck's Hill,'" the veteran replied.

Jackson nodded, recognizing the current password, one

that even Marie didn't know. He glanced at Falcon, who moved to block her view.

"Jessop, the man you were supposed to meet..." the soldier whispered harshly. "He's dead."

"Dead?" Jackson met pale brown eyes that had suddenly filled with tears.

"They killed him."

"How do you know?"

He wiped at his eyes with the back of a dirty hand. "Because I buried him. Jessop was my son. He bought into this for a while. When he realized its madness and tried to back out, it cost him his life."

"Who killed him?"

"You know who. Thompson's men."

"So they're real?" Jackson pressed coins into the soldier's filthy hand. To anyone who saw them, it would appear that he was simply offering money and sympathy to one of the South's bravest, now left destitute.

"Of course they're real. When will you damned Yankees stop underestimating us? Thompson's Raiders are real and they're growing in numbers by the day," the soldier growled under his breath.

"To what avail?" Jackson began to walk again, as if attempting to rid himself of the beggar. "The war's over."

"This isn't about states' rights anymore. It's about hatred. Vengeance."

"Where's Thompson?"

"I don't know. My son wouldn't tell me. You need to see a man named Spider Bartlett in Birmingham, but he won't be in place until next month. He's one of Thompson's men. Or so Thompson thinks." The old soldier winked.

"Bartlett in Birmingham," Jackson repeated.

"Thank ye for the coin. It will buy a bottle of comfort.

Strong drink's all that keeps me going now. The world's not what it was…nor ever will be again.''

The soldier disappeared into the bustling crowd. Marie slipped her arm through Jackson's, her eyes slanting with pleasure. "It was him, wasn't it?" she whispered in his ear. "He was just a little late."

"No, it wasn't him."

"You're lying."

"We'll discuss it later."

"Jackson." She clutched at his arm as strain and annoyance made her voice strident.

He shook off her hand. "I said, 'later.'"

"How long?" Cameron barely whispered, her voice raspy.

Taye tipped the glass of water to her lips. "Eleven days."

Cameron squinted at the bright light that seeped from behind the closed drapes. "Eleven days? Almost two weeks." She took another sip and then lay back on the bed again, exhausted from just that little bit of exertion. "It seems like we arrived only a few minutes ago."

"You were very ill." Taye set down the glass and brought a damp cloth to her sister's forehead.

Recalling her symptoms, Cameron suddenly lowered her hand to her flat abdomen. "The baby?" she whispered.

Taye smiled, wiping her forehead and then her cheeks. "Fine. Naomi thinks it was the water. Evil spirits." She rolled her eyes indicating she wasn't sure she believed such superstition. "I don't know. We all drank the water that night at dinner. But Naomi says your soul is weaker because you're carrying the baby." She removed the cloth and dropped it into the washbowl beside the bed. "I think she's full of voodoo nonsense." She lifted her shoulder in a shrug. "But I boiled the water anyway and you did seem to get better. We're drinking only boiled water as well."

Cameron gazed around the shabby hotel room. It had been cleaned up in the time she had been ill, but the wallpaper was still faded and torn, the draperies still tattered. At least it no longer smelled of kerosene smoke and mold. "Where's Naomi?"

"Gone to the market. Since you fell ill we haven't dared eat the food here at the hotel. Naomi has been cooking for us in the fireplace." She nodded toward the glowing coals. "It makes the room hot, but at least no one else had been poisoned."

"Ngosi?"

Taye smiled. "He's fine on his mama's milk. Getting bigger by the day."

Cameron smiled and settled back on the pillow again. She wanted to ask if Taye had heard from Jackson, but that was silly, of course. He was in New Orleans. He thought she was in Baltimore, safe and sound. "I want to go home, to Elmwood, Taye."

"In a couple days. Naomi said you need to get your strength back before we travel again. She's been to the train station several times and she thinks she's figured out a way to get us to Jackson."

Cameron reached out and took Taye's hand in hers. "Thank you so much for taking care of me," she whispered.

"Don't be silly." She squeezed Cameron's hand and then got up, fussing with the wash bowl. "I didn't do anything for you that you wouldn't do for me under the same circumstances."

Cameron sat up to study her lovely sister through new eyes. She had once thought Taye weak, but she was as strong as any Campbell. Perhaps stronger because of her mother's heritage. "I hope that's true."

"Of course it is. Now hush this talk and let me get you something to eat. Naomi has made a savory lentil soup I know you'll want to try."

Cameron lay back on the pillow, thankful her father had loved a woman like Sukey enough to bring a sister like Taye into the world.

12

Jackson returned to Baltimore just after dawn. When he entered the house, all was still quiet. He didn't see a soul, except for a sleepy houseboy, as he slipped up the staircase and into a guest bedroom to bathe before he went to Cameron.

The boy brought up hot water and Jackson shaved and washed the grime of his unsuccessful trip off his body. As he dressed in clean clothes, he contemplated what he would say to Secretary Seward when he met with him tomorrow. The contact had never shown himself on the riverboat and the trip had been a waste of time. He still knew nothing more of Thompson than he had two weeks ago and he was becoming frustrated.

Jackson felt it was his duty to support and aid the president in any way he could, out of loyalty not just to him, but to his fallen predecessor.

The house was still relatively quiet, but he now heard stirrings downstairs in the direction of the kitchen as he walked toward his bedchamber. No doubt Naomi had the women buzzing around the house, preparing for the day. She had turned out to be an excellent housekeeper, perhaps because she did not see herself as a slave any longer, as many of his employees still did.

As Jackson walked down the silent hallway, he decided he'd spend the day with Cameron doing whatever she wanted to do. He'd shop, ride in the park, even go out to see those damned horses of hers, if that would make her happy. He owed her that much. Perhaps his undivided attention was what she needed...and a little gift.

He halted at his bedchamber door and drew the small black velvet bag from inside his coat. He opened the drawstring top and pulled out an emerald eardrop to admire it. He knew Cameron would love the acorn-sized earbobs, and the deep green color would complement her red hair beautifully.

He dropped the jewel back into the bag and rapped lightly on the door. "Cameron? Cam, honey, it's Jackson. I'm home."

He turned the doorknob, thinking he would surprise her by waking her up, or perhaps leaving the velvet bag on her pillow beside her.

Just before he pushed open the door, he spotted Addy coming up the back staircase carrying an armful of clean linens. "Capt'n!" she cried, looking as startled as if she had seen a ghost.

"'Morning, Addy. I just got back from my trip." He nodded toward the slightly ajar door. "Mrs. Logan isn't awake yet, I take it?"

Addy's mouth opened and closed but no words came out. Something was wrong.

Jackson flung open the bedchamber door.

The lush bedchamber, with its velvet draperies and brocaded bed curtains, was empty. Their massive carved bed was made.

Cameron was nowhere to be seen. No teacup marred the

bedside table. Not a single book or petticoat lay discarded on the floor beside the bed.

"Addy!" he shouted. He needed to think there was a perfect explanation for Cameron's absence at eight in the morning. She'd risen early to ride before the summer sun was too hot. She had an early appointment with a dress-maker.

But the tightness in the pit of his stomach told him that was not the explanation. That little bitch, he thought. "Addy, where is Mrs. Logan?" he barked, knowing the answer, but needing to hear it anyway.

"Gone," Addy squeaked, hugging the sheets in her arms.

"Gone!"

Addy cringed as if he were going to strike her and Jackson glanced away, forcing himself to calm down. His head was suddenly pounding with anger, his fists balled at his sides. But he had no right to direct his anger at anyone but the woman who deserved it.

"Where did Mrs. Logan go, Addy?"

"Mississippi, we think," she whispered. "Miss Taye and Naomi, too."

Jackson tightened his fists at his side again, but he didn't raise his voice. "How long?" His mind raced. Maybe she had just fled the house. Maybe he could catch up to her. Maybe...

"Near two weeks."

"Two weeks? And no one sent word to me?"

Addy's voice trembled. "We didn't know where ya was, Capt'n. Everybody said it was a secret."

He turned his back to her. Of course, no one could have contacted him. He had left that way purposefully to spite Cameron. "You can go, Addy," he said quietly.

Jackson heard her run down the back steps as he closed

the door behind him. Alone in his bedchamber, he ripped the velvet bag out of his coat and threw it on the floor. He brought the heel of his boot down hard on the bag and felt the gratifying crunch of the jewels beneath his foot. Clenching his jaw, he ground them into the floor. One earring shot out of the bag and he took a long stride, crushing the last gleaming green gem beneath his boot.

Jackson wasn't satisfied. He stared at his empty bed and then caught his image in Cameron's floor-length dressing mirror. He met his own volatile gray-eyed gaze. "Son of a bitch," he muttered. "Looks like I'm going to Mississippi."

"I can't tell you what to do, Thomas. I can only remind you of what the town looks like right now. What kind of people are roaming the streets these days." As Jackson spoke, he tacked up his horse. Silently, Falcon saddled a horse in the stall next to him. "You've been there, Thomas," he continued grimly. "It's not a place for decent women these days."

Thomas seemed to squirm in his muddy brown frock coat. "I simply cannot believe Taye left that message saying she and Cameron had gone to New York." His Adam's apple bobbed. "I just assumed it was true because you left for New Orleans so abruptly and—"

"And Cameron was pissed with me."

"I can't believe Taye would deceive me that way."

"Sure you can believe it." Jackson checked the girth one last time, forcing himself to take his time to treat the horse gently. "Cameron said," he mimicked, "'Jackson says I can't go to Mississippi. I'm going anyway because I'm a spoiled, selfish, little papa's girl who won't grow up.' She looks at Taye, and says, 'Do you want to go to Mississippi?' And Taye jumps on board without thinking twice.

It's the way it's always been with those damned sisters,"
he said sourly.

"But Taye understood clearly my concerns of her going
there, even after we had wed." Thomas coughed and pulled
out a handkerchief to press to his mouth. "It's so unlike
Taye to be so irresponsible."

"Not when my wife is involved," Jackson said bitterly.

"Well, I just don't know," Thomas mumbled into his
handkerchief. "I've an important appointment this afternoon. A man who is considering hiring me on retainer for
his shipping business will be locating in New Orleans. The
initial fees alone would be enough to open my offices
again."

"Look, Thomas, why don't you just stay here? Take care
of your business and let me go to Jackson and bring the
women home. I can slap Taye around for you, if you like."

Thomas glanced up, folding his handkerchief, his face
solemn. "I would never hit a woman, and I would hope
you would not, either."

"I was joking, Thomas," Jackson said dryly as he threw
his leather bag over the back of his horse and strapped it
on. "I would never strike my wife or any other woman.
You know me better than that." He shook his head. "Not
that Cameron hasn't tempted me. Isn't tempting me now."
He made a sound of frustration in his throat. "Damn it,
what she was thinking? Doesn't she realize that she's risk-
ing her own life? And Taye's?"

"We must go, friend, if we are to catch the train," Falcon interrupted from the other stall.

Jackson glanced over. Falcon was always so quiet that it
was easy to forget he was there. Jackson was glad he was,
though, glad he would be accompanying him to Mississippi. Falcon would be his voice of reason as he had been
so many times in the past.

"I'll send you a telegram as soon as we find them, Thomas. They're probably safe, camped out on the ballroom floor at Elmwood, wishing to God they had listened to us." He clamped his hand on the other man's arm. "Try not to worry. We've got two tough women there, and Naomi is with them. I'm sure they're fine."

Thomas stepped back to allow Jackson by with the horse, and he stood in the barnyard as the two mounted.

"We'll be home soon," Jackson said, tipping his hat to Thomas.

Jackson and Falcon rode out of the yard and turned north toward the railroad station. If they hurried, they would make the next train to Richmond.

Falcon glanced over his shoulder as they rode past the front of the house. "He is a good man."

"Thomas?" Jackson settled in his saddle. "He is. He was loyal to Senator Campbell, and he's been a good friend to me."

"He is a good man, but he is not the right man for Taye."

Jackson stared at Falcon, but there was no further explanation from his companion, and he knew there would not be. At least for now.

Taye clasped Cameron's hand, forcing her to tear her gaze from the train window. They had grown used to the scenery by now, but they had not grown immune to its horrors. "We should go back to Baltimore," Taye said firmly.

"I'm not going back," Cameron said, feeling hollow inside.

"I knew this was a bad idea from the beginning," Taye went on. "I was being selfish when I agreed to come. I wanted to get away, so I agreed to come here with you, not considering the harm it could do. When you got sick in Richmond, I should have insisted we return home.''

Cameron's gaze strayed to the window again as she stared at the abandoned houses they passed, the fallow fields. The farther south they had traveled, the more dispossessed black men, women and children they had seen walking along the roads and rail tracks. Without a way to earn money to feed themselves or put a roof over their heads in the drizzling rain, they were left to wander the roads and scrounge or steal what they could find to eat.

As she stared at a huddle of black women along the roadside, dressed in rags, dragging children along beside them, her heart twisted until she thought it would break. Slowly the train chugged by them and they looked up at her with hollow eyes.

There were soldiers, too. Soldiers everywhere. Those dressed in blue seemed to have fared the best. They were on the train, on horseback, or at least in buckboard wagons, slowly making their way north toward home. But the Confederate soldiers, dressed in tattered rags of gray, walked south in hole-ridden shoes with little or no food. Those men looked at her with empty eyes, eyes of surrender, of defeat.

Cameron thought she had experienced sadness before, but scenes like this, what she had seen from the train window, were heart wrenching. Jackson's words had been conservative when he said the South was devastated.

When the war came four years ago, Cameron understood intellectually why it had to be fought. Her father, though a Southern senator and planter, had been a staunch supporter of the antislavery movement. She understood that the dream to set men and women free might come to war. But never, in her wildest dreams, had she ever considered the price Americans—Northerners and Southerners—would pay for the conflict.

"Why did the South hang on for so long?" Cameron whispered, watching the group of women and children disappear from her view. "Why did they let the soldiers do this?" she murmured.

"Cameron!" Taye patted her hand to get her attention. "You have to listen to me. We don't have to go to Elmwood. We don't even have to get off this train. The conductor says it's returning to Richmond from here. We can just stay aboard and—"

"No," Cameron said, feeling as if she were waking from a dream. "I have to go. I have to see Elmwood again. Then I don't know what I'll do."

Taye sighed and glanced at Naomi, who held Ngosi on her shoulder, patting his bottom.

Naomi rolled her dark eyes heavenward. "Well, we're here," she muttered. "Pullin' into the station, or what's left of it. We might as well find us a room, at least for the night. Miss Cameron don't need to be sleepin' on this train again. Not with her being so ill such a short time 'go."

The baby continued to fuss in his mother's arms and Cameron reached out. "Let me take him, Naomi. You rest a minute."

Naomi handed the infant, swaddled in a red blanket, to her mistress and Cameron cuddled him against her. The warmth of the baby, the weight of him in her arms, was somehow comforting, and she thought of the child she carried.

Taye watched Cameron. "You're certain this is what you want? You don't think it will be worse, actually seeing Elmwood, now that you know what it will be like?"

Cameron shook her head. Ngosi was beginning to quiet. "No, I need to see my father's home."

"Then we'll get a room at a hotel. We'll have some supper and in the morning we'll hire a carriage to take us out to Elmwood. We'll see Elmwood, then we'll return to the train station.'' Taye ignored Cameron's frown and continued. ''And we'll take the next train north, no matter where it's bound.''

Cameron didn't argue with Taye. There was no need to tell her sister that she had no intention of boarding this train again. Go home to Baltimore for what? she thought stubbornly. To what? A husband who lied to her? Had abandoned her? He could rot in hell. She had her own money, her own home. She and the baby would just stay in Mississippi.

The whistle sounded and the train began to slow. It jolted and jostled Cameron; she cradled Naomi's baby tighter as he drifted off to sleep.

Cameron prayed the Jackson hotels had fared better than those in Richmond. She wanted a bath and a warm meal and she wanted to sleep the night without fearing there were cockroaches scurrying over her in the darkness.

She knew just where they would go. The Magnolia was a well-respected hotel with a fine dining room that was run by Mr. and Mrs. Pierre from Atlanta and their two adult daughters. If Cameron recalled correctly, Annie had just married before the war began. She had been a sweet girl, Cameron's own age, who had often spoken to Cameron at church on Sunday mornings.

At last the train ground to a halt and Naomi stood. Cameron handed her the sleeping baby and she watched with fascination as Naomi tucked her son into the cloth sling that held him warm and safe against her body. Cameron had never seen a white woman carry her baby that way, but it made such complete sense to her that she decided she would do the same with her own child. She cared little what others would say. Why would it matter as long as she and the infant were content?

Passengers began to disembark and Taye reached out to Cameron. "Ready to go?"

Cameron rose without her sister's assistance. "I'm fine. Yes, I'm ready. I do hope Mrs. Pierre has something tasty for supper. I'm starved."

The three women disembarked from the train into an open field where the tracks ended a quarter of a mile from the train station—a parting gift from the Union army. A lump rose in Cameron's throat at the first glimpses of home as she shouldered her own bags and picked her way through the mud with the other passengers.

A stench rose up out of the mud and Cameron fought the churning in her stomach. With every step that brought her closer to the train station in the twilight, she could not stop staring at the changes in Jackson, Mississippi's appearance since last she was here.

She had followed the progress of the war in Mississippi after her escape north in September of 1861, but grainy photographs and black print on white newspaper couldn't, she realized now, accurately describe the devastation to the capital city.

In early May of 1863, General Joseph Johnson was sent by the Confederate Secretary of War to Mississippi to defend Jackson against the two Union army corps. Under the command of Sherman and McPherson, the Union army was advancing on Mississippi. With only six thousand troops available to defend the town, Johnson evacuated it. The Confederate troops engaged in battle with the enemy and endured mortar fire until the evacuation was complete. At that time, Johnson was ordered to disengage and withdraw. The Union troops quickly moved in, cut the railroad connections with Vicksburg and burned part of the city.

The scent of charred wood filled Cameron's nostrils as a warm, light rain began to fall. She could almost see Johnson's retreating army dragging wearily out of the city in defeat, hungry and dejected, and the Union soldiers riding in victorious. She could see in her mind's eye the blue-uniformed soldiers riding up and down the beautiful streets of her hometown, setting fire to the buildings.

Cameron was so lost in her thoughts that she nearly stumbled over the carcass of some large animal she could not identify. It had to be the source of the stench in the field. Flies rose up and buzzed around her head and she stifled her gag reflex. Taye grabbed her arm and steered her around the dead, swollen corpse.

Arm in arm, they reached the train station and walked through a hole in the back wall to the main reception area. The station had fared poorly in the war, but it was still standing, and reconstruction on the exterior walls had already begun. Inside, the paint was peeling and the walls were smoke-colored and gray. As the women crossed the dirty floor to exit onto the street, Cameron tried not to think about what a pretty train station it had once been, or how much she had enjoyed embarking from here on trips to Washington, D.C., with her father. Those years were gone, relegated to memory.

The sun had disappeared beyond the horizon by the time the women stepped onto the street, and it was just as well. Cameron wasn't sure how much more they could take in one day. At least in the darkness, the truth could be left in the shadows.

"The Magnolia is a few blocks away," Cameron said, feeling a sudden surge of strength inside. It was time she took charge, time she started acting like Senator David Campbell's daughter returning home. "It will be nice to see a familiar face."

As the women walked down the street, they kept their gazes focused ahead, trying not to look at the burned buildings, the shattered windows, the evidence of mortar fire everywhere.

Even in the falling darkness, Cameron could make out the hollow frames of burned-out houses and stores, abandoned carriages, the charred remains of furniture. Garbage littered the streets and sidewalks.

The moment Cameron walked around the corner, she halted and stared up at the hotel—or what was left of it. The shutters were gone, the porch razed. Because the hotel was brick, it still stood, but appeared abandoned.

"No," Taye murmured.

Cameron exhaled in frustration. "Not The Magnolia, too," she whispered. "What did I expect?"

"We'll have to find somewhere else," Taye said. "And soon." She glanced over her shoulder warily. There were many men on the street, but few women.

A mangy dog trotted by the women, baring its teeth.

"Shoo!" Naomi hissed and waved her arms at the mongrel.

"Cam," Taye whispered, obviously afraid.

"Wait! I think I see a light." Cameron gazed up at a window on the second story. "Maybe the Pierres are still here."

"The hotel doesn't look open," Taye whispered. "We should go."

"Go where?" Cameron asked. "Don't be a goose, Taye. If we can't sleep here, we may have to sleep in the train station. Now come on."

Cameron walked onto what remained of the porch, pointing to a hole burned through the floor. "Careful." She pushed open the front door and stepped into the once elegant receiving hall, now watermarked and smoke stained. "Hello?" she called. "Mrs. Pierre? Mr. Pierre?"

Cameron listened to the silence of the once busy hotel,

trying to ignore the eerie feeling making the hair rise on her arms.

"Spirits," Naomi murmured, making a voodoo sign of protection with her hand.

"Nonsense," Cameron snapped. "Mrs. Pierre!"

The scrape of a door opening sounded hollowly from upstairs and timid footsteps followed. "Someone there?" called a feeble voice.

Someone holding a kerosene lamp appeared at the top of the carved, winding staircase.

"Mrs. Pierre? It's Cameron Campbell."

"Cameron Campbell?" The old woman came slowly down the stairs, gripping the rail. As she drew closer, Cameron's jaw dropped in shock and she had to force herself to smile. "Mrs. Pierre, it's so good to see you."

The once plump, dark-haired woman was a mere shadow of herself. Her hair was a thin shock of white standing on end, and she wore a tattered dress, too faded to tell the color, which appeared several sizes too large.

Mrs. Pierre reached out a thin, trembling hand. "Cameron Campbell." She spoke as if she were seeing a ghost from the past.

"And look, I've brought my sister Taye," Cameron said cheerfully. "And this is Naomi, a dear friend."

Mrs. Pierre's gaze flickered to Naomi and a look of disapproval crossed her lined face.

Cameron ignored her. She knew that old traditions would change slowly here in the South. "Where is Mr. Pierre? Your daughters?"

"Mr. Pierre died. Battle of Vicksburg. God rest his soul." She crossed herself. "Alison died in childbirth last year."

"I'm so sorry," Cameron whispered. Alison had only

been a year older than Cameron. "And Annie?" She was almost afraid to ask.

"Oh, Annie." Her tired mouth lifted into a smile. "She'll be home shortly. She works for one of the army captains in town. Washes, cooks. I have her little one upstairs."

"She has a child?"

"Brett. He's three. His father, Annie's Charles, was captured and sent to prison—Fort Delaware." She shook her head. "Terrible place…terrible. We never heard anything of him again." She pressed her thin lips together. "Dead, of course."

The old woman's words lay heavy on Cameron's heart. A part of her wanted to weep for what Mrs. Pierre had lost, what all Southerners had lost, but she couldn't be weak. She had a responsibility to Taye and Naomi and the baby.

"Mrs. Pierre, I was wondering if we could rent a room for a night or so. I've come back to Elmwood."

The woman lifted her head as if hearing sounds no one else could hear. She gazed into the darkness of the empty hotel. "We've been closed for business since the evacuation. What Sherman didn't steal, he burned," she said bitterly.

Cameron exhaled. It was fully dark outside now and they were all exhausted. Surely there was some room here they could use. "Mrs. Pierre, I have money. We'd be willing to take whatever you can offer in the way of a bed and meal."

"Union money, not that worthless Confederate paper?" she asked, her eyes lighting up with interest.

"Yes, real money. I'll pay you well. It's just that we've come so far—from Baltimore. And we're tired. We just need somewhere to sleep the night where we'll be safe."

"The room would be meager, nothing like The Magnolia once sported."

"Anything, just a roof over our heads."

"I've got a room on the third floor with a mattress," Mrs. Pierre said hopefully. "Maybe a sheet and a blanket."

"That would be fine. Perfect," Cameron said excitedly.

"No food, though. Nothing to make. We ate the last of the turnips for supper, Brett and I. Annie eats at the captain's place before she comes home."

Cameron sighed with relief as she herded Taye and Naomi farther into the entranceway and closed the door behind them. "I'll go out for something to eat as soon as we're settled. Thank you, Mrs. Pierre. Thank you."

Mrs. Pierre had not exaggerated when she said the room would be meager. She managed to find another lamp, and when she lit the room, Cameron almost wished she had not.

The flowered wallpaper was peeling and the once polished wooden floor was rough and splintered. Night air blew in through broken panes, and the sounds of the street below drifted in. The furniture was all gone except for the remnants of a wooden chair that someone had broken for firewood. In the corner of the room was a bare mattress on which Mrs. Pierre spread her one sheet and blanket. The room smelled of mouse droppings and mildew, but at least it was not a bench in the train station.

"I...I can get you a table," Mrs. Pierre said shakily, obviously embarrassed.

"We'll get it ourselves," Cameron answered kindly. "This will be fine. After sleeping sitting upright on the train, that mattress will feel like clouds in heaven." She walked the older woman to the door as Taye and Naomi came in and put down their bags.

"Now, you go back to your grandson, Mrs. Pierre. If we need anything, we'll call." Cameron pressed several bills into the old woman's hand.

"I never thought I'd live to say this, but you're a saint, Cameron Campbell."

"Nonsense. Good night."

After Mrs. Pierre was gone, the women scrounged the rooms up and down the hallway and found chairs, a table and a wooden crate for Ngosi to sleep in. Once they set up the room, Cameron went into one of her bags, got more money and slid her pistol into her dress pocket.

"I'll get us something to eat. I won't be long, I swear it."

Naomi sat down on the mattress and lifted the baby to her breast. "You be careful, girl."

"Of course." Cameron gave an exaggerated smile.

Taye worried her hands. "You want me to go with you? You haven't been on your feet a whole week yet."

"I'm fully recovered and strong as an ox, puss. I want you to stay here and see if you can find anything else that resembles bed linens. Some dishes, too." She walked to the door. "And fresh water. There are a couple of candles there on the table. Mrs. Pierre said that the pump still works in the kitchen downstairs. Pump some water and boil it. We'll take no chances until we know the wells are safe here."

Taye followed her out into the hall. "Are you sure it's safe to go out alone?"

"I was born and raised in Jackson, Mississippi," Cameron said proudly. "I've a right to walk these streets. Besides, I have my friend here." She patted the pistol in her pocket. "Now don't worry your pretty little head. I'll be right back."

Cameron's words sounded braver than she actually felt, and by the time she had walked half a block from The Magnolia, she was beginning to regret her decision. The street was pitch-dark except for light that glimmered in dirty windows. Starving dogs roamed the streets and an occasional wagon went by, its driver huddled on the front bench.

There had been a drinking establishment, O'Shea's, on the next corner that Cameron guessed would still be open, if anything was. No matter what happened in life—wars, death, devastation—men still needed their liquor. She had never been inside herself; her father would never have permitted it. But she guessed that if it was open, she might be able to buy some food there.

"Hey, missy."

Out of the corner of her eye she saw a shadowy figure move in the alley.

Instinctively, Cameron stepped sideways, away from the man. But she wasn't fast enough.

"You hear me talkin' to you?" the voice said as a hand shot out of the alley and caught her wrist.

Cameron opened her mouth to scream, but another hand clamped over it and she was lifted off the sidewalk and dragged into darkness.

13

Cameron bit down on the man's hand and he grunted in pain. At the same instant, she sank her elbow into his stomach with all her might. If she could just reach the pistol in her pocket...

Another grunt. A foul curse. "So that's how you like it, eh, missy? Rough?" he muttered. "All righty. I can give ya rough."

He slapped her so hard that her head spun, and she had to close her eyes to fight a wave of nausea.

Cameron could smell whiskey on his breath, sour body odor on his clothes. She struggled frantically as he dragged her deeper into the alley, but he was too strong for her.

"Going somewhere, sir?"

Cameron's eyes flew open. "Jackson?" she croaked from beneath her captor's hand.

"Release her and you live," Jackson stated stoically. Jackson must have been holding a pistol on Cameron's captor. She couldn't see in the dark, but the man stiffened and loosened his grip on her.

"Hold her another second longer and I put a bullet through your head," Jackson warned, as matter-of-factly as if ordering a brandy, but in this alley, he was judge, jury and executioner, if he so chose.

Cameron's captor must have known it because he released her so suddenly that she tumbled forward. She hit the muddy ground, hands down, but scrambled up quickly.

As she got to her feet, Jackson hurled himself through the darkness, slamming into her attacker. She heard the sickening crunch of breaking bones and cartilage as her husband punched the derelict square in the nose.

"Jackson!" she screamed.

He hit the man with such force that they both tumbled to the ground, Jackson on top of him. Again and again Jackson threw one punch after the next.

"Jackson," Cameron cried. "You're going to kill him!"

"Killing him isn't good enough," he raged, throwing a punch.

Either her words or her presence must have reached Jackson because he ceased pummeling the man. "Cameron, move," he said. "Get back."

Pushing away from the men, she stood, pressing her back to the damp wall of a building.

Jackson got up, dragging the dazed man with him. "You all right?" he asked her.

"Yes. Yes, I'm fine," she panted, brushing herself off. "Really. He just scared the wits out of me. He didn't touch me. I swear to God he didn't."

"All right." Jackson moved in the darkness, dragging the man with him, holding his pistol to the man's head. "Now, we walk slowly out of this alley and across and down the street," he ordered. "I believe there's a jail cell with your name on it. Cameron, you stay behind us," he grunted. "This man makes one move I don't like and I'm going to blow his head off."

Once on the street, Cameron fell in behind Jackson and

his prisoner, who walked with his hands high on his head. She could see his face had been beaten to a bloody pulp. Would Jackson have killed the man if she hadn't stopped him? Was this the man she had married?

As they walked down the street in silence, Cameron's heart pounded in her chest. She was nearly as afraid now of Jackson as she had been of the man who dragged her into the alley. Not that she was afraid he would hurt her; he wouldn't. Now, she simply feared his anger.

Her husband had been right, so right. This place was too dangerous for an unescorted woman. If Jackson hadn't come, Cameron didn't know what would have happened to her. Rape? Kidnapping? Worse? She felt faint at the thought of it.

He halted in front of the brightly lit jail. Through the window, she could see several blue-uniformed soldiers playing cards on an elegant cherry dining room table. The soldiers had been left in every major town in the South to protect its citizens and see that the laws of the Union were enforced. By writ of the president, Mississippi remained under martial law.

"Can you wait here one moment for me, Cameron?" Jackson asked, his anger and sarcasm thick in his voice. "Or do I need to haul you inside, too?"

"No," she breathed. "I'll wait right here." Her words sounded bold, though she was feeling anything but. She waited for her husband, hugging herself, trembling with a mixture of apprehension and the sudden chill she felt in her bones.

In less than five minutes, Jackson walked out of the jail-house. "Do you know who that was?" he demanded, grabbing her by the arm and hustling her down the street none too gently.

"N-no."

"A carpetbagger, a rapist the authorities have been trying to capture for two months. A few weeks ago he took a young girl off the next street over, raped her and then beat her half to death with a club before tossing her naked and bleeding into the street."

Cameron bit down hard on her lower lip. "I'm sorry," she whispered.

"Guess you would have been sorry if he had raped you," he said cruelly. "They say she was a pretty fifteen-year-old schoolgirl before he got his filthy hands on her. Now she's gone mad, she's blind in one eye and her face and her future are ruined. Doesn't even recognize her own father or brother. She howls and curls into a ball whenever a man comes into the room."

Tears filled Cameron's eyes. How could she have brought Taye and Naomi with her without thinking this through? "How did you know where to find me?" she gulped, fighting the tears.

"It wasn't hard to figure out where you had gone, once I arrived home to discover you had run away."

"I didn't run away," she corrected him, shoving aside his hand. "Anyway, I meant *here*. How did you find me on the street?"

"Goddamn luck, that's how I found you. My train arrived in Vicksburg a couple of hours ago, and I came by horseback to Jackson. I asked someone in the train station if they had seen you. You weren't hard to spot. You were the only white woman fool enough to be on the street after dark. I followed you to The Magnolia."

"Taye and Naomi?"

"They're fine. No thanks to you. Falcon helped them gather their belongings. It's not safe to stay at The Magnolia. For God's sake, Cameron, Mrs. Pierre doesn't even have locks on the door of that hotel. After dark, these

streets are crawling with vermin. That's why Union soldiers
are still here.''

"You said that Taye and Naomi were gathering their
things?" She dared a look up at her husband. Even on the
dark street, she could see the fury in his face, the way his
sensual mouth was pulled taut and his gray eyes were
barely slits. Her voice lifted hopefully. "Are we going to
Elmwood?"

"No, damn it, we're not going to Elmwood," he exploded. He grasped her shoulders as if to shake her. "Can't
you get it through that stubborn damned head of yours,
woman? Elmwood is in ruin. *There is no Elmwood!*"

She bit down on her lower lip, but refused to yield to
him. "The house still stands," she challenged.

He gazed down at her, and for a moment she feared his
response. But he gave none. Instead, he grabbed her arm
and started down the street again.

At The Magnolia, Cameron said goodbye to Mrs. Pierre
and thanked her for the offer of the room. Taye and Naomi
had already gone on with Falcon to a residence on the edge
of town that Jackson had apparently purchased during the
war—another secret he had kept from her. Because Union
officers had been billeted and had operated from there,
Jackson explained, the house had been spared when Sherman and McPherson marched through. It was fully furnished and even had a small staff.

Jackson gave Mrs. Pierre several more bills, in thanks
for taking his wife in. She tried not to accept them, but he
flattered her the way he had always been able to flatter
women, young or old, beautiful or plain. In the end, the
gray-haired woman slipped the money into the pocket of
her faded dress.

On the street, Jackson untied his horse. "Can you ride?"
Before she could respond, he went on.

"And don't tell me you're just fine. Taye told me that you'd been ill in Richmond." He chuckled without humor. "A touch of dysentery is probably what saved your damned life. Had you arrived here two weeks ago—" He let his sentence go unfinished, leaving her to be reminded of the man in the alley.

Cameron drew herself up, stiffening her spine. "I am fine," she said stubbornly. "And I didn't have *dysentery.* It was a little stomach ailment, and Taye ought to keep her tattling mouth shut. Of course I can ride."

He lifted her onto the horse as if she weighed nothing and then climbed up in front of her. To keep from falling, she had to wrap her arms around his waist. She tried not to allow any more of her body to touch his than necessary, but it was so uncomfortable that in half a block she gave up and hugged him tightly, resting her cheek on his warm back.

They rode in silence to the edge of town, then up a long lane to Atkins' Way. While not as palatial a dwelling as Elmwood, the manor house seemed a magical place in the midst of Mississippi's devastation. Even in the dark, Cameron could see that the spacious front lawn and the boxwood hedges were neatly trimmed, and that the L-shaped two-story frame house had recently been painted white with green shutters. She could smell the new paint on the humid night air.

Jackson rode up to the front veranda and dismounted, then lifted Cameron down. A young black boy rushed to lead the mare away.

"Heavens, I need a bath," Cameron said as she lifted her skirts and hurried up the steps in front of Jackson.

Without waiting for him, she opened the front door and a thin, ebony-skinned girl popped up off a chair just inside the door. She looked no older than twelve or thirteen and it appeared as if she had been sleeping at her post. "Good evenin', ma'am. Capt'n. We got word you was comin'."

"Good evening, Patsy. This is my wife, Mrs. Logan," Jackson said crisply. "Please escort her to the master bedchamber. Her bags were brought by Mr. Cortés and should already be in her room."

Patsy dipped a curtsy, swishing a bright new white apron. "This way, Mrs. Logan," she said, hurrying across the Italian-tiled marble entryway to the grand curving staircase. Cameron slowly turned in a circle at the foot of the stairs, taking in her new surroundings.

The house seemed tasteful and welcoming, as far from the ravages of war as the earth from the moon. The hall passageway was spacious enough for dancing, although not as large as the entry area in Jackson's Baltimore town house. Sparkling white plaster walls rose above the painted chair rail and finely crafted wainscoting. The draperies on the stair landing were a thick velvet, echoing perfectly the pale gold of the painted woodwork. Two antique straightback chairs and a Queen Anne blanket chest stood against one wall. Above it hung an English hunting print in a lovely gilt frame.

To her right, through an open doorway, Cameron could see an elegant library with a marble fireplace, round walnut gaming table and three chairs, a settee and a piano. The other doors leading off the hall were closed, but she could easily imagine them leading to the front parlor and dining room. It was a Southern house like many she had known in her childhood, a house built and furnished for gracious living, one that would have been unpretentious and unremarkable ten years before. Now, in this time and place, Atkins' Way seemed a treasure.

"I's born right here on this plantation. My mama was the housekeeper," the young girl prattled. "She done passed, God rest her soul, and now I'm to take over her duties.'' She beamed proudly.

Cameron offered a smile as she grasped the walnut railing to climb the staircase. She was suddenly worn to the bone, she realized, not just physically, but emotionally as well.

As she reached the second floor, she saw that the wall at the head of the staircase was dominated by a mirror as wide as a man was high and twice as tall. It was framed in gold gilt with tiny cherub faces carved into each of the corners.

At the sight of herself in the massive mirror, Cameron self-consciously tucked a lock of wilted hair behind her ear. She looked a fright.

"I try not to look,'' Patsy whispered as they passed the mirror and headed down the hall.

Cameron had to smile. Tonight it was good advice.

"This room gonna be yours while yer here, Mrs. Logan.'' Patsy pushed open a white-paneled door halfway down the well-lit hall. "Mrs. Atkins always called it the Garden Room, on account of all the pretty roses on the walls. She come from a place called Ing-land where her father grew the prettiest roses.'' She spoke as if repeating a magical fairy tale she had heard a hundred times before.

Cameron entered the massive bedchamber that was papered in hand-painted red roses with delicate green leaves. Filmy drapes, the same color as the leaves, hung across a panel of four French doors that opened onto the second-story veranda and enclosed the four-poster bed, as well. There were carved rosewood chairs, a Chinese writing desk, a mirrored vanity and large chiffarobe, all so lovely and delicate that Cameron wondered how they had survived a house full of soldiers.

"Miss Taye asked me to have the tub sent up.'' Patsy

pointed to the large copper bathing tub in the corner of the room. "She said ya was to call her if ya needed her. Hot water be up in just a snap. You want me to help you get undressed? You look like you beat worst than a rug."

"No. Thank you." As Cameron walked past the bed, she brushed her fingertips across the gauzy bed curtains. It was warm tonight; she had forgotten how warm Mississippi could still be after dark. "Just the bathwater and a little something to eat. Some tea and toast perhaps."

"Yes, ma'am. Comin', ma'am."

Patsy backed out of the room, closing the door behind her, and Cameron wandered to the window. She drew back the whispery curtains to stare out into the darkness. Down the road, toward the east, she could see a speckle of lights along the woods line perhaps a mile away, and she wondered what they came from. There were no structures that she could remember so far from town.

When Patsy returned with two young boys carrying pails of water, Cameron pointed out the lights. "Patsy, it's been almost four years since I've been here, but I don't recall anything lying in that direction. Where are those lights coming from?"

Patsy left the boys to fill the tub and came to the window. "That? That's J Town. That's where negras who got nowhere to go is livin'. It's a bad place, Mrs. Logan. You don't want to go there, not even in the light of day. Mostly men livin' there ain't found work. Those men lookin' for trouble." She lifted her hands, palms upward. "You free the negras, they got to go somewhere. Ain't like there's a boat headed back to A-fri-ca. I'm just thankin' Jesus that the cap'n bought up Atkins' Way after Mr. and Mrs. Atkins died, 'cause I got a place to lay my head. Not everyone I know so lucky."

Cameron let the curtain fall. The girl was right; it was a

matter that most antislavery advocates hadn't given much thought to. Once slaves were set free and released from their tasks in the fields, in the slave owners' homes and shops, where *did* they go?

"Bath's ready, missus."

"Thank you, Patsy. Now if you'll just unhook my gown, you can go. I'll call you if I need you." She turned her back to the young girl who did as she was asked and then shooed the boys with their buckets out the door.

"Towels and soap right there for you, missus," Patsy said as she disappeared, closing the door behind her.

Cameron sat on the edge of the bed and pulled off her boots and stockings. She lay back for a moment, and the bed felt so good that she was tempted to go to sleep without the bath. But she knew she desperately needed it, so she rose and stripped off her layers of dusty, dirty clothes. Leaving them in a pile on the floor, she climbed into the warm tub and sighed with relief as she slid down. She leaned back, closed her eyes and let the scented water rise right to the tip of her chin. It felt so good that she feared she might drift off to sleep right where she lay.

As she rinsed her long hair, Cameron heard the door open. "Just put the tray on the table beside the bed, Patsy. I'll call you if I need anything else tonight."

"Yes, ma'am," Jackson said sarcastically. "Anything else I can get you, Mrs. Logan?"

Cameron's eyes flew open.

Jackson entered the room carrying a serving tray of food. He pushed the door shut with his elbow and took the tray to the bed, as instructed.

"Turn your bed, perhaps, Mrs. Logan?"

Cameron lay back again and closed her eyes. "I thought you were Patsy."

"I'm definitely not Patsy." His voice was edgy. He was still angry with her. Very angry.

Well, let him be, she thought. He was the one who'd lied about Elmwood. He'd left her no choice but to come here alone.

Still, she was apprehensive. She knew he was not pleased at having to come all the way to Jackson from Baltimore when he was so busy, and she knew he held her responsible.

She listened as he moved around the room preparing for bed. He removed his coat and hat, his boots and the pistol he wore holstered at his waist. She heard him drag a chair toward the tub and he seated himself beside her. He said nothing, just sat there looking at her.

When Cameron could stand his scrutiny no longer, she opened her eyes. "What do you want, Jackson?"

"I'm waiting for the explanation you owe me."

"I don't know what you're talking about." She closed her eyes again and pretended to relax, though every nerve she possessed was on edge.

"I think you do."

Again the silence, which he knew made her crazy.

She opened her eyes. "What explanation?" She gestured angrily, slapping the water and splashing it on the floor. "I think it's pretty self-explanatory."

"I suppose you're right. You were angry, so instead of discussing the matter with me later, at a more appropriate time, like a mature adult, you took off the second I was gone. You endangered yourself, and others, including our child—"

"I did not *endanger* the baby," she countered. "And I had tried to discuss Elmwood with you for weeks." She sat up in the tub. "Since the day you came home, Jackson, you wouldn't listen to me. And what right have you to say anything about me running away?'' She flicked water at him. ''What do you think you were doing when you took off for New Orleans on your *mission?*''

He leaned over, bringing his face to hers. ''I wouldn't *agree* with you because you weren't being reasonable. You were acting like the spoiled papa's girl that you are, demanding to have your way. Well, it's time you grew up, *sugar.*''

''How can I be a spoiled papa's girl? My father's dead!'' She hit the water hard with her hand and splashed droplets of water in his face.

He reached into the tub, scooped up a handful of water and splashed her, drenching her hair and face.

''Oh!'' Cameron sputtered, wiping her eyes with her hands so she could see again. ''You see. I can't talk to you.'' She stood up in the tub, water streaming off her naked body. ''You call me spoiled and say I must always have my way, but you're no different than I am. You won't listen to anyone. You want everyone to do as you order, as if we are your little army and you are the commander in chief.'' She half saluted. ''Well, I've had enough of your orders, Captain Logan.'' She gave him a hard shove, to push him out of her way, and lost her footing in the water-filled tub.

Jackson caught her wet and slippery body in his arms and lifted her out of the bath.

''Put me down,'' she ordered, struggling against him.

He sat down on the chair, ignoring the fact that she was getting his clothes soaking wet, and reached for one of the large bath sheets folded neatly on a chair. Cameron tried to escape, but he pinned her between his muscular thighs, and she couldn't get away.

Jackson wrapped the cloth around her and began to rub vigorously while she still struggled to escape.

"Leave me alone! Do you hear me? I want you to go. Leave this room this instant!"

"You'll not put me out of my bedchamber again, my dear. Not ever."

"Well, we'll just see about that," she spat, bracing both palms against his chest, leaving water marks on his linen shirt as she tried to shove him again.

Jackson opened the large cloth sheet and wrapped it around her tightly, pinning her arms to her sides.

"Let go of me, Jackson, do you hear me?"

Ignoring her protests, he lifted her into his arms and carried her to the bed.

"Jackson, if you don't release me this moment, I swear I'll scream, and every man, woman and child in this house will be at that door."

"Close your mouth, Cameron, before I wrap something around that, too."

He dropped her suddenly onto the bed, and she gave a gasp of surprise. She was so damned angry with him that she could tear him ear to ear with her fingernails. Yet, as he leaned over, drawing his face to hers, she felt her heart skip a beat and her pulse quickened. She groaned in frustration as she tried to free herself from the tangle of damp linen.

Would it always be this way between them? The anger, the ugly words and then the passion that came upon them so suddenly that they could not control their desire?

No. This is not how it would be!

"Jackson—"

He covered her mouth with his, silencing her, taking her breath away. He was wet and warm and smelled of that inexplicable combination of tobacco, maleness and, somehow, salvation.

She freed her hand and slipped it over his wet shoulder

to his thick, corded neck. He was leaner than he had been before the war, more solid and muscular.

She didn't want to argue. She didn't even want to talk. She just wanted to feel his mouth on hers, taste his tongue, feel his hand between her legs in that place that already ached for his touch.

Cameron pulled his head to hers and parted her lips to accept his thrusting tongue. He tore at the bath towel, unrolling her so that he could send it flying off the bed to land in a wet heap on the floor.

Naked under him, she arched her back, needing to feel his weight on her, pressing her into the feather tick. He threaded his fingers through her wet hair and kissed her again and then again.

Cameron pushed at the fabric of his wet shirt, slipping her hands beneath it to feel his skin, the rippling muscles of his chest, the nubs of his nipples.

Jackson groaned and she licked his lower lip. He bit back ever so gently and lowered his mouth to the hollow of her throat. She arched her neck, feeling her nipples harden, even before he took the first in his mouth.

In response, he took her nipple and the areole full into his mouth. She rolled her head on the pillow, gasping with pleasure. Her fingers found his thick hair and she guided his mouth in encouragement.

He took the other nipple, first teasing it with tiny bites, then into his mouth. She moaned. If possible, since her pregnancy had begun, her breasts were even more sensitive than they had been before. As he suckled, he cupped the breast, massaging it, lingering until time seemed to stand still.

Cameron glided her fingertips over his back and shoulders, down his chest and under the fabric of his shirt again.

He slid his hand from her breast and moved it over her belly, that would soon grow round, and then lower.

Fiery heat built at the apex between her thighs as his hand slowly slipped down. She parted her legs and her entire body trembled, quaked, with anticipation.

His long, strong fingers found the mound of bright-red curls, the soft folds of her flesh and the tiny nub from which all sensation seemed to emanate.

"Cameron," he whispered as he stroked. "If you would just let me love you. Let me be the man to you I want to be."

She closed her eyes, clinging to him, and groaned. It would be so easy to surrender to Jackson. To give him what he wanted. What she wanted, no, needed, desperately.

But—

She sat up suddenly and shoved him back with both hands. "No," she cried panting.

Startled, he sat back on the bed, his hair falling forward over one eye. "No, what?"

"No, I won't do this." She scrambled to cover her nakedness with the sheet she pulled out from under him. "I won't let you do this to me. This is how you always get your way, Jackson. Taking…taking advantage of me," she sputtered. "And I'm not going to play your games any longer."

He stared at her hard, his gray eyes narrowing. "You're saying you still won't—"

"I won't," she cut in. "Not until you and I come to some sort of mutual agreement."

He slid off the bed and reached for his trousers. When he spoke again, his tone was harsh. Hurtful. "You know this is a man's right. A husband's right."

"Your right?" she scoffed. "And what of my rights?"

"You deny me my entitlement to sleep with you," he muttered, "and maybe I'll just—"

Cameron rose on her knees, gripping the sheet. She was still trembling all over, but now it was from anger rather than desire. "You'll what?" she demanded.

He grabbed his shirt off the floor and punched one arm through the sleeve as he walked to the door. "Then I may just seek my comfort elsewhere."

Cameron climbed out of bed, dragging the sheet behind her, but it was too late. Jackson was already out the door.

The door slammed with a resounding sound and she halted in the middle of the room. "Go ahead!" she shouted, swiping at the tears that rolled down her flushed cheeks. "Seek your comfort elsewhere! I just can't imagine who the hell would have you!"

14

In the morning, Taye slipped downstairs and glanced both ways in the entrance hall before hurrying across the Italian marble floor to the richly furnished dining room, with its wide pine plank floors polished by years of service to a honey patina and scattered with worn but exquisitely woven Turkish carpets. The floral velvet draperies that flanked the three twelve-paned windows were drawn back so that sunlight poured into the room, reflecting off the silver pitchers, tureens and serving platters that lined the Irish hunt board and causing the crystal glassware to shoot sparks of light.

If she hadn't been so hungry, if the tantalizing smell of fresh sausages and sweetened hominy had not tempted her so, Taye would have remained in her bedchamber with her tray of tea and cold biscuits.

Finding Falcon Cortés at their door last night at The Magnolia had been a shock. She'd known Jackson would come after Cameron; she'd suspected that was part of the reason Cameron had taken off the way she did. Taye even half hoped Thomas would come for her. But Falcon?

Just the thought of him brought a heat to her face as she remembered the kiss they had shared in the garden two weeks ago. Shared? They had not *shared* a kiss. He had stolen it from her!

"Good mornin' to ya, Miss Taye," Patsy said, carrying a porcelain-covered dish to the sideboard beside the heavy mahogany dining room table. "There's candles under the dishes so everything stays hot. Ya help yourself to whatever ya like. There's more in the kitchen. Cap'n Logan, he lets Cook buy enough food for Sherman's army," the young girl said, wide-eyed with pride.

"Has no one else come down?" Taye picked up a delicate china plate edged with pale pink roses. French or German origin, she mused. Fit to grace the table of royalty. The sterling silverware, each piece bearing the monogram *C,* was polished to a high shine. The service was English, obviously very old and lovingly cared for. She couldn't help wondering how the flatware had come to reside on the table of Jackson's manor house, and what family had been forced to part with a precious piece of their past.

"No, Miss Taye," Patsy replied. "Ain't no one come down yet, but I suspect they will soon. Cap'n Logan, he like his big breakfast." On her way out of the dining room, she halted in the doorway. "Whenever he come when the war was on, he always had him a big breakfast before he left."

Taye lifted the lid of a silver serving dish and helped herself to a scoop of fluffy eggs. She would eat quickly, hopefully avoiding Falcon, and then return to her room and wait for Cameron. Surely Cameron would know why he was here and when he would go. And the sooner the better, as far as she was concerned.

Taye lifted another lid to find tiny buckwheat hotcakes.

"Your face is bright when you smile," came a husky male voice from the doorway. "You should smile always."

Startled, Taye dropped the lid onto the serving dish with

a clatter. "Oh, goodness." She blinked and reached for the lid again. She refused to let him rattle her. He simply didn't have the right. "Good morning," she said in what she hoped was a neutral tone.

"Good morning to you, also. Did you sleep well in your bed?"

She turned to Falcon, who had picked up a plate and come to stand beside her. "It's none of your business how well I slept in my bed, sir, and it's rude of you to ask."

"White men and women are very strange, do you know that?" He slipped a long, thin knife with a bone handle from the belt around his waist and stabbed a fat piece of sausage.

As Taye watched in fascination, in horror, she wondered how he had not noticed that she was not a white woman, but a mulatto.

"They will talk all day and into the night of that which means nothing, and yet they cannot speak of everyday matters. They talk, talk, talk, yet they cannot speak of what is nearest their hearts. Have you noticed that about white men?"

He said it as if excluding her from the faction; so he had noticed she was different. Taye wasn't sure if that pleased or concerned her. She took a step away from Falcon and scooped up a piece of toasted bread, more to be doing something than because she wanted it. The appetite which had brought her downstairs had suddenly evaporated. "I haven't the slightest idea what you speak of," she said haughtily.

"I think that you do." He smiled as if he knew some secret about her as he lifted one of the sausages on the end of his knife and bit a piece off.

Taye flounced away, taking a chair on the far side of the dining table. As she slid into her seat, she could feel her pulse racing. She felt giddy, almost light-headed. Where were Cameron and Jackson? She prayed they would appear soon to rescue her. She didn't want to dine with this dark-haired, dark-skinned interloper. He was rude, spoke inappropriately and took liberties he had no right to take. But she wasn't just going to run upstairs, either. She wouldn't give Falcon the satisfaction of knowing he had chased her away.

She glanced up at him. His back to her, she could see the outline of his broad shoulders and narrow hips. His hair, as black as a crow's wing, was tied back with a strap of leather. He wore soft suede boots that came nearly to his knees. He looked completely out of place in the dining room in this elegant home in Jackson, Mississippi.

And yet he made her skin prickle with excitement…made her feel so aware…so alive…

"You can ride with me to Elmwood, or I'll go alone," Cameron told Jackson coldly as they descended the curved grand staircase. They'd met in the hall by accident. She didn't know where he had slept last night and she didn't care. "But I'm going and no one is going to stop me."

"Not me or Grant's army," Jackson said, equally snappish. "Fine. We ride to Elmwood, *together*. But first, I'm having something to eat. I'm starving. And I'm warning you, if you try to leave without me, I'll tie you to the damned dining room chair."

At the bottom of the staircase she passed him, head held high, and strode away. Jackson halted, grabbing the carved newel. Damn her! Did she realize how beautiful she looked this morning. Even as angry as he was with her, he could not deny that her cheeks glowed with color or—

He swallowed and groaned silently as memories of the previous night rolled over him. He could still smell the womanly scent of her body…still taste her. Jackson's mouth curved downward in a frown. God, he wanted her badly. But he wouldn't force her. He had meant what he said last night. And if she was going to deny him the physical pleasures of their marriage bed, he would seek them elsewhere. Marie would never have denied him. Never.

Cameron entered the dining room, suddenly realizing she was starved. Since her illness, her appetite had seemed to return twofold. "Good morning," she announced.

Taye was seated at the far end of the dining table. Beside her was Falcon Cortés, Jackson's friend from the war. Cameron found him a bit disconcerting. She had never met an Indian before. He did not act or speak like other men she knew and was, therefore, an unknown. Cameron preferred to know what, or who in this case, she was up against.

"Good morning," Taye said, popping up from her chair. Her voice sounded high and oddly strained.

"Morning, puss. Mr. Cortés." Cameron nodded politely, looking from his face to Taye's. Did they know each other? They couldn't possibly, and yet—

"Please," Falcon said, rising from his chair. "I am called Falcon by my friends."

Cameron nodded as she picked up a plate. "Falcon it is." She began to stack bacon on her plate. "Did you get enough to eat, Falcon? I hope the fare was to your liking."

"It was good, thank you." Falcon hesitated. "But there was no raw bear meat."

It took a moment for Cameron to realize the straight-faced man was joking. Jackson laughed first, then Cameron. The moment she laughed, Falcon smiled.

Taye plopped down in her chair as if annoyed.

Still chuckling, Cameron filled her plate and joined the others for breakfast.

It was after ten by the time Jackson at last completed his meal and announced he was ready to go to Elmwood. When Cameron stepped out the front door to join her husband, she frowned at the open carriage that had been parked at the veranda steps.

"We're not going by horseback?"

He opened the carriage door for her. "After last night, I would think you might have come to realize that maybe it's time you slowed down and began acting like a married woman who will soon be a mother."

"And I suppose married women with children take carriages."

"Usually."

Cameron crossed her arms over her chest. "I should have made a run for it when I had the chance," she said sourly.

"And I should have tied you to the dining room chair when I had the chance."

She made a face at him. "You know, my riding won't hurt the baby." She met his gaze defiantly. "Having a baby is what a woman's body was made to do. Do you know we had slaves who gave birth in the evening and returned to the fields the very next day?"

"Commendable. I'll keep that in mind. Should I want to plant tobacco, I know you'll be available."

She glowered at him as she accepted his hand to help her into the carriage. "Don't think you've won the battle here, Captain. This is merely an insignificant skirmish."

"Duly noted."

As Cameron settled on the front seat, Taye came out the door. She had changed into a simple, pale blue traveling gown that looked quite fetching on her. It matched her eyes perfectly.

Jackson helped Taye into the carriage. As she sat down, Falcon appeared from around the house on horseback. He was riding a massive black steed that looked, Cameron noted, as if it had German blood in it.

"He's beautiful," Cameron breathed, turning in her seat to get a better look at the stallion, in awe of the magnificent creature.

"I told Falcon you would appreciate him." Jackson swung into the seat and lifted the reins.

"Is he going, too?" Taye asked, indicating Falcon with a tip of her delicate chin.

Her comment was so unlike her that Cameron stared at Taye. "Why?" she asked quietly. What had she missed in the dining room this morning? Or had something happened last night? Jackson said Falcon had escorted Taye and Naomi to Atkins' Way. Had the man taken advantage of her in some way? "Is there a problem with Falcon?"

Taye looked down, adjusting the folds of her gown with exaggerated effort. "Certainly not," she answered stiffly.

"Falcon and I may be entering into a new business endeavor." Jackson urged the team of sleek horses down the dusty drive. "He may be here at Atkins' Way for a few weeks."

Business? Cameron wanted to ask Jackson. She knew very well that the only business that Indian was conducting with Jackson was spying business. Just what the two men were up to, she didn't know. To her, it appeared Falcon was currently acting as a bodyguard, riding as he was behind the carriage, twin pistols on his belt.

The four took the road to Elmwood, riding mostly in silence. Cameron saw more of what she had viewed from the train: burned houses and fields, neglected meadows, boarded-up windows and untended gardens. Only, now she was home. Now she knew who had lived in each house, who had owned each plot of land, each mill that was now silent. By the time they reached the long drive, lined with elms that would lead home, her heart was heavy.

Jackson halted the carriage on the grown-over driveway that four years before had been hardened dirt, packed down over the years by frequent visitors and daily farm vehicles. "I think we're going to have to walk in," he said, setting the brake.

"I'll ride ahead," Falcon offered. "Cut a path."

Cameron climbed out of the carriage, not wanting Jackson's assistance. Now that she was here, she wanted to run up the drive the way she and Taye and Grant had so many times as children.

But then she realized that neither her father nor Sukey would be there on the veranda to greet her with open arms, and tears gathered behind her eyelids. Her father had been her whole world, and Sukey, Sukey had become her mother after her own mother's death. In truth, a better mother than the refined, distant Suzanne had ever been.

"The trees survived," Taye observed as they walked up the lane in the path Falcon beat down for them on his horse through the waist-high grass. "From the train windows we saw so many beautiful old trees that had been cut from drives and yards, just because soldiers had been too lazy to walk into the woods for firewood."

Cameron gazed up at the tall elms that stretched high into the blue sky on either side of the driveway and offered a canopy of bright green leaves to shield them from the hot sun.

The elm-lined drive brought back a shower of memories. She remembered being a little girl of six or seven and running down the lane, pulling a kite her father had bought for her. She remembered the summer Jackson first came to Elmwood, riding up this lane and into her life. Then there had been that terrible night four years ago when she and

Taye returned home to find Grant ranting and raving—and the tragic events that had followed.

She squeezed her eyes shut against the pain of the recollection.

"At least that's something to be thankful for," Cameron mused aloud, pushing aside the memories.

They followed the bend in the drive, and the house rose up suddenly before them, as if rising from the ashes Cameron thought it had succumbed to. She halted and lifted the back of her hand to her mouth as she gave a little cry...of horror, mixed with relief.

The mansion's exterior white paint was as faded and water stained as an old discarded dress. Many of the giant glass-paned windows were shattered, eyes that could no longer see. The front porch sagged in places beneath leaning columns that had once stood straight and tall as soldiers.

The lawn was overgrown, a jungle of thistles and weeds. There were overturned wagons without wheels, fallen trees and remnants of rotten canvas where an army had erected tents on the front lawn. To the side of the house, buzzards circled, and there was the stench of something large and rotting.

But it was home. *Home.*

Taye slipped her slim hand into Cameron's, and Cameron squeezed it.

"I want to go inside," Cameron said firmly.

"I'm not even certain the structure is safe." Jackson pushed his way through the weeds toward the front porch. "Be careful in the ballroom. Someone built a campfire in the middle of the room and burned through the dance floor."

"You coming?" Cameron asked Taye.

Taye smiled bravely. "I think I'll go to my mama's grave first, if you don't need me."

Cameron considered offering to accompany Taye to Sukey's grave, but she sensed Taye would not welcome her. Sukey had died attempting to cross the Pearl River to escape with other slaves. She had been shot by slavers. But both women knew that Sukey's life had been over well before she had attempted to flee. She had never been the same mentally after the senator had died from the *fall* off his veranda the night the Southerners fired on Fort Sumter.

Cameron knew that Taye needed to go up the hill to where the slave quarters had once been, just as she, herself, needed to enter her father's office. She knew that they each had ghosts to lay to rest.

Jackson eyed Falcon, who waited on horseback, and Cameron knew he would be certain Taye was safe. "You go," Cameron whispered, patting her sister's hand.

"I'll be up in a few minutes." Taye brushed her lips across Cameron's cheek, smiled and walked away.

Jackson offered the security of his hand from the warped porch steps and Cameron accepted it for the sake of common sense. As she crossed the wide veranda, she gazed up at a nest of chirping starlings. "It's only been four years," she said. "Why does it look like it's been ten?" she murmured.

At the front door, Cameron twisted the loose knob and it opened, unlocked. She took a breath, almost afraid to step inside.

She forced one boot in front of the other. "Oh," she murmured as she entered the entry hall that towered two stories overhead. Her mouth was dry and her heart pounded against her rib cage.

The black-and-white marble tile beneath her feet was marred and chipped. The yellow-papered walls with their once majestic magnolias were water stained and peeling. Broken crates were scattered across the floor and her mother's French gold-gilded mirror was gone. The carved grand staircase was missing its hand-carved newel post that had been in the shape of a pineapple, and the steps, once polished to a sheen, were badly scarred.

But if Cameron closed her eyes, she could see the hall exactly the way it had been before the war. She remembered coming in through the front door the day that Jackson had arrived to discuss the impending war with her father. She could see herself wearing her grass-stained riding habit, and Taye, in her pretty yellow gown, begging her to change before meeting the men in her father's study.

And if she kept her eyes closed very tightly, if she held her breath, she could almost hear her father's muffled laughter from his study.

Cameron opened her eyes, fighting the lump that rose in her throat. "Looks like she's still standing to me," she said sarcastically.

"Cam—"

Ignoring him, she hurried down the hall, wanting to see the entire house, attic to cellar. But there was one place she needed to go first—her father's study. She dragged her fingertips along the wallpaper, noting the smudges of soot; someone had burned fires in the middle of the floors. Why hadn't they used the fireplaces? "The place looks *structurally* safe enough to me."

"Cam, listen to me. It's not just the house I'm concerned with. Damn it, can't you see it's not the only reason it's not safe for you to stay here?" Jackson followed her down the hall. "Wasn't last night enough? The South has changed. This is not a safe place for you, or for any woman right now."

Cameron barely heard his words as she reached her father's office door, pushed it open and halted at the creaking threshold. Floor-to-ceiling mahogany bookcases were turned over and most of her father's precious books were gone. Burned for fuel, Jackson had told her.

The senator's great Elmwood carved desk stood on end blocking the veranda door, and his chair was missing. The maps of Mississippi and the United States were gone, torn from the walls.

But the room still smelled faintly of her father and the memory of him filled her heart. "Papa," she whispered under her breath.

"Oh," she cried, suddenly crestfallen, "my grandmother's desk is gone." She walked over to the place where it had stood and stared at the empty space. The desk had not been of particularly fine construction, or of great monetary worth, but she'd always loved it because her father's mother had brought it from Scotland. After her father died, she and Taye had found proof that Taye was his daughter in the desk. They had also discovered jewels he had hidden to provide Taye with money so that she could live safely and independently.

In a way, the desk was Cameron's life, filled with compartments, some that made her very happy and some very sad. "It's gone," she whispered, lowering herself to the floor. She looked up at Jackson who stood in the doorway. "My grandma's desk is gone. Burned for firewood, I suppose." She lifted one shoulder and let it fall in dejection.

Jackson stood over her, looking uncomfortable. "You need to think about that plantation I've bought on the Chesapeake. I want you to look at the plans I have for the addition on the house. If you could just see it, I know you would love it."

She leaned back on the paneled wall and covered her face with her hands, ignoring him, feeling as if every ounce of energy had been sapped from her. As if she were walking through a nightmare. "Don't speak of that place again."

As she pressed against the dusty wood panel, it seemed to give a little. She gazed down at where she rested her hand and pushed again. "What in heaven?"

"What is it?"

She turned around, rising up on her knees. "This panel of wood in the wainscoting, I think it moved."

Jackson kneeled beside her. "I don't think—" He pushed the wood with one hand. "Damn if it didn't."

"It's a secret door or something." She pushed it a little harder. The wood squeaked and a panel not much larger than a Bible magically swung open.

She thrust her hand into the dark hole in the wall. She couldn't see anything, but beneath her fingertips, she felt a familiar object. Leather binding.

"It's a book!" she breathed. She jiggled it, trying to release it from where it was wedged inside the wall, but it stuck.

"Let me try."

Reluctantly, Cameron pulled her hand out of the wall and allowed Jackson to thrust his inside. He grimaced, then pulled a dusty, leather-bound book from the secret compartment and handed it to Cameron. She sat down on the floor and lowered the book into her lap. Brushing her hand across the dark blue leather cover, she wiped away cobwebs and dust.

Apprehensively, she opened the book, and on the very first page she recognized her father's distinctive handwriting. "Oh," she breathed, seeing the date.

"June 7, 1817. Elmwood Plantation, Jackson, Mississippi. I begin to write today because today my life has changed forever," she read aloud.

She looked up at Jackson. "I think it's a...a diary. My

father's diary from 1817. He would have been only twenty years old and just returned from William and Mary College. He hadn't even married my mother yet.'' She lowered her head to read on.

''My life has changed today because I have met a woman who makes my heart sing.''

Cameron pressed her lips together. It was difficult for her to think of her father younger than she was now, young and in love with the woman who would be his bride two years later. At that moment in time, David Campbell had his whole life before him—a marriage, children, a seat on the United States Senate floor.

She bit down on her lower lip and read on, aloud. *''Today we received a new shipment of slaves, and Papa sent me to Jackson to bring them home in a wagon. Mother's palsy is worse and she has need of additional workers in the kitchen. I accepted on two males and two females. It is impossible to say exactly how old they are, but they all appear to be between fourteen and twenty years of age. Of course, there is nothing extraordinary about the events of today. We buy slaves often. What is extraordinary is the striking young woman among them called Sukey. I think I have fallen in love with her.''*

15

Stunned by what she had read, Cameron slammed the diary shut. "Oh, heavens," she breathed. "Oh, heavens." She felt as if she were a child again and had just listened in on a very private conversation she shouldn't have. Her own father's private conversation.

"You didn't realize your father had known Sukey that long," Jackson said. It was a statement, not a question.

Cameron shook her head, understanding what had not been said. Jackson had known. How or why, she didn't comprehend, but this was not the time to ask. She wasn't even sure she wanted to know. The revelation that David Campbell had known Sukey since he was twenty years old made her realize that she hadn't been as close to her father as she had always perceived, and that suggestion was distressing.

"Papa never spoke of his relationship with Sukey." Before Jackson could ask what she knew would be his question, she met his gaze, almost feeling as if she had to defend herself to her husband. "No, of course I didn't ask. I knew she was his mistress, everyone knew. I simply assumed—"

"Sukey performed a *service?*"

She scowled, not appreciating his tone of voice, not appreciating him even being in this room with her. "You're not from the South. You can't possibly comprehend our traditions. It's the way it's done here. I'm not saying I ever agreed with the practice, but it was what was done."

"Cameron?" Taye's voice echoed in the hallway.

"In Papa's study," Cameron called out.

Taye walked through the door and gazed around the room, her face falling at the sight of their father's favorite room in such a sad state. "The desk is gone," she said softly, her attention settling on the empty space on the wall behind Cameron.

"Yes, but look what I've found." Cameron scrambled off the dirty floor and rushed to her sister, the diary cradled in her arms. "It was behind a panel in the wall. Hidden all this time. Taye, it's Papa's diary and it starts here at Elmwood when he was just twenty." She flipped through the pages, showing her sister the dates as they fluttered by. "Look, it goes on for years and years."

"Papa's diary?" Taye knitted her brow. "You're not going to read it, are you?"

"Of course I'm going to read it. Listen to this first entry." She searched for the page. "Papa talks about meeting your mother. Did you realize he was only twenty and Sukey was seventeen when she came to Elmwood?"

Taye laid her hand on her sister's, closing the leather-bound book. "You shouldn't read this, Cameron. It's not right." She met Cameron's gaze, her blue eyes troubled. "If he had meant for you to read it, he'd have given it to you."

"He didn't know he was going to die," Cameron scoffed.

"It doesn't matter." Taye walked to an overturned ladder-back chair and righted it. "It's wrong to read something so personal."

"Don't you want to know what our father's life was like? What kind of man he was?"

"I already know what kind of man he was." Taye walked out of the study, her petticoat swishing behind her. "I'm going upstairs to see my old room."

"Well, I'm going to read it." Cameron pushed the precious diary into Jackson's hand. "We'll take it back to Atkins' Way."

"Certain you're not opening Pandora's box?" he asked.

"This couldn't have been an accident," Cameron insisted. "The diary was meant for me to find. It's a gift from my father, something to fill the hollow of his absence."

"Taye apparently didn't agree with you."

"Once she's had time to think about it, she'll realize that I have to read Papa's diary. He would have wanted me to."

Jackson shook his head. "Cameron Logan, you are the most stubborn woman I've ever known. You take the bit in your teeth and charge ahead without ever considering that you just might be wrong and someone else might be right."

"Nonsense." She shook her head. "Just be careful with that. I don't want anything to happen to it until I get a chance to read it."

"Where are you going now?" He watched in perplexity as she hurried out of the room.

"Upstairs, of course." She disappeared through the doorway. "I'm not going to run off if that's what you think. I'll find you when we're ready to go."

Jackson stood in the center of the late Senator David Campbell's office and listened as Cameron's footsteps died away.

He should have anticipated her escape to Mississippi and stopped her before it got this far. He didn't know how he was going to tear her away from Elmwood now. He knew how Cameron thought. Though she saw the condition that the house, the town, the entire South was in, she still didn't fully understand. Despite her age and all she'd been through, in many ways she was still naive and incredibly spoiled. Her way of life was gone.

The question was, how was he going to convince Cameron of that? Diary still in hand, he walked to the window he recalled standing at only two weeks before Fort Sumter had been fired upon. He pushed up the cracked sash and stared out through the dirty glass at the dilapidated yard. Weeds poked through the floorboards to flower as if taking possession of the area where the Campbell family had once dined on balmy evenings.

He sighed as he digested all he saw: the rundown veranda, the weedy yard, the overturned wagon that had been abandoned by soldiers when it lost a wheel. From this vantage point, it all seemed so hopeless to Jackson. Not simply the restoration of Elmwood Plantation, but the South itself. President Johnson swore the Southern states would be rebuilt; he was already beginning to implement his Reconstruction plan, though it was not fully realized yet. He'd told Congress that it would take time, but the South would rise from the ashes. He maintained that Americans would once again be united under a single front now that the Union had been restored. But staring at this yard, knowing what it had once been, Jackson wondered. Could a country that fought a civil war and then assassinated its own president ever stand united again?

Jackson walked away as doubtful of that notion as he was of the idea that Cameron could ever return to Elmwood and live the life she had once led. Rebuilding would take a lifetime. Hell, three lifetimes. The South that his wife was looking for would never rise from the ashes again. His lips tightened in a hard line. And it was probably for the best. Some things about the old South were too rotten to ever want to replace.

Cameron sat on a stone bench in the tangle of vines and weeds that had once been Elmwood's rose garden. Her mother had imported the roses from Europe and planted them in the style of the old English rose gardens. Despite the weeds and bugs, the garden was still beautiful, just in a different way than it had been before. And if she closed her eyes and inhaled the scent of the flowers, she could picture it just the way it had been when Papa was alive.

Cameron caught sight of Jackson walking around the corner of the house and waved.

"Ready to go?" he asked. "I think Taye has had enough sun and memories for the day. She's been cleaning up her mother's grave for the last hour."

"I know. Just a minute more." She lifted her hand to shade her eyes from the sun as she looked up at him. "Do you have the diary?"

"Taye is taking it back to the carriage now. Falcon will walk with her to be sure she's safe. There's no telling what kind of ruffians could be hiding out here."

"Do you know why Taye is acting so oddly with Falcon? They don't know each other, as far as I know."

He stood stiffly in front of her. She knew he was angry about the previous night. About her coming to Mississippi, about Elmwood, but he certainly couldn't be any angrier with her than she was with him.

"I think they met at the ball," he said.

She furrowed her brow. "Something doesn't seem right. It's not like Taye to be angry with someone she's just met."

"It's possible her feathers are just ruffled," he offered carelessly. "Falcon may have flirted with her."

"May?" It was just like Jackson to provide as little in-

formation as possible, no matter what he knew. "What's that supposed to mean?"

"Only that they met in the garden the night of the ball. I wasn't there so I can't say what happened, but Falcon asked me about her later." He rubbed his forehead as if he had a headache. "Look, do we have to talk about this now?"

"Yes, we have to talk about this now," she snapped. "You told Falcon that Taye was engaged to Thomas, didn't you?" When he didn't answer immediately, she eyed him, her ire rising. "Didn't you?"

"Of course I did."

His answer seemed sincere enough, but Cameron still felt he was keeping something from her. She would speak with Taye about Falcon tonight, and if necessary, speak to Falcon herself. Taye and Thomas intended to marry. They were perfect for each other, and she didn't want a man like Falcon Cortés muddying the waters.

"Well, I'm glad you set Falcon straight," Cameron announced, trying to calm her anger.

"Oh, most assuredly."

She couldn't tell if Jackson was being sarcastic or not, but she wasn't in the mood to fight with him about this. Not today. Instead of pressing him further, she gazed out over the tangled garden, allowing the nostalgia of the day to wash over her once again. It felt good to be in her mother's garden, even if most of the roses were gone now. It felt good to feel near to those she had loved, especially her father whom she still missed so much.

"I cannot believe we found Papa's diary," she mused aloud. She wanted to say it had been worth the horrendous trip south, just to lay her hands on the book, but she bit her tongue. There was no need to provoke Jackson.

"I don't think I'll read it all at once," she said to herself as much as Jackson. "I think I'll read it passage by passage, day by day, as I rebuild Elmwood, savoring Papa's words, his thoughts, his experiences.''

Jackson turned abruptly away from her for a moment, then turned back. "Cameron, I wanted to wait and talk about this tonight in private, but—" He raised a hand but let it fall to his side.

"But what?" Her voice immediately took on a defensive tone. "What did you want to talk to me about?"

"Look, we're not staying," he said bluntly. "We are not staying in Jackson, and you are not rebuilding Elmwood. You're going home where you belong."

She sprang off the stone bench, her hands on her hips. "This is my plantation, my house," she seethed, unable to contain her anger. "Somehow I'd thought you would change your mind. I thought that once you saw me here, saw how I feel about my family home, you would understand. But I see now, with striking clarity, that you don't understand and you never will. You don't want to. You have no right to tell me where I can and cannot go, Captain Jackson Logan."

"But you're wrong there, Cameron." His voice was cold. "As my wife, you have a legal obligation to do as I say. By legal *right,* this all became mine—" he extended his arms "—when you married me."

His gray eyes darkened to a stormy black and Cameron realized, an instant too late, that she had pushed him too far.

"In fact," he continued, his voice taking on a cruel tone, "while I may not be able to *legally* force you to submit your body to me, it is within my *legal* rights to sell this worthless place if I wish."

"You bastard, you wouldn't dare!" She flung herself at him, hitting him with the full force of her body. She would have hit him with both fists, but he caught her wrists and forced them to her sides.

Cameron could feel her whole body shake from head to foot. "You wouldn't dare," she repeated, feeling his betrayal.

"I will if you continue to act like a damned fool, jeopardizing your life and the life of my child."

He caught and held her gaze, and she wondered at that moment what had ever made her think she could make this marriage work. What had ever made her think he truly loved her?

Cameron held herself stiffly, biting down on her lip until she tasted her own blood to keep from flinging names at him. "Let me go, you bastard."

"Are you going to behave yourself?"

"Let me go," she croaked.

He let her go and she turned and ran. She ran through the garden, around the front of the house and down the elm-lined drive. If he followed, she didn't hear him. Halfway down the driveway, her lungs near to bursting, she slowed to a walk. But when she spotted the carriage, she lifted her skirts and ran again.

"Cameron, what's wrong?" Taye said, rising off the rear bench seat.

"We're done here for today." Cameron grasped the side of the carriage and hauled herself up onto the seat beside Taye.

Falcon hurried to dismount and come to her aid, but by the time he reached the side of the carriage, Cameron was up and sliding onto the front seat to take the reins. "Back," she ordered, pulling evenly on the leather straps.

"What are you doing?" Falcon demanded, attempting to grab the horses' harnesses.

"Get out of my way," Cameron shouted. She yanked

the six-foot leather buggy whip from its compartment and raised it over Falcon's head.

He lifted his hands in surrender and stepped back.

She called out again and the horses followed her command. They backed in their traces out of the drive and onto the main road.

"Cameron, please," Taye cried. "You're frightening me."

"Hang on," Cameron told her.

"Where do you think you are going, crazy woman?" Falcon shouted after them. "How is Jackson to return to the house?"

"I don't care," she shouted over her shoulder as she urged the horses and carriage forward.

16

Once Cameron was a safe distance from Elmwood, she pulled back on the reins and slowed the careening carriage, calling soothingly to the horses.

"Are you all right?" Taye breathed, climbing onto the bench seat beside her.

Cameron stared straight ahead at the rutted road. "I'm fine." She took a calming breath and looked to Taye. "I've done it again," she murmured, truly feeling a sense of remorse.

"Done what?"

"Jackson was right about one thing. I shouldn't have let you come with me. It was wrong for me to subject you to the danger here in Mississippi, and it was wrong of me to snatch you away from Thomas. Now I've done something dangerous again, taking off in this carriage the way I did. It could have overturned."

"Now wait one minute, Cameron Campbell Logan. We are not children anymore and I am not the little sister tagging along who you have to feel responsible for."

"But I begged you to come. You knew it wasn't a good idea."

"I came to Mississippi of my own free will," Taye said

firmly. "Everyone seems to forget that Mississippi, that *Elmwood,* is my home, too. And what is this talk of you taking me from Thomas?" she scoffed. "It's been over two weeks and I'm not even certain he knows I'm gone yet."

"Oh, Taye, you know that's not true."

"It's not like he came barreling to rescue me the way Jackson did you, is it?"

Cameron met her sister's gaze, shocked by her sarcastic tone of voice. She wasn't quite sure what to make of this fiery young woman. "I... I'm sure Thomas wanted to come. Jackson probably told him to stay in Baltimore, that he would fetch you."

Taye gave an unladylike snort. "As if a pack of runaway horses would have kept Jackson from boarding the first train south, once he knew you were gone."

"Taye." Cameron transferred both reins in her right hand and covered her sister's hand with her left. "Have you and Thomas quarreled?"

Taye gazed straight ahead, over the heads of the horses to the countryside they were passing. "No, of course not," she sighed, some of her energy seeming to seep from her voice. "It's just that—"

"Just that what?" Cameron knitted her brows.

"I don't know. I just...don't feel the way I thought I would feel about him. About us marrying."

"Does this have anything to do with Falcon Cortés, because if it does—"

"It has nothing to do with that man," Taye interrupted. "What would possibly make you think that?" She began to concentrate on arranging the folds of her blue traveling gown, which was now covered with the dust of her mother's grave. "Mr. Cortés means nothing to me. I barely know him."

Cameron wasn't sure if she believed her, but she could

tell by the high pitch of Taye's voice that she would get nothing more from her sister on the subject right now.

"Well, I want to apologize to you," Cameron said, turning onto the main road leading back toward the town of Jackson.

"Whatever for? I told you. I'm not a child to be cared for by my master's daughter—*the grand lady of the plantation*—any longer."

This was the first time Cameron could ever recall Taye referring to her position in the Elmwood household. It suddenly occurred to Cameron that it might have bothered Taye that she had been David Campbell's daughter, too, yet, because of the color of her skin, no one had acknowledged her in the way Cameron had been acknowledged. Suddenly her heart ached for the child Taye had been. Taye had never fit in among the other slaves, but she had never been a Campbell, either.

"What I meant," Cameron said gently, "was that I was sorry I haven't been there for you these last weeks. You came to Baltimore for my sake and I was so happy to see you, happy to know that you and Thomas would wed. Then I got so caught up in my own problems." She sighed. "And I have to admit, I was a little angry with you."

"Angry with me? Whatever for?"

"It seemed as if you just came into the house and took over. The ball, shopping for my gown... I wasn't used to you being so...so capable."

Taye grinned at her sister and patted Cameron's knee. "Well, I suppose you will just have to get used to it. Your little Taye is all grown-up and maybe more like her big sister than any of us would care to admit." Her blue eyes sparkled mischievously. "Now tell me what on earth you and Jackson are quarreling about that will force him to walk all the way back to Atkins' Way or be carried like a boy on the back of Falcon's horse.''

Cameron concentrated on arranging the leather reins in her bare hands, determined to keep her emotions in check. ''This isn't going to work out.''

''What isn't going to work out?''

''Jackson and me.''

Taye gave a laugh that was without humor. ''Surely you don't still think he's cheating on you with another woman!''

''We haven't even discussed that,'' Cameron said. ''It's just not going to work.'' She couldn't look at Taye for fear she would cry. ''We want different things.''

''That's the most ridiculous thing I have ever heard. You and Jackson are the most perfectly matched couple I've ever met. He loves you passionately.''

''The only thing he *loves* is controlling me,'' Cameron argued. ''He thinks he has the legal right to tell me where I can go and what I can and cannot do. He tells me that if he is not welcome in my bed, he'll go where he is welcome. Well, I have news for him. He can have his other woman! He can have me thrown in jail for all I care! I'm staying here and he isn't to stop me.''

Taye sighed and shook her head. ''Oh, Cameron, I'll grant you one thing, you are fervent in your convictions.''

''This is my home,'' Cameron argued. ''Don't you think I have a right to come home?''

''What I think right now is that you should go back to Atkins' Way, take a long bath, drink a tall glass of lemonade, eat a little something and then rest. A woman carrying a baby tires more easily than she realizes.''

''I'm not tired,'' Cameron argued. ''And I don't want to rest. I have a million plans to make. I have to locate men willing to work for me so that I can begin to rebuild Elmwood. I want you come to my room so I can tell you my plans. See what you think."

Taye looked away, her gaze lingering on the overgrown countryside. Through the trees, she could see the Pearl River as it wound its way through a grove of willow trees. "Jackson will return soon enough," she said, as much to herself as Cameron. "And when he does, I have no intentions of being near."

Cameron fully intended to begin drawing up plans for the rebuilding of Elmwood immediately, but by the time she reached Atkins' Way, she wasn't feeling well. Maybe Taye was right: maybe she did need to lie down and rest for a few minutes.

"What's wrong?" Taye asked as the two sisters climbed the grand staircase side by side.

"I don't know. Suddenly I feel…weak. A little dizzy. It must have been the sun."

"I told you that you needed to lie down," Taye chastised in her mother hen tone as she slipped her arm around Cameron's waist. "Now let me tuck you into bed and have Patsy bring up a little something for you to eat."

At the top of the stairs, Cameron caught her own reflection in the massive gilded mirror and couldn't help noticing how pale she appeared.

Taye continued to fuss, leaving Cameron in the doorway of the master bedchamber so that she could prepare the bed for her sister.

Cameron slid her hand low over her abdomen. A lump rose in her throat as she realized that part of her discomfort was coming from cramps similar to those she sometimes experienced with her monthlies. Biting back a cry of fear, she looked to Taye, who was busying herself pulling back the bedcovers and fluffing the goose-down pillows. After the baby had survived her illness in Richmond, she had thought that surely—

"Get Naomi," Cameron cried.

Taye glanced up, a pillow she was fluffing cradled in her arms. "What?"

Cameron pressed her hand to the doorjamb, lowered her head and closed her eyes as she stroked her abdomen. She had never been so terrified in her life. Not when the slavers had chased her. Not when her brother had held a pistol aimed at her head. "Get Naomi, Taye. Please hurry."

"What do you mean I can't go in?" Jackson demanded. He reached out and grasped Taye's arm none too gently. "Taye, you know I care for you, but you will not come between my wife and me. Not this time. Because this time, she's gone too far."

"Jackson, listen to me." Taye didn't struggle.

When she met his gaze, he realized her blue eyes were filled with tears. "What is it?" he asked, releasing her arm. "What's wrong, Taye?"

"You can't go in right now because Naomi is examining her."

"What are you talking about?" Jackson growled. He tried to reach around her to the doorknob, but she blocked his way. For such a slight, gentle woman, she could be tenacious. "Naomi is examining Cameron? Examining her for what?"

The moment the words were out of his mouth, he wanted to drag them back and swallow them. As the realization of what was happening behind the closed door seeped into his mind, his heart, he wished he could take it all back.

Jackson's arms fell to his sides. "Not the baby."

Taye nodded slowly, tears splashing down her pretty

cheeks. "I'm sorry, Jackson. Naomi says this happens sometimes, more often than we realize."

Jackson turned away from the door, numb. "I shouldn't have argued with her. I shouldn't have said the things I said. Not last night. Not today." He put one foot in front of the next, going down the hallway as if sleepwalking. "I shouldn't have upset her the way I did. I made her run. Made her take off in the carriage."

"No. No, this isn't your fault, Jackson. You mustn't think that." She followed him down the hall, taking his cold hand in her warm one. "Jackson, this is no one's fault. Just God's will."

"God's will? God's will!" Jackson pulled away from Taye and drew back his arm. He threw his fist as hard as he could into the gilded mirror at the top of the landing and stood in the rain of shattering glass.

Cameron lay curled up on her side, her knees drawn to her chest. Silent tears slipped down her face and dampened the pillow beneath her head.

Naomi sat on the edge of the bed and rested her hand on Cameron's hip. Even through the bed linens, she could feel the heat of Naomi's gentle hand.

"Feelin' better?"

Cameron nodded, not trusting herself to speak. Her miscarriage had been swift, almost anticlimactic. And now, after two cups of Naomi's strange-tasting tea, the cramping was already beginning to ease.

"It's your body's way of sayin' this jest ain't the right time. Nuthin' more. There'll be other babies, Miss Cameron, I can promise you that."

Cameron didn't answer, but the mere thought of another pregnancy made her want to cry all over again. She had wanted this baby, loved this baby so much. How could Naomi talk of another?

"Now ole Naomi understand ya don't feel much like talkin' right now, so ya jest let me do the talkin'. Now, some women start thinkin' right off they did something wrong, that they brought this on. But ya got to understand the laws of nature, sweetness. This was jest a soul not meant to be. From the look of yer bleedin', this happened days ago, probably weeks. Maybe even before ya got sick in Richmond. This is jest yer body's way of cleanin' things out, preparin' a new nest."

"Maybe if I hadn't taken off in the carriage that way..." Cameron said in a very small voice.

"Stuff and nonsense, Miss Cameron. You grew up on a plantation. You know how tough women is, how strong." She continued to rub Cameron's hip rhythmically. "And don't be givin' me nothin' about slave women bein' different. Noah been readin' that Bible of his to me at night and he say God created us all to be like Himself. Way I see it, God made all women strong, stronger than men in ways that count." She reached up and brushed Cameron's hair off her face. "Wasn't no little buggy ride gonna loosen that baby less there was somethin' wrong with it in the first place. It's your God's way of givin' us them perfect little babies like Ngosi."

Cameron glanced up at Naomi through teary eyes, wanting desperately to believe her. "Do you truly think that's so, Naomi?"

"'Course I do. Every woman goes through this sooner or later, black, white, green."

Cameron didn't know how, but she smiled. "Thank you for being here, Naomi. For taking care of me. I don't know what I would have done without you."

Naomi smiled down at her. "Didn't I tell ya my bones sent me? That I knew ya needed me."

Cameron drew back her mouth in fear. "You knew this was going to happen?"

"'Course not, Miss Cameron." She began to stroke her hair again. "But even if I did, wouldn't be nuthin' you or me could do about it." She sat back on the edge of the bed. "Now why don't you just hush and rest? You want I should send the captain in?"

"No. No, don't do that." Cameron half sat up in bed. Naomi had helped her dress in a fresh nightgown and tied back her hair. "I'm not ready to see him. Not yet."

Naomi patted her shoulder. "Now don't be gettin' yourself in a twist, Miss Cameron. This ain't the place for a man tonight anyway. Men got no business in women's 'fairs."

Cameron rested her head on the pillow again, feeling incredibly sleepy, and wondered if it was the events of the day or something in Naomi's tea that caused it. "Naomi?" she said, letting her eyes drift shut.

Naomi had begun to clean up the room. "Yes, sweetness?"

"Please don't call me Miss Cameron anymore."

"You want me to call you Mrs. Logan?" Naomi's voice rose in pitch.

"No," Cameron whispered. "I want you to call me Cameron. I was wrong not to have asked you to years ago." She opened her eyes and smiled sleepily. "You and I have been through a lot together, haven't we?"

Naomi smiled. "That we have. That we have."

And then Cameron closed her eyes and drifted into a dreamless sleep.

Taye slipped down the rear servant's hall toward the kitchen, carrying a kerosene lamp to light her way. It was late, after midnight, and she had just left Cameron's bedside. Cameron hadn't wakened in hours and Naomi said it would be morning before she did.

Taye was worn out emotionally and physically, but she was hungry, too, and if she didn't get to something to eat, her grumbling stomach would keep her awake all night. Maybe just a bite of pie, a cup of cool milk, and she'd be satisfied and ready for bed.

She pushed open the kitchen door and was surprised to see the glow of light coming from inside. One of the servants must still be up. But Taye didn't need someone to make her a meal; she could do it herself. She set down her lamp on the preparation table in the middle of the room and reached for the pie safe door.

"It is late and yet you are still awake."

Taye spun around. Falcon seemed to be everywhere she turned. Was he following her? Of course, that was a silly notion. He had been in the kitchen first.

"Good evening." She turned back to the pie safe and opened the door, the sweet smell of apples, cinnamon and cloves filling her nostrils.

"How is Mrs. Logan?"

Taye pressed her lips together, uncomfortable even responding. Women didn't usually discuss such personal matters as miscarriages with men. "She...she is sleeping. Naomi says she will be fine." She grasped a pie pan and slid it out, taking it to the table. Against her will she lifted her lashes to gaze at Falcon. His words had struck a chord in her. "It's kind of you to ask," she whispered.

"I know this is hard for Mrs. Logan. Even the loss of the possibility of a new soul breaks our hearts. Brings tears to our eyes and those who have gone before us."

Taye studied his obsidian eyes. She wasn't used to men speaking of tears...or feelings, either. "Our logic tells us this happens for a good reason and yet—'' She left her sentence unfinished.

''And yet,'' he continued for her, coming around to her side of the table, ''we cannot help but wonder what could have been. Who could have been.''

Taye nodded slowly, the pie held tightly in her arms.

Without breaking eye contact, Falcon took the pie pan from her and set it on the worktable. ''You are a good sister. A good friend. I hope she knows that.''

She couldn't look away from him. She was mesmerized by him, by his voice, the rich woodsy scent of his skin.

''Mrs. Logan must be proud to call you her friend,'' he continued. ''I know that I would be.''

Taye's lower lip trembled. Suddenly she feared she was going to burst into tears. Her heart ached, not just for Cameron and Jackson but for that little soul that would never be.

''Shh,'' Falcon soothed. He reached out to take her into his arms and she was powerless to resist. She knew it was wrong to let him touch her with such familiarity; she belonged to another. And yet she could find no resistance in herself. His black eyes were pools of hypnotizing water that drew her deeper, closer, with every passing moment.

Taye didn't realize Falcon was going kiss her until it was too late. His mouth brushed hers ever so gently, like the wings of a mysterious, dark moth, and still she was powerless to pull away.

Taye's lips parted of their own accord. Her pulse quickened and her eyelids fell. The heat of him, the scent of him, the feel of his mouth on hers... She tasted him, drank him in.

Taye slid her arms up over Falcon's broad shoulders. She heard herself sigh...no, *moan* as his kiss deepened.

Thomas's kiss had never made her moan.

Falcon molded his body to hers, pressing his groin to her hips, and even through the layers of fabric of her gown, she could feel his maleness.

She should have been shocked, horrified. Instead, her heart skipped irregularly and a heat began to fan from her most intimate part. More than a heat, it was an ache.

Taye felt herself sway in Falcon's arms. Before she was ready, he drew back. His gaze met hers again and for a moment she feared she would beg him for another kiss.

But the spell was broken. She gave a little strangled cry of mortification and turned and ran to the safety of her bedchamber.

17

Jackson hesitated outside the bedchamber door. It was past noon and he had not seen Cameron since the previous day at Elmwood. Last night Naomi and Taye had kept him out, and then this morning he had told himself that she needed time alone. He convinced himself that this bedchamber wasn't the place for a man, and that she needed her rest. But he knew he had to face her.

Jackson had spent a sleepless night downstairs in Charlie Atkins's library, sharing a bottle of scotch and war stories with Falcon. He had drunk more than his fair share of the liquor, and he had the blinding headache to prove it.

Falcon had tried to talk to him about Cameron's miscarriage. He had spoken some nonsense about God's will and the human desire to control it, but Jackson had silenced him and changed the topic to the new Smith & Wesson rifles being manufactured.

Jackson lifted his hand to grasp the white glass door-knob, then let it fall to his side again. He needed to collect his thoughts before he saw Cameron. He needed to prepare himself. What did he say to her? Simply apologizing for arguing with her, threatening her, saying he would seek solace in another woman's arms, making her so ill that she had lost the baby, seemed almost sacrilegious. How could she ever accept an apology from him?

Sometime toward dawn, Jackson had realized he couldn't possibly force Cameron to return to Baltimore now. Not after what had happened...after what he had done. He was still concerned for Cameron's safety in Jackson, but he would simply have to keep her safe. He'd do what he could personally to protect her, and he would look into what the local law enforcement was doing to make the streets safer for everyone.

He would have to go to Birmingham in a few days and follow that lead, but once he had tracked down Thompson's Raiders, his government work would end. He would go to Washington, and he would tell Secretary Seward that he had given enough years of his life for his country; it was someone else's turn. As for Marie... Her image floated through his head, but instead of the feelings of desire he had fought only days ago on the riverboat, he felt nothing. Nothing but regret.

When he went to Washington, he would tell her he would not work with her and he would not see her again, thus removing further temptation. Considering what had happened to his wife, it was the least he could do.

Jackson once again lifted his gaze to the paneled bed-chamber door before him. He dreaded going inside. He hated the prospect of looking into Cameron's amber eyes, knowing he was responsible for the loss of their baby. But he had to get it over with. He'd stay five minutes, tell her about the architect he had contacted this morning who would be out to speak with her about the renovations to Elmwood just as soon as she was receiving.

Jackson rested his hand on the cool doorknob. Before he pulled away again, he rapped on the paneled wood with one hand and turned the knob with the other.

"Yes?"

It was Cameron's voice, husky and surprisingly strong, considering her ordeal.

Naomi swore to Jackson that his wife was fine. She said that Cameron would be up and out of bed within the week, but he needed to see so for himself. He needed to see that she had not died in a pool of blood in her bed, as his own mother had.

Jackson was by no means a coward, but his gut twisted as he walked through the door.

"Jackson," Cameron murmured.

Her voice cut him deeply.

"Good afternoon," he said formally.

She was lying back in the bed on a pile of pillows, dressed in a filmy, pale blue sleeping gown. Her long, copper hair was parted and pulled back in two thick, silky plaits. She looked seventeen again and as sweet and innocent as the day they had first met.

"How are you feeling?" he asked awkwardly.

She closed her father's diary and placed it on the rosewood table beside the bed. "Well. Thank you." She sounded equally ill at ease.

Jackson walked to the bedside, but not too close, his hands stuffed into the pockets of his pressed trousers. "So...you're feeling better?" He wanted to meet her gaze, but he couldn't. He just couldn't bear the thought of seeing the accusation he knew would be in those amber eyes.

"I really am. Naomi says I should rest a few days, but I'm not sure how long I can stand to lay abed."

He nodded and then a silence stretched between them, a tense stillness that resulted from words exchanged that could not be taken back no matter how badly either party wanted to. She was his wife, but right now she seemed a stranger to him. The intimacy they had once shared was gone, perhaps forever.

And it was his fault. He had done this to her. To them. How could she ever forgive him? he wondered desperately. And why would she? If she felt half the empty void that loomed in his gut, how could they ever mend the damage he'd done?

"I see you're reading David's diary." He pointed lamely.

She nodded, brushing her fingertips over the smooth leather. "I promised myself just an entry a day, but I can't help myself. Papa was very poetic in his youth." She smiled at a memory. "I had never thought of him that way before. Listen to this."

He watched as she lifted the book, opened the cover and turned a page. He was so mesmerized that he barely heard the words Cameron read to him. She appeared so angelic lying in bed in her sleeping gown. Years seemed to have fallen away from her face, a face he could have fallen in love with all over again.

How could he ever have thought that Marie could hold a candle to Cameron? he mused, a tightness spreading in his chest.

"It is as if my eyes have opened for the very first time. The scales have fallen away," Cameron read slowly. *"She is the most beautiful woman I have ever seen, with skin the color of rich cocoa and eyes of polished alabaster."* She lifted her gaze to look over the top of the book at him. "So far, he's barely spoken a word to Sukey. David Campbell shy. Can you imagine?"

She gave a little laugh that, instead of pleasing him, made his heart ache. Cameron had the most beautiful laugh, so full of life and all its possibilities. A laugh she could have shared with their child if he had not been such an idiot.

Jackson stared at the floor.

Cameron closed the diary and hugged it to her chest. "Don't you want to sit down?" she asked hesitantly. "A chair?" She brushed her hand across the coverlet. "Here on the bed?"

He shook his head. "No. No, thank you. You should rest."

"I'm already bored with resting."

"I just wanted to tell you that we'll be staying here in Jackson." He did not look at her for her reaction. "I own several businesses in town—bought during the war—that could use my attention. Also, some property between here and Vicksburg." He didn't tell her that from here it would be easier for him to track down Thompson's Raiders, especially if they were in the Birmingham area. There was no need to worry her, especially when this would be his last assignment for the State Department.

"What of your ships in Baltimore?" Cameron asked. "I thought you needed to be there."

"Josiah is quite capable, probably more capable than I am. I'll have to go to Alabama, then return to Baltimore to make the arrangements sometime in the next week, but then I'll be back." Damn! He sounded so formal. He might have been speaking to a casual acquaintance rather than the woman he loved...the woman who had once loved him.

He dared to glance at her. She was nodding, but she didn't lift her head to meet his gaze.

"I also wanted to tell you—" He cleared his throat, staring at the white bed coverlet. "A Mr. Jasper is willing to meet with you as soon as you're up to it. He's an architect who can help you make plans for rebuilding what was lost at Elmwood. Not only can he draw plans, but I understand he is an expert in structural integrity. If any of the walls or the roof need additional stability, he can tell you.''

"Thank you," she said softly.

His gaze strayed to the open window. The drapes had been drawn back to let in the bright sunshine, the panes lifted so that the warm, humid breeze drifted through the chamber. He wondered how it could be so bright and cheery in the room and he could feel so cold and disheartened.

Jackson stuffed his hands into his pockets again. "I should go. Rest, and I'll speak with you this evening."

A lump rose in Cameron's throat as she watched Jackson retreat from their bedchamber. She had waited most of the day for him to arrive, had even considered sending Patsy to fetch him. And at last when he had come to her, he had acted like a polite, detached stranger. He hadn't even mentioned the baby.

She hugged her father's diary to her chest and bit back a sob as he closed the door behind him, leaving her alone. She didn't know if she wanted to lay her head down and cry or chase him down the hall barefoot, in her bedclothes, and hit him with something.

She knew he blamed her for the miscarriage. Why else would he not meet her gaze?

"I'm sorry, Jackson," she whispered as tears slipped down her cheeks. "I'm so sorry."

"Jackson, I need to speak with you," Taye said, approaching him near the barn. He stood at a white-painted fence, leaning over it, his forearms resting on the top rail. He had shed his coat and cravat and opened his shirt, looking more like the stable hand in the center ring than the famous war hero he was.

He turned to her. The sun was just beginning to set over

the horizon, casting a shadowed light over his worried face. Taye knew how upset he was over the loss of the baby. She just hoped he and Cameron would be able to get through this and allow the unfortunate event to strengthen their marriage rather than weaken it.

"I need to return to Baltimore. Right away," Taye told him, gazing into his eyes with utter determination. "I need to...see Thomas."

"Is something wrong?" He came off the fence.

"No, of course not." She pressed her lips together and clasped her hands. "It's just that I left without being truthful about where I was going and I need to make amends." It wasn't really a lie. She did need to make amends with Thomas. There was no need for Jackson to know that she also needed to go to remind herself of who she was—and to get away from Falcon. "And that was wrong of me," she continued. "I want to tell him how sorry I am."

And she was sorry. Just as sorry as she was for kissing Falcon the way she had last night. Inside, Taye trembled. She was so confused. For the last four years all she had thought about was being with Thomas. Seeing him again. Marrying him. And now that they had been reunited, nothing seemed like she had thought it would be. Things were not as they had been four years ago when they had stood in the moonlight on the deck of Jackson's boat and held hands. The feelings just weren't the same.

Taye's first thought was that it must be Thomas. Thomas was different than she remembered him. That was it. That was what was wrong. But if she was honest with herself, she had to admit he had not changed. He was still the same quiet, studious gentleman that he had been. It was *she* who had changed.

So this was all her fault, and it was up to her to right it. If she could just be with Thomas again, she knew she could fix things. The kiss last night with Falcon...it had been impulsive. It meant nothing. Taye had been tired and drained emotionally. She had been vulnerable, and that man had taken advantage of her.

"You needn't go to Baltimore, Taye," Jackson said.

"No, you don't understand." She twisted her hands. If she had to, she would go without Jackson's approval. "I—"

"He's coming here. Possibly already on his way."

"Coming here? Coming for me?"

"Well, to see you, of course. And you knew he was considering reopening his father's offices here in town. We— Cameron and I will be staying a while and I assumed you would want to stay with her. I sent a telegram to Thomas this morning suggesting he join us and begin work on the offices. From what I hear in town, people are desperate for good legal advice right now. This place could use a good lawyer like Thomas."

"So he's coming here," she said softly.

"I'm sorry, Taye, about the big engagement ball we promised you back in Baltimore, but given the circumstances, I think we need to remain here in Jackson. Cameron needs time to heal and I think Elmwood would be the best balm. I hope you'll understand."

"No, no," Taye said with relief. "It's quite all right." Truthfully, the thought of a great public announcement of her and Thomas's engagement frightened her.

Taye reached out to brush a leaf from Jackson's shoulder. Thoughts of herself faded as she studied his handsome face etched with lines of sadness. "It's good of you to change your mind about staying. I understand your position, but being here might very well be what Cameron needs to recover."

"Whatever makes her happy," he said walking away. "Anything."

* * *

Cameron remained in bed for four days and on the fifth, rose at her usual time, had tea in her room and dressed, with Patsy's help. Cameron had not slept well the previous night. She had spent hours staring at the painted tin ceiling, replaying, in her mind, every argument with Jackson since his return home.

He had asked her to slow down. He had wanted her to stop acting like the young restless woman she had once been and more like the married matron she was supposed to be. Cameron didn't blame herself for the miscarriage—what Naomi said made sense—but Cameron knew that Jackson wouldn't understand. She knew he blamed her. Why else would he have taken so long to come to her after she lost the baby? Why else had he not met her gaze a single time when he had finally come to their bedchamber? Why else had he not only not touched her, but never even mentioned the baby?

Cameron gazed at herself in the mirror and pinched her cheeks for color. She didn't know what to do about Jackson. Should she confront him? Shout at him that the miscarriage wasn't her fault and that no one was to blame? Should she tell him there would be other babies? Or did she just let him be for a while?

Since Jackson's return from the war, she had dealt with her husband by aggressively confronting him with her concerns. It hadn't worked. Look what had happened when she asked him about those rumors of another woman. It had only put them at odds and driven a wedge between them. Maybe if she backed off, he would come around. Maybe if she gave him some time to think, he would realize that she'd wanted this baby as much as he had. That this wasn't her fault.

In the meantime, she would concentrate on Elmwood.

Just the thought of restoring her ancestral home made the ache of losing the baby a little easier to bear. As she crossed the room to go, she fought against the fear that Jackson would not come around as she hoped. That he would truly seek solace in another woman. In *that* other woman. She was afraid that what she had said to Taye, about their marriage not working out, might be true. But Cameron simply wouldn't think about that possibility right now. She had her father's diary to comfort her. She had an architect to meet with this afternoon at Elmwood to keep her occupied. Somehow she would get through the day.

"Jackson has set up an account in several of the shops in town." Taye spoke to Naomi as she climbed out of the carriage with the aid of a hired man from Atkins' Way whom Jackson had sent to escort them into town. "He says he wants to support as many businesses as possible, so feel free to buy whatever the household needs. Any large items, you can have delivered."

Naomi, dressed brightly in a yellow-and-gold skirt and a blue bodice, her hair tied in a multicolored turban, nodded. Once Jackson made the decision that he and Cameron would remain in Mississippi, Naomi had taken over as housekeeper and was already directing the servants and whipping the home into shape. "You want I should meet you at the train station?" Naomi asked.

Taye opened her blue parasol that would protect her from the beating sun. The pale blue fringe on it matched the fringe on her day gown and her cap. Cameron had called the little French cap *beguiling* on her. Taye hoped Thomas would think so. "Yes. Jackson said that Thomas's train is due at three. Noah and several servants from the Baltimore house have accompanied him."

Naomi grinned, baring perfect white teeth. "Can't wait

to see my man," she said huskily. "Ya don't realize how much ya miss a man until you're parted from him."

Taye smiled. She was anxious to see Thomas, too, but she feared her feelings didn't match Naomi's. Taye wanted to see Thomas so that they could begin their relationship anew. She wanted to concentrate on their plans for the future. She would have preferred to have returned to Baltimore to distance herself from Falcon and whatever foolish attraction she had for him, but if Thomas had decided to return to his father's law office, Taye certainly couldn't protest. He had made it clear from the beginning that returning to Mississippi was a possibility.

"I'll see you at three then," Taye said, lifting her pale yellow petticoats to step over a mud puddle.

Naomi grabbed a soft-sided basket from the carriage floor, which she would use to hold her purchases. "Where you goin', Taye?"

"I thought I would look at fabrics at Madeline's old place, if she's open. Most of the draperies at Elmwood will have to be replaced, and I promised Cameron I would see what I could find. I thought I'd ask around about some seamstresses, as well."

Naomi waggled a finger at their escort, an ebony-skinned young man of fifteen or sixteen with large dark eyes and a metal ring in one ear. "You keep an eye on Miss Taye, Moses, you hear me? You carry any bags she got and you keep the filth off-en her." She shook her head in disgust. "Got bad people roamin' the streets these days. Hardly safe for decent folk, white or black."

"Yes, Miss Naomi," Moses said, obviously eager to please. Employment for a young, recently freed slave didn't come easily, and Moses seemed to recognize what an opportunity he had, working for the Logan family. "I won't let nothin' happen to Miss Taye, I swear it on my mama's grave.''

"Don't be swearin' on your mama's grave." Naomi slapped his face lightly with her palm and then fingered the gris-gris bag she always wore around her neck. "You let your mama rest in peace. Ya got to live up to yer own responsibilities, boy."

"Yes, ma'am." He nodded rhythmically. "I'll do my best, ma'am."

"And don't be callin' me ma'am, either. Ya call me Naomi." She started down the wooden sidewalk. "And you need somethin', you come to me."

"Yes, ma— Naomi. Anything you say."

Parting from Naomi at the carriage, Taye picked her way down the sidewalk, trying to avoid the rubbish that still blocked the street in places. As she walked, she couldn't help but notice the stares she was attracting. White and black faces alike gawked at her, and for an instant she wondered if her gown had come unbuttoned or something equally embarrassing was taking place.

Then it occurred to her, in sudden shock, why they were staring. Before the war, everyone had known Senator David Campbell, known that Taye was his housekeeper's mulatto daughter, to be treated with the same respect due his daughter. But the people on the street were strangers.

These people—shopkeepers in their doorways, freed slaves wandering the street—were all wondering why a young dark-skinned woman like herself was dressed so grandly. They were wondering just how she had reached such a position so quickly. They were immediately distrustful of her.

It had never been like this in the North, but as she walked down the street she began to remember what it had been like to live here in Jackson. No one had dared speak ill of her for fear of the senator's wrath, but she had never been considered a lady of Mississippi society, as Cameron had been. She had never been anything but the senator's little mulatto curiosity.

Taye spotted Madeline's and sighed with relief at the sight of the signpost announcing that the shop was open. Taye slipped inside, a bell ringing overhead, and was pleased to spot Mrs. Madeline Portray at once.

"Mrs. Portray," Taye called, waving a gloved hand.

For a moment, the middle-aged woman stared at Taye without recognition.

"It's Taye," Taye announced. "Taye Campbell from Elmwood."

The older woman's eyes lit up. "Oh, my, so it is. So it is." She rushed over in a bustle of crisp petticoats. "It is so good to see you, my dear. We had heard at the very beginning of the war from, oh, I don't know whom—" she fluttered a thick, short-fingered hand "—that the senator had laid claim to you on his deathbed."

It wasn't exactly how it had happened. The senator's death had been...sudden. It hadn't been until months later that Taye and Cameron discovered that she was also David's daughter. But Taye saw no need to explain it all to the shopkeeper. What mattered was that she be recognized for who she was, a Campbell, just like Cameron.

"Is Miss Cameron here, as well?" Mrs. Portray questioned.

"She is. We've come back to Elmwood, at least for the time being. Cameron hopes to restore her."

"We heard she married that dashing Captain Logan." Her bushy brows furrowed as her plump, rosy cheeks expanded. "My goodness, he wasn't killed in the war, was he? I lost three sons you know, and Mr. Portray lost his left leg to gangrene."

"I'm so sorry to hear that, Mrs. Portray. No, the captain was not killed in the war. He's here in Jackson. He's purchased the old Atkins place. That's where we're staying, at least for the present."

"Well, I'm certainly glad to hear that some of the county's finest families are beginning to return." Mrs. Portray's gaze wandered as she spoke and Taye glanced over her shoulder to see what she was looking at.

There was a young black woman with her back to the two of them, touching something on a counter.

The shopkeeper's brows shot up. "Ever since I hung my shutter again, I have had a terrible time with these coloreds stealing from me," she whispered harshly beneath her breath. "They'll rob me out of house and home if I don't keep an eye on them. If you'll excuse me…" She hustled up the aisle, her slippers tapping on the wooden floor.

"May I help you, miss?" Mrs. Portray asked haughtily.

"No. I just want to pick out some buttons," the young woman in a battered, lavender-plumed hat answered. She was dressed better than most of the negro women Taye had seen on the street, but her clothing was obviously well-worn and most likely secondhand. Her dress was inches shorter in the back than it should have been, and the bodice was so tight that her dark, round breasts rose high on her chest, revealing far more bare skin than was appropriate for midday.

"Picking out some buttons to purchase or to steal?" Mrs. Portray harrumphed.

The woman turned to face the shopkeeper and Taye stared at her. For a moment she studied the round face, trying to place it. "Efia?"

The girl looked up. She had a pretty face, colored by

rouge on her lips. She also had the shading of a black eye on her right cheek.

"Miss Taye?" the girl cried out in astonishment.

Taye rushed forward. "Efia, I can't believe it's truly you!"

18

Taye opened her arms to the young girl Naomi had be-
friended just after the war began. Efia and her twin sister,
Dorcas, both slaves, had been attempting to reach safety in
the North and had accompanied Taye, Cameron and Naomi
on the long trek on the Underground Railroad.

Mrs. Portray took a step back. "You...you know this
young female?"

"I do." Taye closed her arms around the thin woman,
pleased to see she was alive and well. They had parted one
night in a field somewhere in Maryland. Efia and Dorcas
had gone across the bay to Delaware to join family, while
Taye had traveled on with the others to Baltimore. "And I
can vouch for her honesty," Taye insisted, meeting Mrs.
Portray's gaze.

"Well..." The matron took one look at Taye's face and
realized that if she wanted the Campbell sisters' business,
she had better back off. Even if the chit was stealing, the
loss of a few buttons would be nothing compared to the
loss of the income Taye and Cameron might bring in.
"Well, you two just visit and let me know if you need
anything." She backed away, returning to her position behind a counter where she cut cloth.

"How are you?" Taye stepped back and squeezed Efia's hands between her own, noting that they were rough from harsh soap. "However did you get back to Jackson? I thought you were in Delaware."

Efia lifted a thin shoulder, her gaze taking in Taye as she spoke. "Things didn't work out there, so I jest come home. Got me a man who takes real good care of me." She smiled, revealing a broken front tooth. "I'm sure ya know him. Clyde Macon. He was the overseer at the Filberts' place."

Taye's face fell, but she quickly lifted her mouth into a half smile. She did know Clyde Macon, a white man from Florida, though only by reputation. Before the war, he had been known in the county as a brutal, unjust overseer and was thought to have been responsible for the disappearance of more than one young slave girl. Rumor had been that he liked sex with very young girls, ten to fourteen years old, and that he liked it rough.

But Efia obviously seemed pleased by her circumstances, and it *had* only been rumor.

"So you're making out well?" Taye asked.

Efia shrugged. "Well enough. Better than most of the negras for certain. At least I got a roof over my head and food in my belly."

Taye nodded. "It was dreadful to return home and see what's happened to our town. To Elmwood."

"I best be getting back." Efia began to move toward the door, clutching a black velvet drawstring purse. "Clyde don't like me out much."

"It was good to see you," Taye called after her as Efia opened the door, a tiny bell ringing over her head. "I know Cameron and Naomi will be pleased to hear that you're safe and well. I'm sure we'll see each other in town again."

Taye watched as Efia passed the shop window and disappeared from sight. She was concerned with Efia's black eye and broken tooth. Knowing the reputation of Clyde Macon made her all the more suspicious. Yet, Efia did seem happy, Taye thought. She was probably worrying for nothing.

"What can I show you, Miss Taye?" Mrs. Portray hustled around the counter. "I have a lovely silk damask, the color of your eyes, just aching to be made into an evening wrap."

"Where you been?" Clyde snapped from the sagging front porch of the hastily built one-room shack in J Town. He rose out of a stolen cane rocking chair and set one of his new hound puppies gently back into a basket with its mother.

Clyde was an ugly man with a receding hairline, plump, hairy arms and a perpetual stain of tobacco juice down his beard-stubbled chin. He was mean, too, with the men who worked for him, with their neighbors and especially with Efia. Sometimes she wished she was that bitch hound in the basket on the porch. He showed the dog far more kindness than he had ever offered her.

But when she'd returned to Mississippi after running from the law in Delaware, Clyde had taken her in. At first, she had thought it was going to be a business arrangement. She had thought she was going to cook and clean for him and his men, and he was going to pay her in cash. She had been naive to believe those were the only duties he would require of her.

Efia hurried up the muddy path toward the house, carrying a cloth feed sack of food in each arm. The mile walk from Jackson to J Town had been hot, lugging the bags of cornmeal, flour and lard, especially as she was dressed in her best Sunday gown and shoes, both of which were too tight. She knew that the feather in her hat was drooping with the heat and humidity, and the sweat that trickled from her armpits was staining the fabric of her gown. That knowledge was upsetting enough to nearly bring her to tears. She had worked hard to make the money to buy this gown and matching hat and shoes from the used shop on the edge of town. Harder than any woman should have to work, especially flat on her back.

"I told ya I had to go into town to get flour to make biscuits." She rushed up the steps, circumnavigating Clyde, hoping to avoid a cuff as she went by.

"The boys are hungry. Ain't nuthin' to eat here but friggin' corn pone that got worms in it."

She walked through the open door that allowed a hot breeze to filter into the main room. It also allowed the flies free access.

The "boys" were the band of ragtag men, bad men, black and white and mixed race, who worked for Clyde. Many of them had nowhere to go and slept on the shack floor. She was expected to cook for them and clean up after them.

"I got salted beef, too. I'll whip up some beef and gravy over biscuits in no time. Ya know ya like how I make it."

"I was hungry an hour ago!" He followed her through the doorway, giving her a push between her shoulder blades.

Efia caught herself before she tumbled to the floor. She had stopped by Orpa's on her way through the winding road of J Town and traded eggs for the stolen buttons. She didn't want to break the precious eggs. "I'll make it up to ya, Clyde." She lowered the bags to the fine cherry dining table he'd stolen from one of the nearby plantation homes. She didn't know where it had come from. Didn't care.

"Damn straight you'll be makin' it up to me." He

walked up behind her. "'Cause my pecker's been itchin' since I got up."

Clyde clasped her around her waist and knocked her up against the table. She closed her eyes with a grunt as her thighs banged hard into the wood.

Clyde lifted up her lavender skirt and the lace petticoat she wore. She hadn't bothered paying the thirteen cents extra for the drawers. A girl like her didn't need drawers.

Efia heard Clyde drop his pants and his belt buckle hit the floor. She thought to suggest they move onto the narrow bed they shared behind the curtain she'd strung up. Anyone who walked by the shack would be able to see them through the open doorway, but she was afraid of angering him any further. She'd set him off last night because she had spilled dishwater on the step, and she'd received a black eye in payment. It hurt like hell and she didn't want another, so she kept her mouth shut.

Clyde pushed hard on her back and she bent over; her stomach rolled. She knew what he wanted. He liked it that way because he said she was tighter. She thought he liked it because he realized it hurt her.

Efia knew better than to cry out, though. That was how she had gotten the broken tooth a couple of months ago, protesting against his unnatural desires.

Efia squeezed her eyes shut against the pain and gripped the table. Her thighs bumped against the edge, making a rhythmic, banging sound as Clyde grunted.

Trying to block out the sounds, the feelings, she thought of Taye. Taye with her light-colored skin and blue eyes. Taye with her fancy parasol with the fringe that matched her hat, and a new surname to go with it. A white surname, Campbell. The best in the county, maybe in all of Mississippi. What had Taye done to deserve all that? What had Efia done *not* to deserve it?

Resting her cheek on one of the cloth feed bags full of groceries on the table, Efia hoped Clyde would be careful when he was done. She didn't want him staining her dress.

After a delicious meal of trout and new potatoes, and conversation among Jackson, Falcon and Thomas, Taye was anxious to escape. Cameron had taken her evening meal in her room, saying she was tired, but had insisted Taye join Thomas and the other men. Cameron didn't want her to miss an opportunity to be with Thomas their first night together again.

Taye would have preferred to have eaten with Cameron in the privacy of her bedchamber. Sitting with Falcon and Thomas, pretending nothing had happened in the kitchen between her and the Cherokee, had been difficult. Through the entire meal Taye had concentrated on Thomas, trying to anticipate his every need, while attempting to ignore Falcon. But it had been difficult to disregard him when he had stared at her through every course. Taye only prayed the other men hadn't noticed.

"Would you like to go for a walk outside?" Taye asked Thomas as he helped her slide from her dining chair.

"Outside?" Thomas looked startled.

Taye lowered her voice. "It's a pleasant evening and… and we could be alone for a few minutes. I've missed you." And she had. Thomas had become a good friend over the years. She appreciated his opinions and enjoyed general conversation with him, something many women could not say about their husbands-to-be. She only wished she had missed him the way Naomi had missed Noah.

At the train station Naomi and Noah's behavior had been totally improper. He leaped off the train before it even halted, ran across the platform and grabbed her up in his arms. They had kissed right there in front of everyone,

mouths locked in passion. They had laughed together as if
there was no one in the world but the two of them.

Thomas had kissed Taye's cheek as if she were a distant
relative and inquired after her health. He hadn't even chastised her for leaving Baltimore so suddenly without telling
him of her intentions.

Taye knew very well that Thomas was not the kind of
man who would make a scene in such a public place as the
train station. She only wished that he had at least *wanted*
to sweep her in his arms. Just *one* hungry look from him
would have contented her.

"Please," Taye whispered. "Just one loop through the
garden. A lot has happened this week. I want to tell you."

"I suppose we could go for a walk." He glanced with
uncertainty in the direction of Falcon and Jackson, who
were already retiring to the study for brandy. They were
heatedly discussing the rebuilding of the railroad necessary
to begin trade in the South again.

The whole subject seemed utterly confusing and a bit
overwhelming to Taye, but she could tell by the look on
Thomas's face that he wanted to go with the men and par-
ticipate in the discussion. It hurt that she could be won out
so easily by talk of a length of rail track.

"Just a short walk," she pressed, smoothing his sleeve.
"And then I'll leave you men to your talk of President
Johnson's Reconstruction plan."

His brown-eyed gaze settled on hers and he smiled
kindly. "The fresh air will do me good. Should I send for
a wrap for you?"

She laughed. "Goodness, no. Have you forgotten how
warm a July evening is in Mississippi?"

Arm in arm they walked out through the open French
doors in the parlor and onto the winding garden path that
had been laid with small, pale stones.

"I want to tell you how sorry I am for leaving Baltimore without telling you I was going." Taye held his arm tightly, preventing him from pulling away if he tried. "I shouldn't have lied to you that way."

"It's quite all right. You forget how long I've known Cameron. She can be impulsive. And very persuasive when she wants to be."

"I know. That's why I came—because of Cameron." They walked around a flowering shrub and she inhaled its fragrance. "But I should have taken you into consideration. After all, we are going to be wed. Soon, I hope," she dared, gazing at him.

"Yes, well…considering the, um, circumstances, Jackson and I have agreed there won't be a formal engagement ball."

"I told him it was fine," she said quickly. "I don't mind. Really I don't. In fact, I think I prefer it this way. We should just get married quietly, with Jackson and Cameron present."

"I'm going to very busy these next few months, Taye. My father's building is in shambles, and I've already received messages from two gentlemen wishing to employ my services. There's no hurry, is there?"

Taye halted on the stone path and turned to face Thomas. There was something about his tone of voice that was unsettling. Had he changed his mind? If so, why? She wanted to ask, but she couldn't bring herself to do it. Perhaps because a tiny part of her nearly sighed in relief, and that made her feel immensely guilty.

Maybe Thomas hadn't changed his mind at all. Maybe it was just what he said, that he would be busy. No time to think of a new wife and setting up housekeeping.

"Of course, there's no hurry," she rushed on. "Whatever you think best."

He smiled and lowered his head, but again kissed her cheek instead of her mouth.

"Jackson has invited me to stay here at Atkins' Way while my family's home is cleaned, repainted and prepared. I told him I would have to check with you first. I wouldn't want you to feel uncomfortable, my being so near. I know I was staying in the same home with you in Baltimore, but this could be months."

"No, no, that will be fine," she said quickly. *It will keep my mind off Falcon,* she mused, guilt seeping into her veins again. *Off the feel of his heat and the taste of his mouth on mine.* Just thinking of him sent a tingling to her nether regions and a flush to her cheeks. "I know you'll be busy in town but we can see each other in the mornings, perhaps, and then for the evening meal, of course."

He began to walk again, leading her along. "I fear I can't make any promises. I'll be very busy, but I will certainly do my best not to neglect you."

Taye nodded, afraid to speak for fear her disappointment would be plain in her voice. She didn't simply want to not be neglected. She wanted Thomas to *want* to be with her. She wanted him to want to cover her face with kisses. To touch her, or at least fantasize about touching her.

"Tell me of the plans for the offices in town," Taye said, pushing such thoughts from her mind. "Do you think you have to put a new roof on?"

Cameron sat on the edge of her bed in the light of a single bedside lamp and listened to the sound of Jackson's boots as he walked down the hallway in the opposite direction of her room.

He had come in to ask if she needed anything, but he did not indicate he had any desire to remain in her presence a moment longer than he had to. He hadn't even closed the door when he came in.

And now he had retired for the evening, to one of the guest bedrooms, and Cameron would sleep alone again.

She fell back on the pillows, lying on top of the coverlet, and stared up at the dark ceilings. She knew she had put Jackson out of her bed to begin with, but she wanted him to *want* to be here with her. Even if they couldn't make love right now. Of course, she couldn't very well force him to stay, could she? And she would never beg him.

With a sigh she rolled onto her side and reached for her father's diary to read the next entry.

It's been three days since I brought the new slaves to Elmwood. Papa has conveniently placed me in charge of the new arrivals. I am to be sure they are properly housed, fed and put to work. "Slaves are to be treated well," Papa reminded me this morning at the breakfast table. "They are expensive investments and must be treated like valuable property."

It occurred to me that he had not spoken of the fact that they were also human beings deserving of compassion and decency, but I didn't dare speak up for fear he would delay my departure. I intended first to look in on the new arrivals, then Sukey. Saving the best of my day for last.

I found her by the river, squatting near the water's edge. She was washing out a piece of brightly colored fabric. It was not until I stood there at the woods line watching her that I realized she might even pay any mind to me. To her, I might be nothing more than another master.

She must have heard me because she turned and looked up. I smiled. She smiled hesitantly in return and I knew that she too felt something between us. Some spark.

"Hello," I called cautiously, not wanting to scare her.

"Hello," she returned, her smile widening.

And that was when I knew that, in time, she would love me.

Cameron closed the diary and held it to her chest for a moment, feeling almost as if she were holding him again. She glanced at the clock on the mantel. It was getting late. She knew she should try to sleep, but she wasn't sleepy yet. Just one more entry, she told herself.

Today I have learned a good lesson in the mettle my Sukey is made of, she read in her father's masculine hand-writing. *I came upon her completely by accident. I was riding to inspect one of the sugarcane fields and saw three women gathered alongside a field. Mr. Wright, one of our foremen, was holding another woman down on the ground. I heard Sukey's voice even before I saw her. She spoke slowly, but her voice was strong. Defiant. She was admonishing Mr. Wright, telling him that he should be ashamed of himself.*

I heard the young slave woman on the ground cry out and saw her kick furiously at him, but she could not escape Mr. Wright because he had straddled her and pinned her to the grass, holding her hands over her head. I immediately dismounted with a shout. Attempting to use my father's most authoritative voice, I demanded to know what was happening.

One of the women called my name, but she was so distraught that I could barely understand her words. She was weeping profusely as were the others, all but my Sukey. When she saw me, there was a light in her eyes that made me want to reach out and take her in my arms. I did not, of course. I have to be very careful that no one suspect my feelings for her. I'm not sure at this point that even Sukey knows the depth of my feelings for her.

I asked Sukey what had just transpired, and she replied that Mr. Wright had tried to take advantage of Sugar, the woman on the ground. Despite the intensity of the moment and my unease with the situation, I couldn't help but notice that Sukey did not speak like the other slaves anymore. Her speech has improved tenfold since her arrival. Is it our talks late at night when we walk the woods? Has she been learning unbeknownst to me? If so, she is a quick study, and the mind behind that beautiful face is swifter than even I have suspected.

Mr. Wright, of course, was furious that Sukey would dare to appeal to me, or for that matter, that I would ask a slave's recounting, rather than a white man's. Mr. Wright called my Sukey a lying bitch and told her to keep her black mouth shut. But Sukey did not back down in fear. Instead, she glanced up at me. I sensed immediately that it was a test. She wanted to see if I am the man I profess to be.

I looked at my foreman and then the frightened girl still lying on the ground, trembling with fear. Her gunnysack dress had been torn to reveal her small, firm brown breasts. She could not have been more than fourteen. My temper flared. I wanted to strike Mr. Wright with my fists, to inflict pain on him as he had so thoughtlessly done on these help-less women. Instead, I commanded him to bring Sugar to her feet and apologize at once.

When he protested, I could no longer control myself. I grabbed his arm and yanked him so hard that he stumbled back and nearly fell. Sukey immediately went to the young girl's side and helped her up, using her hands to shield Sugar's bare breasts from my eyes.

I turned on Mr. Wright once again and demanded an explanation for his behavior. He began to immediately make excuses, saying that he had sent these lazy women to the fields to pick bugs off the plants and that Sugar had attempted to run off. He claimed that he laid hands on the woman to keep her from escaping, nothing more. Sukey shook her head in protest. Still holding her friend in the *safety of her arms, she declared unflinchingly that Mr. Wright was lying. She said that he had, indeed, sent them to pick weevils, but then he'd called Sugar out of the field to come to him. Sukey said they heard Sugar scream and ran to her aid. They found her struggling with the foreman.*

As Sukey presented the women's side of the story, Sugar was crying, but it was a soundless cry. Tears ran down her dirty, tanned cheeks. It seemed to me that her tears were as genuine and heartfelt at that moment as those of any other woman. And with that realization, I could help but accept that she was as human and worthy of humanity as I.

I reminded the foreman of my father's feelings about his employees forcing themselves on the female slaves. As I spoke, I could feel myself growing more outraged by the moment. All I could think was, what if this had been Sukey I had come upon, pinned to the ground? I feared I could have pulled my revolver from my holster and shot Mr. Wright dead, and that side of myself I had never seen before.

Mr. Wright proceeded to protest his innocence hotly, asking me if I could believe the word of negra girls over him. I looked into Mr. Wright's filmy green eyes and knew that he was lying. And I knew that he was afraid. I told him to go to Mr. Melbourne, the overseer, for transfer to a men's detail, effective immediately. I moved closer to him, poked my finger into his chest and threatened that if I ever saw him near any of our slave women again, he would be out of a job. Not just at Elmwood, but in all of the damned state. I shouted at him, telling him to get out of my sight.

The women remained huddled together and watched as Mr. Wright got on his nag and rode away. I turned back to Sukey, who had sent her friend into the arms of the other women.

I spoke quietly to my Sukey, not wanting the others to hear my tone, telling her what a brave thing she had done. She looked up at me, her face so solemn, and replied that she was not brave, she had only done what was the right thing to do. When her brown-eyed gaze met mine, I felt a flutter in my heart. I knew she was talking not about herself, but about me. She thought I was brave.

And my heart went from fluttering to singing.

19

Cameron walked to the end of the mahogany dining table, carrying her breakfast plate with her. Bright sunlight poured in through the open windows, and the rich, comforting smell of freshly turned soil from the vegetable garden filled her nostrils. She had forgotten how much she loved the rich scent of Mississippi earth, how it breathed life into her.

She hesitated at the sideboard laden with fried meats, egg pieces and sweet pastries, then glanced at Jackson who had his head bent, absorbed in a newspaper. In the sunlight, she spotted a touch of gray in his dark hair and was taken aback by it. Then she reminded herself that he was twelve years older than she. Balancing her delicate china plate, she studied him and decided that perhaps the gray made him even more attractive. Had they been strangers in a crowded ballroom, had she been unwed, she wondered if he was a man whose company she would have sought. Would he have asked her to dance?

Cameron took her place at the far end of the mahogany table and picked up her napkin. "What news is there?" she asked.

Jackson didn't look up from his paper. "General Hoffman, Commissary General of Prisoners, has agreed to send an expedition of men to the prison camp in Andersonville, Georgia, to attempt to identify and mark the graves of Union soldiers buried there.''

"Their graves are unmarked?'' she asked quietly.

He glanced over the edge of his paper, giving her a look as if he thought her an idiot. "The Southerners did not put marble headstones on the prisoners' graves when they buried them. They dropped their remains into trenches in mass burials.'' He returned to his paper. "But at least there was some recording of the order the men went into the pits. The Secretary of War seems to think there will be some success in identifying the graves.''

Cameron nodded, taking a bite of corn muffin, though she was not particularly hungry. "Taye tells me that you're leaving tomorrow for Birmingham,'' she said after several minutes of silence.

"Yes.'' He did not lift his gaze from the newspaper as he spoke. "Falcon has agreed to remain here and serve as escort for you and Taye.'' He turned a page. "Two days ago the Coverdale farm three miles from Elmwood's west boundaries was robbed in the middle of the night. A band of men broke into the house, took money by gunpoint and raped the wife and sixteen-year-old daughter.''

Horrified, Cameron pressed her napkin to her mouth. If her husband's intent had been to shock her, he'd succeeded. But if he'd wanted to discourage her from rebuilding Elmwood, he would hope in vain. She was made of sterner stuff and no longer a stranger to senseless violence. The war years had fired her will and tempered it until it burned as hard as steel. She may have been a girl when her father fell to his death from that balcony, but no more. She was an intelligent woman who knew when to pick her battles. She really didn't want Falcon following her every time she stepped foot from this house; she truly needed her inde-

pendence right now. But she was no fool, and the reality
of the home she had returned to was hitting her hard. The
news in the local paper worried her, as well.

Only four years ago, Jackson had been a city where any
woman, black or white, could walk down the street safely.
Now Cameron even sent an escort with Naomi when she
went to town.

"I thought I would take the carriage out to Elmwood this
morning." She pushed a piece of sausage around her plate
with a silver fork much like the one that had come from
her mother's own silverware. Physically, she was recover-
ing well from the miscarriage, but she didn't yet feel up to
riding. "I would be interested in knowing what you think
of mine and the architect's plans."

He lifted his head from the paper, meeting her gaze for
the first time since she lost the baby. She couldn't read his
face, hadn't been able to decipher it since she'd come from
her sickbed. But at least he was willing to look at her.

"If you have the time, of course," she said, feeling silly
that her heart fluttered when she spoke to him. It was if
they were strangers again and she was tentatively testing
the waters around him.

"I'm meeting with a banker at one."

"We could go now," she said quickly, searching his face
for any sign of forgiveness. "Or later. Of course, it's not
necessary that you come at all," she finished, feeling the
need to protect herself.

He picked up his cup of black coffee. Naomi had managed to find the chicory coffee Cameron had told her he
liked and the aroma was heavenly. "If you feel up to it, I
could go this morning."

No smile. No enthusiasm in his voice.

Cameron stabbed the piece of sausage and stuffed it into

her mouth as she rose from the table. "Just let me get my pen and paper and ink and my bonnet. I'll meet you outside."

The carriage ride from Atkins' Way to Elmwood was uneventful. They passed several wagons and carriages and encountered neighbors, many of whom were just returning to the area. Cameron spoke gaily as if life with her husband was perfect, as if she were the mistress of Elmwood again, as in the days before the war. She promised each and every woman she knew that she would call on them soon, or told them that they "must come by Atkins' Way for afternoon refreshment in the near future."

They also passed several groups of freed slaves, carrying what they owned on their backs. Like the men and women Cameron had seen from the train, they seemed lost, forlorn. In every face, she looked for recognition of someone who had lived at Elmwood, but to no avail.

On the ride to Elmwood, Cameron and Jackson didn't speak much, and when they did it was of inconsequential matters. But at least he was speaking to her again.

Jackson approved of allowing Noah to oversee the workmen she was hiring to begin restoration of her family home. He asked for any instructions she might have for the household staff in Baltimore, requested what she would like him to bring back for her, which gowns, which jewels. He wanted her to make a list for him, and Addy would see that all the items were packed in Saratoga trunks for shipment to Mississippi.

When they reached the elm-lined drive, Jackson was able to take the carriage all the way to the house. He had hired men to clear not just the driveway, but the entire grounds surrounding the house and the outbuildings still standing. Her beautiful barn where she had stabled her Arabians was gone, of course. It was that structure she and Jackson had seen burning the night they fled from the soldiers. But the architect had listened well to her description and seemed confident he could design the barn as it had been before.

Jackson set the brake on the carriage and Cameron waited for him to help her down. Physically, she no longer felt weak. As Naomi said, a woman's body was like a patch of green briers. Give it a little peace, a little sunshine, and it will spring back tough as ever. The bleeding had nearly subsided and her strength was almost what it had been before. But emotionally, she felt fragile, as if she might shatter into tears at any moment. Just the touch of Jackson's fingertips as he helped her down was somehow comforting.

His gray-eyed gaze accidentally met hers as she stepped onto the grass, and she stared up at him, wanting desperately to say something, anything, to narrow the gulf that yawned between them. But in the end, she didn't know what to say and he seemed unwilling or uninterested in meeting her halfway.

Cameron turned away and strode toward the front porch, her tone light and focused on the subject at hand. "All the pillars save this one can be repaired," she explained, resting her hand on one corner pillar of the front porch that appeared to have been hit by stray mortar. There had been no battle on Elmwood's grounds, but apparently there had been some sort of target practice. "And this can be replaced, once the second floor veranda is shored up."

Jackson nodded, following Cameron as she made her way around the house, pointing out broken windows, missing shutters and a crumbling chimney that had also been damaged by practice mortar fire. As he walked, he made a few comments, but did not seem interested in engaging in conversation. Cameron reminded herself that at least he was here, and that made her hopeful.

"The kitchen is, of course, the greatest obstacle." She

made her way through the blackened rubble where the herb garden at the back door had once been. "I'm told that the easiest thing to do will be to tear what remains of the kitchen off the back of the house and rebuild the entire structure. Mr. Jasper says it is truly a miracle the fire didn't spread to the rest of the house. He says the fact that my grandpapa had the forethought to make the wall between the kitchen and main house brick saved Elmwood." She opened of arms. "Of course, look at this mess. It will take weeks to clean it up."

"What's left of the kitchen can be burned or buried," Jackson observed. "Once it's cleared, construction can begin."

Cameron stepped into the charred remains of the kitchen and uprighted a portion of a table on which kitchen maids had once rolled piecrusts and cut biscuits. The scent of burned wood became strong as she disturbed the table and the acrid smell stung her nose. Beneath it, she found a dish, miraculously in one piece. She pulled a lace handkerchief from her sleeve and rubbed the plate to reveal a purple iris painted on the china. "Oh, heavens. Look at this. It's one of my mother's morning dishes."

Something hit the ground just in front of her and she looked up, startled. There was nothing overhead but the blue sky. What could have fallen? Seeing nothing above or before her, she glanced at her feet. There was a small, pale stone at the toe of her boot that had not been there a moment before. She recognized the stone as being one from the bed of the Pearl River; she and her brother and Taye had collected them as children. She looked back at Jackson, but he was moving a blackened beam to reach something.

Cameron rubbed the plate in her hand again, revealing another iris. *Plunk.* This time a stone hit the remains of the table with a distinct sound. She looked to Jackson. He had heard it, too.

He raised his hand, warning her to stand still. He was suddenly acutely alert. He set one of the iris-patterned breakfast plates down carefully and withdrew the ivory-handled pistol from the holster he wore on his hip.

Cameron stood motionless, her mother's plate held fool-ishly in front of her as if it could somehow shield her from harm. It had not occurred to her that someone might be here at Elmwood, not when everyone in the area knew she and Taye had returned to their birthright.

Jackson eased up to stand beside her. "Where did it come from?" he asked quietly.

She shook her head, staring in the direction of where the kitchen had been attached to the main house. When she had first come here, burned timbers had blocked the doorway from the kitchen to the hall, but they had been hauled away. She could now walk from the ruins of the kitchen into the main house. "I'm not sure," she whispered. "But I think it came from there." She nodded toward the doorway.

Jackson took a step forward and a stone struck him squarely in the middle of the chest. "Ouch. Son of a bitch!" He grabbed Cameron and pulled her behind him. "Where the hell is it coming from?" Keeping his gaze fixed on the doorway, he gave her a push. "I want you to get back to the carriage."

"No," she protested loudly. "I want to know who is trespassing on my property!" She darted around Jackson and rushed for the door.

"Cameron, you damned fool," he cried out, running af-ter her. "You want to get yourself killed?"

"With pebbles?" she demanded, more annoyed than afraid. "If whoever this is really meant to hurt us, he'd have done it by now." She turned away from him.

"Hello?" she shouted. "Hello? Who's there? I am Cameron Campbell and this my home. I demand to know who—"

Another pebble whizzed by, dangerously skimming her cheek, and struck Jackson again. This time he cursed in French.

Cameron caught a flash of color and movement inside the house and she ran through the door and down the hall. Footsteps sounded in front of her, but the intruder had a head start. She didn't get a look at him.

"Stop," Cameron called, running past her father's study door. "No one is going to hurt you."

"Cameron, come back here!" Jackson shouted.

"Wait," Cameron said. "I just want to talk to you!" She caught another flash of bright blue fabric as the person disappeared around the corner, into the front hallway. It was a woman's skirt.

Jackson passed Cameron at a run as they entered the front entryway.

A woman—no, a child, her gamine face nearly hidden by a tangle of red-blond hair, bounded up the grand staircase.

"You! Stop," Jackson shouted, taking the steps two at a time."

"Be careful," Cameron shouted, grasping her skirts in both hands to follow him. "Don't hurt her!"

"Don't hurt her?" Jackson growled over his shoulder. "She could have taken my eye out."

At the first landing, he caught a handful of the intruder's dress in one fist, but his struggling quarry screeched like a trapped wildcat and tore free, leaving him holding only a handful of tattered blue fabric.

Cameron glimpsed a flash of scabby knees and dirty bare feet as the girl darted away.

"Damn it, we just want to talk to you," Jackson hollered, taking up the chase again.

"Jackson, don't. You're scaring her!" Cameron's throat constricted as tears of compassion sprang to her eyes. She had no idea why she was no longer angry with this starving waif who had invaded her family home, but the girl seemed so pitiful in the ragged, oversize blue dress that had been hacked off at the knees.

At the top of the stairs, the girl raced down the hallway in the direction of the guest bedchambers. Cameron heard a door slam, immediately followed by the pounding of Jackson's footsteps and then the splintering of wood.

"Jackson, don't hurt her!"

She followed him through a storage room door he'd broken open, to another door that slammed shut as she entered the room.

"Where does this lead?" he demanded, twisting the knob violently. It wasn't locked, but when he pulled, it wouldn't open. The intruder had jammed something beneath the knob to keep it closed.

Cameron stared at the door. "It's one of the attics." She herself had tried the same door earlier in the week and it had stuck then, too. At the time, she had made a mental note to send one of the workmen upstairs to loosen the door. Had the child blocked it then? Had she been up in the attic when Cameron had been here before?

Jackson grabbed the doorknob, steadied himself with one foot against the wall and jerked on the door. It flew open and he nearly fell back. "Stay here," he ordered, scrambling up the narrow staircase.

Cameron ran after him. Holding her skirts in one hand, placing the other hand on one rough-hewn stair tread at a time, she climbed into the attic where she'd not been for years.

The moment she reached the top of the stairs, she knew the child had been here for some time. Weeks at least, perhaps months. A small table that had come from the parlor was set with Cameron's mother's silver tea service. There were two chairs at the table, as if the little thief was expecting a guest for tea. An area had been set up under the tiny eaves window as a bed with a mattress from one of the bedrooms below and a curtain for a bedcovering.

"Where is she?" Jackson panted, standing in the center of the attic where his head nearly brushed the beams beneath the peaked roof.

It took a moment for Cameron's eyes to adjust to the dim light that came from the small window. The attic was cluttered with three generations of the Campbell family's discarded chairs, trunks and crates. She saw an old spinning wheel, a freestanding dress rack, a dressmaker's mannequin used for fittings.

"I know you're here," Jackson growled. "We've got you trapped, so you might as well come out."

Cameron's gaze drifted carefully from one shadowed object to the next. She spotted another chair, a table of some sort, a pile of hatboxes. Then something caught her eye. She looked back at the table and smiled.

"Damn it, Cameron, I told you to stay downstairs. You shouldn't be running or climbing steps yet!"

As Jackson protested loudly, she slid one foot in front of the other, easing toward the table. When she reached its edge, she slowly bent at the knees to squat, balancing herself with one hand on the dusty table's edge.

Cameron's gaze met another's.

The young girl blinked.

"It's all right," Cameron said softly. "We won't hurt you." She offered her hand. "Why not come out where I can see you."

After a moment, she hesitantly took Cameron's hand. It was obvious to Cameron that she did so not because she wanted to, but because she knew she was trapped.

"That's right. Just come out where we can see you better," Cameron urged gently, as if the girl were a startled colt. "Just here in the light where I can get a look at you."

The child allowed herself to be led out from under the table and into the wide beam of sunlight in the middle of the room. Her face was smudged with days of dirt, as was the hacked-off blue gown that looked like some New Orleans tart's dress. Her bare knees were skinned and grass stained.

"Goodness, how old are you? Ten, twelve?" Cameron questioned, holding fast to the dirty hand. Between the dirt and the dim light, it was difficult to guess her age.

The girl smelled as if she had not bathed in weeks, and she was desperately thin. Even in the feeble light, her protruding collarbones and sunken cheeks were evident.

The girl pulled away slowly, her gaze locked with Cameron's.

"Can you tell me your name?" Cameron asked, making no quick movements for fear of startling her.

"Lacy," the child answered, still seeming undecided as to whether she would bolt again or not. But she pushed a hank of matted hair out of her face and boldly remained where she stood. "My name is Lacy Campbell."

20

Cameron stared in shock at the girl's filthy, waiflike face. Lacy *Campbell?* Of course, it was a coincidence, their having the same family name. But a cold stab of intuition in the pit of her stomach suggested it was not. There was something about this girl—the way she spoke, the way she held herself—that put Cameron on edge. "What did you say?"

"Ya deaf?" the girl challenged, dropping her hands to her narrow hips to reveal in one hand a wooden slingshot made from a Y-shaped tree branch. Suddenly her timidity had been transformed into a bravado Cameron knew wasn't quite genuine.

"Hey," Jackson growled at Lacy. "You'll be respectful."

The child never acknowledged Jackson, never blinked.

"I said I'm Lacy Campbell!" she repeated, meeting Cameron's gaze with childlike defiance. "And this here is my house, too."

"I want you to pack whatever is yours and go now," Jackson told Lacy. "Go now and don't come back, and I won't call the authorities and have you arrested."

Lacy's wide, intelligent eyes were the color of green

grass flecked with shades of honey. Those wary eyes—
somehow hauntingly familiar—watched Cameron.

"I said, I won't bring the authorities if you go now."
Jackson reached for her arm, and Lacy jumped back as if
she'd been stung.

"Jackson, no." Cameron stepped between them, sepa-
rating them. Still studying Lacy carefully, she turned her
back to her husband, speaking softly, as she might approach
an unbroken colt. "You're mistaken," she told the girl.
"This is my house. My sister's and mine. My father left it
to us when he passed away."

Lacy shook her head, setting her jaw, glaring back with
eyes too old for her face. "Might be yore'n, but it be mine,
too," she said stubbornly.

Cameron offered her hand again. "My name is Cameron
Campbell." She twisted to glance at Jackson and then
turned back to the girl again. "It was Campbell before I
was married. Now I'm Cameron Logan, of course."

"I know who ya are." Lacy whipped her tangled mass
of red-gold hair and made no move to accept Cameron's
hand of introduction.

"You do?"

Lacy nodded. "Seen ya in town, a'fore the war. Ya and
the mulatto. Y'all always wore pretty dresses and pretty
bonnets. Ya were the one with them fancy horses."

Cameron's brow knitted. She was certain she had never
seen this girl before, but then four years ago the child could
have been only eight or so. She might have looked quite
different. "Do I know you?"

She shook her head. "Don't reckon ya do."

"And you say you have a claim on Elmwood Plantation?
That's impossible, of course. The fact that we share a family name is simply coincidence. My half sister Taye and I
are the last of the Campbells in Mississippi. In all of the

United States. We have no relatives here. You would have to take a ship across the ocean to a place called Scotland before you met another of my father's blood relations.''

Lacy folded her arms over her chest and the folds of her gown gaped at the bodice to reveal bare, freckled skin, nearly hidden by more dirt than Cameron would have thought possible for one child to possess. Lacy Campbell was wearing no undergarments; it was plain to see that whatever her age, she had not yet begun to grow breasts. ''I knows what I know.''

Cameron thought for a moment. She realized the girl's claim was untrue, naturally. If Lacy had seen her and Taye in Jackson before the war, it was probably wishful thinking. But there was something about those flecked hazel eyes that told her there was more to the girl's tale, a story Cameron feared she didn't want to know.

''Are you hungry?'' Cameron asked, veering off the subject of Lacy's claim.

'''Course I'm hungry. Nothin' in the garden 'hind the kitchen. A few stray beans and onions in the old slave garden. Once in a while I get me a rat or a bird.''

Cameron winced. ''Well, let's go downstairs and I'll get you something to eat. I brought food with me and I'll share.''

''Cameron.'' Jackson's fingers closed over her forearm and he turned her, forcing her to look at him. He lowered his voice. ''You shouldn't do this. I understand you feel sorry for her, but girls like this are all over the South. You can't save them all. We should give her some money and send her on her way. She can mean nothing but trouble, and more trouble is something we don't need right now.''

Cameron glared at Jackson, wondering exactly what he meant by that, but she didn't ask. This wasn't about her or him, or the trouble between them. It was about this half-starved, homeless urchin who was barely more than a child. Where was his heart?

Cameron pulled her arm from Jackson's firm grasp. "Let's go downstairs," she told Lacy, mopping her perspiring brow. "It will be cooler outside."

Lacy followed Cameron down the attic stairs, with Jackson bringing up the rear. At the bottom of the grand staircase, Cameron told Jackson, "There's a dinner basket in the back of the carriage. Would you bring it to the veranda?"

"Cam, it's barely eleven—"

"We can eat there. We'll drag a table and some chairs out. Papa and I used to eat on the veranda all the time."

He stood on the marred Italian tile staring at her. "I'm not leaving you alone with that urchin. She could harm you."

"With her slingshot?" Cameron snatched the weapon from Lacy's hand.

"Hey!" Lacy protested.

"Just for safekeeping. I'll give it back to you," Cameron promised, slipping the slingshot into the waistband of her navy riding skirt. She glanced at Jackson. *"Please?"*

He grunted and walked out the front door, leaving it open.

By the time the scowling Jackson had returned with the dinner basket Naomi had packed, Cameron and Lacy had carried a wooden table and three unmatched chairs they had found overturned in the ballroom onto the veranda. It was nothing like it had once been, not the veranda or the house or the once neatly manicured garden before them, but it was still home and that thought warmed Cameron's heart.

"I'm not hungry," Jackson grumbled, dropping the basket in front of Cameron. "I need to get back to town."

"If you have to go," Cameron said to Jackson. "Go."

She waved her hand. "Take the carriage. Send it back for me later."

"I'm not leaving you here with her!"

Cameron arched an eyebrow. "So you'll wait until after we have our dinner?"

Jackson walked away to stand by the open door to the house and glare at them.

Cameron ignored him. "Let's see, what do we have here?" She pulled several pieces of fried chicken wrapped in brown paper from the basket. "Chicken. Cheese. Pears. Oh, and Naomi's lemonade. You're going to love this, so sweet and yet so tart at the same time."

Lacy sat on a chair and stared with wide-eyed wonder at the food Cameron spread out on the table.

"Please, eat," Cameron said. She watched as both of the girl's small hands darted out.

Lacy somehow managed to grab two pieces of chicken and a pear, all at the same time.

"Unless you'll like to wash up first," Cameron suggested, watching as Lacy gnawed ravenously on one piece of chicken, while clutching the other tightly in her filthy hand.

"Don't need no washin'," Lacy said between mouthfuls.

Cameron picked up a pear and, tossing it in the air, caught it and took a bite. "So you say Elmwood is yours. How so?"

Lacy chewed on the gristle from a drumstick. Taking one last look at the bone, she deemed she was done with it and threw it over her shoulder. "Ya don't look stupid. I tole ya. 'Cause I'm a Campbell, too."

Jackson made a derisive sound behind them.

Cameron watched in amazement as the discarded bone flew into the garden and landed on the weedy path. She didn't know where the poor girl had been raised, but the young woman's manners had obviously not been addressed.

Cameron had to drag her attention to Lacy again. "So you are a Campbell, are you? Long-lost cousin of mine, I suppose?"

Cameron's mouth twitched with amusement when Lacy didn't answer. The child had probably heard that the Campbell heiress was home and that she was planning to restore Elmwood to its former glory. She was here to see what she could get from the Campbell family. "So you're not a cousin?"

"Nope." Lacy munched on the pear, then took a bite from the second piece of chicken. "Yer my aunt."

Cameron nearly choked on her pear. She didn't know what she had expected the girl to say, but that wasn't it. She swallowed the mouthful of fruit. "You can't expect me to believe that you are my niece?"

Lacy nodded. Pear juice ran down her chin and her lips were shiny with grease. "Ya gonna eat that other chicken?" She stared at the piece left on the paper. "It's real good."

What appetite Cameron had was gone. She set down her half-eaten pear. "Help yourself." She leaned forward, elbows on the table, studying Lacy. "How could you be my niece?"

"Grant Campbell's daughter."

Cameron sat back suddenly in her chair, as if her brother's ghost had just floated onto the veranda. She took a deep breath, brushing off the strange feeling that had come over her at the mention of her brother's name.

Lacy was lying, of course. Grant had had no children. "My brother died without issue," Cameron said coolly. "He had no children, legitimate or otherwise."

"None ya knew 'bout, I guess." Lacy threw the other

bone over her shoulder. "'Course, the other Mr. Campbell, he knew."

Cameron shot out of her chair. "Mr. Campbell? Which Mr. Campbell do you speak of?"

"The father." Lacy licked her fingers noisily. "Yer father."

"I think we've heard enough here," Jackson said. "She needs to go, now, Cameron."

Cameron held up a finger to Jackson. "No. That's impossible," she insisted, turning back to Lacy. "My father knew nothing of a grandchild. You're lying."

Lacy shook her head. She was finishing off the pear, smacking her lips, eating it core and all. "Mama said ya'd say I was a big fat liar. But I ain't." Her hazel-eyed gaze, which suddenly looked startlingly like Grant's, met Cameron's. "But ya dig down in yer belly, ya know I ain't."

Cameron pressed her hand to her mouth. "Who was your mother?" she demanded. "How old are you?"

"Be fourteen come the turn of the year, and my mama's name was Morrie. Maureen Matthews. She worked at The Dog-Ear Saloon."

Cameron remembered The Dog-Ear vaguely, though it had closed down years ago when the proprietor was shot and killed in a barroom brawl. It had been a seedy place where men played cards, drank...and apparently amused themselves in other ways. "So, your mother was a—"

"Cleanin' woman," Lacy said, meeting Cameron's gaze, daring the older woman to say otherwise.

The girl had a lot of guts for someone her age.

Lacy spotted a scrap of crumb from the chicken batter and licked her finger to pick it up with. "My mama cleaned for old man Carter, but he didn't pay much. Mama said Mr. Campbell was nice to her, least at first. Bought her pretty baubles."

"You mean Grant? My brother."

Lacy nodded. "Mama said he was young then, had a draggin' leg and wanted to make up for it. Thought he was a big stud."

Cameron blanched. Grant had had a limp. He'd fallen from one her horses when he was twelve and broken his leg so badly that it had healed shorter than the other. After the injury her brother's personality had changed for the worse. He spent the rest of his life trying to make up for his physical weakness by bullying others.

Lacy wiped her greasy mouth with the back of her hand, then dragged it down the front of her stained blue gown. "'Course, he lost interest once her belly got swolled up, Mama said. He stopped comin' 'round. Tole her she looked like an ole sow."

Cameron couldn't believe what she was hearing. How could Grant have fathered a child and then simply ignored her? But inside, she knew what kind of man her brother had been. She knew the kinds of things he had done.

"If this is true, though I'm not saying I believe you," Cameron warned, raising one finger, "why didn't your mother ever come to us? How did I not know about you?"

"She did come. She come to this house when I was still a babe on the tit. Mr. Carter had put her out on account of my cryin'. Mama couldn't get no work done. Grant Campbell turned her away," she said, making no attempt to hide her hatred. "But then old Mr. Campbell, *Senator,* Mama called him—" Her face lightened. "He come to the Dog-Ear and give us money. Put us in a nice place over the apothecary's. He brought money every month, for years till—"

Cameron gripped the back of the chair, lost for a moment in that terrible night here at Elmwood. "Until he died," she murmured.

Lacy nodded. "At first, Mama thought he just forgot about us, there bein' a war and all, and him being such an important man, but then we heard." She lowered her gaze to the table. "And we was sorry 'cause he was a good man."

Tears gathered in the corners of Cameron's eyes. David Campbell *had* been a good man, and this young girl was living proof. "What happened to your mama?" Cameron asked.

"Jesus," Jackson barked. "You believe this horseshit?"

Cameron sat down in the chair again and waited for Lacy to speak.

"She couldn't find no work. Not when the fightin' started. We couldn't stay above the apothecary's no more, so we started sleepin' here and there. When soldiers come to town, blue or gray, they give her food for washing their clothes, sewin'." The girl's gaze flickered to Cameron's, her pain obvious. "Sometimes they wanted other tendin'. Men things."

Cameron trembled. Lacy's mother had sold her body to soldiers to feed her child. To feed Senator David Campbell's granddaughter. It was an appalling story, so appalling that Cameron knew in her heart of hearts that it was true. It had to be. It all made perfect sense. Grant had fathered a baby when he was fifteen. To protect the Campbell name, the senator had quietly taken care of the child and her mother. If he was alive today, he would still be fulfilling that obligation he felt.

"Where's your mama now?" Cameron asked.

Lacy stared at her dirty hands in her lap. "She got sick. Bowels wouldn't stop runnin'. Big ole sores on her paps and arms. I tried to help her best I could. Tried to get us food. I even stole some tea and a fancy teapot, but she died anyway," the girl finished softly.

"And you've been on your own ever since?"

Lacy nodded. "I come here sometime in March." She half smiled. "Before Mama died, I used to lay beside her and make up stories about us livin' in this grand house. Drinkin' lemonade on the veranda like this," she said feigning importance as she swayed her thin shoulders. Then she gave a girlish laugh, lost in the memory.

"And so you came here after she died."

A shrug. "Didn't know where else to go."

"And you've lived here alone all this time?"

Lacy nodded. "I made me a place up there in the attic. Found food best I could. If anyone came—" she pointed to Jackson "—like your man did month back, I jest hid till they was gone."

"But then I returned home," Cameron offered.

"And all of a sudden the place was hoppin' like Main Street on the Fourth of July before the war," Lacy said. "Workmen comin' and goin'. You and him down in the garden shoutin' at each other."

Cameron felt her cheeks color. Lacy had been watching them the day she and Jackson had argued?

"I've had enough of this," Jackson said from the doorway. "I'm going back to town and you're coming with me, Cameron. I don't care where she goes."

Cameron took her time getting from her chair to repack the basket, saying nothing. When her task was complete, she carefully pushed the chair under the table. "Get whatever you want from the attic and meet me at the carriage out front," she told Lacy. She turned to Jackson, daring him to object. "You're going home with me."

21

Cameron walked into the parlor to find Taye and Thomas seated across from each other, each deeply engrossed in a book. Jackson had opened the French doors and stood out on the veranda, staring into the darkness.

"Heaven knows how she could be afraid to sleep alone in the bedchamber." Cameron spoke to no one in particular. "She was sleeping alone at Elmwood in the attic, for heaven's sake. But Naomi placed a pallet on the floor for one of kitchen girls' daughters, and finally both girls are sound asleep."

Taye looked up from her book. "I'm glad Lacy is settled. Now you should sit down and put your feet up. You've had a long day."

Thomas smiled mildly in Cameron's direction and continued reading. Jackson was either so lost in his thoughts that he hadn't heard her come into the parlor, or he was ignoring her.

"I feel quite well, thank you. Tomorrow we'll need to go into town and see what we can do about getting Lacy something to wear. I thought we could buy a couple of used gowns until we can have some made for her by a seamstress."

"I'll go if you like." Taye smiled. "I thought I might visit Thomas in his office tomorrow. He tells me they've made great progress." She glanced over at him, but he didn't look up from his legal tome.

Cameron walked past her sister and patted her shoulder. "I knew I could count on *you,* at least." She eyed Jackson, who still paid her no mind.

"We could make a day of it. I have several other errands," she said as she crossed the parlor and walked onto the veranda. She had changed out of her riding skirt and into an apple green bombazine with V'd sleeves that fell to her elbows. The gown had a low décolleté, suitable for evening, and showed her rounded breasts rather nicely.

Cameron walked to the rail to stand beside Jackson and tipped her head back to feel the warm, humid breeze, inhaling the heavenly scent of honeysuckle on the air. "Where's Falcon?" she asked, trying to choose some neutral ground on which to speak with her husband.

"Don't know. Left after supper."

"Probably a woman," she remarked lightly.

He didn't even smile. "I doubt it. Falcon keeps mostly to himself."

She lifted one shoulder. "Well, he is free to come and go as he pleases, and I certainly don't have need of a guard here in the house."

"I wouldn't be so sure, Cameron. There was another raid on a farm not too far from here two nights ago. They burned the barn, took the man's horses and chickens, killed and gutted his pregnant sow in front of his children."

Cameron shook her head. "Jackson, the war is over. Why—"

"These men think they've been pushed into it. They believe the war gave them no other choice. There are no jobs, no money—"

She studied Jackson's shadowed face. "You're defending the marauders?"

He scowled. "No. No, of course not. These men and others like them have to be stopped if the South is to recover. I'm only saying that this is a more complicated matter than most realize.

"I'm going back to Baltimore tomorrow."

Cameron glanced at him, her stomach knotted. "So soon?"

"You don't need me here. I've business to attend to."

Cameron turned to face him, unable to control her anger. "So it's Washington again, is it? Or is it that woman? When you said we would be living here in Mississippi, I assumed you would have to return to Baltimore on occasion for your shipping business. If you'd listened to me weeks ago, you would have known that was to be my suggestion all along. But I also assumed, Jackson, that by moving to Mississippi, you'd be done with this damned spying business."

"Would you not say that quite so loud?" he demanded under his breath, looking to see if anyone had heard them.

"I don't care who hears me! I don't want you to go on any more missions for the State Department."

His face was so void of emotion, his tone so cool, that his words were hurtful. "We don't always get what we want, do we, Cam?"

She groaned in frustration. "If you're talking about Lacy, why don't you just say you don't want her here? She's a Campbell, Jackson. We can't hold it against her that she's Grant's child."

Cameron sighed, staring into the darkness. She knew Jackson was angry about Lacy, but she wasn't going to budge where the young girl was concerned. She knew in her heart of hearts that Lacy was Grant's daughter, therefore her niece. The senator would expect Cameron to take care of her brother's by-blow. Jackson, of course, thought she had to see proof. How could she explain to him that the proof was in the girl's eyes, in the sadness mixed with pride Cameron had heard in her tone of voice when she spoke of her grandfather, the *senator?*

"Lacy is lying, Cameron."

"She can't be lying! She knew too much to make it up."

He laughed humorlessly. "Anyone who has lived in this town, or *knows* anyone who lived in this town, could have repeated the things she knew about Grant and your family."

"You're wrong. It sounds too much like my selfish, cruel brother not to be true."

"I'm not going to argue with you about this, Cameron," Jackson said abruptly. "Not tonight."

"Good," she snapped. "Because the discussion is over. Lacy stays."

"I don't know how long I'll be gone. I've transferred money to an account at the bank in town."

"I don't need your money. You forget, I have my own."

"Falcon has agreed to stay here and keep an eye on you," he continued, ignoring her comment. "You and Taye are not to travel anywhere beyond the plantation's gates without Thomas or someone appointed by him accompanying you."

Cameron opened her mouth to protest, but he grabbed her arm roughly. "That's not a wish, it's an order. Falcon has his instructions. You disobey me, you'll be under house arrest. Trust me, he'll do it. His loyalty is to me, not the blessed Campbell name."

His fingers bit into her arm. "Stop treating me like a child," she demanded.

"As soon as you stop acting like one."

Cameron searched his gray eyes for a glimmer of the love she had seen in them only a few short weeks ago. When she didn't see it, she wondered if it had ever been there to begin with.

Jackson released her arm and Cameron pressed her lips together, filled with anger, hurt. "If that's all you have to say, then, I suppose I will go to bed." She stared at the toes of her apple green slippers and recalled the night Jackson had pulled them off and tossed them across the room in his haste to make love. "I'll see you when you return."

"I'll send a telegram to let you know how long I'll be. It could be a couple of weeks."

Cameron longed to tell him that he was her husband and he belonged here with her now. But then she remembered that he had only agreed to allow her to stay as consolation for the loss of the baby.

She left the parlor without speaking again and retired to her bedchamber. At least there she would find the solace of her father's words.

"David, no," Sukey said softly. "We must not."

I clasped her hand tightly, leading her through the woods along the river. Golden moonlight lit our way like a magical sprinkling of fairy dust. I knew no one would miss us. My father and mother were at a ball at a neighboring plantation and thought I was in bed with a stomach ailment. Sukey had completed her duties in the dairy where she worked and would not be missed, either.

I glanced back at her and just that glimpse of her beautiful rounded face and rich cinnamon eyes made my heart skip a beat. "We're almost there. Wait until you see this tree."

I led Sukey off the path. A hundred yards from the riverbank was an ancient cypress tree whose branches had grown until they reached the forest floor, making a perfect hiding place, like a curtained room. I held back a handful of branches and she stepped through, completely trusting in me.

"So dark," she whispered.

I stepped through the branches. "I brought some candles and something to eat. I thought we could have a picnic." I turned and bumped into her. Suddenly we were nose to nose. I could feel her light, sweet-smelling breath on my face.

"Sukey," I whispered.

She brushed her hand across my chest. I knew I shouldn't, but I couldn't stop myself. If I didn't taste her at that moment, I would perish. I lowered my head and brushed my lips against hers tentatively, almost expecting lightning to strike.

It did, but not in the way I expected.

Her lower lip trembled. She, too, knew this was forbidden.

"David," she whispered.

"Shh," I breathed. And then her lips parted and she took me hungrily. I knew then that there was no turning back.

Efia knew Clyde had returned home when she heard the bitch hound on the front porch begin to bark excitedly. It was well after midnight and she was already in bed, dressed in the only shift she owned. It was so hot tonight that she was tempted to sleep naked, but she didn't dare. That was too big an invitation to Clyde, too big an invitation to any of them.

"Fee!" Clyde hollered.

She didn't want to get out of bed. She was tired and her back was sore from lugging crates from a wagon into an abandoned house not too far from town off the road to

Vicksburg. Efia didn't know what had been in those crates and she didn't want to know. She didn't know what Clyde and his boys were using that abandoned house for, and she didn't want to know that, either.

"Fee!" Clyde called again. "Where the hell are ya?"

He was drunk.

The coonhound howled and then whined in greeting to her master. Efia heard Clyde stamp up the steps. There were others with him. She could hear them laughing, then the sound of their dirty boots on her clean floor as they entered the shack.

"Got anything to eat?" Clyde barked. "Fee, where the hell are ya? Don't ya hear me callin'?" He ripped back the curtain that hid their bed.

Efia shrank back, trying to cover her bare shoulders with a torn sheet she had found in the dump. Someone had lit the kerosene lamp on the table. The men were dragging out chairs, laughing at some private joke. They were all drunk. She could see that one had brought moonshine in a crock jug, and another, a particularly nasty soul, was wearing what looked like a brand-new yellow frock coat.

"Where you been, Clyde?" she asked, shrinking back from him against the wall. "What you been up to? The sheriff and them soldiers already been through J Town once this week."

"None of yer damned business what I been doin'. Now get up and get me somethin' to eat."

When she didn't move fast enough, he grabbed her by the arm and dragged her out of the bed.

"Let me get dressed, at least," she murmured. "I'll make ya up a nice pot of greens. I got fatback."

"Ain't no need for ya to get dressed." He smacked her hard on her bottom. "Ain't nuthin' of yours my boys ain't seen before." He laughed and the others echoed.

"Now get on," Clyde ordered, "before I put this boot up your skinny, black ass. Rustle up some pone an' blackstrap 'lasses to go with them greens. I got me a taste for sweets tonight."

Efia hurried barefoot to the stove and pulled a rusty pot from a crate against the wall. As she grabbed handfuls of fresh greens from a basket, she eyed the men.

Someone had pulled out a deck of cards and five of them, including Clyde, sat down to play. There were others out on the porch; she could see the glow of their pipes burning and hear their crude talk.

At the card table, Bucky was wearing a fancy black top hat like one Efia had seen in the hat shop window in town. As she tossed kindling into the stove to bring up the flames, something glittery around Pot's neck caught her eye. It looked like a woman's necklace.

Efia didn't dare ask where any of the stuff had come from. In town, she had heard about the thieves who were terrorizing the county. She knew where the clothes and the jewelry were coming from, but it wasn't her place to say anything about what was right or wrong. She knew speaking up would get her nothing but a shallow grave.

Efia turned to the stove. As she stirred the greens with a stick she had peeled the bark off of, she thought of Taye Campbell at Atkins' Way. She didn't know what made her think of the beautiful mulatto, but she wondered what she was doing right now. Probably sleeping in a proper nightgown in a big bed with clean sheets that smelled of sunshine.

Clyde caught the hem of her shift and drew it up slowly, showing the men a peek of her bare ass. Efia turned around and swung the stirring stick at him, taking care not to actually hit him. If she hit him, he'd knock her to the floor with one punch and likely take out a tooth.

The men howled with laughter and Clyde caught the hem of her thin shift again. He was like that, like a mean little boy bully. He never grew tired of the same stupid joke. He'd do it over and over again, not caring who he hurt or how much he hurt them.

"Fee, I got to go out and take a piss," Clyde said, his words obviously meant for his audience. "Think you could hold my cards for me?" He slipped his hand beneath her shift, trying to stick his cards between the cheeks of her bottom. The men burst into another round of vulgar laughter and one rocked riotously in his chair.

Clyde would have managed it had she not sidestepped his hand when she felt the cards touch her skin. "Careful," she warned, grabbing the pot. "Water's boilin' for the greens. Don't want to burn you."

Clyde slapped his hand of cards on the table and walked out the door, still laughing at his own cleverness. Efia caught a glimpse of him standing on the edge of the porch, watching his stream proudly as it arced into the darkness.

Efia had heard a rumor in town that Taye Campbell was engaged to the lawyer, Thomas Burl. A white man. Efia had herself a white man, too, but she guessed that Taye's didn't piss off the porch into her flowers, and that didn't sit right with Efia. It didn't sit right one bit.

Jackson sat in the rear of a seedy tavern on the poor side of Birmingham, Alabama, sipping a mug of homemade beer.

Jackson felt a twinge of guilt that he was here instead of in Mississippi. His duty was to be at Cameron's side while she recuperated, but she didn't want him there. That was plain enough. She had barely batted an eye when he told her he had to go. If she'd asked him to stay, or even protested, he might have sent Falcon in his place to find this

Spider Bartlett. But Cameron had said nothing. All she had done was nod and then excuse herself to see to some pressing matter with the household.

So here he was, drinking warm ale on a hot night, dressed in one of his servants' clothing. He had a two-day beard and the dust of the road on his hands and face, the taste of it in his mouth. Last night he had slept in a burned-out church, surrounded by a sea of white wooden crosses from the nearby cemetery. A couple of discreet inquiries in a blacksmith's shop and a whore house had led him here.

A black man approached his table. "I hear yer lookin' for Spider. Who you?"

Jackson caught the glint of a knife nearly hidden by the folds of the man's dirty shirt and willed his body to remain relaxed. He wore a pistol in the rear waistband of his pants, another in his boot, and could quickly reach them if he had to. "Who's askin'?"

The black man grinned. "This'll go a whole lot faster if one of us trusts the other."

Jackson calmly reached for his ale. "You're the one carrying the blade, friend." He paused. "Buy you a drink?"

The man glanced around, noted that no one was paying him any notice and slid onto the bench across from Jackson. "You don't think a free black man can do somethin' for his country, too, Captain?"

Jackson looked at him over the rim of the wooden mug. "These are dangerous times. A man has to be careful."

"A black man, even more careful." He chuckled. "Name's Spider."

"I understand, *Spider,* that you might have some information for me concerning a certain soldier."

"This certain soldier got a name?"

"Thompson."

"You lookin' to join him?"

Jackson gazed intently at the man. This was always the crux of his spymaster conversation. Sometimes he had to play from both sides to get the information he was looking for. Jackson didn't know if Spider was with Thompson or against him, but he made an educated guess. "I'm looking to stop him before he does anything stupid."

Spider shook his head, reaching for Jackson's ale. "He's got a lot of men on his side. A lot of people feedin' him and his men, hidin' 'em, helpin' 'em gather arms and munitions. Not just in Alabama, either. Mississippi and Virginia, too."

"I need to know what he intends to do with this army he's building."

Spider offered a half grin and lifted the mug to his mouth. "You go to one of his meetin's and his men talk about showin' Washington what for. They talk about restorin' honor to men's names. Settin' the government on its ear."

"Assassination attempt?"

Spider lifted a massive shoulder. "Could be, but I don't think so. Too many men. We're talkin' an army here."

Jackson studied the man across the table from him. "You think they mean to march on Washington? Or attack?"

A young man with blond hair and a wicked scar across his forehead appeared from the dingy darkness of the tavern. "Spider, we got to go," he whispered urgently, glancing behind him. "You know you can't get caught in here, talking to the likes of him. You'll be swinging by that big fat neck of yours before dawn."

Spider drained the last of the ale and slapped the mug on the table. "Thanks."

"No. Thank you." Jackson slid his hand across the table and lifted it to reveal a pile of coins.

Spider looked at the money for a long moment. "That's not the kind of man I am."

Jackson glanced at his raggedy, dirty shirt and battered shoes. "Perhaps your family—"

"My family is dead. I do this because I believe in this here government we got in Washington. 'Cause I got to." He tipped an imaginary hat. "I'll see what I can see for ya, Captain."

Jackson half rose from the table as Spider disappeared into the dark. "How will I find you?"

There was laughter. "Ah, Captain Logan, we'll find you."

22

"I won't be long," Taye assured Cameron as she stepped from the carriage. "I realize Thomas is very busy, and I simply want to stop by and see how the offices are coming."

"Take as long as you like," Cameron assured her. "Lacy and I will go down to the dress shop, and I'll send the carriage back for you."

Lacy sat beaming on the leather seat beside Cameron, visibly thrilled to be riding in a carriage.

"Oh, that won't be necessary," Taye answered quickly as she popped up her pink-and-white parasol. "I can walk. It's only a short distance."

Falcon frowned and Cameron caught his eye in understanding. "I'll send the carriage back for you, Taye." She waved. "Have a lovely time."

"Have a lovely time, Aunt Taye," Lacy mimicked, practicing her manners.

This morning Taye had listened as Cameron spent ten minutes at the breakfast table teaching the girl how to properly say good morning. Taye found the idea of Cameron instructing Lacy on manners both amusing and ironic. In their younger years, it was Cameron who had argued and fought against decorum, and Taye who had always attempted to steer her in the right direction.

Taye eyed the young girl seated beside Cameron, hoping fervently that her sister knew what she was doing with this hoyden. The child was uneducated, ill-mannered and had the temper of a bee-stung she-bear. Cameron insisted the girl truly was Grant's by-blow. Taye just hoped that her sister was correct and that she hadn't bitten off more than she could chew.

Right now, of course, Lacy was sitting beside Cameron behaving quite perfectly, hands folded in her lap as instructed. Maybe she did just need guidance, as Cameron suggested.

Taye watched the carriage pull away, still making a point to ignore Falcon. If he was going to stare at her like that right here in public, she was certainly not going to encourage him.

Adjusting her straw bonnet, edged in pink ribbon, Taye walked across boards that had been laid down for clients and opened the door to Thomas's law office. The first room was a reception area, which had been recently painted a pale peach and still smelled of wet paint. Someone was pounding nails elsewhere in the building and she could hear the steady rasp of a saw.

"Thomas?" she called.

She heard a cough and someone clearing his throat. It was him. He'd been coughing since he arrived in Jackson, and if it didn't ease soon, Taye was going to insist he see a doctor.

"There you are," she called, following a narrow hall to the room she knew would be his private office, once the rear wall, damaged by Sherman's shelling, was replaced.

Workmen had been cutting wood on the floor and she had to lift her pink petticoats to step over a pile of sawdust.

"Thomas," she called cheerfully when she spotted him near the new window. He had a guest, a dark-haired, distinguished-looking gentleman with a small mustache that barely covered his lip.

"Taye," Thomas said, wiping his mouth with his handkerchief and stuffing it into his pocket. "So kind of you to stop in."

She smiled, thinking he truly did seem pleased she was here. "I hope I'm not interrupting." She patted her new hairstyle, a delicate chignon.

"Of course not. I was expecting you. Mr. Gallier, let me introduce you to the late Senator David Campbell's daughter, Taye Campbell."

Taye froze. *The senator's daughter?* Was that how Thomas was introducing her? The senator's daughter and not his fiancée?

The gentleman reached for her hand, then halted and stared at Taye. Several uncomfortable seconds passed before he blinked and then nodded politely. "I apologize, *mademoiselle,* it is only that you remind me greatly of someone else. Someone lost to me. It is a pleasure to meet you," he said with a strong French-Creole accent.

"*Oui,* a pleasure to meet you, as well." She allowed him to kiss her gloved hand, forcing herself to continue to smile politely though her heart plummeted. Why would Thomas not introduce her as his fiancée?

"Mr. Gallier is a potential client, Taye. He knew Jackson from the war. It was kind of him to stop and see the progress on the offices, don't you think?"

Taye kept the smile plastered to her mouth. "Kind, indeed."

"Well, I must go, but I will return when next I come to Jackson, *oui, Monsieur* Burl? And we can further explore my options."

"Yes, yes, of course." Thomas pumped his hand eagerly. "I look forward to seeing you. Once you send me those files, I can begin work immediately."

Mr. Gallier bowed to Taye and replaced his bowler. *"Au revoir."*

"Well," Thomas said, clasping his hands as the Creole gentleman exited the building. "Are you having a good day?"

She studied him, hoping she had misinterpreted his earlier words. Perhaps he was just nervous about having a new client and had blundered the introduction. After all, Thomas had never been particularly adept at polite conversation. Perhaps he had realized his mistake, but simply hadn't been able to figure out how to correct it gracefully. Any of those minor breaches was forgivable. What would not be forgivable would be Thomas intentionally keeping their relationship a secret because she embarrassed him.

"I was having a nice day until I came here," Taye said, staring at her intended.

His brows knitted. "Whatever do you mean?" He rubbed his balding head with his hand, nervously.

She took a step closer to him, not wanting to share their conversation with the workmen she could hear in the office beside them. "You introduced me to Mr. Gallier as David Campbell's daughter."

"Well, yes. Most heard during the war. It's old news, Taye. I sincerely doubt anyone would—"

"You introduced me as David's daughter, but not as your fiancée."

His face pinkened immediately, and while Taye had hoped she had made a mistake, she knew by his reaction that she had not. Her heart seemed to tumble until it reached her pink slippers. "Thomas, why would you do that?"

"I...I don't know," he confessed. "It was on the tip of my tongue to say we were engaged. Truly it was." He began to cough and pulled out his handkerchief. The coughing continued for a full minute, a nasty racking cough that seemed to come from deep inside him.

She waited until the fit subsided. "But you didn't say it?" she questioned.

He squirmed, wiping the corners of his mouth. "I'm sorry, Taye. It was wrong of me. It's only that I have just returned to Jackson, and there are many here who have suffered a great deal. They are trying desperately to retain what they can of their old way of life and—"

"And they don't believe a white man should marry a negra wench?" she challenged.

"No, no, it's not that. It's just that—" Thomas hung his head. "Yes, I suppose that is it," he whispered. "I'm sorry."

He did seem remorseful, but that didn't ease the ache in Taye's chest. "You ought to be ashamed of yourself." She wanted to cry, but she bit back her tears.

"I am." He bobbed his head. "I am, Taye. It...it was an error in judgment. I do love you."

"And you still want to marry me? Because if you don't, Thomas, you should say so now." It took him a moment longer than she liked for him to answer.

"Of course I still want to marry you." He pushed his handkerchief into his trouser pocket and reached for her hand. "It's only that...it's harder than I thought it would be."

She pulled back, not wanting him to touch her. "What is harder than you thought it would be?"

He wouldn't meet her gaze. "Being here. Talking to so many people who have lost so much. I know it's wrong but...but you can see how they would blame the freed slaves for all that's happened to them.''

"But, Thomas, what does that have to do with me?" Taye demanded. "My father freed me and my mother years ago. I didn't start this war!"

"I know." Thomas shook his head sadly. "I know. Please don't be angry with me, Taye. I don't know that I could stand to have you angry with me. It's just that you're so strong and me...I'm weak," he murmured. "It's your Campbell blood, I suppose."

"No, Thomas. You're wrong. You're not a weak man." As she tried to convince him, she tried to convince herself. "Why, think of all the things you did in the war. You're a brave man. A hero."

"Jackson," he whispered. "It was all Jackson. I did it for him. I did it all with him. I've got no spine of my own."

Taye sighed, a sadness filling her. He was right. She didn't want him to be, but he was. "You were a brave man to admit to me that the color of my skin does concern you," she said softly.

"Please let me make it up to you," Thomas begged. "Don't go away angry."

Her anger was gone now, but in its place was the empty ache she knew too well. It was an ache she had hoped Thomas could fill, but realized now that he never could. "I think we should talk of this later, when we've both had time to think," she said kindly.

He bobbed his head, seeming relieved that she was going. "You're right. Of course you're right. I...I'll see you this evening. Perhaps we can go for a walk after we dine."

Taye turned and walked out of the office and he let her go. She pulled her handkerchief from her sleeve and pressed it to her damp eyes. She had been sure that marrying Thomas was what she wanted, and now she felt like a boat adrift in the sea. Halfway down the hallway, she nearly ran into Falcon.

"Oh!" Taye cried. "I didn't realize you had come inside." Her gaze met his and she realized he must have heard at least part of her conversation with Thomas. "You were listening!" she accused.

"I was waiting for you as Cameron instructed me."

Taye turned on her heels and strode through the reception area to the door, too wrought with emotion to know what to do or what to say, mortified that Falcon had heard what passed between her and her betrothed—if he was still her fiancé.

She hurried across the boardwalk.

At the carriage, Falcon grasped her around the waist and lifted her up before she could protest. She plopped down in the front seat and slid over to make room for him.

"I am sorry," he said quietly as he released the brake and urged the pair of bays forward.

"Whatever are you sorry for?" she snapped, covering her pain with anger as she had seen Cameron do so many times. "You didn't do anything wrong."

"I am sorry that in this place, a woman can be judged by the color of her skin. My people have suffered from this prejudice, as well."

Taye turned to him, and for the first time she realized that of all the people she knew, this was the one person who could truly understand her position. "Jackson said your mother was Cherokee," she said softly.

He nodded. "She is dead."

"I'm sorry."

He turned and looked at her and Taye felt as if she stumbled, fell into the dark pools.

"I believe that you are," he said and covered her hand with his.

As they rode down the street, his hand on hers on the seat between them, Taye wondered what she was going to do. She wondered just what her choices were and whether Falcon played a part in them.

Thomas stood in the empty office and stared at the door Taye had just walked through, not believing he had done that to her. How could he have been so weak, so unkind?

Taye had never been anything but good to him. She had offered her love to him on the boat that night in the Gulf of Mexico, the first woman who had ever loved him. And this was how he repaid her?

He began to cough and pulled out his handkerchief, coughing so hard that he sank into a chair in the corner of the room. It was getting worse. He had tried several concoctions from apothecaries in Baltimore, all sorts of nasty smelling and tasting droughts, but nothing seemed to ease the symptoms.

He coughed until he thought his lungs would burst, and finally the seizure ended. He patted his mouth with his handkerchief, trying to think what he would say to Taye tonight when they went for their walk.

Perhaps he should move back into his parents' home. Several rooms had been cleaned and were fit for living. Living apart from Taye would give her some time to think. He had told her he would marry her, and if that was what she wished, he would keep his promise. But now that she had seen him for the man he truly was, he hoped she would think long and hard on the proposition. And if Taye decided she would not marry him…

He glanced at the white handkerchief, now dotted with red specks of blood, balled in his hand.

Perhaps it would be for the best anyway.

* * *

Jackson nodded to the servant who had shown him into Secretary Seward's private library and then closed the door behind him.

The Secretary of State was seated near a cold fireplace, a book on his lap. The dark-paneled room seemed appropriate to Jackson; it smelled of pipe tobacco and knowledge.

"I apologize for interrupting you at home, sir," Jackson said, standing stiffly and tucking his hands behind his back. "Your personal secretary said you did not intend to go into your office in the next couple of days, and I needed to speak with you. Information came through only this morning that warrants I leave at once for Chattanooga."

"Jackson, please." Seward waved him closer. "Enough of the apologies. Mostly I remain home to pacify my wife. She fears I'm back to work too quickly." He lifted one hand. "A small inflammation in one of my wound sites. It's nothing." He gestured. "Please sit down. How can I help you? If you need to go to Chattanooga, you know we have monies and men at your disposal. You needn't ask my permission."

"Actually, sir, that's why I've come." Jackson did not sit.

"You've need of finances? Men?"

Jackson shook his head. "I need permission to work alone. Falcon Cortés has remained in Mississippi to guard my wife and—"

"Ah, I see now. We speak of Mrs. LeLaurie," he said. Seward's expression grew solemn.

Jackson stared at the expensive but well-worn oriental carpet beneath his feet. For the last week he had done nothing but debate what to do about Marie. He knew he could not see her again. It was the least he could do for Cameron. And while Jackson did not want his personal business to interfere in state business, he felt he could no longer work in close contact with Marie. It was not in his best interest, and therefore, in this case, not in the Union's best interest. If Seward wanted him to track down Thompson and his raiders, it would be on his own.

Seward reached for his pipe. "So the rumors—"

"Will." Jackson addressed the Secretary of State carefully. "My wife has recently had a miscarriage. You know how hurtful gossip can be. Rumors don't have to be true to cause injury to others."

Seward studied Jackson for a moment and then nodded. "Mrs. LeLaurie will be removed immediately from the mission."

"If you'd prefer, I can step down. I—"

"Jackson, I'll be frank." Seward pinched a bit of tobacco from a tin and pressed it into the bowl of his pipe. "You are not the first gentleman who has found Mrs. LeLaurie difficult to work with. She's an excellent operative, but she— Let's just say she enjoys making these assignments more *personal* than necessary. You are not the first man who has come to me with this concern. And although she has excellent contacts, this was one of my concerns when we accepted her offer to assist us at the very beginning of the war. Shall we say her reputation with married men *preceded* her?"

Jackson could feel the heat of embarrassment color his cheeks. He was not the only man caught in Marie's web? Somehow that made him feel better. It was no excuse, though it salved his conscience. He didn't want to hurt Marie, but better her than Cameron.

"In truth, I already have another assignment for her," Seward went on. "One she'll be far more suited to, in New Orleans, involving some brothels."

That was the first time Jackson realized Seward didn't

like Marie. Never had, apparently. With a jolt, it struck him that he hadn't liked her, either. Not really. The sex that one time had been good but... Or had it? Had he ever felt with Marie what he felt with Cameron, his wife, the woman he'd sworn before God to honor and protect with his life?

Damn, he'd been weak. He'd let need and circumstances compromise his sense of right and wrong. There was no whitewashing the truth. And no changing what had happened, only what would. No more Marie, he swore silently, and no more like her, *ever.*

Seward cleared his throat and tamped down the tobacco. "Is there anything else I can do for you, Jackson? I'm sorry to hear about your wife's ill health."

Jackson shook his head, hoping he hadn't made too much of an ass of himself. "I leave for Chattanooga within a day or two." He took a step back, feeling as if a great weight had been lifted from his shoulders. "Thank you for seeing me, sir."

"I'll contact Mrs. LeLaurie and make her aware of the change in plans."

"No," Jackson said. "I...I need to speak with her myself. If it's all right with you, of course, Mr. Secretary. I'll tell her of the change of assignment and let her know that she can see you for the details of her new mission."

"Take care of yourself," Seward offered as Jackson backed out of the library. "And take care of that wife of yours. I only had the pleasure of meeting her once, but I knew her father and I know what mettle the Campbells are made of. She is a beautiful woman, and intelligent. A man would be fortunate to have such a woman at his side."

"Thank you, sir. I agree with you. I am very fortunate to have her. Good night." Jackson closed the door behind him. Now that this was done, he was anxious to see Marie and put an end to whatever it was they'd had. Perhaps then he could go back to Cameron and make amends.

If it was still possible.

"Jackson, love." Marie swept into his private study on the first floor of his Baltimore mansion.

She was as stunning as always, dressed to attend the opera in a pale gold silk gown that bared her shoulders and most of her lovely breasts. A headdress of tiny feathers and golden beads adorned her ebony hair. She was a goddess from an ancient civilization, come to walk the earth for a single night. "I came as quickly as I could when I received your message."

Jackson looked beyond Marie to Addy, who had shown his guest in and was now standing in the doorway scowling, her loyalty to her mistress plain on her face. It was obvious to Jackson that Cameron had earned the devotion of his staff in his absence. Cameron had told him that this house wasn't her home. Hell, apparently it wasn't his anymore, either.

"You may go, Addy," Jackson said.

She backed up, pulling the brass doorknob.

"But leave the door open," he called.

Addy made a point of pushing the door fully open again, all the time scowling at Marie.

"Heavens," she huffed. "These negroes have certainly gotten on their high horses since this Thirteenth Amendment was introduced in Congress, haven't they? The next thing you know, they'll be saying it gives them the right to vote!"

Jackson rose from behind his desk, studying Marie's beautiful face. Looking at her now, he saw a hardness he had not seen before. Had it always been there?

"I'm sorry to disturb your evening. I know you're bound for the opera," he said stiffly.

"For you, Jackson," she purred, "I would walk through the dry desert. Climb the steepest—"

"Marie," he interrupted, not in the mood for her manipulations. "This won't take but a moment." He did not come around the desk to greet her as would have been proper. He didn't know if it was because he feared he might still find her willing body tempting, or because suddenly she disgusted him.

How could he have been so foolish as to think that she had ever loved him? During the war, when she had been proclaiming her love for him on those lonely nights when they had hidden in abandoned homes and barn lofts, she had been telling other men precisely the same thing. How could he have been such an idiot? Hadn't he left her years ago because she had shared her *affections* with another man while still proclaiming her devotion to him?

"Has there been word of Thompson?" she asked, watching him carefully. She seemed surprised by his tone, unsure of what to make of him. "I can be ready within two hours."

"Marie, you've been assigned elsewhere." He glanced at the paperwork spread across the mahogany desk that had been his father's before him.

"Reassigned?" She pursed her red lips in a seductive pout. "Whatever do you mean, Jackson?"

"My words seem self-explanatory. I will continue to investigate Thompson's Raiders. Secretary of State Seward has a new assignment for you."

"He can't reassign me." She started to walk around the desk to him. "I'll simply tell *Mr. Secretary* that—"

"Marie. This wasn't Seward's idea. It was mine."

She halted, her dark eyes widening. "What?"

"I told Seward I didn't want to work with you any more."

"Oh, heavens, Jackson, don't tell me your wife—"

"Leave my wife out of this," he snapped, anger building in the pit of his stomach. "I don't want to work with you any longer because I find I cannot stand the sight of you."

She drew back, a flicker of pain in her dark eyes, but then her face hardened. "You cannot do this," she whispered under her breath. "Men do not cast aside Marie LeLaurie."

"No? Then, consider this a first, Marie. I'm leaving Baltimore tomorrow. I don't know when I'll be back." He glanced around the book-lined study. "I don't know that I'll be returning at all."

"Now wait one moment, Captain Jackson Logan," Marie snapped. "I will not stand for this kind of treatment from you." She grabbed the pressed black lapels of his evening coat. "We're not done until I say we're done, and if you don't come to your senses, I'll—"

"You'll what?" he demanded icily as he closed his hands over hers and forcibly removed them from his coat.

"I'll tell your wife," she threatened.

Jackson had known when he called Marie here tonight that she might say that. But surely she wouldn't travel all the way to Mississippi to speak to Cameron. From what Seward had said, Jackson gathered Marie had other married men to pursue.

"You'd better not," Jackson cautioned, meeting her gaze.

"Or what?" she challenged in a shriek. "What will you do?"

He walked away from her, headed for the door. "It's not me you have to fear," he said, strolling out of the study. "It's Cameron Campbell. Addy," he called. "Please show Mrs. LeLaurie out."

23

"We saw Efia in town today," Cameron told Taye.

Taye looked up from the book of Longfellow poems she was reading. She had reread the same page three times. "Did you?"

"She asked about you." Cameron sat on a chair with Lacy in front of her on a footstool. She was attempting to brush the months of tangles from the girl's wild red-blond tresses.

"That was kind of her." Taye smiled, only half listening to Cameron.

Thomas had sent a message late in the afternoon that he would be unable to return in time to join the women for supper. A pressing business matter, he explained, before apologizing profusely. What truly upset Taye was that she was not terribly disappointed. Guilt had set her nerves on edge. She didn't want to be unkind or ungrateful. She truly wanted to be the person her mother had raised her to be, but inside she was fighting to become her true self. She just wasn't sure yet who that was.

To add to her discomfort, while Thomas had been unable to attend supper, Falcon had been pleased to join them. He came wearing a red flannel suit coat with shiny silver buttons that would have looked ridiculous on any other man, and yet on him, was strikingly handsome.

After behaving like the Southern gentleman Taye knew he was not, escorting the women to the dining room and pulling out their chairs for them, he had entertained Cameron and Lacy with tales of the West where he had ridden with herds of buffalo and climbed cliff walls of ancient dwelling homes built by Indians long gone.

Falcon was confident, self-assured and, she realized, actually amusing when he so chose. He seemed to feel passionately about the adventures he related and his enthusiasm was contagious. No matter how hard Taye tried to ignore the man, when he spoke, she could not help but be riveted to every syllable. When he described them, she could not help but feel the dry desert sand beneath her bare feet or hear the pounding of the buffalo herds' hooves as they rounded the crest of a hill.

And when his dark-eyed gaze met hers across the table, she could not smother the fire that he kindled inside her. Just a glance, a word from him, and Taye's insides crackled with an unidentifiable energy. She could barely sit still, fidgeting more than Lacy did. She could barely eat. All she could think about were the kisses she and Falcon had shared and the feel of his hand on hers in the carriage today. He had been understanding and comforting without being judgmental and she couldn't help but appreciate the kindness he had offered.

Taye dragged her thoughts away from Falcon to focus on what Cameron was saying. She was chattering on happily, and Taye was glad to see that with each passing day, she was becoming more herself again. "It was really rather odd," Cameron was saying. "Efia asked about Thomas, when you would be marrying and where you would be living."

"I'm sure she was just curious." Taye forced a smile. "Would you like me to try a hand at Lacy's hair?" she asked, changing the subject.

"No!" Lacy rose off the stool with the comb caught in her hair, her hazel eyes suddenly round and wild. "Cameron will do it."

"All right." Taye lifted her hands, speaking softly. "It's all right, Lacy. I was just offering to help, that's all. Cameron can do it and I'll watch."

"Sit down," Cameron gently told Lacy, pressing her hand on the girl's shoulder. "Else I'll rip the hair right out of your head."

Lacy eyed Taye cautiously, but eased down onto the stool again.

Lacy did not seem to be any more fearful of Taye than any of the other women in the household, but she definitely felt an affinity with Cameron. The men in the house, however, were a different story. It was obvious that she greatly distrusted men. When Jackson had attempted to help her down from their carriage upon their arrival at Atkins' Way, she'd tried to bite him. It had taken Cameron, Naomi and Taye and a stick of hard candy to get the girl out from under the carriage seat where she'd retreated when Jackson set her free.

Taye recognized immediately that the young girl, whoever she was, had probably been abused by men, and she was not upset by Lacy's distrust of her. It was only natural that Lacy would attach herself to Cameron because she had found her. And Taye couldn't help feeling that that was just what Cameron needed right now.

"I think I'm going to bed, Longfellow and I." Taye closed the book and rose. "See you in the morning." She looked to Lacy. "And young lady, you and I will meet after breakfast to begin your first lesson in reading."

Lacy's opened her mouth to protest.

"Now, now," Taye said kindly, but firmly. "We can sit at a table right in the study while Cameron works. You'll be able to reach out and touch her. But schooling you need—" she waggled a finger "—and schooling you will have." She smiled. "And let me tell you, you would prefer my methods to hers." She hooked a thumb in Cameron's direction. "She has no patience whatsoever. She's a terrible teacher."

Cameron laughed, pulling the comb through a single smooth lock of the girl's clean hair. "She's right about that, Lacy."

Lacy offered a tentative smile. "Thank you. Good night… Aunt Taye."

"Good night, sweetheart." Taye blew Cameron a kiss, and with her book tucked under her arm, she walked upstairs.

Taye had nearly reached her room when she felt a hand touch her shoulder from behind.

She nearly jumped out of her skin. "Oh," she cried, half fearing it was one of Naomi's lost souls haunting the hall. She clutched Longfellow to her breast. "Falcon, you scared me half to death." She could feel her heart pounding in her chest.

"I am sorry."

"You shouldn't sneak up on people like that," she chastised, hugging her book.

"I did not sneak up. I only wanted to ask you how you were feeling." He stood in front of her, studying her, not allowing her to break eye contact, no matter how badly she wanted to. "He did not come home."

"It's all right. I understand. He—" She felt herself tremble. She didn't know if it was the emotion of the day, or just having Falcon so near. She was so confused. Confused by her feelings for Thomas and her feelings for this man she barely knew, whom she dreamed of at night.

He took her hand in his warm one and she immediately calmed. She watched, mesmerized, as he lifted it to his mouth and kissed the pad of each finger. With each kiss, a spark of pleasure rushed through her hand, up her arm, to her torso. By the third finger, he had lit a fire in the pit of her belly.

Taye trembled. She didn't understand. How could a man make her feel this way with a mere touch of his lips to a finger?

Falcon finished with her thumb and then brought her hand to his face. Lost in the depths of his ebony eyes, she found herself stroking his shaven cheek, reveling in the feel of his warmth at her touch.

He guided her fingers across his cheek to his chin and up to his sensuous lips. She found herself brushing his lips with her fingertips, recalling the feel of them on her own mouth.

It seemed only natural that he would lean into her, that she would tilt her head, lift her chin, so that his lips could brush hers. She stroked his chin as his kiss deepened and a tiny sigh escaped from her parted lips.

Taye felt her body tense in sweet anticipation as Falcon encircled her in his arms, cradled her in his warmth and strength. When she felt his hand on her waist, she didn't pull away. Nothing mattered but the taste of him. She couldn't get enough. Then, before she could think, before she could stop him, he brought his hand up beneath her breast.

A sound caught in her throat. It was meant to be a protest, but it came out as something else. A sigh…a moan.

Even through the fabric of her gown and underclothes she could feel the warmth of his hand on her breast. She felt her nipple harden, and suddenly the soft silk of her chemise felt like rough old wool against her bare flesh.

He only cupped her breast, stroked it through her gown for a moment before releasing her.

But she wanted more.

Taye dropped her chin, feeling the heat of embarrassment cross her cheeks. Or was it something else, this molten fire pulsing through her?

She didn't know what to say. All she knew was that if she didn't get away from Falcon this very moment, she'd follow him into his room. And then she didn't know what she might do, caught in his spell as she was now.

"Taye," he whispered, and somehow her name sounded like something exotic. Something beloved.

She raised her hand to stop him. "Please. Don't say anything," she whispered. "Not tonight." Then, still clutching her book, she slipped into her room and closed the door behind her, throwing the lock.

For several minutes Taye stood with her back pressed to the door, her eyes closed as she waited for her heartbeat to slow. She listened to the sound of Falcon's steady breathing on the other side of the door. Then she heard his footsteps.

Only once they had died away did she allow herself to open her eyes. "Oh, heavens," she breathed. "What am I doing?"

She flung her book on a side table and walked to the far side of the room where she poured herself a glass of cool water, left in a pitcher by Patsy. It was almost dark outside now, the room heavy with shadows. And it was so hot, hotter than it had been earlier.

Taye finished the glass of water and kicked off her shoes. She stripped off her stockings and then unbuttoned the front of her day gown. She dropped the dress and the constricting corset to the floor in a pile. It was unlike her to make such a mess, but she still couldn't catch her breath. The heat, of course. She needed to be rid of the heavy clothing.

At last, in nothing but her thin, silk shift, she lay out on her bed, on top of the coverlet. The house was quiet. Outside she could hear frogs croaking and the faint call of a night bird.

Taye squeezed her eyes shut, trying to block out the taste of Falcon's mouth on hers. The feel of his hands.

Without realizing what she was doing, she slid her own hand over her breast, imagining it was his. She was shocked to discover that her nipple was still hard from his touch. She brushed her fingertips over the soft flesh and was surprised by the ripple of pleasure that immediately stirred inside her.

She had never felt this way before. Never touched herself before. What had the Cherokee awakened in her?

Taye caressed her other breast gently, then with more purpose. Little ripples of warmth washed over her. Realizing that the source of the pleasure seemed to come from her nipple, she touched it, apprehensively at first, then again. She brushed the hard tip with the pad of her thumb in fascination.

Another ripple of pleasure. Stronger.

Taye closed her eyes and parted her lips, breathing deeply. Her pulse had quickened. Her heart was beating faster, though she lay perfectly still in the darkness.

She lifted her other hand and touched both breasts at the same time. More ripples, ripples that seemed to radiate downward.

Taye's breath became shallow as she slid her hands over her flat stomach with nothing between flesh and flesh but the silk chemise that now clung to her damp, perspiring skin.

Something told her she should stop. She knew she

shouldn't awake these feelings, yet she couldn't help herself.

Taye felt her hand, almost of its own accord, glide lower. She gasped as she brushed the apex of her thighs. She had never realized such feelings could come from *there*.

Using one finger, she boldly outlined the soft flesh of her sex beneath her chemise. With every brush of her fingertip, her pleasure amplified. Her breathing increased.

Suddenly Taye felt as if she were on a mission. She didn't quite know what she was seeking, or how she would reach it, but it was there, just a step or two away.

Taye slid her hand lower to her thighs and slowly lifted her gown. The silk stuck to her damp skin and bunched at her waist.

Her own breath ragged in her ears, she brushed her fingertips across her inner thigh to the source of her pleasure. She nearly moaned aloud and had to bite down on her lip to prevent any sound from escaping.

She let her fingers glide rhythmically over the velvety flesh. She could feel herself growing wet there, softer, more pliable. She felt flushed with the heat. The night air seemed to fill with an odd, but not unpleasant, scent of her dampness.

Taye pressed her lips tightly together and moaned. Without quite understanding why, she moved her hand faster, massaging more deeply.

She couldn't stop now, not even if she wanted to.

She rubbed harder, lifting her hips, moving to the rhythm of her fingertips. Then suddenly, without warning, her sex seemed to burst with unexpected, intense pleasure.

"Oh," she moaned, shocked by what her body had done. She ceased the movement of her hand, now wet, and let it fall to the bed. ''Oh,'' she breathed. ''Oh, goodness.'' Her pulse was beginning to slow to a more normal pace.

Suddenly tired beyond reason, she rolled onto her side and drifted off to sleep with thoughts of a dark-skinned man with a gentle smile and magical hands.

24

Taye waited at the bottom of the grand staircase, the rhythmic ticking of the six-foot-tall cherry grandfather clock matching her heartbeats as she watched for Thomas. She felt foolish walking on tiptoe and hiding behind the stairwell as if she were a thief in the night, but if she wanted to speak with him privately, this was the only way—short of holding him hostage in his law office.

For the last two weeks, at precisely eight every morning, he had walked down the staircase and out the door without speaking to anyone. He rode straight to his law offices, and there he remained until well past supper time. When he did see Taye, no doubt by accident, he always spoke politely, inquired as to her health, but he never crossed the line into anything even remotely personal. He did not mention the incident in his office with Mr. Gallier.

In the first days after their confrontation, Taye thought Thomas just needed some time to think. But more than a week had passed and she was tired of waiting for him to initiate the conversation. If he wasn't going to do it, she would.

Taye heard him cough upstairs, then his light, precise footsteps sounded in the upper hall. She nibbled on her lower lip. Just before he reached the bottom of the staircase, she stepped out of her hiding place.

"Taye?" Thomas jumped and then looked so surprised to see her that, for a moment, she feared he'd run back up the stairs.

"Thomas." She smiled, trying to calm him. "Good morning. I was wondering if you had a few minutes. I could get you something for breakfast."

"No, no, thank you. That...that's very kind of you," he stammered, his Adam's apple bobbing, "but I'm not terribly hungry."

"A cup of coffee, perhaps. Tea?"

He shook his head, his gaze shifting to the front door. She knew he was trying to figure out how to reach it and escape from her. "No, thank you. I really should be getting to my offices. I have a new client coming at nine and I must be thoroughly prepared."

Taye was tempted to step aside and let him go. She had no right to interfere in his business; she shouldn't be worrying him further. He was already so tired that he was beginning to look sallow and thin. "Thomas," she said gently, but firmly, grasping his arm to prevent him from getting away. "This will only take a minute, but we truly *do* need to speak." She studied his face and waited.

At last, he reluctantly shifted his solemn brown-eyed gaze to meet hers. "I suppose we do, don't we?" he agreed softly.

She nodded. "Why don't I walk with you to the barn? These days this house seems to have ears." She smiled. "I don't know how Lacy does it, but she knows what's happening in everyone's life within a two-mile radius of this house, from mine and Cameron's, right down to the old lady from J Town who delivers eggs twice a week."

Side by side, they walked out the front door and followed

the path that led to the stables. Though it was only eight in the morning, the scorching heat of the August sun beat down on them and Taye wished she had worn her bonnet. "We've both had some time to think and I was just wondering—" Suddenly she didn't know how to say what she needed to say. She wasn't even truly sure she wanted to know the answer. She exhaled and started again. "I was wondering if you had rethought our...original intentions."

His apprehensive gaze flickered to hers and then away. "You're having second thoughts and I understand that," he replied quickly.

She was surprised by his response. Surely he wasn't going to put this all on her? He was the one who had admitted to denying her in front of a client because her heritage embarrassed him. "We're not talking about what *I* want right now, Thomas. We're talking about what *you* want."

If Thomas would have declared his undying love for her at that moment, Taye had made the promise to herself that she would do everything in her power to make him happy. She would make their relationship work because he was a good man and because it would have pleased her father. She would have made herself and Thomas content because it would please Cameron whom she loved so dearly.

But Thomas did not answer immediately, and she felt her throat constrict, knowing her fears had not been unfounded. The idea made her sad. At the same time she felt a sense of relief. "Thomas," she said softly.

"I think we should both take some more time," he hedged. He pulled his handkerchief from his coat and pressed it to his sweaty forehead. "I intended to tell you today that I would be moving back into my family's home. It...it's now presentable." He wiped his mouth with the starched white fabric. "I will, of course, still see you when I have the time."

He looked so pitiful that she couldn't selfishly force him into a decision this moment that would affect them both for the rest of their lives.

She lowered her head. "All right. If that's what you think is best. We... We'll take a little more time."

"Now that that has been settled—" he tucked the handkerchief away, looking immensely relieved "—I had best be on my way."

"Thomas, wait." She grabbed his coat sleeve. "Have you seen a surgeon about that cough?"

"I have indeed, and he says it's nothing to concern myself with. Change in the climate is all." He gave a quick smile. "I must be off. Have a good day, dear." He made no move to kiss her goodbye, as he once would have. Not her cheek, not even her hand.

She stood in the stark, bright sunlight and watched Thomas disappear into the barn, wishing she were anywhere but here.

"What the hell you doin' woman, makin' all that damned blessed noise!" Clyde jerked the curtain aside and climbed out of bed, hitching up his britches.

"I'm sorry," Efia said, lowering her head submissively. "I jest thought ya might want a nice breakfast." She turned the bacon in the frying pan over with a fork. Hot grease spat and burned her hand. She jerked it back, sucking on her thumb. "I got fresh eggs and bacon, and I saved ya a biscuit from last night." She offered a smile. "Why don't ya sit yourself down and let me pour ya some coffee?" She walked to the table, fork still in hand, and pulled out one of the chairs invitingly.

Clyde eyed her as he plopped down in the chair and pulled up one drooping suspender over his bare chest. "What's gotten into ya, Fee?"

"Nuthin'." She poured a cup of thick, black coffee at the stove and carried it to him, taking care not to slosh it on the table. He hated it when she spilled coffee. "And here's yer sugar." She slid a small paper bag with a spoon in it across the table to him.

Going back to the stove, Efia fished the three fat strips of bacon out of the pan and placed them on a plate that was painted with purple flowers. Stolen, of course, but she liked it anyway. She deftly broke four eggs into the pan and the grease spat up again.

At the table Clyde dumped a third spoonful of sugar into his coffee, slurped off the spoon loudly and dug for more sugar. "Where's the boys?" He glanced around.

"Gone fishin' down to the river. They wanted to wake ya, but I said let ya sleep. I know ya must be tired, stayin' out so late at night."

Clyde brought the spoon down hard on the table, making her jump in her skin. "What's that 'sposed to mean? Huh? It's none yer friggin' business where I go at night."

"I was jest sayin' ya looked tired last night." She flipped each egg, careful not to break the yolk. "That's all."

He eyed her and took a long noisy slurp of the coffee.

When the eggs were cooked, with the yolk still runny the way Clyde liked, she slid them carefully onto the plate beside the bacon. Adding the biscuit, she walked the breakfast to the table and placed it and a fork before him.

"Salt."

She ran to the shelf over the kitchen and snatched up a saltcellar.

"More coffee."

She went back to the stove, picked up the coffeepot and refilled his cup. Then she stood back and watched while he slurped runny eggs off his plate and mopped up yolk with the baking powder biscuit. He belched loudly and reached for his coffee.

"I was thinkin', Clyde," she said, hoping she had chosen her time carefully.

"Uh-huh?"

"I have to go to town to get something, and I was wonderin'—" She paused, thinking she didn't want to get slapped; maybe she should keep her mouth shut. But she wanted that hat so bad. "I...I was wonderin' if maybe ya had a couple cents for me, bein' as how I washed all them boys' clothes and made them all them meals and they're payin' you to—"

"What the hell ya jabberin' 'bout?" Clyde spun around in his chair, staring at her. "Ya askin' me for money?"

She nodded.

He jumped out of his chair, slamming it back so that it tipped, hitting the floor.

Efia flinched, but she didn't move. Clyde loved to bully a person, but if they stood up to him, sometimes they got what they wanted. "I need twenty-two cents," she said bravely. "I got the rest saved up myself."

He walked up to her, pressing his nose to hers, breathing his sour breath in her face. "Ya need twenty-two cents for what?"

"A hat." She set her jaw. "A blue hat."

"Hell, you don't need no blue hat, Fee." He shoved her back, but not so hard that she hit the stove. "Yer pretty already. Ya don't need no hat." His bitch hound wandered in the open door. He walked over to her and crouched down to scratch her behind her ears.

"But I want the hat," she said softly, staring at his back, wishing she had the nerve to grab that butcher knife off the shelf and plunge it into his back.

"I said you ain't getting no twenty-two cents, and ya

ain't gettin' no hat. No, she ain't, is she?'' Clyde crooned
to the dog. "Now get that bacon grease cooled down and
let Sally here lap it up. 'Cause she's a good girl, ain't she?''
he said to the dog.

He talked nicer to the dog than he talked to her.

Efia turned her back and grabbed the frying pan with a
piece of rag to keep from burning herself. She wanted to
whack Clyde in the head with it. Instead, she carried it out
to the front porch to cool on the rail. She said no more
about the blue hat, but she thought about it. She thought
about it hard and imagined herself riding in a fancy fringed
buggy, wearing that hat.

"No!" Cameron heard Lacy squeal from down the hall.

"Cameron," Naomi shouted. "Cameron, you best git
this naked girl before I take a switch to her lily-white bottom!''

Cameron marched down the hall in her stocking feet,
smoothing the light fabric of her foulard Garibaldi bodice.
She was trying to get dressed so that she could give Lacy
her riding lesson, but she'd already been interrupted twice.
First Patsy had wanted to strip her bed to wash the linens,
then Taye had stopped by to ask about hiring two more
bricklayers for the kitchen addition at Elmwood.

Taye had volunteered to oversee all the new employees,
and Cameron had thankfully turned over the task. Between
rebuilding Elmwood and trying to manage Lacy, it was
good to have Taye's sturdy shoulders to pass some of the
responsibility to.

"Miss Cameron!" Naomi bellowed again. "You hear
me callin' ya? I ain't got time for this nonsense."

"What in heaven's name is going on here?" Cameron
strode over the threshold of Lacy's room just in time to see
the girl rip a dress from Naomi's hand and scramble up

onto the bed. There, she balanced herself, arms spread wide, ready to spring like a wildcat if anyone moved toward her.

"Tell her," Naomi insisted, speaking to Cameron as she shook her finger at Lacy. "Tell her that young ladies wash under their armpits in this household *every* morning, else they don't put on their new dresses."

"Lacy, apologize at once for snatching that dress from Naomi's hand." Cameron's voice was calm.

"It's mine," Lacy said stubbornly. "Ya gave it to me."

"I don't care. I will not have you treat Naomi this way. Now apologize or I'll take a pair of scissors to that gown here and now."

Lacy seemed to consider whether or not Cameron would do it, before finally uttering a hasty "Sorry."

Cameron sighed. "I'll take care of this, Naomi. Thank you."

"Captain done tole you this was a bad idea," Naomi muttered under her breath as she ducked past Cameron and went out the door. "Ain't no way that wild thing could ever be a Campbell."

"What did you say, Naomi?" Cameron glanced down the hall. "Were you speaking to me?"

"'Course not," Naomi answered haughtily. "But it wouldn't matter if I was, 'cause you wouldn't listen."

Cameron rolled her eyes as she stepped back into the bedroom. In many ways, Naomi ruled this house, and everyone knew it, including Cameron. She needed Naomi to run Atkins' Way and care for the household Jackson had sent from Baltimore, plus the people who were already here. And the huge household of servants and workers seemed to be increasing every week because Cameron found it too hard to turn away hungry people who were willing to work for food and shelter. No, Cameron couldn't afford to anger Naomi.

"Lacy! Please get off that bed," Cameron ordered, knowing she had to be patient with her young charge. "Young ladies do not stand on top of a bed in nothing but their chemises—" Cameron blinked, shocked "—and where are your drawers, young lady?"

The way the sunlight poured in through the open windows, one couldn't help but see that the hoyden wore nothing beneath the thin silk undergarment but what God had given her.

"They ain't no need—"

Cameron sent Lacy such a look that the girl started again. "There is not a need," Lacy said, lifting her eyebrows haughtily as she corrected her speech, "for anyone to wear long underdrawers when it's this hot."

Cameron spread her arms wide in exasperation. "But I can see Christmas!"

To Cameron's surprise, instead of throwing one of her temper tantrums, Lacy fell onto the bed in laughter. "See Christmas!" She kicked her legs, laughing wildly. "See Christmas. You're funny, Aunt Cammy. You're real funny."

Lacy's laughter was contagious. It was so good to hear someone laugh in the house. "*Very* funny," Cameron corrected, chuckling as she walked to the bed and plopped down beside her charge.

Lacy rolled onto her back, still clutching the new yellow sprigged gown Cameron had had made for her. "You're *very* funny," she mimicked obediently. "I like you."

Cameron's gaze fell to Lacy's as the young girl stared up at her aunt. Smiling, Cameron tucked a lock of bright red hair behind her niece's ear, touched by her simple words. "And I like you, Lacy," she said softly.

Lacy turned onto her stomach and propped herself on her elbows, suddenly deep in thought. "Ya do?" She looked up at Cameron, her bright hair falling around her like a curtain of spun gold. "Honest to Moses?"

The tears that welled in her eyes surprised Cameron. Lacy reminded her of herself, years ago. Bright, inquisitive, ready to conquer the world and have everyone at her beck and call. Once Cameron had wanted to have it all—wealth, respect, admiration. Now all she wished for was the one person she feared she would never have again.

"Now wash at the basin and dress." Cameron rose from the bed. "And you can leave your drawers if you like, but I'll warn you, you'll not be terribly comfortable when riding astride." She halted in the doorway and looked back at Lacy who had dutifully climbed off the bed to go to the washstand. "Trust me. I've tried it."

"I don't understand why I can't go to town alone," Taye said in exasperation as she moved over on the carriage seat and made room for Falcon. Did the man have eyes in the back of his head? She had just wanted to sneak away for an hour and go to town to visit Mrs. Pierre and her daughter.

Falcon grinned. "You know why I cannot allow you to go alone. My friend has trusted you to my care."

Taye tried to keep her shoulders still as the carriage lurched forward so that she would not have to brush against Falcon's broad shoulder. "You could send one of the men. It's really not necessary that you come every time I go to town. You've already made it quite clear to every man, woman and child you meet that I'm to be treated with kidskin gloves. Heavens, everyone is afraid to say boo to me."

Falcon eased the carriage onto the road and slapped the reins so that the horses' manes danced in the warm breeze.

"I know that I could send another, but I do not want to."
He glanced sideways at her. "I want to escort you because
I want to sit at your side. I want to hear your voice in my
ear and smell the scent of your hair."

His words made her warm under her collar; she ignored
them. "You mean to tell me you enjoy following me from
shop to shop, carrying my bags?" She adjusted her blue
leghorn bonnet, smoothing the white curtain that fell over
her dark hair in the back.

He eyed her again. "I would carry *you* from shop to shop
if you asked me."

Taye laughed at the idea of the big Cherokee carrying
her in his arms from the ribbon shop to the grocer and then
down to the bank.

He lifted a dark eyebrow, obviously not understanding
what was so amusing.

"I'm sorry," she chuckled, pressing a fingerless lace
glove to her bodice. "I don't mean to laugh at *you*, Fal=
con." She brushed her hand against his arm as if it were
the most natural thing, and from the look on his face, her
innocent touch did not go unnoticed.

She looked shyly away, but left her fingertips on his arm.
Something was happening between them, something she
could feel far better than she could explain. With each day
that passed, Taye had felt further from Thomas...and closer
to Falcon.

At first, she had tried to tell herself that these feelings
were only natural. Thomas, her supposed intended, had
slighted her. It was only normal to lay one's attentions on
a man who seemed interested. But it went deeper than that.
This man beside her was beginning to fill a deep need that
she had not even realized existed.

Falcon was actively pursuing her, but not any way that
she was familiar with. He rarely paid her compliments on

her musical ability or her adeptness at playing cards. He
was not interested in the books she read or the languages
she was fluent in. There were no silly flirtations behind
fans, no slightly risqué innuendoes. He spoke very little
compared to most courting men, but when he did, his words
were alarmingly honest and always from his heart. He gave
her gifts, but not perfumed soaps or sheet music. One night
he left a beautiful red feather on her pillow, another time
a shiny black stone.

Falcon Cortés was nothing she had thought she'd wanted
in a man. And yet, he was everything.

"Whatcha gawkin' at?" Clyde barked to Efia. "Get yer
black ass in this wagon afore I leave you behind!"

Efia stood frozen at the hitching post, watching as Taye
Campbell rode by in her pretty fringed buggy, that handsome redskin driving her wherever she wanted to go. She
was wearing the blue bonnet! Efia's blue bonnet! The one
she had seen in the window!

Hot, stinging tears filled her eyes. She wiped at them in
anger as she longingly watched the carriage roll by.

Taye looked like she thought she was queen of the ball,
holding her head high, with that blue bonnet on her head,
like she was better than Efia.

"Ya know her?" Clyde asked, noticing Taye. "Right
pretty piece of ass, ain't she?"

Efia dashed at her tears again, grabbed the side of the
buckboard and hauled herself up. If she waited for Clyde
to help her, it would be a cold day in hell. "I know 'er, all
right. Uppity bitch," she snarled. "You do, too. You'd
know that if ya had a head, ya stupid cracker."

He spun around to slap her but she ducked and he
missed. She knew she was headed for a whoopin'; she'd
been sassy with him all day, but she didn't care. "That's

Taye Campbell, the half darkie Senator Campbell whelped on his housekeeper."

"I'll be damned," Clyde remarked, watching her go by. "And jest how do ya know her so well? She don't 'zactly look like the kind of gal that travels yer road."

Efia sighed as she leaned against the buckboard's seat. "I tole you this, remember? She helped me and my sister. We was on a boat. We walked from Biloxi to Jackson." She thought about their return to Elmwood, about what had happened. She narrowed her eyes. "Then we walked from all the way to Maryland, me, Cameron Campbell and her." She gave a snort. "God knows, I ought to know 'er. Slept beside 'er many a night."

Efia eyed Taye across the street, just stepping down from the carriage with the help of the Indian. The blue bonnet matched her eyes almost perfectly and it made Efia sick.

If only that cheap bastard Clyde have given her that money, she'd be the one wearing that bonnet to town instead of Taye. "Yes, sa', I know a thing or two 'bout Miss Taye that others be shocked to hear," she muttered.

"You sure this is where they're supposed to be?" the man beside Jackson whispered, his pipe glowing red as he inhaled.

Jackson slid his rifle over his arm, adjusting its weight on his shoulder. He stared into the darkness at the warehouse across the street. It was guarded by two Union soldiers, a private and a sergeant. The sergeant had gone off to use the latrine half an hour ago and hadn't been seen since. The private was busy trying to build a house of cards on a barrel, by the light of a single lantern.

The lone eighteen-year-old didn't know it, but he was guarding a storehouse of ammunition waiting to be shipped back to New York. Inside were enough explosives to burn

Atlanta again. What it was doing in Tennessee, no one seemed quite sure of. After receiving word from Spider that the Tennessee warehouse had been targeted by Thompson's men, it had taken Jackson three days to find someone in the Union Army who knew what was in the warehouse. Once that had been established, it had taken another three days and a stack of paperwork for someone else with enough authority to order the transport of the army supplies north to safer grounds. The train was due in the following morning. With any luck, Thompson's Raiders wouldn't make it in time. However, what were the chances that they weren't aware of the scheduled morning transport, too?

Jackson was laying bets that Thompson's men would be here tonight. If they came, he was hoping to get lucky. Men arrested for treason were often willing to talk, even to give up their commanding officer to avoid hanging from a noose or rotting in a military jail.

"Ain't nobody coming, boss," the man behind him, a lieutenant, complained. "We've been out here more than four hours and—"

"Shh," Jackson hissed, a sound on the street catching his attention. "Put out the pipe."

The young officer on loan to Jackson did as he was ordered, but it was obvious he found his night duty with a civilian a wasted night's sleep. He tapped the bowl on his heel, making a soft clicking sound.

Jackson stared into the black night, wiping the sweat from his upper lip. His gaze flitted from each post where his men were hidden. He prayed they were all awake, their weapons in hand because he knew in the pit of his stomach that this was it.

A horse nickered in the street. The sound of hoof beats muffled by rags tied to the animal's feet echoed in his head. In his mind's eye, Jackson could see the wheels of the approaching wagons turning. Still seeing nothing, but almost certain he caught the scent of unwashed bodies on the humid, hot night air, he slid his rifle to his shoulder.

The only light on the street was that of the private's lantern. He was working on the second story of his card house.

Jackson was concerned about the private. He had originally attempted to replace the guards on the warehouse with his own men, but then had discovered that some of the local soldiers were likely in on the theft, either by working directly for Thompson or by simply being paid off. He hadn't been able to risk word getting to Thompson that he was onto him. The sergeant's mysterious disappearance seemed to suggest he was the one in on it, which meant the private might not be. Jackson only hoped that when the time came, he could reach the boy before Thompson's men did.

Out of the corner of his eyes, Jackson saw the first wagon approaching from an alley. Behind it, he thought he saw a second vehicle. Before he realized what was happening, a man stepped out of the darkness that surrounded the barred warehouse doors and walked into the lantern light.

The private's house of cards fell as he whipped around. His attacker reached out, drawing a glimmering steel blade against his neck. The cards fluttered to the ground like rainfall as the young man's body slumped into the dirt. Jackson gave a whistle and his men charged from all corners of the darkness. It was sooner than he would have liked to attack, but he would have no more senseless deaths if he could help it.

Shots rang out from both sides, filling the night air with streaks of light and acrid smoke. The men on the wagons, many dressed in ragged gray uniforms, abandoned the vehicles and took off on foot, firing over their shoulders.

"I want as many alive as possible," Jackson shouted as

he rushed across the street to the private crumpled on the ground. Shots fired around him, ricocheting off of the warehouse, as he went down on one knee to feel for a pulse. There was none.

Jackson rose up, swinging his rifle around to bead in on a man who had darted between the wall of the warehouse and an abandoned building. "Drop to your knees and I won't shoot," he ordered.

"Long live Thompson's Raiders," the man cried, taking off.

Jackson lowered his rifle a notch and squeezed the trigger. He hit his opponent squarely in the back of the knee and the man went flying head over heals.

Already the gunfire had slacked off. His men were wrestling the would-be thieves to the ground. Besides the private, it looked like he had only lost one other man. Another was down on the ground, injured, but with only a superficial wound on his arm.

Jackson supposed that wasn't bad for a night's work, considering how many could have died if Thompson's men had been able to make off with even half the munitions and explosives in the warehouse. Still, even two lives were too great a price when the war had already cost so many.

Jackson wiped his mouth on his shoulder in disgust. He was sick to death of this work. Sick to death of death. He just wanted to go home, home to Cameron—if there was a home left for him there.

25

He was coming home. At last, Jackson was coming home. Cameron stood outside the telegraph office and reread the telegraph clenched in her gloved hands. After weeks of secrecy and his brief, impersonal telegraphs from places like Chattanooga and Memphis, he had sent word that he'd be arriving at the week's end. But now that his return was at hand, she didn't know whether she was anticipating or dreading it.

"My husband will soon be gracing us with his presence, Taye," Cameron murmured, tucking the telegraph into her drawstring reticule.

The two women stepped back, allowing three ragtag Confederate soldiers, still partially in uniform, to pass them. They were thin, sad men with hollow eyes; one, missing a leg from the knee down, walked on a peg with the aid of crutches.

Once the men had safely passed, Taye linked her arm through Cameron's and hurried her down the wooden sidewalk. "That's wonderful. You see, I told you he would come home. Now, Falcon says we have to hurry. It's getting dark and he wants us safely tucked away by the time night falls."

Cameron frowned as she allowed her sister to lead her along. "Falcon," she harrumphed. "That man is entirely too dramatic, don't you think?" She peered into Taye's face, hoping she might discover something of the clandestine relationship she suspected between Taye and the Cherokee.

Taye glanced away, focusing on the boards that had been placed on the ground to keep the hems of ladies' petticoats and crinolines from dragging in the mud. "There was another attack by that gang of ruffians last night, this time just outside of town. They grow bolder every day. Another rape and beating. The woman did not survive," she said gravely.

"I cannot understand why the soldiers can't track these blackards down. They just transferred an army captain here. I thought he was supposed to deal with this." Cameron's amber eyes flashed with anger. "I mean, damn it, how difficult can it be to find them? They must be selling the goods they're stealing. And surely they talk of their escapades. Most men can't keep their mouths shut when they commit a crime. It's how they're always caught."

At the buggy, Falcon offered a broad hand to help Cameron up and then Taye. "You probably already know this," Cameron told Falcon, "but Jackson is coming home."

"This is good," Falcon said in that soft cadence she had grown accustomed to. "It is time Jackson returns to his responsibilities. A man cannot make amends so far from his lodge."

Cameron saw Taye's and Falcon's gazes meet in silent communication and wondered if they'd been talking about her and Jackson behind her back. She would have to speak with Taye on the matter. Of course, the question was, why was Taye talking to Falcon about such personal matters to begin with? Exactly what was her relationship with the

Cherokee? She was supposed to be marrying Thomas, though that union seemed to be up in the air, too. Thomas had moved out, and they only saw him infrequently. Taye rarely mentioned him, but when pressed, she insisted they were still engaged. Cameron didn't know what was going on inside Taye's head and she didn't like it one bit.

Taye was still young and naive in many ways. She did not understand how a man like Falcon Cortés could lead an unsuspecting innocent astray. And the closer Cameron watched, the more obvious it was that there was something between them. Fortunately, Jackson would be home Friday and she could tell him of her concern. Perhaps it was time the Indian was gone.

He was nervous, Jackson realized as he stepped off the train. He was coming home to his wife, so why was he so damned worried? He'd put an end to whatever it was that he'd had with Marie and Cameron need never know. Surely Cameron had had time to think during the weeks he had been gone. As her body healed, she most certainly would have come around to forgiving him for what he had done. For what he'd trade his immortal soul to undo.

As he walked through the train station, a single leather bag in his hand, Jackson half hoped Cameron would be there waiting for him in the apple green gown he liked so much, the one that showed off her voluptuous breasts and accentuated the rich color of her auburn hair. He pushed through the throng of men and women greeting family members and welcoming long-lost friends home. He imagined seeing her from afar, as pretty as she'd been the day he'd fallen in love with her all over again. He fantasized about opening his arms and having her run into them, contemplated what it would be like to go Atkins' Way to share an intimate dinner with wine and candlelight and then carry her to bed and make love to her all night long.

It was foolish whimsy, of course. He hadn't said in his telegram which train he was coming in on, or even from what town. Still, when he spotted Falcon near the outside door, he couldn't suppress a sense of disappointment.

"Falcon," Jackson called, offering a hand.

Falcon put his arms around him, and Jackson was both surprised and embarrassed by the lump of emotion that rose unexpectedly in his throat. He had not realized that a man could give another man comfort this way.

"Friend," Falcon said simply.

Jackson stepped back, uncomfortable with his emotional response to the Cherokee's embrace. "It's good to see you."

Falcon nodded, staring with those obsidian black eyes of his, eyes that seemed far wiser than their years. "I came in the wagon to pick up barrels for Naomi. I hope you do not mind the transportation."

Jackson chuckled. "Sounds like Naomi has the household under control."

"She does. And Noah has taken charge of rebuilding the kitchen at Elmwood. They are good people."

Jackson scowled. He couldn't help but think it was Elmwood, damned Elmwood, that had brought about all this trouble to begin with. If Confederate soldiers had just burned the damned plantation house to the ground four years ago, he'd still be in Baltimore with his wife, and they would still be expecting a child.

Jackson threw his bag into the back of the buckboard and climbed onto the seat beside Falcon. "I have a lot to tell you. I know my messages have been cryptic. They had to be that way, of course."

"Are you close to finding Thompson and his men?" Falcon released the brake, lifted the reins and the farm wagon rolled forward.

"Close on more than one occasion, but Thompson is smarter than we suspected. And these Southerners have a sense of devotion to their lost cause that goes beyond what we Northerners can understand. People are hiding these men, good people who should know better. We caught some of his men attempting to raid one of our warehouses. I was hoping one of the men would provide us with some valuable information, but it's been a dead end, so far."

Jackson watched the store windows go by, taking notice of all the changes in the town in the nearly five weeks he had been gone. He knew the process would be long and difficult, but the president's Reconstruction plan was a good one. He also noted how many more Confederate soldiers roamed the streets than a few weeks ago. He had read in the paper yesterday that more Northern prisons had been emptied—Hart's Island, Camp Chase, Fort Delaware. When the prisoners were set free, they simply began to walk south, praying they'd reach home before they died of starvation.

"If we find this Captain Thompson, do you think that will be the end of those who follow him?"

"I think so. Spider has been a valuable contact. From what I've been able to pick up, many who served under Thompson during the war are devoted to the man rather than to the cause. I can't help thinking that many of them are probably hoping our government will put an end to this last stand, so they can go home."

"Tell me what you need me to do. I'll do it."

Jackson grinned. "You know, you'd make a damned fine wife."

Falcon chuckled, tugging on the long, black braid that

hung down his back. "You are not the kind of man I would marry, I am sorry to say, friend."

The two men laughed and then settled into conversation. Falcon updated Jackson on the local band of men who had still not been captured and seemed to be growing bolder by the day. He spoke of the increasing size of the household at Atkins' Way and the number of freed black men and women and homeless soldiers they had employed. Neither man brought up the women both knew were on the other's mind.

Efia stood in front of the jailhouse in her best dress, thinking not only of the blue bonnet, but of all the bonnets she had seen in her lifetime and wanted and could never have. Through the window, she watched two blue-uniformed soldiers drinking coffee from tin cups. She couldn't tell what they were saying, but she could hear their laughter. Why did her life always feel this way, like she was standing alone outside while everyone else was inside, smiling and happy?

Efia wasn't dumb enough to think that money was the only thing that could give a person happiness. She knew that the color of her skin would be a disadvantage the rest of her life. But Taye Campbell's skin was almost the same color, and look how far she had gone.

Efia reminded herself once more of the blue bonnet perched on Taye's head, then walked through the door of the jailhouse.

A blond soldier with a bushy mustache sat behind a big table, reading a newspaper. He didn't even look up at her. "Help you?"

Efia glanced over her shoulder at the door, clutching her purse strings with every bit of strength she had. If she walked out now, nobody would be the wiser.

"I said, could I help you?" He glanced over the top of the paper, looking her up and down. Judging her.

"Yeah. I was wonderin'—"

"What's that?" He lowered the paper to the table, giving Efia his full attention. "You're goin' to have to speak up."

Efia pressed her lips together and met the young soldier's gaze. "Do y'all pay for information?"

"What kind of information?"

"'Bout crimes. 'Bout crimes people do but don't get caught."

She had his attention now. He pressed the palms of his hands to the newspaper. "What kind of crimes?" He turned his head. "Captain Grey, could you come out here?" He looked back to Efia. "You can tell our captain."

Efia shook her head. "Nope, I got to know how much yer payin' first."

"That depends on how serious an offense you're talking about." He hooked a thumb. "If you're talking about stealing hens out of a neighbor's henhouse, we've got no time for that. If you're talking about real criminal offenses—" he leaned closer "—something can be arranged."

"I'm talkin' 'bout a serious crime," she said, staring him down. "I'm talkin' 'bout murder."

At the house, Falcon let Jackson out at the pillared front, then he drove the wagon around to the back to unload the barrels Naomi would use to store the pickles she was making in the summer kitchen. Jackson walked up the steps to the veranda and in the front door. There was no one there, but the house buzzed like a beehive on a warm Sunday afternoon. Voices rose from everywhere, from the kitchen and the ballroom, from upstairs, and even through the open windows. Out on the side veranda, through the parlor, he could see a young boy he did not know sweeping grass clippings.

Jackson walked up the grand staircase, eyeing the place where that magnificent mirror had hung at the head of the stairs. Someone had replaced it with a large oil painting of horses grazing in an open field, but there was a faint fading of the wallpaper that revealed the outline where the mirror had once been. Passing the picture, he remembered the sound of the shattering glass and the feel of his breaking heart.

As Jackson walked down the hall, he squelched the impulse to call out to Cameron. What if she refused to come to him, or worse yet, hurled insults at him? He had no desire to share their problems with a staff the size that Falcon said Jackson was now supporting. At the bedchamber door, he halted. It was slightly ajar. When he listened, he heard movement inside.

"Cameron?" He pushed open the door in time to see the little imposter, Lacy, scramble off the bed. Clutching a schoolchild's blackboard to her chest, she glared at him with startled eyes.

Jackson looked around, but Cameron wasn't there. "Where is she?" he demanded.

At least the chit was dressed decently now in a light blue gown covered with yellow flowers. It even looked as if someone had attempted to tame that wild frizzy hair.

Lacy thrust out her lower lip and lifted one thin shoulder. "Don't know."

"Don't tell me that," Jackson snapped, his words coming out harsher than he intended.

Lacy took a step back.

He halted, realizing he was scaring her. He didn't like her being here. He didn't believe her story that she was a Campbell for a moment, but he didn't want to scare her or harm her, either. She was just a child, a child who had obviously had a difficult life. "I know you know where she is." He held up his hands to show he would make no move toward her. "Just tell me."

"Elmwood" was the only word Lacy muttered.

Jackson strode out of the bedchamber. *Elmwood.* Of course. Where else would she be? How could he have been so foolish as to think she might have been here waiting for him when her precious Elmwood beckoned?

Jackson walked down the grand staircase.

"Jackson, it's so good to have you home." Taye smiled, meeting him at the bottom of the staircase. She kissed his cheek and he returned the gesture.

The moment she drew back, her gracefully arched brows furrowed. "Oh, dear, Cameron. I'm sorry. She's not here. She wanted to be here when you returned, but she had to go out to Elmwood. There was—"

"Of course she did," he interrupted dryly.

"Jackson, where are you going?" Taye stood at the staircase and watched him cross the front hall that echoed his footsteps.

He yanked open the front door, thinking this was not how he had envisioned his homecoming. "Where do you think?"

"You're sure everyone is all right?" Cameron climbed over fallen timbers at the barn site, carrying a bucket of water she had drawn from the well to give the tired, dirty workers a drink. As she stepped over the freshly sawed boards, water sloshed up onto the bodice of her apple green gown. The water was cold and felt good, considering the heat.

"Everyone is fine, Miss Cameron." Noah, shirtless, lifted several timbers that had fallen to the ground and began to stack them neatly. "Now stop worryin' yerself. Jake, he got a broken leg, and Pouty done wrenched his neck. The rest of 'em got nothin' but skinned knees and a year of their lifes scared out of 'em. Ain't nothin' Naomi can't set right."

Cameron halted and lowered the bucket to the ground. The workmen had been putting up the south wall when a piece of timber had apparently snapped. The entire frame of the wall had come tumbling down on top of them. When one of the young boys had arrived at Atkins' Way to tell her what had happened, no one had known how seriously anyone had been injured. Noah had simply sent for his mistress immediately.

"Look, here, jest like I said." Noah carried a six-foot-long board to her. "Broke off right at the knot. Them boys shoulda looked over these here boards better before they nailed 'em in."

Cameron sighed in relief as she watched the last of the workers settle into the wagon Noah would drive them home in. Naomi sat on the tailgate, washing a man's bloody knee.

Cameron dipped her hand into the bucket and drew it across the back of her neck, savoring the feel of the cold water trickling down her sweaty back. She had ridden here at breakneck speed, the first time she'd been back in the saddle since her miscarriage.

The sound of a horse galloping up the drive made them both turn to see who was approaching.

"Oh, no," Cameron groaned, recognizing the rider. She smoothed her hair that had tumbled hopelessly from her chignon. "It's Captain Logan. I completely forgot in all the confusion. His train must have arrived."

Watching Jackson ride across the barnyard, straight for the new stable, Cameron's mouth went dry, and she felt tingles of excitement skitter down her spine.

"Good afternoon to ya, Capt'n," Noah said, lifting his hat as he walked to the wagon to load his toolbox.

"'Bout time you come home," Naomi muttered.

"You hush, woman," Noah hissed, waving his hat at her. "Stop yer sassin'."

Jackson shook his head as he dismounted, then ground-tied his mount. "I understand you're both doing a fine job keeping everyone in line for me."

Noah grinned as he walked around the wagon. "Jest doin' my job, Capt'n. You ready, Naomi?"

"I'm ready. Let's get these boys home."

Cameron stood a hundred feet away watching Jackson as the wagon turned and headed down the drive, leaving them alone. She wanted to lift her skirts and run toward him, wanted to fling herself into his arms and tell her how sorry she was for everything. But her feet wouldn't move.

It took longer than an eternity for Jackson to finally turn toward her.

Slowly they moved closer.

"You...you're home," Cameron stammered.

"Falcon picked me up at the train station." He lifted one hand and let it fall, halting before he reached her.

She nodded. "I...I wanted to be at the house when you arrived, but—"

"I'm sure you did," he said sarcastically.

Cameron's half smile fell and her hackles went up instinctively. "I did!" She looked at him, amber eyes blazing. "You know, I've had a lot of responsibility here while you were gone, traipsing all over Tennessee and Alabama and God knows where—" she flung up one hand "—doing God knows what."

He blinked and looked down, twisting his mouth into a frown. "I could say that I wouldn't have been in any of those places and you wouldn't have been here if you hadn't left Baltimore in the first place." He paused. "But I won't say that."

Cameron wanted to pick up the water bucket and fling it at him. She wanted to grab one of the broken timbers and hit him across his thick head. Instead, she just stood there and stared at him.

Cameron heard Jackson curse under his breath. Cursing her?

"Cameron—"

He held her gaze. His eyes were stormy, but there was something there....

"Jackson..." she whispered.

He pulled her roughly into his arms and she didn't fight him. "Cameron, Cameron, what are we doing? Is this really the way we want things to be between us?" he groaned. "Is this how we will let it end?"

She couldn't answer.

Then, God bless him, Jackson lifted her chin and covered her mouth with his.

26

Jackson caught Cameron around her waist and pulled her against him. The pressure of her mouth, the scent of her skin, was so intoxicating that he felt dizzy, as if he had consumed glass after glass of scotch.

"Jackson," she murmured as she parted her sweet lips.

He wanted to say he was sorry for what he had done, for how he had acted, but the words wouldn't come. He could only murmur her name. "Cameron. I've missed this."

Missed her, or missed her in his arms? Cameron wondered. She knew they were two different things. She would have asked, but Jackson thrust his hot tongue into her mouth and she closed her eyes, relishing the taste of him. Right now, she would take him any way she could get him.

As Jackson kissed Cameron, his hand spanned her hip and then closed around her tiny waist. It was hard for him to believe that she had carried his child. Did he dare hope she could do so again?

Cameron leaned into him, encouraging him, and he slid his hand upward to cup her breast.

She moaned.

In so many ways, Jackson did not understand this woman

who was his wife, but he understood her body. He understood her needs, perhaps because they were so like his own. He massaged her breast through the layers of her gown and underclothing and she thrust one long, lean leg between his thighs.

It was Jackson who moaned this time as she rubbed her knee against the bulge in his breeches that grew with every passing second. "Do you want to go into the house?" he panted, knowing he wouldn't be able to wait until they returned home to consummate this passion.

"We don't have to. No one is here but us." She threaded her fingers through his hair and pulled his mouth down to hers again. "Love me, Jackson," she whispered.

There was a desperation in her voice that brought a tightness to his chest. "Always," he muttered, dragging his mouth over her chin, down the length of her neck to the damp, hot valley between her breasts.

Somehow, it seemed right to Jackson to make love here at Elmwood, in the place where the stable would be rebuilt. This was who his Cameron had been, who she would always be, no matter where she went or what she did.

Her gown was wet with water, and it felt cool alongside his cheek, against the heat of her bare skin as he pulled at the bodice of the thin summer fabric.

Cameron reached around to the back of her gown and tugged at the buttons, her breath heavy in his ear. She loosened her bodice to offer him better access to her breasts, and he stroked her creamy flesh greedily.

She cradled his head as he nuzzled, and he was rewarded with a tip of rosy flesh. He laved her nipple and she moaned in encouragement, thrusting her hips against him.

Cameron grasped the lapels of his coat and pushed it off, dropping it carelessly to the grass. She tugged at his starched shirt until she pulled it from the rear of his cambric trousers. Then she slipped her hands beneath the linen shirt. Her fingertips found the small of his back and sent tiny pulses of pleasure rippling over his bare skin.

She swayed in his arms. "We're going to fall," she said.

"We won't." He opened his eyes to find her laughing.

Still encircling him in her arms, she sank to her knees in a puddle of green lawn and crisp white petticoats, pulling him down with her.

The sun was setting in the east over the lines of swaying elm and oak trees, but the grass was still warm from its radiance and its heat seemed to seep into his very bones.

Jackson lowered his head over hers and drew in her amber eyes. One at a time, he pulled the bone pins from her hair and let them fall to the soft grass around them. He ran his fingers through her thick, glossy tresses until it was a curtain of red tumbling over her shoulders.

She rested her forehead against his chin and slid her hand over his thigh, taking her time. He groaned as her fingertips brushed the swell of his loins.

"You said you missed me," she breathed, tipping her head back to look up at him. "Is this what you've missed?"

"Yes..."

"And this?" She slid her practiced hand lower and brought it up to cup his soft flesh, making him tremble all over.

It suddenly occurred to Jackson that if he was not careful, he would end this encounter long before Cameron's needs were met. He forced himself to brush her hand aside, and he lay on his back on his coat, pulling her down with him.

Cameron stretched out over his chest and pressed her hipbones to his, grinding against him.

"Tease," he grunted as, in one motion, he flipped her over and changed places with her.

She flung her hands back over her head and stretched

like a cat, gazing up at him with heavy-lidded amber eyes. Grabbing handfuls of bright grass, she threw them at him and they were both showered in green clippings. A piece fell in his hair and she caught it between her fingers, laughing.

"Like this," he told her quietly, "with your hair down, and this mischievous smile on your lips—" he traced her pouting mouth with his forefinger "—you look seventeen again."

"But I know so much more than I did when I was seventeen," she purred. She took his fingertip into her mouth and sucked on it, then bit down playfully.

With a growl of desire, Jackson grasped her arms and pressed them into the soft grass over her head. Holding her down, with one hand on both her wrists, he pushed her bodice off her shoulder and took one hardened nipple between his teeth. He tugged gently and then teased its very tip with the point of his tongue.

Hot, tingling desire pulsed through Cameron's veins as she pulled her arms from Jackson's grasp to run her fingers through his thick dark hair and guide his mouth to her other breast.

Cradling her in one arm, he rolled onto his side, taking her with him so that they faced each other. Jackson's mouth twisted hungrily against hers and she drew a finger downward from his chest, over his belly to the waistband of his trousers, where his shirt had been pulled free. The tip of her finger traced the narrow line of dark hair that disappeared beneath the cambric.

"Touch me, Cam," he encouraged and then he glanced up. He found her smiling at him, a tenderness in her eyes that he desperately needed. Still holding his gaze, she unfastened his trousers and slid her hand beneath the straining fabric. He shuddered as she grasped him firmly, her hand hot and sure, and he let his eyelids close.

Cameron stroked Jackson rhythmically, slowing when his breath came too quickly, then increasing the speed of her caress again when he had settled. She teased his senses until her own soared, until she thought she could not bear another moment without feeling him deep inside her.

"Jackson," she whispered.

He knew what she wanted. He gently pushed her hand aside and grasped the hem of her gown. His fingers trailed her pale inner thigh and she felt herself melting into the warm grass. She held her breath, her skin tingling in anticipation, as he slid his hand closer to the place that now throbbed, damp with desire for him.

At last he cupped the bed of bright red curls with the palm of his hand and she raised her hips to meet that caress. "Come to me," she begged, parting her legs, her voice strained and throaty.

Jackson covered her body with his again and the force of his hardened member against her bare leg made her moan aloud. He took her in one motion. A shudder went through her and she cried out, tightening her fingers on his shoulders. One stroke, just one, and she was already tumbling in bright peaks of pleasure.

Jackson stilled for a moment, allowing her to catch her breath and acclimate herself. Then he began to move again, knowing just how she liked to be stroked. He varied his rhythm and the length of his caress, teasing her, taunting her, until she writhed beneath him.

He arched his back and caught the hard, erect peak of her breast in his mouth. She cried out again, this climax even harder. She felt every muscle in her body tighten, then relax, then tighten again as pulses of pleasure surged through every fiber of her being.

Jackson lowered his head over Cameron's and kissed her tear-stained cheeks. He brushed a ringlet of hair off her forehead and kissed the spot where it had been.

Cameron opened her heavy-lidded eyes and drank in his smile. Then she raised her hips to his and he began to move again. Staring up into his dark-pooled gray eyes, she lifted her hips again and again, feeling how close he was to fulfillment, hearing it in his breath. Suddenly she felt herself balance on the edge once more. She tried to hold back, but she couldn't. She wrapped her arms around Jackson's neck and pulled him hard against her...deeper.

She cried out as her entire being seemed to tumble and then burst into bright shards of hot white light and pleasure. She heard Jackson groan in release and felt his entire body shudder as ripples of ecstasy washed through him.

After a few moments they lay still, listening to each other's breath as it came easier. Jackson eased from her body and rolled onto his side, gathering her in his arms. Darkness was falling quickly, and she could no longer see the forms of the barn timbers, which stood around them.

Jackson kissed her damp cheeks, the tip of her nose, her love-bruised mouth. She opened her eyes and reached up to stroke his cheek. "Welcome home," she murmured.

"Do I look presentable?" Cameron asked Jackson as she tried to smooth the hopelessly wrinkled bodice of her gown. He had helped her locate her hairpins, scattered in the grass, and she had done an acceptable job of tucking her hair back into its chignon, but the skirt of the apple green gown was hopelessly grass-stained. She was concerned that she might not be able to slip into the house at Atkins' Way and change before anyone saw her.

"You look beautiful," Jackson assured her as he plucked

a tiny leaf from her hair and dropped it to watch it flutter to the ground.

She cut her eyes to him. "What do you know? A man who has just had his way with a woman outside in the light of day will say anything."

"Just about," he teased. "Especially when he's hoping for another go after supper."

The heat of the blush that crept across her cheeks pleasantly surprised Cameron. Jackson had once been able to make her redden. If he could do it again now, perhaps there was a chance they could go back to where they had strayed, and mend their relationship. "I'm going to go upstairs and change. I could meet you in the parlor for a glass of wine before supper, if you like."

He leaned forward, pressed a kiss to her lips and opened the front door for her. "I would like that very much."

Jackson looked both ways as they stepped inside the lamp-lit marble hall and Cameron hurried for the grand staircase. "Are you certain it's safe for me to come inside, no one hiding in wait to shoot me with their slingshot?"

She spun around, already halfway up the stairs. "Jackson, please, I thought we weren't going to talk about Lacy tonight. That was your suggestion, wasn't it?"

They had ridden their horses slowly back to Atkins' Way, enjoying their time together. They had briefly discussed Lacy, then agreed to disagree on her for the present. Neither broached the subject of the terms they'd parted on, nor did either mention the baby they had lost. As they had ridden down the drive, they'd also agreed they would call a truce for the night. Tomorrow they would see what the day brought.

Jackson grinned happily, lifting his arms high in surrender. "A chardonnay or a burgundy, my dear?"

"You pick." Cameron started up the stairs again, her

skirts bunched in both fists, feeling happier than she had in months. Jackson had said she looked seventeen again; tonight, she almost felt like it. "I'll be down shortly."

Jackson wandered into the parlor and walked out onto the veranda to lean on the railing. He smiled to himself in the darkness, pleased with his homecoming. Cameron hadn't said anything, but he felt that while she might not have forgiven him for what had happened yet, she was on her way. He drew in a deep breath. If Cameron forgave him, perhaps he could forgive himself.

"Good even', Capt'n."

Jackson turned to see Patsy standing in the doorway. "Good evening, young lady."

She smiled shyly and swished her white skirting. "Someone to see you at the door, Capt'n. A Capt'n Grey. He got a soldier uniform on."

Jackson frowned. He knew John Grey vaguely. He was a career soldier from New Jersey who'd recently been assigned to the Jackson jailhouse. Grey, and Union soldiers like him, would remain in place until every Confederate state was in compliance with all federal and constitutional laws and was accepted back into the Union. Jackson had no idea why John Grey would be here to see him, though.

He strode out of the parlor and into the front hall.

"John." Jackson offered his hand, taking note that two more soldiers escorted the army captain.

"Captain Logan, good to see you again, sir."

"What can I do for you?" Jackson asked. "Don't tell me you've finally decided to accept my invitation for a drink on my veranda."

The army captain slipped a piece of paper from his uniform and gazed down at it. It was obvious that whatever his mission, he was uncomfortable with it. "I'm sorry to say it's official business that brings me here, sir. I've a writ for Taye Campbell's arrest.''

"I'm sorry," Jackson said, thinking he must have misheard. "What was that?"

Captain Grey took a strangled breath and repeated himself. "I have orders for the arrest of Taye Campbell, daughter of Senator David Campbell."

"Oh, my God!" Cameron said from the top of the staircase.

Jackson looked up.

"What is this about?" she demanded, racing down the stairs as quickly as she could in a belled crinoline. She had dressed in a lovely beige-and-white silk evening gown that revealed her bare shoulders and the swell of her breasts quite nicely.

"I don't know," Jackson said. He turned back to the captain, keeping his voice low and calm. "I believe there's been a mistake, sir. One which I'm sure can be quickly righted."

"No mistake," Grey said. "There is only one Taye Campbell of Elmwood Plantation in Jackson, Mississippi."

Cameron reached the bottom of the staircase and hustled across the marble floor, shaking a teakwood lady's fan at the army captain. "Arrest Taye? That's the most ridiculous thing I have ever heard. What has Taye done? Bought too many bonnets? Fed too many starving women and children from our back door?"

The captain kept his gaze locked on the paper in his hands. "Ma'am, she's to be arrested for the murder of your brother, Grant Campbell."

Taye stood in the upper hallway, her back pressed to the floral papered wall. She couldn't breathe and for a moment feared she might faint.

She touched her hand to her breast and felt her heart pounding as if it might spring from her chest. Her breath now came in short pants.

"Taye?" Falcon strode down the hallway toward her wearing a faded red shirt with silver buttons that she loved on him. "You look as if you have seen an evil spirit. What is wrong?"

She reached out to him, covering his mouth with her hand for fear the soldiers below might hear him. "S-soldiers," she whispered.

His dark brow furrowed. "I do not understand." He took her hand, whispering. "Come to my room and tell me what is wrong. I will fix it, if it is in my power."

She pressed her lips together, her eyes filling with tears. She shook her head furiously.

He stepped closer, slipping his arm around her waist. "Tell me."

Her lower lip trembled as she searched for the right words. How could she tell Falcon? Would he hate her when he learned what she had done? That, she couldn't bear. "There are soldiers downstairs," she breathed, her mouth close to his ear. "They have come to arrest me."

He held both her hands in his and gazed down at her, his black eyes filled with compassion. "For what?"

"The murder of Grant, Cameron's...our brother."

"That is ridiculous. You should not be afraid. We will go to these men and tell them they have made a mistake."

Tears ran down her cheeks as she shook her head no again. She stared at the floor. "I can't go down there. I can't face them."

"Why?"

Slowly Taye lifted her lashes. "Because I did kill Grant Campbell. And if I had to, I would shoot him all over again."

27

Cameron stared at Captain Grey for a moment, lost in memories better left buried. Taye *had* shot their brother Grant. It was a plain fact that both she and Taye had simply tried to forget.

Taye had killed him on that hot August evening four years earlier, and Cameron and Jackson had buried his body in Elmwood's graveyard, beside his father. There had been no funeral, no prayers said over the grave, no tears shed. There was only relief, relief to feel safe at last.

After Taye and Cameron fled north to safety, Jackson had quietly let it be known in town that Grant had died and been laid to rest. He had then ordered headstones for both Grant's and Sukey's graves and paid to have them set in place. No one in the town had liked Grant enough to even ask how he had died.

Cameron's lower lip trembled and she bit down on it until the metallic taste of blood seeped onto her tongue. She gazed at Captain Grey. He knew nothing of Grant Campbell; he knew nothing of the evil, vile man Grant had been.

It had been Jackson's opinion that Grant's passing from this earth had gone too easily. Because he'd not wanted to see Elmwood's slaves freed and his own luxurious life altered, Grant had knowingly pushed his father over a second-story veranda rail to his death. He had sold off Elmwood's slaves, then sent slavers to hunt those who tried to escape. Sukey, Taye's mother, the love of Senator Campbell's life, had been shot and bled to death on the banks of the Pearl River trying to flee the men Grant had hired. Not satisfied with the evil he'd wrought, Grant had then attempted to auction Taye's virginity in a Baton Rouge whorehouse. Who on this earth could have argued that Grant Campbell did not deserve to die for those offenses?

But Taye had not shot her half brother for the crimes he had already committed. No, she'd done it to save Cameron. And Cameron was as certain now as she had been that night, that Taye would never have killed for any other reason.

Cameron tried to push the memories aside, but she couldn't. Suddenly she could feel the perspiration trailing down her back; she could smell the scent of the honeysuckle near her father's balcony. In her mind, she could still see her brother leaning over the rail, their father's pistol gripped in his hand, his eyes wild with madness.

Grant had stood on the same bedchamber balcony he had pushed his father from and shot at her. He missed the first time, but in her heart of hearts she had known he would not miss the second time. Driven by hatred, greediness, lust and jealousy, he would kill his own sister.

Taye must have known Grant would not stop until Cameron lay in a grave beside the senator and Sukey. She had stepped from the falling darkness and fired one shot, killing him instantly.

"How dare you come into my home, Captain?" Cameron flared, the reality of the situation startling her as sud-

denly as a slap on the cheek. "How dare you come here
spreading these lies?"

"Ma'am, I'm only doing my job. This is a serious
charge, and justice must be done. Especially now when we
are trying to return the states to—"

"Serious charge!" she interrupted. "Instead of chasing
after ghosts, why aren't you hunting down the men who
are raiding this county? How many women will have to be
raped? How many will die before you get off your lazy
a—"

Jackson laid his hand gently, but firmly, on Cameron's
forearm and squeezed, effectively silencing her. "May I ask
how this has come up? Grant Campbell passed away in the
summer of '61. That was four years ago."

"All I can tell you, sir, is that evidence has come to
light. We would not being doing our job if we did not take
this matter seriously."

"What kind of evidence?" Cameron demanded, her
mind spinning. No one could have known that Taye shot
Grant. No one but Naomi, perhaps, who had been at the
house. But Naomi would never have told; Cameron would
bet her life on it. Grant had been holding Naomi prisoner
here in Elmwood as his sex slave, chaining her to the bed
at night to prevent her from escaping.

"I cannot say what evidence has been presented,
ma'am." Captain Grey looked to Jackson, perhaps for a
male's sense of reason. "If you could call Miss Campbell,
she'll have to come along with us, Captain."

"You're going to take her to jail?" Cameron tapped the
army captain with her fan and he flinched. "You're going
to lock her up with men who steal and rape?"

Captain Grey looked to Jackson. "Arrangements will be
made to be certain that she is safe and has as much privacy

as can be allowed. If you don't mind me saying so, sir, you should hire a lawyer for Miss Campbell immediately."

"A lawyer?" Cameron's eyes grew round with insult. "Let me tell you, sir—"

"Cameron." Jackson met her gaze meaningfully. "Please go upstairs and bring Taye down."

"Surely you don't mean you're just going to turn her over to them?" She stared at him in disbelief. He knew Taye had killed Grant, but he also knew Grant's reputation, what kind of man Grant had been.

"Captain Grey is not accountable for the charges," Jackson said quietly, his voice ominous. "We cannot hold him responsible. Now bring Taye down, or these gentlemen will be forced to search the house and drag her out." His gray eyes met hers. "Is that what you want?"

His words chilled her to her core. Her first reaction was one of anger—at the soldiers, at Jackson—but she knew they were right and fought her anger. Once charged, Taye had to face her accuser, whomever that might be.

Jackson laid his hand on the small of her back and gave her the tiniest push toward the grand staircase. Cameron wanted to be angry with Jackson, but she couldn't be. He had helped them hide Grant's unnatural death. He had taken care of the gravestones. And more importantly, he had never again spoken of the incident.

"I'll bring her down," Cameron said softly, fighting a sense of defeat as she took the stairs slowly. They would have to hire a lawyer quickly. Taye could not languish in jail.

Would Thomas defend Taye? More importantly, would Thomas defend her once she admitted to him that she was guilty?

At the top landing, Cameron turned right down the hall toward the multiple guest bedchambers. She halted at

Taye's closed door, breathed deeply and then tapped on the paneled wood. "Taye?" she called softly.

"Aunt Cameron?" Lacy called from behind the door.

"Lacy? Where's Aunt Taye?" Cameron pushed open the door to find Lacy dressed in one of Taye's favorite gowns, the blue silk with scalloped skirting trailing along the floor.

"Aunt Taye said I could put on any of her gowns, long as my hands was clean." She swished the skirt of the blue silk and spun in a circle. Minus a petticoat and crinoline, the dress yawned like a flower opening its petals.

"As long as your hands *were* clean," Cameron corrected, distracted by Taye's absence. "Lacy, where is Taye?"

Lacy danced her way across the polished floor, taking no heed of the gown as she trampled over the hem. "Aunt Taye is teaching me to waltz." She lifted her hands to an invisible partner and practiced her smile, her hazel eyes bright with excitement. "You want to dance with me, Aunt Cam? My mama was a good dancer."

"Lacy, listen to me." Cameron tossed her fan to Taye's bed and walked to her charge, grasping both of Lacy's hands in her own. "I need you to tell me where Taye has gone."

Lacy pressed her lips together as if they had been glued with sap from a tropical gum tree.

"Lacy Campbell!"

The girl somehow pressed her lips tighter. "You can torture me and hang me by my thumbs, I ain't telling," she mumbled, her words garbled by her sealed lips.

"I *am not* telling." Cameron reached out and grabbed her arm. "Listen to me. I am not playing, Lacy. I need to know where she is this minute."

Lacy thrust out her jaw. "I promised I wouldn't."

Cameron exhaled, realizing that this was not the way to

deal with Lacy. "I'm sorry," she whispered, throwing her arm around her niece's thin shoulders. "It's just that some men are here to talk to her and—"

"Soldiers, they come to arrest her. She was smart to run 'cause they ain't gonna—are not going to," Lacy corrected, "listen to anything she says. Not a negra girl like her."

"Lacy! Taye is not—" Cameron caught herself. Taye *was* half African, and Cameron knew in her heart that while that should make no difference in a court of law, it might. Only last night she had read her father's words in his diary.

Sukey's skin is as dark as polished ebony, and I have been brought up to believe that that alone somehow makes her of less worth than myself, a white man. But when I look into her dark eyes, I know it is I who am not worthy of her.

Cameron bit down on the lip that she had already bloodied. She needed Lacy to grow up believing that the color of one's skin, the circumstances of one's birth, should not matter. It was what her father had taught her and what he would have taught his granddaughter had he been here today.

"It's not true, Lacy. Taye has a right to a trial. A trial of her peers. There she will be innocent unless she can be proven guilty."

"Well, I don't know if she was the one who killed my papa or not, but I can tell you, Aunt Cameron, there won't be no negra girls on that jury you're talking about. And no women, neither. I lived on them streets. I know who your justice is for and who it ain—isn't. And it shore ain't for negra wenches what shot a white man to death."

Cameron threw her arms around Lacy and hugged her tightly, knowing the child, wise beyond her years, hit closer to the truth than she realized. "I'm sorry," she whispered.

"Your father did die the night they are talking about, but they don't know the circumstances."

Lacy didn't return the embrace, but she didn't try to escape, either. "I'm not upset 'bout him, Aunt Cam. Mama said he was a futterin' bastard who deserved to die by havin' his pizzle rot off."

Had it been any other time or place, Cameron would have laughed. "I'm sorry, anyway." She pulled back to gaze into Lacy's eyes, trying not to see Grant in them. "Now can't you tell me where Taye went?" she whispered.

Lacy shook her head. "And not who she went with, neither."

And with that, Cameron knew her sister had run and who she had run with.

She spun on her heels and hurried from the room. "I have to go back downstairs. You stay here."

"You think I could put a little of that red stuff on my cheeks?" Lacy called after her.

"No." Cameron shut the door loudly and hurried to the staircase. There, she took a breath and slowly descended the steps, as if making her first appearance at a ball. "I'm sorry, gentlemen, but I was mistaken," she said sweetly when she reached the front hall. "My sister does not seem to be at home."

Captain Grey looked to Jackson and frowned. "What's the meaning of this, Logan? I came this way, after dark, so as not to cause Miss Campbell any undue anguish. But I will not be toyed with. I am here for duty's sake, and fulfill it I shall."

Jackson turned to Cameron. "She's not here, dear?"

Cameron shook her head, meeting Jackson's gaze. That was when she realized he had known something before she had, probably before she went up the stairs looking for Taye. "I don't know where she could be, but I will ask the servants. You see, sir,'' she said, smiling sweetly, ''Captain Logan only returned to Mississippi on the afternoon train. He and I were inspecting Elmwood Plantation, my father's home, and we had only just returned when you came in. I assumed my sister was here at Atkins' Way, but I'd not yet had time to speak with her.''

''We'll have to search the place,'' Captain Grey said stonily.

''Of course.'' Jackson stepped back and gestured grandly. ''Two stories. The servants' quarters are over the kitchen, and there are also men residing over the barn. If we can be of any assistance, please let us know.''

''If you don't mind, ma'am, could you ask your servants where Miss Campbell might be?''

''Yes, Captain.'' She smiled her most generous smile and hurried off to the kitchen. She knew she had to speak to Naomi, not about Taye, but about the night Grant died.

Cameron gripped Naomi's lean hand in hers and led her out of the kitchen into the darkness of the small, paved herb garden.

''I don't know where's she gone,'' Naomi said, wiping her hands on her white apron. ''So no need to ask.''

Cameron glanced at the house that loomed behind them, on the lookout for the soldiers. ''I don't want to know where she went, at least not yet.'' Cameron stared into Naomi's dark eyes. ''You know why these men are here?''

Naomi lifted her shoulder slightly. ''The kitchen ain't so far from the front hall.''

''Naomi, I need you to think carefully back to the night Grant died.''

Naomi's face tightened and her lips drew back in a half sneer. ''One of the best nights of my life, 'scuse me for sayin' so.''

"I need you to think back. Were Dorcas and Efia anywhere near the house?" Cameron tried to recall, but her
memories were sketchy as to where the others had been.
"Hadn't Taye and the twins gone down to the stables, or
to the slave quarters to look for food?"

"I think that's where they said later they was. Don't
know fer sure, 'cause I was in the house tryin' to set myself
free." Naomi rested one hand on her hip as she thought.
"But I know didn't no one see what happened but you and
Taye. Them silly girls didn't even come up to the house
after they musta heard the gunshots."

"I didn't think so, either."

Naomi looked to Cameron suspiciously. "But that little
negra girl Efia is here in town again."

Cameron nodded.

"Got to be her tellin' tales." Naomi fingered her gris-
gris bag. "I knew them wenches was nothin' but trash. And
her takin' with Clyde Macon after what he done to them
little girls." She made a clicking sound between her teeth.
"Like sleepin' with Ghede Satan himself."

"Well, I know that Taye is frightened, but she shouldn't
have run. It just makes her look guiltier."

There were unfamiliar sounds in the kitchen and both
women turned to gaze at the open door. The soldiers had
entered the room to search it.

"What ya gonna do?" Naomi whispered.

"I don't know, Naomi. I just don't know. Once the soldiers are gone, Jackson and I will probably ride in to see
Thomas. Then we've got to find Taye and convince her to
turn herself in." She shook her head, hating to think of
how this might all play out. "Considering the fact that Taye
was the housekeeper's daughter and Grant was the senator's son, a Southern jury isn't going to like it. There's a

lot of bitterness in this town against your people. A lot of anger no one knows where to lay.''

"Might not matter why she killed him or whether or not he deserved it twice over,'' Naomi whispered.

Cameron rested her hand on Naomi's shoulder. "I should go inside. I don't want to look suspicious.''

Naomi pulled off her apron and tossed it into a bush. "And I'll be takin' a little ride into J Town to pay a call on a young lady.''

Cameron grabbed her hand. "You can't go to J Town, not alone after dark. They say no woman is safe there.''

Naomi smiled slyly. "You got a look at my man lately, girl? He four feet wide and got arms on him like tree trunks,'' she said proudly. "Don't know no one not give him a wide berth.''

"All right, find out what you can. Thank you.'' Cameron squeezed her hand and released it, then headed for the back door.

"Ain't nothin' Naomi can't do for her girls.''

Cameron smiled, thankful once more for the friend she had found in such an unlikely character.

28

Cameron entered the kitchen through the rear door.

"There ya are, Miss Cameron. Theys lookin' for ya upstairs." Patsy twisted her bony hands in her apron. "That girl of yours gone crazy-wild."

Cameron hurried out of the kitchen and into the main house, following the sounds of Lacy's shrieks.

Jackson met Cameron at the top of the stairs, pointing down the hall toward Taye's bedchamber and the source of the commotion.

"Lacy!" Cameron called, hurrying down the hall.

"Get away from me!" Lacy screamed.

Cameron heard the sound of shattering glass and one of the soldiers ducked out of the room. "Captain Grey told me to look everywhere," he said sheepishly. "I have to look under the bed."

"Give me a moment, sir." Cameron stepped through the doorway and ducked just in time to miss a glass hurled at her head.

The drinking glass exploded on impact with the doorjamb, and glass and water sprayed Cameron. "Lacy Campbell, get off that bed this minute and stop throwing things."

Lacy stood perched on the center of the bed, her eyes

wide. "Aunt Cam," she gulped as she lowered the crystal water pitcher in her hand. "I didn't get ya, did I?"

Cameron walked to the bed and jerked the pitcher out of her hand. "Get down this instant." The girl was still dressed in Taye's blue gown, her cheeks and lips now bright red with lip pomade. "Because if I have to come up there after you," Cameron threatened, "you will not be pleased." She set the pitcher down safely on a table.

"I didn't want 'em in here, Aunt Cam," Lacy explained softly. "I don't like soldiers."

Cameron offered her hand to help her niece down, softening her tone. "I don't suppose you do," she said, recalling what Lacy had told her about the soldiers and her mother. "Now come with me. They need to search this room. Taye's not here, so they're not going to get her tonight," she reassured her quietly. "It's going to be all right."

Lacy clasped Cameron's hand, and Cameron was surprised to find that the small hand was shaking. Lacy was a feisty little girl, but in many ways, she was still just that, a little girl.

"You've searched the master bedchamber?" Cameron asked the soldier.

He bobbed his head, stepping back to give the glass-hurling hoyden a wide berth.

"Then I'll take her in there. I apologize for her behavior, but her experiences with soldiers have not been the best."

"Yes, ma'am. No need for us to bother you. You go right ahead."

Cameron put her arm around Lacy and escorted her down the hall. Jackson still stood at the top of the stairs.

"I'm going to take Lacy to our room until they're gone," she told him. "They must have frightened her."

"Frightened *her?* Hell, it looks like she did a fine job of scaring that poor boy out of a year of his life."

Cameron eyed him but bit her tongue. "Come find me after they're gone," she whispered.

Cameron left Jackson to deal with the soldiers and escorted Lacy to the master bedchamber. "You have to learn to be more ladylike," she admonished. "Campbell girls do not stand on beds and throw chamber pots."

Lacy set her jaw. "He asked me if he could come in, and I told him hell no!"

Cameron had to hide her smile. "Ladies do not curse, either. Now let's get this gown off you." She walked to one of her clothing trunks and pulled out a pretty yellow sleeping gown, embroidered with violets.

Lacy allowed Cameron to help her remove Taye's blue gown and her underclothes and pulled the sleeping gown over her head. Cameron then led her to the washstand and offered her a linen washing cloth, studying her face. "I told you, no rouge."

"Weren't rouge."

"Of course it's rouge. Wipe it off."

"Nope. Nothin' but some spit and a 'lil red paint offen that red rose wallpaper."

"That qualifies as rouge," Cameron insisted firmly.

Lacy sighed dramatically and obediently dipped the cloth into the water and scrubbed her face. "My mama used to wear paint."

Which is exactly why I don't want you wearing it, Cameron thought. *Look where face paint got her.* She didn't say it aloud because she didn't want to hurt the child or tarnish her memory of her mother.

"You've still got some there." Cameron touched the corner of Lacy's mouth. "I'm going to call for a tray for your supper and I want you in bed." She pointed to her own oversize four-poster.

Lacy's face lit up. "Will ya—you read to me? From my grandpapa's journal?"

Over the last few weeks it had become a habit with them to curl up in the evening and Cameron would read to Lacy. Sometimes she read from the Bible, although heaven knew the child had no religious upbringing whatsoever, or from one of the many books from the library. Occasionally, she read to her from David Campbell's diary. Taye still insisted she had no right to hear of the private life her mother and father shared, but Lacy, like Cameron, was fascinated by the passages.

"We shall see." Cameron stuck her head out the door to call for Patsy and saw Jackson coming toward her.

"Need something?" he asked.

"I was looking for Patsy. I want her to bring up a tray with some supper for Lacy."

He rested his hand casually on her waist. "You should eat, too. You look thin."

"Are the soldiers gone?" she asked, instead of responding to his remark.

"On their way out. Grey is pretty angry. He expected to come to the house and have her go with him peaceably."

Cameron lifted her lashes. "She must have heard us from upstairs."

He nodded.

"You think she went alone?" she asked, pretty certain she already knew the answer.

He shook his head.

She sighed and rubbed her temples with her thumb and forefinger. "This was one of the things I needed to discuss with you, Jackson. As I told you earlier, Thomas has been acting very odd. It's not just that he moved back to his family's plantation. I can't get him or Taye to tell me a thing, but I know they've had a falling-out.'' She gestured. ''I suspect he's ill, too. The coughing has gotten worse.''

''And Falcon?''

Again, she sighed. ''Neither Taye nor Falcon have said a word to me, but I know there's something going on between them. I see the way they look at each other when they think I'm not watching.''

''I thought something like this might happen,'' Jackson mused.

''And you didn't say anything? You didn't try to stop Taye from ruining her life?''

He met her gaze, his gray eyes steady, solemn. ''When you decided you would have me, could anyone have changed your mind?''

The way he said it tugged at her heart. They both seemed to ache for what had been lost. Or maybe only misplaced?

She pressed her lips together and glanced at the floor. ''I suppose not,'' she conceded.

''Well, in case you haven't noticed, Taye is more a Campbell woman than anyone is giving her credit for.''

''I just don't want her to make any mistakes. I don't want to see her hurt.''

''I don't think anyone does.''

''And Thomas... I feel so badly for him. He was so loyal to Papa and he has been so good to us.''

''That doesn't mean we can hand him Taye as a reward.''

She looked up at him again. She had never thought of it that way before. ''I suppose. Well, anyway, wherever Falcon and Taye have gone, we've got to bring them back. Running only makes Taye look guilty.''

''She is guilty.''

Cameron pushed the heel of her hand into Jackson's

chest. "Don't you say that," she snapped, looking up and down the hall to be sure no one had heard him.

"Damn it, Cameron, I didn't mean I thought she should be held accountable. If I'd been there, I'd have blown the bastard away, too, with less excuse."

"Well, it's not up to us, now. None of it is. We just need to bring her home."

"I'm going to talk to Thomas just as soon as the soldiers are gone."

"I'll go with you." She turned to go back into her chamber for a wrap.

He caught her arm and halted her. "No. Let me go alone. I'm going to have to tell Thomas that she left with Falcon. No need for you to be there to witness it. You stay here, in case Taye comes back. Besides—" he nodded in the direction of the bedchamber door left ajar "—I think you've got your hands full already."

"Oh, Jackson, if you would just give Lacy a chance," she said softly, "I think you'd really like her." She hesitated. "I see a lot of me in her."

"Your mother wasn't a whore, and you know who your father was."

"That's something else you and I need to discuss. I had Thomas do some investigating after you left town. He spoke to some people who had known Maureen. He's of a mind that Lacy might well be Grant's daughter. So everything Lacy told us was true. About her being at the saloon, about her mother losing her place above the pharmacy."

"Can anyone prove undeniably that she's Grant's daughter?"

Cameron shook her head. "No, but—"

He pressed a finger to her lips. "We agreed we wouldn't argue about her tonight. I need to get to Thomas."

Cameron grasped the doorknob, wishing she could go

with Jackson, but understanding that it made more sense for her to stay. A silence stretched between them. She was searching for that sense of intimacy she had felt this afternoon at Elmwood, but Jackson was now set on a mission, and he was all business.

"I'll wait up for you. I want to know what Thomas says."

He nodded. For a moment he acted as if he wanted to kiss her goodbye, maybe hug her. Instead, he turned away and walked back down the hall.

Cameron swallowed the lump in her throat and went back into the bedchamber to join Lacy.

"Today we began the spring planting. It's hard to believe Sukey has been here almost a year. It is amazing to me how quickly time passes when one is happy," Cameron read aloud.

She glanced over the edge of the diary to see Lacy sound asleep, her red-gold hair spread across the pillows on the big bed.

Cameron smiled and then glanced at the clock on the far mantel. Almost midnight. Jackson had been gone a long time. Her gaze returned to her father's diary and she flipped through several pages. She had read this section to Lacy because there was nothing inappropriate for her to hear. But now that she was asleep, Cameron was anxious to continue where she had left off the previous night.

I do not know how it happened. I was not as careful as I should have been. Not patient enough. Papa caught me sneaking out of the house to meet Sukey. When he demanded to know where I was going, I could not lie to him. I confessed my relationship with Sukey.

Cameron bit down on her lower lip, trying to imagine how her father must have felt that night, so torn between loyalty to his father and loyalty to the woman he loved, but would never be permitted to truly have.

Papa surprised me, Cameron read on silently. *He did not chastise me for lying with one of our slaves. He only suggested that I be more discreet. He said my mother would be distressed to learn that her son was, indeed, growing up and had the same urges as other men. I wanted to ask Papa if there had ever been a slave woman or someone else forbidden to him who he had loved, but the subject changed so quickly that I did not have the chance.*

After he gave me his permission to sleep with Sukey, he casually announced that he had made an agreement with another Mississippi family...for a marriage contract between their daughter and me. My heart seemed to break and crumble as he related the details. I am to marry Katherine Parnell within the year....

Cameron closed the diary in her lap and squeezed her eyes shut against her tears. In her father's words, she could feel his pain, and somehow, a part of it became her own.

''Well, looky what we got here.'' Clyde Macon walked out onto the rickety porch of the shack Naomi had been directed to. Sour lamplight spilled from the house. The smell of cooked cabbage was strong.

Naomi knew the man; everyone in the county did. And as far as she knew, they all despised him, black and white.

''Evenin','' Naomi said, swallowing the bile that rose in her throat. Just looking at his ugly, leering face made her want to vomit on his muddy boots. ''Yer missus at home?''

Clyde chuckled and scratched behind the ear of a hound pup he held cradled in his arm. ''My missus? That's pretty funny. And who might you be?'' He looked her up and down lasciviously.

The man made Naomi's skin crawl. There wasn't a curse

mean enough or harmful enough to cast on him. "Not your business who I am." She set her hand on her hip. "Is Efia here or no?"

"Feisty one. I like 'em feisty!" Clyde drawled.

He took a step closer to her and Naomi sidestepped him. "Ya see that big man sittin' on that horse in the shadows there?" Naomi asked.

Clyde peered around her.

"Wave to Clyde," Naomi called to Noah.

Noah waved and Clyde took a step back. Obviously he'd not noticed Noah. "Fee! Get your lazy ass out here. Can't ya see ya got a visitor?"

"What ya talkin' about, Clyde? I thought ya wanted me to beat up them—" Efia stepped out of the shack onto the porch, wiping her hands on a filthy, tattered apron. Oddly enough, she appeared to be wearing a new gown. She halted midsentence.

The moment Efia stepped onto the porch, she knew why Naomi was there. Naomi also knew in the same moment that Efia had told the soldiers that Taye killed Grant.

"I need to speak to you," Naomi said softly, her anger evident under her breath.

Efia's gaze darted to Clyde. "This is women's business. No need for ya to stand there and stare."

"Women's business? What kind of women's business?" Clyde asked suspiciously from the doorway.

"Efia's got a little problem with her bleedin'. Ya want me to whip ya up a potion, too?"

Clyde blanched and backed in through the door. "Don't be takin' long, Fee. I want my biscuits."

Naomi waited for Clyde to disappear inside and then fixed her dark gaze on Efia. "What have ya done, girl?"

"I don't know what yer talkin' about." Efia's voice trembled. She was afraid of Naomi.

"Ya know jest what I'm talkin' about, carryin' tales to the law!" Naomi accused.

Efia shook her head frantically. "I don't know what yer talkin' about. Get off my porch."

"Don't know what I'm talkin' about?" Naomi grabbed her bony wrist and fought the urge to shake some sense into her. "Ya didn't see nothin' that night. Ya didn't even know the devil was dead till ya saw him go in the ground the next day."

Efia pressed her full lips together. "I ain't 'sposed to talk about it. They said I'm a 'fishal witness, and I ain't to talk to none of ya." There was a hint of defiance in her voice as she jerked her arm from Naomi's grasp.

"Ya ought to be ashamed of yerself," Naomi hissed. "Taye Campbell fed yer black ass and dragged ya over half the South then north to set ya free and this is how ya repay her?"

Efia's lower lip trembled. "I know what I seen."

Naomi scowled. "What did they give ya to tell this lie?" She looked at the dress. "Money? How much money is worth yer soul, girl?"

"Get away from here," Efia challenged. "Ya come again and I'll tell the sheriff. And don't be think' about puttin' any spell on me, either!"

Naomi shook her head in disgust. "Spell?" she said softly, backing down the steps. "I ain't throwin' a spell at ya. I ain't wastin' good breath on ya, Efia, 'cause ya done dug yer own hole. No good comes of this kind of meanness."

Naomi turned away and lifted her arm. Noah pulled her up behind him and they rode off, leaving Efia to stand on the sagging porch alone in the darkness.

Jackson tiptoed down the dark hallway. It was later than he had expected to be, and the entire household was quiet.

He'd talked a long time with Thomas. Immediately jumping at the chance to defend Taye's honor, Thomas had insisted that he, along with a team of the finest lawyers in the country, would defend her.

Thomas almost seemed relieved, not shocked or surprised, when Jackson revealed that Taye had left with Falcon. He had then told Jackson something that now weighed heavily on Jackson's mind, on his heart.

Jackson stared at the closed bedchamber door. He had promised Cameron that when he came home he would tell her what Thomas had had to say, but right now, all he wanted to do was climb into bed and sleep with her in his arms. He knew that their lovemaking earlier this evening would not solve all their problems, but he hoped that it was enough balm to begin the healing process. If Cameron could just forgive him, perhaps they could repair the damage and begin anew.

He turned the glass doorknob and walked in to see a single lamp burning by the bed.

He smiled at the sight of Cameron asleep on her side, her father's diary cradled in her arms. Her hair hung loose in waves of bright red light around her head, and she wore a thin sleeping gown that had slid up to reveal a good deal of one shapely thigh.

His smile turned to a frown when he noted the second sleeping form in the bed. Lacy.

He ground his teeth. He didn't understand why Cameron couldn't see that the girl was only trying to take advantage of her. She was no more Grant's daughter than he was! Cameron was too softhearted, seeing this young girl as a lost colt, not the clever, opportunity-seeking chit that she was.

Knowing he couldn't carry Lacy to her room without a commotion, Jackson gazed longingly at Cameron again. He needed so badly to lie beside her and hold her. But he didn't want to disturb her sleep. He walked to the bedside and carefully removed the diary from his wife's arms, setting it by the bed. Then he blew out the lamp and left the room in silence.

29

The following morning Cameron lay in bed for a few moments, drifting in that pleasant place between sleep and consciousness, where all the edges of life seem softer. She dreamily recalled the smell of the grass beneath her and the arch of the stable framing overhead, as she and Jackson had made love the previous evening. Remembering the touch of his fingertips on her skin, the taste of his mouth on hers, she smiled and stretched lazily.

As she opened her eyes, though, the reality of the previous night jolted her. The soldiers' visit, Taye's disappearance.

Cameron turned her head on the pillow, and her heart sank even further. It was not Jackson who lay beside her sleeping peacefully, as she had dreamed, but Lacy.

With a sigh, she rose. A thousand thoughts went through her head as she dressed in a simple pale-blue-and-yellow gown and swept her hair into a chignon low at the nape of her neck.

Perhaps Jackson was not even here. Perhaps he had stayed with Thomas, who was overwrought by the news of the charge against Taye. Or maybe the situation had changed during the night. What if Falcon and Taye had been caught trying to leave town?

Downstairs, Cameron found Jackson on the veranda, drinking coffee. He glanced over a newspaper when she stepped outside. He wore dark breeches and a starched white shirt, but no cravat or jacket. He looked younger than his forty-odd years, with his dark hair still damp from bathing and his chin freshly shaven.

Cameron inhaled the heavenly aroma of crepe myrtle blossoms as she stepped outside. The scent brought back memories of a lifetime, sweet and bittersweet. Perspiration prickled the skin on the back of her neck; it was going to be another hot Mississippi day.

"They say the Thirteenth Amendment, giving black men their freedom, will be passed by congress before Christmas," Jackson said to her, turning the page of his newspaper. "And a fourteenth amendment will not be far behind that will make anyone born in this country a citizen no matter what the color of his skin."

Jackson did not rise to kiss her good morning, and Cameron was immediately on edge.

Why hadn't he joined her in the bed last night? If he had wanted to begin sleeping with her as man and wife again, wouldn't he have come to her bedchamber? If he had really wanted to sleep with her, would a fourteen-year-old street urchin have stopped him? Once, a team of wild horses, a regiment of soldiers, an entire civil war would not have stopped him.

She slid into a chair across from him, not certain if she was angry or just hurt. She reached for the pressed linen napkin folded neatly in front of her. "President Lincoln would have been pleased."

"That he would have." Jackson turned another page.

Patsy appeared to pour her mistress's coffee. "Captain

says no breakfast for him, Miss Cameron. Says ain't no one else here to make breakfast for, but you and the girl. You want me to tell the kitchen to get their skirts movin'?''

Cameron shook her head as she watched the dark coffee pour into her porcelain teacup. "Just some biscuits and jam, Patsy."

"Yes, Miss Cameron."

Cameron added sugar to her coffee and sipped it, glancing over the rim of the delicate cup at Jackson. "You saw Thomas last night?"

He nodded. "He wants to represent Taye. He believes a jury will be more likely to find her innocent if she is defended by her fiancé, a man they know from the county." He reached for his own coffee cup, setting aside the newspaper. "He intends to contact colleagues today to build a team of lawyers."

She lifted a brow. "So he thinks there is merit to this ridiculous accusation?"

"He is afraid that because Reconstruction is just beginning, the government will feel they must move cautiously with a case like this." He hesitated. "Cam...the truth is, I've learned that there's a price on Taye's head. Five hundred dollars for the slave woman who killed her master—dead or alive."

"That's barbaric! Besides, my father set Sukey and Taye free years before he died."

"I understand."

"Grant was never Taye's *master*."

"I understand that, too."

"But it's so unfair to Taye. How could anyone—"

"Cameron," Jackson interrupted, leaning forward on the table. "I'm not expressing my own opinion, but rather what an all-white Mississippi jury might say. What the Southern newspapers and conservative Republicans might say. For

God's sake, I don't hold this against Taye. Grant tried to auction her virginity in a whorehouse. It's difficult to see why she didn't murder him sooner.''

"That's not how it happened," she retorted hotly. "She would never have shot him if he had not been shooting at me. And now you tell me her life is in danger for that?''

"Cam, it's silly to argue over this when you and I are on the same side. We both know damned well that this was a form of self-defense because Taye was defending you. All I'm saying is that we must proceed cautiously because a jury might not see it that way right now.''

"How is a jury to say what happened?'' she demanded. "No one was actually there but Taye and me.''

"No one but you and Taye, and Naomi and Efia and Dorcas. You forgot the sisters.''

She glanced up, fighting to regain her composure. "I didn't, but the girls weren't actually there. They couldn't possibly have seen anything. Naomi went to see Efia last night, anyway.''

"I have already spoken to Naomi this morning. You two were correct in your guess. Efia wouldn't really say anything, but Naomi is certain she is the one who went to Captain Grey.''

"Why?'' Cameron demanded. "Why would she do such a thing to Taye? You know what we all did for those two girls.'' She shook her head, thinking back to the weeks they had spent together. At that time, nothing they had said or done indicated Efia would ever turn on Taye this way. On them.

"We don't know why. But the South is crawling with desperate men and women who would kill their own sister for that much hard money. We've got to find Taye and Falcon before anyone else does.''

"Falcon will protect her.''

"With his life, but he's only one man. If we don't straighten this out, Taye could spend the rest of her life running. We have to find them. But we need to be cautious. We don't know what kind of case Thomas intends to build. We wouldn't want to hinder his efforts."

"We have to go looking for her today."

Jackson shook his head.

"Why not? Fleeing only makes Taye look guiltier in the eyes of the law," Cameron said. "And now, if she's in danger of being murdered, we have to—"

"I want to give Thomas time to gather his thoughts and come up with a plan."

"And what if we do find her? Do we bring her back to face trial? Who's to say something terrible won't happen to her here?"

Jackson's face hardened. "If and when we find her, I'll take care of her. I promise you that much."

"But how?"

"I don't know yet, but I'll think of something. This is what I do, Cam. What I've been trained for. One way or another, we'll keep her safe." He paused. "I have a pretty good idea where they've gone."

"You do?" Her gazed flickered to his. "Where?"

"The fewer who know, the better off everyone will be. Once we come up with a plan, I'll go and fetch her."

"You won't go without me?"

The corner of his mouth turned up in a wry grin reminiscent of their first years together. "I have a feeling I could try, but I doubt I would be successful."

She dared a half smile, and for a moment, just the briefest moment, she felt a spark leap between them. For just that instant, she seemed to be on familiar ground with the man she had once loved more than life itself.

Jackson pushed away from the table and the moment was

gone, just that quickly. "There's something else I need to tell you. It's important that you keep it to yourself, but I told Thomas I would speak for him."

Her brows knitted. "Whatever are you talking about?" She felt a tightening in her chest. Had he and Taye broken off their engagement? She had known something was going on. Why hadn't either of them told her?

"Thomas is dying," he said flatly.

"What?"

"He's dying."

"How—"

He raised a hand to silence her. "I think he has known for some time. He's tried several medical treatments, but none have been successful. I imagine he has been denying the truth for weeks, perhaps months."

Cameron could only stare in disbelief. Thomas Burl, dying? It seemed impossible. He was still such a young man, younger than Jackson. He had been in her life for so many years, steady, dependable. Because of his relationship with her father, she had always known he would be there for her. And now he would not be.

"Consumption," Jackson finished softly.

A chill passed through Cameron as she met his compassionate gaze. She thought of Thomas's coughing fits. Of how thin he had become. How could she have been so blind? She had even asked recently if he had seen the apothecary. But Thomas had insisted he was just working too hard. Why hadn't it occurred to her that he might be seriously ill?

The answer came swift and sure from deep inside her.

For the same reason you couldn't see that Taye no longer loved Thomas.

"No." Cameron willed herself not to listen. She gripped the handle of the delicate china cup. She stammered, trying to recover her composure. "D-does Taye know about Thomas?"

Once, Taye had told Cameron everything. But since Taye had joined her in Baltimore, she knew there had been secrets between them.

Because you stopped thinking about her happiness, Cameron's inner voice accused harshly. *All you could think about was yourself. More than Taye, more than Jackson— even more than your own baby. You had to have your way.*

"She does not know, and Thomas has asked that we not tell her."

"Surely she has to be told!"

"He wants to tell her himself." He rose from his chair. "He has that right. And he has the right to decide when he will tell her."

Cameron stared at the wide painted boards of the veranda flooring. She felt guilty for not having been more perceptive. She felt guilty for being so wrapped up in her own troubles that she had missed the signs of Thomas's illness. But she'd never intentionally hurt Taye. She loved her. "Maybe that's what has been wrong between Taye and Thomas," Cameron said. "I know Taye felt he was not giving her the attention she expected. Perhaps his illness is why he moved home." She looked up. "He knew, but he didn't know how to tell her."

Jackson walked around the table. "I think he was hoping he was wrong. You cannot blame a man for that." He rested his hand on Cameron's shoulder.

She closed her eyes, welcoming his touch. "Could I speak to him?" she murmured.

"Not yet. Give him a few days. He was pretty upset. I don't think he'd told a living soul about the consumption, and now this thing with Taye has happened."

He removed his hand from her shoulder and she opened her eyes, the spell broken.

"So I just have to sit here and do nothing while the state builds a case against my sister for murdering our brother?"

"I'll be home this evening." He walked into the house, leaving her on the veranda.

She couldn't bear to watch him go.

A week later, Jackson halted in front of the bank on his way inside. He offered his hand to a man he had known from the war. Both being in the shipping business, his and Antoine Gallier's paths had crossed several times. Jackson knew he was here in town because Thomas was working on some legal documents for him. In the commotion of Taye's charge of murder, and Jackson's overnight trip to investigate a lead on Thompson's Raiders, however, he had not had a chance to see his old friend. "Antoine, good to see you."

"And you." Mr. Gallier tipped his hat and clasped Jackson's hand warmly. "I must thank you for sending me to Monsieur Thomas. He has been most helpful. He is quite knowledgeable about the intricacies of international shipping."

"I'm glad he could be of aid to you. I told you Thomas would not disappoint. Are you in town long? My wife and I would be pleased to have you join us for supper one evening."

"I am here until week's end, then on to New Orleans before I return home to Baton Rouge."

"What about tonight, then?"

"*Merci,* Jackson. You are too kind. You must know how dreary dining alone can be when one must travel so often."

"What time would be good for you?" Jackson nodded

to a passing carriage as a young lady fluttered a handkerchief. "Seven? Eight?"

Gallier pulled his watch from his pocket. "Let me see,
it is five now—"

The portrait of a woman inside the lid of the gold pocket-
watch caught Jackson's eye. "Damn, Antoine, who is
that?"

Gallier turned the watch so that Jackson could get a better look at the miniature. "*Mon dieu,* this is my dear niece,
Minette." He crossed himself. "May God rest her soul that
lies on the bottom of the sea."

Jackson stared at the young woman's portrait, shocked
by the incredible likeness to Taye Campbell. "I'm sorry to
hear that, Antoine. I must tell you, she looks so much like
my sister-in-law that you could have told me it was she
and I would have believed you."

The Creole closed the gold watch. "*Oui,* I had the pleasure of meeting the mademoiselle last time I was in town.
The similarity was quite unnerving. Of course, I found the
young lady quite charming."

Jackson's mind spun as he considered the absurd thought
that had just struck him. "Could you tell me, Antoine,
when did your niece pass away?"

"It was May of '61, just before your war began. Lost at
sea in the gulf in a terrible storm. *Affreux.* All hands lost.
My own ship." He shook his head sadly. "It was tragic.
My wife was devastated."

"Again, I am sorry for your loss." Jackson touched the
older man's arm, his head reeling with the possibilities. His
idea would never be viable. It was a ludicrous notion, so
ludicrous that it just might work. "Listen, Antoine, would
you consider doing me an enormous favor? A larger favor
than any man should ask of another."

Gallier looked up. "You know I would do anything for

you, Jackson. If it were not for you, my business would have perished during the war. My family would have starved.''

"My proposal would not be entirely lawful, I'll tell you that up front," Jackson warned. "But I swear to you it would be for a good cause. It would mean a great deal to my wife's family. To me."

Antoine smiled slyly. "This would not be the first time I have done something *illégal,* eh, *ami?*"

"I don't understand," Cameron told Jackson. But even as she spoke, she began to toss clothing onto the bed to be packed in her Saratoga trunk. "How can we save Taye by bringing her home to face trial? You said yourself she won't be treated fairly. And what does this Mr. Gallier have to do with her? I've never even heard of him."

"I haven't quite got everything worked out in my mind, but Thomas and I are meeting him in Thomas's offices in an hour. I'll know more once Thomas explains to us the legal ramifications."

Cameron tossed clean shifts, stockings and a corset onto the bed. She paid no attention to what articles of clothing she chose. She wanted to hurry so she'd be prepared when Jackson was ready to leave town.

"I don't understand." She turned to where he stood in the doorway. He hadn't even entered the bedchamber when he'd come to tell her they were going for Taye. "At least tell me where we're going. Where is she?"

"I have a feeling she and Falcon are in New Orleans."

"New Orleans? Why there? We know no one in New Orleans."

He shook his head; she could tell he was already preoccupied with other thoughts. "It doesn't matter. What matters is that we need to get her back here."

"I can be ready within the hour. It won't take me long to pack Lacy's things, either."

He had started to turn away, to go down the hall, but he turned back. "No." He held up his finger to her. "Just you. I will not take that she-beast any further than the end of the drive."

"Jackson—"

"This is nonnegotiable," he interrupted before Cameron could even present her argument. "The girl will stay here with Naomi, or you will stay here with her. I am not traveling with her. I haven't the time to deal with her little fits."

Cameron opened her mouth to argue, but when her gaze met Jackson's, she realized this was a battle she would not win. She had to decide, would she leave Lacy in Naomi's capable hands, or would she pass this chance, not only to find Taye, but also to be alone with Jackson for a few days?

Cameron hated to leave Lacy behind, but she knew she had to go with Jackson. If the only way she could do that was to leave her niece, then Lacy would remain at Atkins' Way.

Cameron pressed her lips together and lifted her lashes to meet Jackson's gaze. In her arms, she clutched a pale yellow petticoat. "I'll be ready in a few minutes."

"Take what time you need. We probably won't even be able to get out of here until morning. I'm not sure if we'll go by train or boat or carriage or all three. I just want you to be ready."

"I'll be ready," she whispered as he strode down the hall.

30

"Something more to eat?" Falcon asked Taye across the tiny courtyard table at a hotel in New Orleans. Candles glimmered on the tables and in the trees, and three dark-skinned men played rich, soulful Creole music from a gallery above them.

"Something more to eat?" Taye gazed at Falcon and laughed. "Tonight you have stuffed me with jambalaya—" she ticked off on her fingers "—quail stuffed with oysters, and shrimp, and now you want to feed me more? I think not." She reached for the glass of wine a beautiful quadroon woman had just brought her. "*Merci,*" she murmured. She met the woman's dark-eyed gaze, so much like her own. "*Vous avez les yeux très beaux.*"

The proud young woman dipped her head and murmured beneath her breath, "*Pas assez que les votres, madame.*"

Taye felt her cheeks color at the compliment. "*Qu'est-ce que ç'est quoi votre nom?*"

"Josette."

"*Merci de vos mots aimables,* Josette," Taye said.

The woman smiled, then slipped away.

"I did not know you spoke the language of the Creole,"

Falcon remarked, watching Taye intently in the flickering candlelight.

She turned her glass, watching the crimson wine slide up the side. "I speak four languages." She glanced at him over the rim. "Cameron's French is barely passable, but our tutor always said I had a gift for languages."

His sensuous mouth turned at one corner. "Is one of those languages, by chance, the tongue of my mother?"

"Cherokee?" She laughed and shook her head. "I'm afraid not. But I do speak the language of your father. Spanish."

"Then if you came to California with me, you could talk about me behind my back to my padre. I do not speak my father's tongue."

"Why not?"

He lifted one broad, muscular shoulder in a shrug. "I grew up among the Cherokee. My mother's father was my father. It was not our way."

"So you did not know him as a boy?"

Falcon shook his head. "I was a young man before I ever laid eyes upon him."

She sipped from her glass, deep in thought. "Then, in a way, you and I are very alike. I, too, grew up without a father. Only he was right there, and I never knew it."

"Does this anger you?"

She thought before she answered. "Anger me? No. It could not be helped. It was not our way." She smiled good-humoredly. "But I long for what I know now that I missed."

Falcon nodded in the direction of the quadroon who had served them. She was now cleaning up another table. "I only speak a little of the Creole French tongue. What did she say?"

"I told her that she had beautiful eyes. She thought I did, too," she finished shyly.

"She is right." He continued to watch her. "You seem very comfortable here. I thought that you would be."

Falcon was right. It seemed odd to her that she could feel so at home in a place so far from home. But here in New Orleans, there were so many men and women of mixed race that, for once, she did not feel out of place. He had noticed the same when he had visited New Orleans with Jackson during the war. Falcon said that that was one of the reasons he had brought her here, to show her that life could be different for her.

She sipped the sweet, fruity wine and set down the glass. Falcon slid his hand across the table to cover hers. "Would you like to dance with me?"

A sweet, mournful song of love found and then lost echoed in the moss-tangled tree overhead, and couples rose to dance arm in arm. It was not a waltz or any other dance Taye recognized; men and women seemed to simply sway to the music, wrapped in each other's arms. It seemed quite risqué to her, and terribly alluring.

"You dance?" she asked, delighted by each new facet of Falcon's personality that she discovered.

He clasped her hand and led her to the bricked patio to join the other couples. "I usually place a war bonnet upon my head and dance around the campfire, but tonight it is too warm for a fire."

She clasped one of his hands and rested her other on his shoulder as she laughed. Under the moonlight, amidst the twinkling stars of candlelight in the trees, Taye could almost forget that she was here in New Orleans because she was running away. Running for her life.

Falcon drew her closer and she rested her cheek on his shoulder. "Do you know what I wish?" she whispered.

"Wishes are not to be shared," he murmured in her ear. "Not with anything but the sky, not with anyone but the mother earth."

"Well, this is one wish I want to share with you." She tipped back her head so that she could look into his ebony eyes. "I wish that I could dance in your arms like this forever."

Falcon brushed his mouth against hers. "Come west with me and we will dance every night under the stars."

She shook her head. "I've been thinking about this all night, Falcon. I don't know that I can do that. I don't know that I can leave my sister. Not without even saying good-bye." And Thomas, she thought. How can I just abandon him without releasing him from his promise?

Taye wished now that she had gone to Thomas the night the soldiers had come for her. At least then, there could have been some sense of conclusiveness in her life. Right now, everything was left undone. She felt as if she could not step forward and could not move back.

The song ended and a banjo began to strum a faster beat. Hand in hand, Taye and Falcon walked back to their table, but there, Taye only picked up her reticule. "Let's go back to the room," she said softly.

Falcon turned his head to meet her gaze and seemed to read some meaning in her words, a meaning she didn't even quite understand.

In the week since they had arrived in New Orleans, Falcon had shown her the sights of the town. They had picnicked in Jackson Square and walked along the waterfront off Decatur. She had seen the ladies of the evening hanging off the galleries on Bourbon Street and strolled through the *Vieux Carré* where Marie LaVeau, the voodoo queen, was sometimes seen at twilight. Taye and Falcon watched the Creole dance to their native music. The two of them ate their fill of the delights Louisiana had to offer and played at gambling tables until late in the evening.

Each night they returned to their hotel on Royal Street where they shared a room. Falcon had said it would be safer if they traveled as man and wife; Taye had allowed him to make that decision. But each night when they retired, she slept alone in the great bed, covered by mosquito netting, and he slept on the floor by the door.

Tonight it would be different. Gazing into Falcon's eyes, she knew she had to return to Mississippi and face her accusers. She knew that she could hang for what she had done, but that didn't matter. She would do it all over again if it meant saving her beloved Cameron.

But without putting an end to the life she had left behind, she had no hope of exploring the possibility of a life with Falcon. Until she made peace with Grant and with Thomas, she would find no true happiness in Falcon's arms.

Falcon took her arm in silence, sensing her need to be alone with her thoughts. Within minutes they entered their lavish suite in the Three Sisters Hotel. He locked the door behind them and tossed his top hat on a chair.

They had both purchased clothing once they had arrived in New Orleans. Taye was wearing a lacy orange Basque habit she had chosen on a whim. Falcon had chosen black trousers to wear with his red coat and had added a black tall hat which made him appear even larger and more imposing.

She laid her gloves on the chair beside his hat and turned to face him. He seemed to be reading her mind, as if she were one of the books from Jackson's library. He reached his hands to her and took hers. They were warm and reassuring.

"Taye," he said softly. "I will take you as my wife here and now, but you must come to me willingly, without regret. You know I could take you far from here, where you would never be found.''

She shook her head. ''I have to go back, Falcon.'' She lowered her head and then lifted it to look at him. ''I know you don't understand, but I must release Thomas from his vow to marry me. And I must answer my accusers in court.''

He frowned. ''I understand the importance of a promise made, but to allow yourself to be arrested...'' He shook his head. ''I fear you will not see fairness in the Englishman's court. I fear that you will be judged by the color of your skin and not your deeds, as I have been many times in the past. As I know you have been.''

She pressed her lips together, feeling the burn of tears behind her eyelids. She was afraid he would be angry with her, but she didn't care. She knew what she had to do. ''I still have to go back.''

Then, to her surprise, he smiled. ''You are a very brave woman, Taye Campbell, brave enough to be a Cherokee maiden.'' He pulled her into his arms and she tipped her chin upward to meet his lips.

They had kissed many times since the night they fled Atkins' Way, but there was something different in this kiss. Something Taye sensed inside herself.

She remembered the nights she had touched herself, dreaming of Falcon. Now she would live those fantasies in the flesh.

She might have her day in court, she might be found guilty and hang for killing Grant Campbell, but she would have this night, she decided. She would have this perfect night with the man she wanted to spend the rest of her life with.

Taye slipped her arms around Falcon's neck and pulled him tight against her. She felt her pulse quicken as she thrust her tongue into his mouth and tasted the hot, dark cavern. There was something about his woodsy scent, the taste of him, something half wild, something that excited her in a way she had never experienced before.

Falcon rested one hand on her rib cage and she covered his hand with her own. Slowly, but intrepidly, she guided it upward until it rested on the swell of her breast.

She sighed as the heat of his warm hand seeped through the filmy fabric of her gown and underclothing. It was so hot and steamy here in New Orleans that no woman wore any more clothing than was absolutely necessary for decorum.

He tugged on her lower lip with his teeth and brushed his thumb over her nipple. Again she sighed, only this time it came out as more of a moan.

Taye was caught between the timidity she had grown up with concerning sexuality, and the compelling feelings blossoming inside her. She wanted so badly not just to be touched, but also to touch. She was not a complete innocent; she had been raised on a plantation. She knew what a man's genitalia looked like, but she wanted to touch Falcon, to see what a man's flesh felt like in her hand.

Perhaps she should have been ashamed, but she was not.

Taye tipped back her head so that Falcon could press his mouth to the hollow of her throat. At the same time, she dared to lay her hand on his thigh and then slide it upward.

"Taye," Falcon groaned, deep in his throat.

The sound of his voice, husky, needy, made her bolder. She slid her hand over until she touched the swell in his trousers and was rewarded by another guttural groan of pleasure.

She slid her hand downward and then upward, stroking him, fascinated by the way he seemed to harden at once beneath her fingertips, despite her lack of experience.

"Taye." Falcon drew his mouth over the swell of her breasts above the bodice of her gown. At the same time, he caught her wrist and halted her caress.

Her eyelids flickered open, and for a moment, she feared she had made a mistake in judgment. Perhaps he did not want to make love with her.

"Taye, I am sorry. I thank you for the gift you offer me, but I cannot take that which is meant for the man you will spend the rest of your life with."

Her breath came so ragged that it took a minute for her to respond. She was relieved that she had not misunderstood and that he did, indeed, want her. "Falcon, I know what I'm doing. I know what I want. No matter what happens to me, I know you are meant to have my virginity," she whispered.

He smiled, a kind smile that seemed sad at the same time. He lifted her hand to his chest, where she could feel his heart pounding. "Your words touch my heart, but I must say no. Not when you still hold your promise to Thomas binding."

Her lower lip trembled. She ached so badly for him at this moment that she knew one brush of his fingertips on her sex would make her explode with pleasure beyond her experiences alone. But she could not force herself upon him if he did not want her.

She lowered her chin, her face growing hot with a mixture of disappointment and embarrassment. She could feel the heat of the humid night prickly and damp on the back of her neck. "You do not want to make love with me, when I am willing?"

He clasped her chin between his thumb and forefinger and lifted it until she was forced to gaze into his eyes. "I did not say I would not make love with you, only that I would not take your virginity until you can give it freely."

When she at last absorbed his meaning, her face brightened in an impish smile. "I had not thought of that," she
murmured. It made sense, of course. If she could please
herself, why could he not pleasure her in the same ways?
Why could she not please him and still remain a virgin?

Taye raised both hands and Falcon pressed his to hers.
Their fingers entwined and he drew closer. He caught her
lower lip between his teeth and bit down gently. She parted
her lips and teased his tongue with hers. Only then did
Falcon cover her mouth with a suffocating kiss.

She laughed deep in her throat as he swept her into his
arms and carried her to the big bed that they had yet to
share. Setting her down gently, he stood and slowly began
to remove his clothing. His boots. His stockings. His red
coat and then the white shirt and cravat.

Taye watched in fascination, the heat building first in her
cheeks, then outward, as he stripped down to bare skin.
The pit of her stomach tightened; her pulse seemed to
pound in her ears. She moistened her dry lips with the tip
of her tongue as his fingers brushed the waistband of his
trousers.

He hesitated.

Taye lowered her eyelids until her eyes were half closed.
"I will see all of you, Falcon. I should inspect the goods,"
she purred, "before I make any promises."

His low rich laughter was the best balm there could be
for her nerves. She watched, unabashed, as he pushed the
black trousers over his narrow, sun-bronzed hips.

Her breath caught ragged in her throat as she saw the
dark patch of hair. Then he sprang forth, larger than she
expected and not nearly so foreign. She smiled and reached
out to him with one hand. "It's so warm in here," she
whispered, half sitting up. "Help me with this tiresome
gown."

Never taking his gaze from hers, he slipped off her shoes
and then her silk stockings. As he undressed her, he lingered, drawing his warm fingertips over her skin, sending
ripples of gooseflesh up her legs. Then he sat on the bed,
facing her, and drew her up by her shoulders. He brushed
his lips against hers in brief, fleeting butterfly kisses as his
fingers found the buttons down the back of her gown.

"For a man, you are well versed in ladies' clothing,"
she teased huskily as he drew the yards of gown over her
head, taking care with the delicate fabric. He took the time
to walk to the far chair and drape the gown over the back.

She watched as he walked toward her, stiff and erect in
his maleness. Taye had always known that she would do
this with someone, but she had always thought of it as a
woman's duty to her husband. It had never occurred to her
until she met Falcon that she would really desire to touch
a man, to feel him inside her.

Falcon sat on the edge of the bed again and helped her
out of her corset and shift. Only once she was utterly naked
did he stretch out beside her in the big bed and draw down
the mosquito netting so that they were enclosed in a magical web.

"You are more beautiful than I had dreamed," he
breathed in her ear. As he spoke, he dragged one finger
between her breasts, over her stomach and upward again in
a lazy circle.

Taye sighed and, without thinking, lifted her hips as his
hand drew lower once more. "You dreamed of me?"

He leaned to press a kiss to the peak of her small, firm
breast. "Every night since I found you in the garden. A
gift sent to me from the heavens."

Her breath caught in her throat as he drew his hand lower
on her belly, then, at the last possible moment, upward
again.

Taye rolled toward him and lifted up to catch his mouth with hers. She was trembling from head to toe, aching. She brushed her palm across his cheek and took his mouth hungrily. At the same time, she slid her hand down his leg and, without hesitation, took his hard, hot flesh in her hand.

Falcon groaned and their kiss deepened.

Taye was fascinated by his sex, by its shape, by its responsiveness, by the soft texture of his skin. She had always thought a woman's body was beautiful, a gift of creation by God, but she had never known how glorious a man's body could be.

Falcon rolled on top of her and she gave a little cry of protest, not yet ready to release him.

He drank in her dark eyes as he slid down her body, dragging his hot, wet tongue in a path, lower and lower. He teased her navel with the tip of his tongue and then rested his cheek on her belly.

Taye could barely catch her breath. Everything was spinning. The room, the bed, her thoughts.

Falcon grazed the bed of dark curls between her thighs with his skilled fingertips and a cry of relief escaped her lips.

"Shh," he murmured. "Slowly. We have all night."

She laughed and closed her eyes, trying to catch her breath as she attempted to slow her pounding heart. He waited a moment and then began to touch her again with light strokes.

Taye raised her hips to meet his hand. Just once he brushed against the swell of pink flesh and she cried aloud with pleasure. He rested his cheek against her belly again, cupping her sex, letting the sweet ripples of pleasure wash over her, drown her.

When her breath came more regularly for a second time, he began to touch her. He stroked her soft, damp flesh with a gentle hand. He wanted to know what pleased her and that thought made her heart swell with love.

Love. She did love him. She knew that now. She not only loved Falcon, but she was in love with him. And that was something very different from what she had experienced with Thomas.

Gradually, Falcon slid down in the bed, kissing a path from her belly downward. The moment she realized what he intended to do, she thought to stop him. But she couldn't. She simply could not stop the need that now seemed to be instinctive.

Taye threaded her fingers through Falcon's thick, black hair, thinking she would permit just one kiss *down there.* But the moment his tongue brushed the dampness at the apex of her thighs, she was lost in sensation. Just one stroke of his tongue—two—and she was moaning aloud again, writhing beneath him.

Again he lay still, giving her time to catch her breath. When she could speak, she reached for him. "Falcon—"

"Shh," he hushed. "I have waited a long time to touch you, to taste you. Do not stop me now." And as he spoke, he had already begun to stroke her, exploring in knowing ways she had not explored herself.

Twice more Taye cried out with satisfaction. At last, when she so tired she could not lift her lashes, Falcon stretched out beside her. He blew out the lamp beside the bed and enveloped her in his arms.

"I love you, my Taye," Falcon whispered in her ear. "Tell me that you love me and I will wait for you until the end of my days."

"I love you," she whispered, her eyes closed. "I want to be with you. Always."

"Then tomorrow I will send word to Jackson. He will tell us what we must do so that we can be together always."

Taye opened her eyes one last time to see Falcon looking down at her and then she drifted off to sleep, content that no matter what happened, she could die a happy woman.

31

Cameron stepped onto the paddle wheeler's deck and took a deep breath of the pungent night air. Heady smells enveloped her, as hot and powerful as moonshine whiskey: rich black soil, verdant walls of vegetation, rotting logs and the eternal river itself, thick and silt-choked, black and smooth as molasses.

The creaking of boat timbers, the rhythmic slap of the paddles and the swish of the bow parting water drowned out the noises of the river that she could feel all around her. But she could hear them in her mind, and they seemed more real than the notes of the piano or the laughter of passengers from the ship's main saloon.

Cameron could imagine the flapping of a night bird's wing, the croaking of frogs and the splash of fish. She could see the faint flicker of lights from houses along the shore and unconsciously strained her eyes to see the faces and figures of the inhabitants.

With only a little imagination, Cameron fancied that she heard the clink of a tin cup against a bucket as lovers shared a cool drink of water at a well, the murmur of a sleepy mother crooning a lullaby to her nursing infant, or the squeak of a worn rocking chair.

"Old Miss," she murmured. "I do love the river so." How could Jackson expect her to live in Washington or Maryland, when she was so much a child of the Deep South? War-torn and ragged, this was still her home, and she cherished the land and the people with every fiber of her being.

Spotting Jackson's silhouette in the moonlight on the far rail of the ship, she hesitated. Obviously he wanted to be alone, else he wouldn't have picked such a secluded place on the boat. Did she just return to her cabin?

After a moment of indecision, Cameron crossed the deck to join him. She pressed her hands to the painted black wooden rail and took another deep breath, thankful to be out of her stuffy cabin.

He glanced at her, then out at the dark, rippling water again. He had been in a pensive mood since they'd boarded the *Magnolia Queen* the previous day in Vicksburg. Before the war, it might have been faster to take the overland route and the train to New Orleans, but like the rest of the South, Louisiana was a wasteland of ruined plantations, fallow fields and destroyed railroads. At the dock where they had boarded, a one-legged corporal, still wearing the tatters of a gray uniform, had told Cameron that one quarter of the males in the South were dead. Three hundred thousand slaves had been set free without work and without a place to rest their heads. When one looked at those statistics, it was no wonder there were not more bands of thieves and murderers like the one preying upon her own hometown right now.

"I'm sorry that I could not acquire more comfortable lodging," Jackson said, not looking at her. He had been unable to secure them a private berth on such late notice, so Cameron was sharing a tiny cabin with Miss Fanny Motterbee and her great-aunt Frances Motterbee. The two women were chatterboxes, elated to have a woman of not only Mississippi society with them, but of Washington, D.C., society, as well. The fact that Cameron's husband was a Yankee seemed of little consequence. The two women were more interested in hemlines and the shape of new bonnets than politics. Cameron had come outside to escape their incessant chatter.

She listened to the hum of the steam engine, which drove the paddlewheel. "The cabin is perfectly adequate."

She tried not to think about the fact that since her husband had returned home, they had not slept together. The first night, when the soldiers had come and Taye had run away, Lacy had slept with her. After that, each night Jackson had gone to one of the guest bedchambers and Cameron had slept alone. It wasn't that she wanted to; she just didn't know how to ask him to return to her bed. Part of it was that she wanted him to initiate the conversation; she wanted him to *want* to be with her again.

"We even have a small window," she said, making conversation. "How are the men's quarters?"

"Crowded." He glanced sideways at her and she saw his mouth turn up in a half grin. A flicker of the man she had known before the war. "Smoky. Loud."

Cameron took a chance and slid her hand over the smooth, polished wood rail to cover his hand. She wanted so desperately to make amends with Jackson, especially now with Taye's life in jeopardy. She just didn't know how to breech the chasm. "Perhaps in New Orleans we could share a room, just the two of us, minus Fanny and Frances and your dozen new friends," she said lightly.

He turned toward her, and in the moonlight she saw the lines of his face that had not been there before the war. Tenderness washed over her. She wished she could smooth away those lines, smooth away the tragedies he had experienced, of which he rarely spoke. But she knew she couldn't alter the past; not the war, not the loss of their baby, not the things she had said to him out of anger or pain. All she could do was press forward, try to right what could be righted, and accept what could not.

Jackson took her hand in his and lifted it to his lips; he stared out at the muddy waters of the Mississippi. "Talk to me," he said, a catch in his voice. "Tell me what you have been doing to pass the time."

"I've been reading Papa's diary."

"Still?" He smiled and rubbed her hand against his cheek.

He had not shaved this evening before supper in the Captain's cabin, and his skin was pleasantly abrasive. Cameron was afraid to breathe, afraid to break the spell. This was the first real intimacy she'd felt with Jackson in weeks, perhaps months. It was true they had made love the evening he returned, but that had been different. That had been about pent-up desires and release. This was subtler, more lasting.

"I would have thought you would be done with it by now," Jackson mused. "I know, had that been my father's diary, I could not have kept myself from reading until I had read every entry."

She leaned against him, pressing her cheek to his shoulder. He smelled so good, so familiar in a comforting way. The scent of the starch of his cravat, the leather of his freshly polished shoes, the faint hint of tobacco and the intrinsic male scent of his skin all combined to send her senses reeling. This was the man she had loved since she was seventeen and barely in her first lady's corset. Surely such a love could not die so easily; surely, *somewhere,* there had to be a spark still left unkindled.

"I'm trying to savor Papa's words," she said softly. "As I read, I not only see him, but I see myself."

Jackson rested his hands on the ship's rail again, but held fast to hers. "Tell me what you read today."

"It was about my parents' wedding. You know, it was arranged."

He drew his lips back in a sardonic frown. "A good businessman, above all, his father."

"Papa wasn't in love with my mother. He barely knew her. But he did as his father asked and married her anyway."

"It's what Southern men do," Jackson remarked.

"But a week before the wedding, he brought Sukey into the house to begin training to become the housekeeper." She spoke in a soft, conspiratory tone, almost as if she were in on the plan with her father. "He actually openly discussed the matter with his father and gained his permission. The only thing my grandfather stipulated was that Papa be discreet."

She lifted her head from his shoulder to gaze up at him. She had his full attention for once and he was listening, as fascinated by the story as she was. "Papa and my mother married and Grant was born less than a year later." She smiled, remembering her father's words. "He said," she quoted from memory, *"Katherine bore a small but healthy son at dawn with little fuss. Both are hearty. I was hoping for a red-haired girl to bounce on my knee, but there will be other children."*

"And then you came along. The daughter every man secretly wishes for."

She smiled to herself, a sadness coming over her. She wondered if Jackson had wished their child had been a boy, as most men wished for, or if he, too, had hoped for a red-haired daughter.

She turned to him. ''Jackson—''

He crushed her mouth with his, taking her by surprise, silencing her words. Turning her in his arms, he trapped her between himself and the rail and kissed her deeply, his tongue delving into her mouth to possess her.

The flames of her need quickly fanned and Cameron slid her palms beneath his coat and up over his chest. In the hot, humid night air, the fabric of his cotton shirt was damp beneath her fingertips.

Jackson took her breath away with his kiss and then drew his mouth down over her chin. She stretched her neck to bare the length of her creamy skin, and a shiver of pleasure rippled through her.

As Jackson pressed fiery, fleeting kisses over the swell of her breasts, she slid her leg between his and brought her knee up to caress him.

Jackson groaned. ''Damn, I wish I could have gotten a cabin for us.''

Cameron arched her back and felt the hard wooden rail press into her flesh, but she didn't care. His mouth felt too good on her breasts. His hand that caressed her through her gown and underclothing was far too delightful.

Their mouths met again, the fevered pitch of their need increasing with every hot, wet kiss.

Jackson caught the hem of her lavender silk evening gown, pressing her back farther against the boat's rail. Cameron laughed, her voice husky in her own ears, and pushed his hand away playfully.

''Jackson,'' she murmured. ''We're in a public place. Someone might see us.''

''And what would they see?'' he murmured, his breath warm in her ear. He tongue darted out to tease her lobe. ''A man holding a woman in his arms? What harm is there in that? You are my wife. It is my duty to show you such affections.''

Again she laughed. She'd be mortified if someone came upon them, but in truth, he was right. Though they were out on the open deck, it was a secluded spot, and there was no one about. Everyone still awake on the boat was busy drinking and gambling.

Jackson grasped her hand and drew it down over the front of his trousers. "You see? I'm in desperate need of you, Cam."

She stroked the bulge of his trousers, sorely tempted. Surely a woman of her age should not be frolicking on a ship's deck, but as Jackson pointed out, they *were* an old married couple.

"If we get caught," she threatened, a thrill running through her at the thought of doing something so daring, "I swear I'll throw you overboard."

He laughed and kissed her again as she reached down to work the buttons of his trousers. His kiss was long and deep and left her breathless again, wanting him as much as he obviously wanted her.

Jackson groaned, resting his chin on her shoulder as she stroked his hard, hot flesh. Then she astonished even herself by grasping her skirts and lowering herself to her knees.

"Cameron," Jackson protested. "You don't have to—"

"Shh," she soothed. "Don't tell me you don't like this."

He massaged her shoulders. "If someone were to come—"

"No one will see us and if they do," she whispered, "I've dropped my glove and am simply trying to retrieve it from the deck."

"Cam, you can't—"

She drew her tongue up the silky skin of his shaft, silencing him until no sound escaped his lips but a guttural moan.

"Sweet God," he muttered.

Cameron's own pulse quickened as she taunted him with the flicker of her tongue here...there. She lifted the soft sacks of his flesh and caressed them gently.

Jackson panted, clutching her shoulders harder, and as his desire rose, so did her own. She caressed with her hand and her mouth, teasing him to the point of breaking, only to back down until his breath eased again.

Cameron fully intended to tease him beyond the point of return, but just when she knew he was close again, Jackson grasped her shoulders firmly and lifted her to her feet. "Cam, stop," he groaned. "You'll be the death of me."

"Death wasn't what I had in mind," she murmured, smiling against his lips. She lowered her hand to his burgeoning shaft again. "It would be all right if—"

"No, no, it wouldn't be all right," he argued, understanding what she was about to say. He grasped her hand, pulling it away and pushed her back against the railing.

It was dark on the deck, but in the moonlight she could still see him gazing into her eyes. The gray orbs were too cloudy with desire to tell what he was thinking, but she sensed a softening in him. He really did still care for her the way she knew he once had.

Jackson began to raise her gown and layers of petticoats and her crinoline. Not breaking eye contact, she took the bunches of fabric from his hands and leaned back on the rail, tilting her hips upward.

His hand found the damp, soft folds of her flesh and she bit down on her lower lip to stifle her own cry of pleasure. "Jackson," she moaned.

Holding her in his arms against the rail, he slipped inside her. She caught her lower lip between her teeth yet again and dropped her skirting so the yards of fabric surrounded them.

Jackson encircled her in his arms and rocked against her. Cameron held tightly to his shoulders, squeezing her eyes shut as great waves of pleasure struck her like ocean water on the shore. Jackson's breath in her ear, warm and panting, only increased her ardor. He moved faster, nearing the brink and Cameron opened her thighs farther, taking him as deeply as she could.

She opened her mouth in a sudden cry of fulfillment and he pressed his lips to hers so that barely a sound escaped. With one last moan, Jackson grew still.

Cameron suddenly felt as if she could not stand. Her legs were weak and her head spun. Her breath was still coming too quickly, her heart pounding.

Jackson withdrew, pushing her gown skirting down, and quickly closed his trousers. Then he opened his arms and she went to him. They traded places at the rail so that he could lean on the sturdy bar and she could lean against him.

Cameron rested her cheek on his chest and listened as his pounding heart slowed to a steady pace. When he kissed her forehead and pushed a lock of damp hair from her cheek, she could smell the scent of their lovemaking on his fingertips and that perfume sent a trill of happiness through her.

Lifting her lashes to look into his eyes, Cameron slid her hand up to Jackson's shoulder. For once, she had nothing to say. He brushed his lips against hers in a gentle kiss and she was content.

"I'd like a room," Jackson said to the man standing behind the large, ornately carved front desk of the Three Sisters Hotel on Royal Street in New Orleans.

Cameron gazed at the elegant lobby and the winding mahogany staircase that led upward. Through arched doorways, she saw a lovely courtyard where guests were being served lemonade and sweets. It was sunset, and the fragrant, tangled magnolia trees had taken on a lovely air of grace in the fading light.

"How long will you and the lady be staying?" the man asked, with a thick Creole accent.

"I don't know. Two or three nights."

Cameron glanced at Jackson. Last night they had huddled on the deck of the paddle wheeler and talked for hours after making love. Jackson had told her his plan to save Taye. It was an impossible feat. Outrageous. But right now, they had to find Taye and get her home to Mississippi to set the events in motion.

"Certainly, sir," the clerk said.

Jackson leaned on the desk. "Could you tell me if you have a guest here by the name of Falcon Cortés?"

"I'm sorry. We do not." The clerk smiled. "Could I have your name, sir, for our records?"

Jackson frowned. "It's Captain Jackson Logan. And Mrs."

The Creole's broad forehead creased. "I am sorry, sir, what did you say your name was?"

"Captain Jackson Logan."

"How odd," the man remarked. "We already have a Captain Logan staying with us. A tall man with a petite, pretty wife. A relative?"

"Looks like we found them." Cameron smiled.

Jackson and Cameron halted at the hotel room door just down from their own. She knocked. Behind the door, they heard sounds. She recognized Taye's voice, though she couldn't hear what was being said. Falcon's voice was a low rumble.

After a long moment, the door opened a crack.

Falcon took one look at Jackson, at Cameron, and opened it to let them in.

"For a Cherokee brave, you don't hide well, friend." Jackson brushed past him.

"You know me too well," Falcon answered, stepping back to let Cameron pass.

Inside the room was a small trunk, obviously being packed. Jackson looked to Taye. "Going somewhere, Sister?"

Seeing Cameron, Taye took quick, light steps and threw herself into her sister's arms. "How did you get here so quickly? We only sent the telegram yesterday morning."

Cameron hugged Taye tightly, then drew back to look at her. "We didn't get your message, but we've come for you. Taye, there's been a reward offered for your return to Jackson, Mississippi, dead or alive." Taye paled visibly as Cameron continued. "But don't worry. Jackson has a plan." She glanced at Falcon, still unsure how she felt about him. But now knowing about Thomas's illness, she was glad there was someone else in Taye's life.

"Jackson and Thomas believe they can fix this whole terrible mess, but you have to come back to Jackson. Now." Cameron glanced at Falcon. "And *you* need to go into hiding, until this is over. After that—" She looked to Taye again. "I suppose that's up to the two of you."

"What Taye speaks is the truth," Falcon said. "We sent word to you yesterday that she would be returning to Jackson to face her accusers." He spoke slowly in the odd cadence Cameron almost found appealing after the months of hearing it. "Tell me about this plan."

Taye clutched Cameron's arms, tears filling her blue eyes as she met her sister's gaze again. "No, we can't talk about me. Not yet."

Taye suddenly looked as if she were going to dissolve

in Cameron's arms. Cameron took Taye's hand and led her toward the bed. "Taye, please don't be upset. I really think Jackson's plan will—"

"No, please. You have to listen to me." Tears ran down her lovely cheeks. "I...I need to tell you—" She hung her head. "How sorry I am for what I did. For killing Grant," she whispered.

Jackson cleared his throat. "Falcon, I've need of a cigar, perhaps some refreshment. Shall we go downstairs and leave the ladies with some privacy?"

"Just one minute, puss," Cameron said gently, giving Taye's hand a squeeze. She followed Jackson to the door and touched his sleeve. "Thank you," she whispered, her gaze searching his. "I think with a little time alone she'll be all right."

"I just want you to be happy," Jackson murmured. "It's all I've ever wanted."

There was something in the sincerity in his voice that brought up a lump in Cameron's throat, and all at once tears filled her amber eyes.

Jackson pressed a kiss to the top of her head and then followed Falcon out of the room, closing the door behind them.

Cameron returned to the bed and sat down beside her sister. She took Taye's hand in hers and rubbed it. Despite the warmth of the evening, her skin was cool and clammy. "Do you want some water?"

Taye shook her head. "No. I...I just want to tell you that I'm sorry. It wasn't out of vengeance for what Grant did to me or Mama." A sob escaped her lips. "I only pulled the trigger because he would have killed you."

Her lower lip trembled and Cameron knew that in Taye's mind's eyes, she was seeing Grant again, standing on their father's balcony, waving the pistol. Grant had raved in madness from that veranda. He had accused Taye and Cameron of ruining his life. He had accused them of stealing their father's love from him. Then he had pulled the trigger. Grant had missed Cameron by inches and had steadied the gun to fire again. Only then had Taye appeared out of the darkness and pulled the trigger.

"Oh, Taye," Cameron cried, wrapping her arms around her sister. "Never for a minute have I blamed you. He killed our father. He killed your mama as sure as if he had pulled that trigger, and he would have killed you and then me." Cameron smiled through her own tears and wiped Taye's wet cheek with her palm in a sister's loving caress. "Now I don't ever want to hear another word of this. I never blamed you. Never." She fumbled in her sleeve for her scented linen handkerchief and pressed it into Taye's hand. "Dry your tears. I'm going to run back to our room, but I'll only be a minute. I want you to hear something."

Cameron gave her hand one last reassuring squeeze and then hurried from the room. Minutes later, she returned with their father's diary.

"I told you, that is private," Taye said, sniffing as she touched the balled-up white lace handkerchief to her puffy red eyes.

"I don't care. I want you to hear this." She set down the book. "But first I'm going help you undress and we're going to climb into this bed. You look like you haven't slept in nights."

For once, Taye allowed Cameron to care for her. She stood like a child in the center of the room and let Cameron strip her down until she stood in bare feet, wearing only a thin shift.

Removing her own clothing, Cameron climbed into the lovely antique bed beside her sister and drew the mosquito netting around them. She then turned up the lamplight beside the bed and opened the diary on her lap. "Listen to this...."

Taye lay back on a pillow and folded her hands neatly across her stomach.

"Today Sukey gave birth to a girl," Cameron read aloud, *"and I cannot cease crying like an old, foolish woman. All I can do is hold her in my arms in the tiny slave cabin and touch her perfect toes, her perfect fingers. I always knew that I would have children and that I would love them. I certainly love my Grant and my Cameron. But this baby, this daughter of my flesh, was born out of love. And for this gift, I thank God Almighty. I only hope that she will grow up to experience half of the joy she has given me this night.*

"Sukey and I will call her Taye."

When Cameron looked up from the diary, tears were running down Taye's cheeks again, but these were tears of happiness.

Cameron set down the diary and blew out the light. She rolled onto her side and wrapped her arm around her sister, the way she had in the days when they were little girls at Elmwood and shared the same bed. "Go to sleep now, puss, and in the morning, everything will look brighter."

Taye's eyes drifted shut. "Don't leave me."

Cameron kissed Taye's bare shoulder. "I won't. I promise. Not tonight, and not when we return to Jackson. You're going to get through this and then you're going to live a happy life." She laid her head on the pillow, closing her eyes. "I just know it."

32

"I can't do this," Taye whispered. Her hands trembled as she slipped them into a pair of buff-colored gloves.

"Of course you can." Cameron adjusted her sister's new leghorn straw bonnet. She smoothed the pale blue grosgrain ribbon that perfectly matched the silk beneath her muslin Canezou and skirt. It also matched Taye's eyes, making her appear all the more lovely, which was exactly what Cameron had been hoping when she picked the ensemble in the first place.

Taye shook her head, worrying her lip. "I'm no actress. They'll see right through me."

"So speak as much French as possible." Cameron held her sister's flushed cheeks between her palms and gazed into her eyes. "I doubt Captain Grey speaks much French. He's from New Jersey."

Two days earlier they had arrived in Meridian, Mississippi, from New Orleans. The train and carriage rides were exhausting, but Jackson had insisted they were necessary to set up the ruse they were about to unfold. No one could know Taye had returned to Mississippi until their plan was set in motion.

Last night, Mr. Gallier had arrived in Meridian and se-

cretly met with Cameron and Jackson. This morning, Taye
and Gallier would take the noon train to Jackson. Cameron
and Jackson would return home from their trip to New Orleans by hired carriage, approaching from a different direction.

Once Taye and Gallier arrived in Jackson, they'd proceed
to The Magnolia Hotel, which was being renovated, thanks
to an ''unknown'' benefactor, where they would be the first
guests since the war. Mrs. Pierre had not even blinked when
Jackson requested she open her doors prior to her originally
planned date. And, thankfully, she had not asked any ques-
tions.

''Now you must be certain to behave as if you have
never seen the town,'' Cameron lectured Taye. ''You do
not recognize anyone, not even me.''

''I know. I know.'' Taye grabbed her sister's hands. ''I
know the plan. I pray that someone will see us get off the
train and this charade will begin. Mr. Gallier and I know
exactly what we're to say. What we're to do.''

''Good.''

Cameron tried to pull away, but Taye held fast. ''Cameron, listen to me. I want you to know that if this doesn't
work—'' Her voice broke and she pressed her rosy lips
together. ''If this doesn't work,'' she repeated firmly, ''I
want you to know it's all right. It's not your fault.''

Cameron raised Taye's slender hands and kissed them
before pulling away. ''Don't be silly. This will work.''

''Cameron.'' Jackson opened the door a crack and called
in. ''We have to go. We should not have stayed this long.''

Cameron planted a quick kiss on her sister's cheek.
''You do this and you'll have a career on the New York
stage.'' She hurried for the door. ''See you soon, puss.''

Cameron forced herself to walk slowly out the door, giving the impression of utter confidence in the plan that had been devised. Only her pounding heart indicated otherwise.

Taye smiled sweetly, her arm settled in the crook of Mr. Gallier's arm as they strolled down the street toward The Magnolia Hotel. As she walked, she tried to think of herself not as Taye Campbell, but as a young woman who lay on the floor of the Atlantic Ocean.

She and Mr. Gallier had arrived on time, had paid enterprising young men money to deliver their trunks to The Magnolia and then had left the train station on foot. Outside the station, Gallier had had to turn down two offers for hired carriages, explaining loudly, for anyone to hear, that he and his niece needed a little fresh air after their long journey. Jackson had stressed the importance of as many people as possible seeing them upon their arrival to town.

"Il fait chaud, oncle," Taye said, attempting to alter her voice slightly as Cameron had coached earlier in the week.

Mr. Gallier smiled pleasantly and patted her arm. *"Il fait plus chaud que Baton Rouge, si c'est possible."*

"Excuse me." An army officer in a blue coat crossed the street toward them.

Taye's breath caught in her throat and she had to force herself to remain calm. She was certain that the man was Captain Grey. She had never seen him—she'd been too afraid to peer down the staircase the night he'd come to arrest her—but Jackson and Cameron had described him.

"Good afternoon, sir," Gallier said, his French Creole accent seeming heavier to Taye than it had been before.

Two young privates followed the captain across the street, three steps behind him.

Grey halted in front of Taye and Gallier. "Are you Taye Campbell?" he demanded.

She drew back as if startled and stared at the army officer. "*Non.* I am Minette Dubois." She carefully accented her English words.

"This is *ma nièce,* my niece." Gallier's wide forehead crinkled. "May we help you, sir?" he asked in a self-aggrandizing way.

"You're not Taye Campbell? Sister to Cameron Campbell?" Grey asked, looking obviously confused.

Taye shook her head pressing her gloved hand to her ruffled bodice. "*Non.* I have…hmm." She looked to Gallier. "How do you say, *accompagné*—"

"Accompanied," Gallier offered.

"*Accompanied,*" Taye repeated like the dutiful student, looking back to Grey, "*mon oncle*…my uncle on his business to this town."

The officer studied her for another moment, then glanced back in the direction of the jailhouse, visible from where they stood. The two privates stood back waiting instruction. "Cabot," the captain barked.

"Sir?"

"Go back to the jailhouse. Bring that woman here."

"What woman, sir?"

Captain Grey made a sound of derision beneath his breath. "The *woman* who just walked into the jailhouse a moment ago and asked us why we hadn't arrested Miss Campbell when she was walking down the main street of town with a man in a black fedora and a dark handlebar mustache. The *woman* who said this was Taye Campbell." He motioned.

"Yes, sir."

"I'm sorry." Grey offered a half smile, but still blocked Taye and Gallier's way on the street. "My name is Captain Grey of the United States Army. I've been posted here in Jackson at the jailhouse. I believe we may have a case of mistaken identity. We're looking for a woman who matches your description. If you could just wait a moment longer, I'm sure we can clear this up."

Taye looked to Gallier. It wasn't hard to appear uncomfortable. She was shaking in her new heeled slippers. *"Oncle, je ne comprends pas. Que veulent-ils?"*

"English," the officer said tersely. "I would prefer you spoke English, ma'am, as I do not speak French."

Taye had to resist a smile. They were hoping Captain Grey would not speak French. *"Je pense qu'il marche."*

"Minette, dear," Gallier said. "The gentleman asks that we speak English and not French."

"Oui, yes," Taye said, batting her lashes at Grey. "Of course, sir. I am sorry for my rudeness."

"My niece has only recently come from France, you see," Gallier explained as scripted by Jackson the previous night. "She was tutored in English, of course, but did not have as many opportunities to practice as she would have liked before joining my wife and I here in the States, in New Orleans."

Taye smiled prettily, still holding on to Gallier's arm.

Captain Grey eyed her. "Just come from France, you say?"

"Oui. Yes," Taye corrected herself.

The three looked up to see Cabot leading Efia across the street. "Of course that's her!" Taye heard her say.

Taye fought the emotions that bubbled up inside her. She had to play the part if she was to have any chance at not being convicted of murder. Not hanging from her neck until she was dead.

"Right there—Taye Campbell," Efia repeated, pointing a finger. "Don't ya see her? I told ya she was walkin' down the street, proud as a peacock in that hat!"

Taye shifted her gaze to Gallier. His dark eyes met hers

and she felt a strange sense of calm. She could do this. She was, after all, a Campbell, wasn't she?

"*Je ne comprends*...I do not understand," Taye said in her best broken English.

"Are you sure this is Taye Campbell?" Captain Grey asked Efia.

"'Course I'm sure!" Efia spat. "Look at her. All dressed up like a white girl, but we know what color her skin really is, don't we? She's black like Mississippi mud, like the rest of us poor niggers."

Taye was taken aback by the hatred she heard in Efia's voice, hatred she didn't understand. Where had this loathing come from? And why? She and Cameron had been nothing but good to Efia and her sister Dorcas. She tightened her grip on her "uncle's" arm.

Captain Grey looked to Taye. "And you say you are not Taye Campbell?"

"*Non,*" Taye cried innocently. "I am Minette Dubois, recently come from the Sorbonne in Paris."

"This is absurd," Captain Grey muttered, rubbing his sweaty forehead.

"I don't know what she's babblin' 'bout in them Frenchy words, Capt'n," Efia cried, waving a hand. "I swear I don't. All I knows is that's her."

Efia stepped toward Taye, who drew back as if frightened by the madwoman.

Efia shook her finger. "She's the one that kilt Grant Campbell in cold blood! I saw it all."

They were beginning to attract an audience. The baker walked out of his shop, his hands covered in flour. Two ladies carrying parasols picked their way across the muddy street to see what was happening. A young boy hung his head out the window of the storefront and called down to his mother to come quick and see. A group of black men who had been standing on the corner began to migrate toward the commotion.

Captain Grey eyed the pressing crowd and assessed the situation quickly. "All right. All right." He raised both hands, stepping between the two women. "Miss, I'm sorry," he said addressing Taye. "I must ask that you accompany me to the jailhouse. Just until we can get things straightened out here."

"She is under arrest?" Mr. Gallier asked, feigning shock. "Why, this is preposterous!"

"Miss—" Grey held out his hand, indicating the direction of the jailhouse. "Please."

Taye gave Gallier a fleeting look and then released his arm. Her heart was pounding inside her chest so loudly that she feared the captain might hear it. But all she could think of was Falcon and the fact that he thought she was as brave as a Cherokee woman. To him, it was the highest compliment he could pay. And now he waited somewhere beyond the town, in hiding, until she could be released and they could be together.

"Oncle?" Taye murmured pathetically. She opened her eyes wide, trying to look like a little rabbit frightened out of his hollow.

"Tout va bien. It's all right, dear," Gallier insisted, his mustache twitching. "I will have my lawyer come to the jailhouse immediately. Surely he will be able to straighten this matter out."

Grey allowed Taye to pass him. "Your lawyer, sir?" he asked guardedly. "You have come to town with your lawyer?"

"Certainly not!" Gallier drew himself up to his full height, most indignant. "I am here in Jackson because this is where my lawyer conducts his business. Mr. Thomas

Burl is doing some work for me. He is an expert in the laws of international shipping."

Grey looked to Taye, perplexed. And perhaps still skeptical.

It was rather convenient that Mr. Gallier, from Baton Rouge, would have a lawyer in Jackson. Cameron and Jackson had argued over whether or not they should use Thomas as *Minette's* lawyer, when he was supposed to be engaged to Taye. They knew it might look suspicious. In the end, Jackson won, saying the benefit of having Thomas stand in court and say this was not his fiancé outweighed the risk of suspicion.

Taye forced herself to breathe slowly as she picked her way delicately across the muddy street at Captain Grey's side, ignoring Efia who followed them, continuing her accusations loudly so that anyone who might listen could hear her.

The men and the women on the street stared. Some knew Taye and were obviously confused. She could see it in their faces, hear it in their whispers. She kept her gaze down, pretending to know no one.

Please let this work, she prayed silently. Please, God.

"Cabot!"

"Sir?" The private hurried to catch up.

"I want you and Tattersaw to go out to Atkins' Way. Bring Captain Jackson here. Surely he can identify this woman, tell us whether or not she is his sister-in-law."

Cameron was lying on her bed on her stomach, reading to Lacy, when she heard one of the many new housemaids let Private Cabot in downstairs. Knowing for certain why he was here, though she could not hear the discussion below stair, Cameron rose to prepare to go to town.

"Finish your letters on the paper, Lacy. No ink smudges, mind you."

"But where are you going?" her charge asked. A quick study, Lacy's grammar was becoming quite good when she wanted it to be.

"I have to go to town." Cameron grabbed her straw bonnet fashioned like a man's boating hat and stood before the mirror to adjust it.

Lacy wrinkled her pretty, freckled nose. In the weeks since she had joined the household, she had put on a little weight and her cheeks had filled out. Thanks to a proper diet, tutoring and decent clothing, the young lady deep inside Lacy was beginning to emerge. With every passing day, Cameron became more convinced, despite lack of evidence, that Lacy was, indeed, her niece.

"I don't like Jackson much," Lacy said matter-of-factly.

Cameron eyed her in the reflection in the mirror. "Pity."

"Why?"

"Because he is my husband—" she skipped a beat "—and I still love him," she confessed. "And I hope that he will be the father of my children."

Lacy cut her eyes to Cameron. "You got a hot bun in the oven again, Aunt Cammy?"

"Lacy Campbell, you will not speak that way!" Cameron turned from the mirror, appearing quite stern. "You should have said, Aunty Cammy, *have you* a hot bun in the oven?"

Lacy threw herself down on the bed and laughed out loud, kicking her feet in a most unladylike manner. "You are so funny, Aunt Cammy. I love it when you tell me funnies."

Cameron smiled and leaned to kiss the back of her sweet-smelling head where her hair had been neatly plaited by Naomi that morning.

"Mrs. Logan?" Cameron heard Jackson call from downstairs. "Mrs. Logan, could you come at once?"

"I have to go," Cameron said, giving a little wave. "When you're done, you may play with Ngosi."

"Goody!" Lacy flung herself down again and reached for the book on the alphabet.

Cameron stepped out into the hall. "Yes, Captain?" she called, walking to the head of the stairs, playing the part of the good captain's wife for the benefit of the audience she knew was below. "Whatever is it?"

Jackson stood at the front door with a young army private who appeared barely old enough to be out of the nursery. "Sorry to disturb you, dear," Jackson called up, "but this young man says your sister may have been located."

Cameron grasped the rail and hurried down the steps. "Is she all right? Oh, thank heaven. I was afraid that frightful redskin had harmed her."

"Captain Grey has asked that I come to the jailhouse and identify her, and I knew you would want to come along. There seems to be some confusion," Jackson explained for the benefit of their audience.

"Of course I'll come. I was going out to Elmwood," she explained, patting the bonnet already on her head. "But I will certainly accompany you, sir."

Jackson turned to the blue-uniformed soldier. "Mrs. Logan and I will be there directly, Private."

"Yes, sir." He backed out the door, closing it behind him.

Jackson offered Cameron his arm, grinning boyishly. "Nice role-playing, Mrs. Logan. I've always thought you had an inclination toward the dramatic arts."

She took his arm, smiling slyly. "Not so bad yourself, Captain Logan."

33

"Captain Grey," Cameron cried, rushing into the jail-house ahead of Jackson. "Thank goodness you've found my sister." She lowered her beige lace parasol, fluttering a sandalwood fan. The late summer heat was oppressive in the small front room of the government building. "I feared the worst when my husband suspected Taye had been abducted by the redskin!"

Captain Grey came out of the chair behind the front desk. "Mrs. Logan." He nodded. "Captain Logan." His gaze darted to Cameron again. "I apologize. I didn't mean for you to bring Mrs. Logan into town in the heat of the day."

"The captain knew I just had to see my sister." She peered around the captain in the direction of the jail cells. "Could I see her, please?"

Looking nervous and unsure of himself, the army captain led Cameron through a doorway that could be closed off with a wooden door, as well as an iron gate. The same young private who had come to Atkins' Way stood guard at the entrance to the jail cells.

"Heavens," Cameron murmured, fluttering her fan. "My poor sister. I cannot imagine what she has been through."

Captain Grey stepped back, allowing Cameron to pass him down an aisle lined with four small cubicles, each barred with iron.

"Taye?" Cameron cried, rushing down the aisle paved in brick. "Taye, my dearest sister."

She halted in front of the only occupied jail cell. The barred door had been left open. Taye sat in a wooden chair that had obviously been brought for her from out front. The moment Cameron saw Taye, her stomach lurched, but she bit down on her lower lip and widened her eyes in surprise. "Oh, heavens. Oh...my. Who are you?"

Taye rose, looking back at Cameron with equal surprise.

"Captain, I thought you said you had found my sister?" Cameron cried.

Captain Grey approached the jail cell. "This is not your sister?"

Cameron looked at Taye again. "Well, I must say there is a slight resemblance, but—" She looked to the captain, lowering her voice and her lashes demurely. "You do realize my sister is half negra?"

Captain Grey waited.

Cameron lowered her voice even further. "This attractive young lady is obviously not of African heritage, sir."

He looked at Taye. "This is not your half sister, Cameron Campbell Logan?"

"Non." Taye fitted her small hands together. "I have never seen this woman in my life, sir."

"Jesus Christ," Captain Grey muttered under his breath. "Captain Logan." He pointed to the cell impatiently. "This is not your sister-in-law, Taye Campbell?"

Jackson stuck his head around the corner of the jail cell, glanced at Taye, then turned to the captain. "Pretty chit, but not Taye."

"May I go, then, sir?" Taye asked timidly.

Captain Grey took one look at Taye and stomped out of the jail cell room and back into the front of the jailhouse, followed by Jackson and Cameron.

As Cameron turned away from Taye, their gazes met for just an instant. Cameron didn't dare speak for fear one of the men might hear them, but she saw the love and concern in Taye's eyes.

"So you have not found my sister?" Cameron demanded at the front desk.

Captain Grey slid into his seat, mopping his wet brow with his hand. "Frankly, Mrs. Logan, I don't know who this is." He looked up at Cameron. "The woman, Efia, says that is Taye Campbell." He pointed in the direction of the jail cell.

"And you would believe a woman from J Town over me? Why, Captain Grey, do you not know who I am? Who my father was?"

"I'm sorry," Grey said, directing his comments to Jackson. "I'll get to the bottom of this. I apologize for bringing you all the way here."

"That's quite all right, Captain. I understand you're doing what is required of you." Jackson replaced his hat. "You will continue to look for my sister-in-law. We fear the worst with Mr. Cortés missing as well." He eyed him, man to man. "You understand?"

"Perfectly." Grey nodded. "Thank you again." He was now obviously anxious to get rid of them. "If I hear anything, Captain, I'll let you know."

With perfect timing, Thomas walked in the jailhouse door with Mr. Gallier just as Jackson and Cameron were going out.

"Oh, Thomas," Cameron exclaimed, pulling a handkerchief from inside her sleeve. "There is no need for you to come in. It's not our Taye."

"Of course it is not this *Taye,*" Gallier blustered. "That is my niece being held unrightfully."

Thomas leaned to kiss Cameron's cheek, and she could not help noticing how thin and frail he now appeared, how pale his skin was. Just seeing him nearly brought tears to her eyes. She blinked and looked to Jackson, thrusting her hand at him. "Suddenly I'm not feeling well, Captain."

"I'm sorry," Thomas apologized, stepping back to let Jackson take Cameron's arm and lead her outside. "Please feel free to take her down the street to my offices. My assistant can get you something cool to drink. Perhaps Mrs. Logan just needs to sit down."

Cameron allowed Jackson to lead her out of the jailhouse and down the street. "You ought to be ashamed of your-self," Jackson teased in her ear. "You're going to drive poor Captain Grey to drink."

"I don't care," Cameron whispered. "So long as he sets Taye free first."

"Miss Dubois," Taye heard Thomas call as he entered the rear of the jailhouse.

She rose from her chair to greet Thomas and bobbed a slight curtsy.

"My lawyer," Mr. Gallier said, introducing him to Taye. "Mr. Thomas Burl. And he assures me, dear heart, that he can straighten this matter out within hours."

"Oh, I do hope so, *oncle,*" Taye murmured for the ben-efit of Captain Grey and the private standing inside the cell room.

Thomas turned to the captain. "I should like to see my client alone," he said sternly.

Grey looked as if he were going to protest, then threw up a hand. "Certainly, Mr. Burl. Take all the time you like.

Judge Mortimer isn't in town, but I understand he will return within the week.''

"Then you will be holding my client until then?"

"She— Miss Campbell," he corrected himself, "has been charged with murder. I don't know who is going to sort this mess out, but frankly it's not up to me, sir." He stepped into the front office behind the soldier and closed the solid door soundly.

It wasn't until Taye heard the door close that she breathed a sigh of relief. "Oh, Thomas," she whispered. She crossed the couple of feet between them and threw her arms around him. He turned his face away and she stepped back, afraid she might cry. "You have every right to be angry with me, to hate me," she whispered. "But please, let me—"

"Mr. Gallier, this is awkward," Thomas said stiffly. "Would you mind giving us some privacy?"

"Of course." He tipped his hat, backing out of the cell. "I will wait by the door to be certain no one comes through or is listening."

Taye waited until Gallier disappeared around the corner before speaking softly. "Thomas—"

"We do not have long," Thomas interrupted.

"But I have to tell you—"

He grabbed both her hands, meeting her gaze with his warm brown eyes. "Taye, I release you."

"What?" She searched his familiar face for meaning.

"I release you from our engagement to be married. When this is over, you understand you must go far from here, don't you?"

She pressed her lips together, fighting tears, and nodded.

"You must go far from here to a place where you'll be safe. Change your name and pass as a Frenchwoman or a Creole. Become someone else. Mr. Gallier has even made the kind offer to allow you to use his dead niece's name. I want you to find a place where life will be easier for you. I fear it will be too long before the South is prepared to accept you.'' He glanced down and then up at her again. "You should go with him."

Taye knew, of course, who he meant. Falcon. She felt her chest constrict with a mixture of pride and pain. Thomas did love her, just not in the way she needed to be loved. "Oh, Thomas, dear Thomas, I didn't mean for this to happen."

"We cannot control who we fall in love with." He offered a brave smile. "Besides, you and I were not suited for marriage, and we both realized that a while ago, didn't we?"

Taye wanted to argue, but couldn't; he was right. The truth just hurt.

"Now," Thomas said, moving on. "You know the plan. I had not anticipated the judge being out of town. I'm sorry, but you may have to spend the night here. I don't think Captain Grey believes Efia, but he's smart enough to realize what a coincidence we have here. He's not making any decision that will exile him to some wilderness fort in the western territories, fighting Indians."

"It's all right," she said quietly. "I'm just thankful you thought of this."

"Me?" Thomas gave a laugh. "I could never come up with such a scheme. Only Jackson could fabricate such a ruse."

"So you think it will work?"

"I do, particularly when Mr. Gallier comes up with his documents and the painting of his niece, Minette, in his pocket watch."

"But this is absurd," she murmured, still not quite believing. "How can you prove that I am not who I am?"

"It is the way the American justice system works. The authorities must prove that you are Taye Campbell."

"And if I'm Mr. Gallier's niece, then what of Taye Campbell? Won't the law keep looking for her?"

"Jackson has great influence. He assures me that, in time, he can convince the authorities that she is dead. Leave that to us, Taye. Let us—" Thomas began to cough and pulled his handkerchief from inside his coat.

Taye stood and watched as his thin body was racked with spasms.

"I'm sorry," Thomas said hoarsely when at last the fit subsided. He wiped his mouth with the handkerchief, folded it and wiped his mouth again.

That was when Taye saw the specks of blood. "Thomas!" She tried to catch his hand, to see the blood, but he stuffed the handkerchief back inside his coat. "You're ill," she murmured, tears filling her eyes. "Seriously ill."

He hung his head for a moment. When he spoke at last, he did not look at her. "I'm sorry. I should have told you."

Taye knew the symptoms. There were many illnesses that could cause violent coughing fits, but only one she knew of where the patient coughed up blood. Consumption. "Oh, Thomas," was all she could say.

"I just—" he shook his head "—didn't have the nerve."

"Have you seen a surgeon? The apothecary?"

He lifted his head at last. "There is nothing that can be done, and you know it. So you see, this all works out for the best. I could not have married you anyway."

Taye threw herself at him, and he tried to step back.

"No, you mustn't."

"I mustn't what?" she said through tears. "Hug an old friend?" She pressed her face into his coat and breathed deeply, trying to set the scent of him permanently to her memory.

His hand brushed her back and then he carefully extricated himself from Taye's arms. "I must go. I should talk to Gallier, and Jackson has taken Cameron to my office. I need to send them home to Atkins' Way so that they do not appear too interested in Minette Dubois's fate."

Taye nodded, blotting her tears with her own embroidered handkerchief. "I wish I knew how I could thank you, Thomas. Not just for this, but for all you've been for me, for Cameron, for my father."

His brown-eyed gaze met hers. "Smile for me," he murmured.

She smiled, though she did not feel like smiling.

"That's thanks enough," he said, and then he was gone.

"Not hungry?" Jackson asked.

Cameron shook her head and pushed her plate away. She had ordered a light supper out on the veranda, hoping there might be a cool breeze, but there wasn't. The night air was stale and the heat still oppressive.

Jackson had removed his coat and rolled up his sleeves. Cameron had kicked off her slippers and stockings and left them upstairs, shocking even Lacy who had had an early supper and gone to bed. "No, I'm not hungry," Cameron said, reaching for her glass of water in which a precious chunk of ice bobbed.

Jackson had somehow managed to acquire an entire wagon full of ice packed in sawdust, which had been placed in the belowground icehouse and covered with more sawdust. He could not have brought Cameron a better gift if he had presented her with diamonds and emeralds.

She sipped her water, enjoying the coolness of the ice

on the tip of her tongue. "You think this is really going to work?" she asked quietly.

"Stop worrying. It's going to work." Jackson pushed his own plate aside, the food only half eaten. "The judge will return, look at the evidence and release Taye."

"And then what?" She lifted her gaze to see Jackson watching her in the candlelight.

"Then she'll have to leave." He paused, his tone surprisingly tender. "But you knew that, didn't you? And Taye knew that when she made the choice to return rather than just keep running with Falcon."

Tears came suddenly and unexpectedly to Cameron's eyes. By her calculations, she had become pregnant the night Jackson returned home, only a little more than two weeks ago. Her monthly was only a few days late, and yet she could tell already by the changes in her emotions that she did, indeed, carry a child again.

"Ah, Cam," Jackson murmured. He reached out to her with both arms and she allowed him to draw her in. She curled up in his lap, not caring how hot it was, just needing to feel his touch.

"She wants to go with him, you know," she said, laying her cheek on Jackson's shoulder.

He rubbed her arm. "That's not the same thing as wanting to leave you."

"I'm going to miss her."

"Of course you are. But you have Elmwood," he reminded her. "And Lacy," he added.

Surprised, she looked up into his eyes. "Does that mean she can stay?"

He didn't answer but she knew his silence was as close as she would get to his approval.

"I really think she is Grant's daughter," she said, tracing his collarbone with her finger. "I can't really explain it.

Sometimes it's just the way she speaks, or the way she looks at me.''

He sighed. ''Our household has gotten so big, what's one more bad-tempered woman?''

She smiled up at him. ''So you don't dislike her anymore?''

''I never disliked her—she's just a child. She's the one who hates me.'' He paused as if he wanted to say something more.

''And?''

''And—'' he continued, ''I have to confess, I *was* a little concerned about how much of your time she would take.''

Cameron couldn't resist a smile as she looked down at him. Just when she thought she knew everything there was to know about this man, she learned something new. It had never occurred to her that he might be insecure in her love for him. ''You were jealous of that little measly girl?''

''Of course I wasn't jealous.''

She laughed and kissed his mouth. ''I never meant to make you think she was more important—that anything was more important than you,'' she dared, thinking of Elmwood. ''It was just that you came home to Baltimore and started ordering me around, telling me what I could and couldn't do, after having been gone so long.''

He tucked a lock of her damp hair behind her ear. ''Maybe Naomi and Taye were right. Maybe it does take some time to adjust to married life.''

Cameron thought about her secret. She wanted to tell him, but she was afraid. What if she started bleeding? What if it wasn't true? She had to wait a few more days.

Cameron sat up and reached for her cold water. When she took a sip, a little dribbled down her chin. Jackson caught the drop of water with his finger and then eased it down her throat. She arched her neck; the cold felt delicious on her hot skin.

"Oh," she whispered. "I think I could bathe in a glass of ice water, right now."

He took the glass from her hand, took a sip and then pressed his mouth to hers. When she parted her lips, cool water passed from his mouth to hers. She moaned with pleasure as their tongues met.

Jackson dipped his fingers into the glass and dripped water between her breasts. Cameron laughed and threw her head back, giving him perfect access to her damp bosom. Jackson accepted the invitation and leaned forward to kiss her cool, wet skin with his hot mouth.

"Mmm," Cameron groaned. "That's nice."

They kissed again as he fished the chunk of ice from her glass and drew it down her cheek, down her neck to the valley between her breasts. The hard, frozen ice against her hot, prickly skin sent shivers of pleasure through her.

"Jackson." She looped her arms around his neck. "Do you think we should retire to our bedchamber?"

"I was wondering how I might gain access again."

"You just had to ask."

He kissed her lips once more and then eased her out of his lap so that he could stand. He dropped the ice cube back into the water glass with a splash. "Should I bring my ice with me?"

She padded barefoot across the veranda, beckoning him inside. "Oh, most definitely, Captain." She lifted her lashes to meet his gaze, her amber eyes glimmering in the candlelight. "Most definitely."

34

Three days later, Cameron woke to the sound of the bedchamber door. Opening her eyes, she saw Jackson, his face lit with hazy morning sunlight, entering the room, carrying a tray laden with a tea service, biscuits and jam.

She smiled up at him as she stretched stark naked atop the bedcovers. It had been too hot the last few nights to wear a stitch of clothing, and the thought of a coverlet was suffocating. "Good morning," she called brightly, elated to have him in her bedchamber again.

Jackson grinned back, closing the door behind him with his foot. This morning he wore canvas trousers and a simple rough-weave cotton shirt, the sleeves cut off halfway down to reveal his muscular bare arms. He must have just bathed because his hair was darker than usual and slicked back in a club at his neck. "Good morning."

"You working this morning?" she asked, indicating the casual clothing. The simple garb made him look younger and far more carefree than a man of his age and responsibilities.

"I was out in the stable. One of the horses had colic."

She immediately sat up with concern. "Should I dress? I can come out and—"

"No, no, the mare's fine. She's up and walking, eating again. I think she became dehydrated in the heat."

Cameron eased back on the pillows in relief.

Jackson set the tray down over her lap. "Sugar in your tea this morning?"

She nodded. The moment she'd lifted her head from the pillow, her head had begun to swim and her stomach had begun to protest. The sugar seemed to soothe both. "It was kind of you to bring this, but Patsy could have done it."

"I know, but I wanted to." He poured tea from the bone china pot into the delicate cup as if he were an old hand at it.

Realizing she was still unclothed, Cameron laid her hand over his to move him aside. "I should get up and dress in something first."

He sat down on the edge of the bed, effectively pinning her in. "I like you much better like this." Again, that boyish grin, the one she had fallen for so many years ago.

"You ought to be ashamed of yourself, making such lewd remarks in the light of day," she half chastised, reveling in his attention. Since he had returned from Washington, things had been so much better between them. They still had not spoken of her miscarriage, but so much tension had eased between them that Cameron was hopeful. Perhaps when this awful predicament with Taye was over, she and Jackson could see their way through to some kind of truce. Perhaps they could even start again and erase the memory of the last few months.

Jackson took one of the biscuits from the tray and spread strawberry preserves on it. "Cam, I need to talk to you."

The tone of his voice made her immediately suspicious. She reached for the teacup, looking up at him. Waiting.

"I have to go to Memphis tonight."

She set down the cup without tasting it. Her stomach had been queasy since the moment she had opened her eyes, but now it was churning. "Why?" she asked softly, not looking him in the eye.

"I can't tell you."

And just like that, the tenderness she felt for Jackson only moments ago slipped away and she was angry with him again. "Of course you can't."

"Cam, you have to believe me when I tell you that this is it. Once this mission is complete, I will hand Secretary of State Seward my resignation. But Falcon sent word to me this morning that he has intercepted a message. It's the lucky break we've been waiting for and I have to go. Now."

"You have to go now? What about Taye?" she flared. "The judge is finally expected back in town today, and Thomas thinks there may be a decision tomorrow or the next day. You can't leave us now. You can't." She meant he couldn't leave *her,* but she couldn't say it. She was afraid to tell Jackson just how much she needed him right now. How vulnerable she felt.

"I'm not *leaving* you," Jackson said firmly. "I'll only be gone a few days. If there was any way I could stay here, I would. But this matter must be dealt with."

"And you won't tell me what?"

"It's not a matter of *won't,* it's *can't.*" He was talking in his captain's voice now. All business, no emotion.

The thought of Jackson leaving now was almost more than she could bear. Did the last few days of happiness mean nothing to him? He had actually sat down with Lacy yesterday afternoon and taught her how to play marbles. Cameron thought the girl was really too old for childish games. But Lacy had been so tickled with the marbles he had brought her, and he had been so patient with her, that Cameron wouldn't have stopped them for the world.

And they had actually talked, really talked, the way they had before the war, before they were married.

Now he was leaving her again.

"I don't want you to go, Jackson."

"And I don't want to go, Cam. Damn it, I don't want to."

He tried to take her hand, but she drew away. It was silly to be hurt, but she was.

"I have to," Jackson intoned, getting up. "I made a promise to serve the Union and the president."

"And what of your promise to me?" She pushed aside the breakfast tray and climbed out of bed, grabbing a night robe from the chair to cover herself. "What about that wedding vow you made?" Cameron didn't know why she felt so strongly, but something inside told her he shouldn't go.

Cameron tied the silk ribbon of the night robe with shaking hands, her anger building. Should she tell Jackson she thought she was pregnant again? Did she want him to stay for the baby's sake or her sake? For theirs?

"Cameron, listen to me." He followed her to the window, where she drew back the drapes to gaze out at the countryside. "This mission concerns the security of our nation. I'll explain everything when I get back. I swear to you, I will. But I truly must go and I must go now."

Her mind screamed the words and it took every ounce of control Cameron possessed not to turn around and shout at him, *If you leave now, you need not come back.* But something in the tone of his voice made her believe him. Or maybe she just wanted to believe him because she wanted to give him a second chance. Give them both a second chance. "All right," she murmured. "Go. Tend to our country. Taye and I will be fine."

He stood behind her in silence for what seemed an eternity and then she heard him turn to go. "I've made arrangements, once the judge dismisses the case, which I know he will, for Taye to simply remain at The Magnolia with Gallier until Falcon and I return," he said from the doorway. "It will look better than if she just leaves town, anyway. Then I suppose she and Falcon will make plans."

Cameron rested her hand on the windowsill, feeling light-headed.

"I'll be back as soon as I can, Cam."

Jackson kept his head down, his face obscured by a broad-rimmed black hat as he filed along the rutted lane, behind the crepe-draped casket. He was suffering in the sweltering Alabama heat, his black wool suit causing him to sweat as badly as all the others making up the pitiful procession. Even the trees along the wooded road seemed smothered by the thick, humid air. Not a breeze stirred a single leaf. The horses drawing the hearse plodded along, their hooves sinking into the sandy soil, their tails flicking too feebly to threaten the greenhead flies that swarmed around team and mourners alike, feasting hungrily on their blood.

The graveyard and the blackened remains of a brick church appeared abruptly in a dark hollow to Jackson's left. The old burial ground was surrounded by what had once been a substantial brick wall. Now the wrought-iron gates leaned crookedly, with vines and green briars clawing at fallen gaps in the enclosure. Weeds grew knee-high between the untended tombstones and precariously sagging monuments.

A stone angel and a waist-high pile of fresh dirt indicated the new grave in an area surrounded by stone pillars with the letter T carved boldly into them. Here, someone had cropped the weeds and set up a pair of rough sawhorses. Four men, including the driver of the hearse, shouldered the cherry wood coffin and carried it to the gravesite, then set the box carefully on the sawhorses and stepped back to allow the mourners to pay their last respects.

Jackson recognized Thompson, flanked by two young

women in black veils. The reports claimed he had two sisters. One of the women began to cry, and Thompson slid his arm around her waist, supporting her weight.

Jackson glanced up in the direction of the large tombstones and above-ground vaults in front of them. Though he couldn't see Falcon and the dozen men he had brought with him, he knew they were there.

Still keeping his head down, Jackson eased into the line of friends and relatives saying their last farewells to Cora Thompson, beloved wife and mother. Behind him, Jackson heard soft, muffled sighs. He slid his hand inside his coat and closed his fingers over the grip of his pistol. He was directly behind Thompson now. One of the sisters kneeled, resting her hands and head on their mother's coffin, comforted by the other sister.

Jackson eased his pistol from his coat and leaned forward to speak quietly in Thompson's ear. "You can walk out of here quietly, with your dignity, or you can walk out handcuffed and shackled," he said softly. "Your choice, Captain Thompson."

The sandy-haired man in his mid-thirties stiffened as Jackson pushed the barrel of his pistol into his back. "I don't think you want to do that, sir," Thompson murmured, still looking down at his mother's coffin.

"No?" Jackson breathed.

"No," came a deep voice behind him.

Jackson felt a pressure of a gun barrel in the small of his back. A smile flickered across his face as he lifted his head to look at the tombstones twenty feet away. Falcon and three more men dressed in black stepped from behind them, rifles aimed. The man behind Jackson lowered his weapon.

"Damn," Thompson whispered. "You'd arrest a man at his mother's funeral?"

"I'd arrest a man at his own funeral." Jackson prodded Thompson with his pistol. "Now step away and take it slowly. I've got another handful of men behind those tombs and six more standing by the hearse. You behave yourself and your men can just disappear. We don't want them. We want you.''

As Thompson began to walk slowly away from the coffin, one of his sisters cried out to him, but he shook his head. "Take care of Alma," he said, indicating the other sister.

The crowd of mourners stood in quiet shock as Jackson led Thompson up the short hill to the line of carriages and the hearse.

"Where are you taking me?" Thompson asked.

"The train station. I've got a dozen soldiers to escort you to Washington, D.C., where you'll stand trial."

"I didn't betray my country," he said bitterly. "My country betrayed me."

"You'll have a turn to speak your piece." Jackson nodded to the soldier who appeared from behind the hearse. "Now, come on, I'll walk you into town. You've got a train to catch and then I'm getting the hell home."

"Wait just one minute. Let me see if I understand this," Judge Mortimer said to Thomas as he stared at the documents spread across his desk.

Taye sat beside Mr. Gallier in the judge's private chambers off the courtroom and tried to remain calm. Since the judge had not returned when first expected, Taye had spent a full week in the jailhouse. It was not so much the accommodations that had been difficult to deal with, as it was not knowing what would happen next. And now that a decision was about to be made, Taye was terrified.

"We are looking for Taye Campbell," Judge Mortimer said, "and this young lady was identified by the witness to the murder as being Taye Campbell."

"That's correct, your honor," Thomas said.

"The witness knew Miss Campbell intimately," the prosecutor explained. "The very idea that this might not be Miss Campbell is absurd, your honor."

"What is absurd," the judge said, not looking up, "is that my desk is groaning with cases, and you are wasting my time, Mr. Johnson." He shuffled through the documents once more, picking one up to read. "Mr. Gallier?"

"Sir?" Gallier stood, his hat and cane in hand.

"This is your niece, Miss Minette Dubois?" Mortimer indicated Taye with a wave of his hand.

"*Oui,* your honor."

"And not Taye Campbell?"

"With respect, *Monsieur,*" Gallier said, "I do not know this Taye Campbell. I came to Jackson to do business with my lawyer and brought my niece along so that she might see something of this fine country beyond my wife's laundry."

A smile twitched within the judge's white beard. "I once had a young female cousin come stay with us. My wife worked her until her hands bled. She was gone in a month."

Gallier chuckled as if he and the judge were old friends. "*Oui,* your honor. You understand perfectly, then."

Mortimer glanced up at Thomas and the prosecuting attorney standing before him. "Gentlemen, according to the documentation before me, and Mr. Gallier's photograph, we have no case against this woman because she is not Taye Campbell."

"But your honor," Mr. Johnson protested, "much of this so-called documentation is in French. I don't know what it says. I haven't had enough time to find a translator."

The judge peered at the young lawyer. "I speak a little French, Mr. Johnson. What is your point?"

"How do we even know these documents are official and not...falsely produced?"

The judge picked up the papers and handed them across his desk to Thomas, then peered intently at Johnson. "Young man, did you by chance know Mr. Grant Campbell?"

"No, sir, I did not."

"Then you are a fortunate man." Judge Mortimer removed his spectacles, eyeing the prosecutor. "Mr. Johnson, in questioning your witness, Miss Campbell's accuser, I find that she did not, in fact, witness the death of Grant Campbell. We do not know how he died because there was no eyewitness. Mrs. Logan reported her brother's death at the time, making no such claim of murder, as claimed by your witness."

"But your honor—"

Judge Mortimer held up one finger, silencing the lawyer. "If we have no claim but your client's that Mr. Campbell was murdered, then we have no case against Miss Taye Campbell—" he glanced at Taye "—or the lovely Miss Dubois. *Mademoiselle,*" he said in what was obviously his best French.

Taye rose and held her hands so that no one would see them shaking. *"Oui?"*

"I apologize profusely for holding you so long in the jailhouse. I hope your accommodations were not too dreadful."

Taye felt her heart skip a beat. He was going to dismiss the case against her. Praise God, he was going to set her free!

"You can go, *mademoiselle.* Please enjoy your stay in Jackson, and again, I apologize for any inconvenience we have caused."

"Merci, merci, thank you, your honor," Taye said in heavily accented English. She dipped a curtsy and accepted Gallier's arm.

Judge Mortimer eyed Mr. Johnson still seated before his

desk. "You are dismissed, sir, and in the future, let me suggest that you be more careful with the cases you bring before me. I do not appreciate my time being wasted in this manner."

Seeming to sense when to concede, the young lawyer came out of his chair, documents tucked under his arm. "Thank you, your honor. Have a good day, your honor." He hurried for the door.

Thomas, Mr. Gallier and Taye also moved toward the door, but the judge stopped them with one hand. "Please, if the three of you would remain just a moment." He waited until the heavy oak door closed behind the prosecutor. "What I'm about to say is, of course, completely off the record. If you repeat this, I will deny it and all three of you will end up behind bars for one thing or another. However, let me say this—"

Taye gripped Gallier's arm tightly.

"I do not know what took place the night Grant Campbell died, don't care to know. As far as I am concerned, it was for the best. For now, there is no accusation against Taye Campbell. She is not a wanted woman." The old judge met Taye's gaze. "But some day, in the future, God knows who might turn up making accusations, truthful or not." He looked to Thomas. "I think it would be best if Taye Campbell were not to reside in the state of Mississippi."

Thomas nodded. "We understand completely, your honor. And should...should we locate Miss Campbell, I will make that recommendation."

The judge reach for a pile of documents on his desk, effectively dismissing them. "Have a good day."

It was not until they had withdrawn from the judge's chambers that Taye, at last, breathed. "Thank you so much, Thomas," she whispered as the prosecuting attorney brushed past them in a huff.

Thomas smiled kindly at her. "I did give a good performance, didn't I?" he asked.

"That you did!" She let go of Gallier's arm and lifted on her tiptoes to kiss Thomas's cheek. "I'll be staying at The Magnolia a few more days." She cut her eyes to Gallier. "My uncle and I would like to invite you to dine with us this evening. I thought I might also invite a woman I met. She was most kind to me upon learning of my detention. A Mrs. Jackson Logan. I understand she is a family friend of yours."

Thomas's mouth twitched. "I should be honored to join you, *mademoiselle*." He took her gloved hand and made an event of bowing to kiss it. And then he was off, and Taye realized that she suddenly had a full life ahead of her again. Now she couldn't wait for it to begin.

"Fee!" Clyde barked from his rocking chair on the front porch. "Got a dang blasted soldier here lookin' fer ya. Got officer stripes and everything," he called in obvious derision.

Efia glanced up from the table where she was finishing up the little sacks Clyde had told her to sew from bigger flour and meal sacks. She didn't know what they were for; they wouldn't carry much. But she didn't ask. She knew better. At the sound of Clyde's roar, she slapped the last sack down on the table and got out of the chair. A soldier? Was that what he had said? What soldier wanted her? She told that man she met at the general store that she didn't sell tail.

"Fee!"

"I'm comin', I'm comin'," she shouted back as she stepped out onto the porch and glanced up. She was startled by who it was. "Captain Grey." She had no idea why he was here, but it couldn't be for anything good.

The army captain remained seated on his horse. He eyed

her harshly. "I just wanted you to know that we do not take kindly to false accusations."

"I...I don't understand," Efia stumbled.

"I think you do. That wasn't Taye Campbell. She's apparently either run off with or been carried off by some redskin. That woman you identified in town was an innocent bystander."

"No, it ain't true. She was lyin'," Efia protested weakly.

"Well, you can guess who the judge believed," the captain said sarcastically. He glanced at Clyde who continued to rock in his chair, a pup on each knee. He looked back to Efia who was now trembling. "And I want you to know I'll be keeping a close eye on you from now on. There've been rumors of you stealing in town."

"I ain't—"

He pointed an accusing finger, silencing her. "You make trouble for me, I can make trouble for you."

Efia pressed her lips together in fear, her knobby knees trembling. She knew now that she should not have gone to the sheriff's office. She hadn't seen Taye kill Grant Campbell. Even if she had, he deserved to be shot. Deserved worse. It had been plain mean-spirited of her to accuse Taye in front of those men. And what had it gotten her? Taye still had the blue hat. And what did Efia have? Nuthin', she thought miserably. Same thing she had had before, only now Captain Grey would have it out for her. If she got caught stealing, she knew she'd be in jail until her teeth rotted and fell from her head.

Efia just stared as the army captain rode off, then turned to go back into the shack to make something up to eat.

"What the hell's wrong with ya?" Clyde slid both pups to the floor and got out of the chair, blocking her way to the door. Clyde's tone was even nastier than usual.

"Ya run to town tellin' tales that ain't even true and bringing the soldiers to my house!"

Efia cringed. "She did kill 'im," she murmured. "I swear on my ma's grave."

Clyde's hairy arm snaked out, and he struck her hard across the cheek. "I got new things cookin' here, don't ya know that, girl? Got a way to make some serious money. I can't be havin' no soldiers stickin' their noses round my place!"

"I'm sorry," Efia whispered, hanging her head.

"Not half as sorry as you're gonna be." He grabbed one of the short plaits of hair that stuck out from her head and gave it a tug. "Now pack yer shit and get out of here!"

She looked up, tears filling her eyes, not so much because pulling her hair hurt, it had, but because she didn't want to go. She had nowhere *to* go. "Clyde, please."

"You hear me?" He let go of her hair and pulled back his leg to kick her.

She tried to step sideways out of his way, and as her foot came down, she heard one of the puppies yipe.

"You bitch!" Clyde exploded. "Ya hurt my pups, I swear to God almighty, I'll kill ya!"

Efia stumbled backward and felt the porch rail press into the small of back. As Clyde threw himself at her, she ducked, folding herself in half, and fell backward off the porch.

"Ya come here, ya little puppy stompin' bitch!" Clyde came lumbering down the steps after her.

Efia landed on her bare behind and scrambled up, pushing her flour sack dress down over her hips. Without looking in Clyde's direction, she took off.

"Come back here, ya little burnt, baked bitch!" he bellowed in rage.

Efia darted around the back of the shack, around the outhouse, into the darkening woods, and ran for her life.

35

"What do you mean you won't stay for supper?" Taye asked, taking both of Cameron's hands in hers.

"I...I'm just not feeling well," Cameron explained. "I'm going to go home."

They stood in a small parlor off of Mrs. Pierre's main dining room in The Magnolia Hotel where she was serving a small feast in celebration of Mr. Gallier's *niece* being released.

"Are you ill?" Taye pressed her cool hand to Cameron's forehead.

"Of course not." Cameron ducked away in the manner she once had when they had been children and Taye tried to mother her. "It's just that right now, the mere thought of baked quail has set my stomach on edge."

Truthfully, she felt fine, she just needed to spend some time alone. Now that the farce of holding Taye for murder was over, her relieved mind turned again to thoughts of Jackson. She regretted not being more understanding when Jackson had left on his mission, more understanding all these months. She had always been so proud of how he had served their country, proud that her husband had actually played a part in preserving the Union. And how very proud, she thought sadly, her father would have been. What had she been thinking? she wondered ruefully. Hadn't it been her father, Senator David Campbell, who had taught her by example about greater service to their country? What had made her think Jackson could walk away from his duties just because she needed him? What had made her think she was more important than the entire country? Cameron was beginning to realize how selfish she had been since Jackson returned from the war, and now that she was carrying his child again, she needed to put that selfishness aside. In the last few weeks, having Lacy to care for had brought her a strength and happiness she hadn't known could come with the responsibility of another.

Cameron looked to Taye. "My stomach is a bit upset but it's nothing that nine months shouldn't cure."

"So you're expecting again?" Taye cried in delight, throwing her arms around her sister. "Oh, Cameron, I'm so happy for you! You see, I told you everything would work out. And what did Jackson say?" Taye stepped back. "I know he must be thrilled."

Cameron lowered her gaze to the rose-embellished carpet, wishing now that she had told him before he left. "He doesn't know."

"Well, there will be plenty of time to tell him when he returns. Falcon sent word that they might be back as early as tomorrow. And then Falcon and I should go," Taye said tenderly. "Despite my new name, and Jackson's intention to lay Taye Campbell to rest as soon as possible, Thomas believes I should take the judge's advice and leave the state immediately."

"I can't bear the thought of you leaving, but I'm so happy for you." Cameron smiled bittersweetly. "Jackson says that Falcon is a good man and that he loves you and he'll take good care of you."

Taye caressed Cameron's arm, her blue eyes suddenly glowing with excitement. "We've talked of going west. He says I should see the buffalo before they're gone. And out there, things are different, people are different. It won't matter that my mother was a slave and my father was the master of a plantation." She clasped her hands wistfully. "Falcon says he will take me to see the Pacific Ocean. We're going to his father's hacienda in California Territory."

"And will you marry?"

"He's asked me," Taye admitted hesitantly. "I need to think on it, but yes, I think we'll marry."

"A toast to my niece," Mr. Gallier called from the dining room. "Where is that niece of mine, Minette?"

"A toast," Thomas echoed.

Taye glanced in the direction of the dining room and lifted on her toes to kiss Cameron's cheek. "Go home if you must, and rest. I'll see you in the morning."

"Good night," Cameron called after her.

Taye halted in the doorway and turned back. "Oh, dear. We sent Noah back to Atkins' Way. He wasn't returning until ten for you. You shouldn't ride home alone in the dark. I can have Mrs. Pierre fetch one of her male servants to escort you."

"No." Cameron waved a hand. "Then someone will have to bring him back. It's not dark out yet so I'll hurry home."

Taye waved good-night, and Cameron left the private parlor and walked into the front lobby of The Magnolia. She was just pulling on her driving gloves when a woman approached her.

"Pardon me, but aren't you Mrs. Logan?"

Cameron glanced up to see a tall, strikingly beautiful woman with rich black hair and ebony eyes, dressed in a lovely burgundy traveling gown. Cameron knew immediately that the woman was a stranger to the town, but she seemed oddly familiar.

"Yes, I'm Cameron Logan." She pulled on her other glove, still trying to put an identity to the woman's exquisite face. "What can I do for you?"

The exotic-looking woman offered her hand, which sparkled with bejeweled rings. "I'm Marie LeLaurie."

As Cameron clasped the woman's hand with her own, the name reverberated in her head. She lifted her gaze to the woman's eyes and pulled her hand away as if she had been stung. "You were at the ball in my home in Baltimore," she accused, recalling seeing her briefly talking to Jackson. Touching him.

Marie continued to smile, but it was not a smile of kindness.

LeLaurie. Cameron *knew* she had heard the name but how did she know it?

Then she remembered the two chattering gossips in the hat shop in Baltimore. The woman they had spoken of had been a Mrs. LeLaurie.

Cameron's stomach clenched. This was the woman they had claimed Jackson had been having the affair with! That lying bastard.

"You know my husband, I believe," Cameron murmured, her anger rising from the pit of her stomach upward until it made her cheeks burn.

"I do, indeed." Marie held Cameron's gaze meaningfully. "Quite well, it gives me pleasure to say."

No further explanation was needed. Cameron knew as sure as she breathed that Jackson and this woman had been involved and perhaps still were. For an instant, the pain of his betrayal was so great that she couldn't breathe. A part of her wanted to turn and run, but she was a Campbell, and Campbell women didn't run.

"Is there something you wish to say to me?" Cameron asked icily.

"Oh, no." Marie laughed merrily, her voice husky and triumphant. "I was merely passing through Mississippi and wanted to meet Captain Logan's wife face-to-face. We've been working together, you know, Jackson and I. A pity I will miss him, but I cannot stay. I have State Department business in New Orleans, but I'm certain I'll see him again soon. Very soon."

Her implication was plain; her affair with Jackson would continue.

Cameron settled her gaze on the dark beauty, her heart pounding. Here she had been chastising herself for how she had treated Jackson in the months since his return from the war, and the bastard had been cheating on her all along. Cheating on her with this...this...

"You common whore." Cameron spoke softly, her eyes flashing with anger. "How dare you?" She stepped closer to Marie LeLaurie and the woman drew back, her dark eyes wide with surprise. Obviously, she hadn't expected Cameron to respond when she confronted her.

"How dare you come here and address me!" Cameron hissed, pressing her finger to LeLaurie's collarbone. "Now let me tell you something! If you ever so much as *speak* to my husband again, I will hunt you down and rip every lovely black hair from your head! Do you understand me? Then I will go to Secretary of State Seward, and I will demand you be discharged from the government's employ and sent away in disgrace for being the lowlife whore that you are." Cameron regarded Marie with utter disgust. "And he will send you packing because he knew my father. Because Secretary Seward respects basic decency!"

"How dare you speak to me that way!"

Marie reached out and slapped Cameron on the cheek. For a moment Cameron was so shocked that she just looked at her. "Do you feel better now, Mrs. LeLaurie? Now, get the hell out of here before I truly get angry!" Cameron demanded.

Marie turned and walked up the stairs.

"Cameron! Cameron, are you all right?"

Cameron heard her sister calling from the hallway, but she couldn't bear to face her, realizing how much Taye must have heard.

Nearly blinded by anger, Cameron ducked around the front desk of the hotel lobby, through a curtain and out a rear exit to the stable yard.

"Cameron!" Taye called, running into the lobby.

"Taye, let her go." Thomas, a step behind her, closed his hand over her shoulder.

"But you heard what that horrible woman said to Cameron," she cried, looking up at Thomas. "Please tell me that wasn't that LeLaurie woman. I'll rip her hair from her head myself." She caught her breath. "Oh, heavens, I have to go to Cameron."

"Let her go, Taye," he repeated firmly. "Give her some time to be alone. To talk to you now would only make it worse," he said.

Taye wiped at her teary eyes. "You knew about this...this creature, and you didn't tell me?" she demanded.

He looked down at her, his brown eyes kind. "Marie is lying."

"This cannot entirely be fabricated. There are too many—"

"Taye," Thomas said sharply. "I am not at liberty to discuss Jackson's personal life with you, but I know for a fact that he has not been intimate with Marie since his return from the war. I suspect that is what prompted this visit in the first place.''

''Then we have to go after Cameron! We have to tell her the truth.''

''She's not going to listen to us. She's not going to listen to anyone, not right now. Give her some time and then we will go to Atkins' Way and see to her, although you know only Jackson can right this now.'' Thomas offered his arm to Taye. ''Now come, let's celebrate your freedom, Minette.''

At the hotel stables, Cameron avoided eye contact with the servants as she ordered her horses to be hitched to her carriage. Shaking inside, but holding back her tears, she waited until the two-seater was ready. Within minutes she was headed out of town.

Jackson had cheated on her. The son of a bitch had lied. Their marriage was a sham and it was over. She shook from head to toe, so angry she didn't know if she could control it.

Through waves of tears, she reached a fork in the road and contemplated which way to go.

When she left Taye, she had fully intended to return to Atkins' Way. It was getting dark, and she knew the roads weren't safe after sunset. But as she approached the road that led out of town toward Elmwood, she couldn't help herself and found the carriage turning, almost of its own accord.

God above, what was she going to do? Her marriage was over. Jackson loved another woman. Taye was leaving. And she was having a baby…alone…without her husband. How would she ever manage?

There was no place to go but Elmwood.

* * *

"All right, boys." Clyde spat a long stream of brown tobacco juice and it splattered on Buster's boot. "Listen up!"

They had ridden into the woods and were well hidden by an overgrown hedgerow that smelled of honeysuckle and something warm. Homey. It made Clyde feel good, like when he rubbed his cheek against one of his puppies' bellies.

"Are ya listenin', Buster and One Arm, or am I puttin' my boot up yer asses?" He waited a moment until all eyes were on him. "Now, here's the idea. It ain't nuthin' tricky, so's ya ought to be able to handle it."

Halfway to Elmwood, Cameron's team suddenly spooked and leaped in their traces, setting the carriage off balance and making it rock violently. She had to pull hard on the reins to keep from careening off the road. "Easy there, easy," she soothed, staring into the hedgerow they passed.

What had the horses seen to frighten them so?

As Cameron peered into the dark, she caught a flash of red out of the corner of her eye. A man running?

She whipped around, to see behind her, and her heart leaped in her chest. Another flash of movement. Another man.

The men rushed her from out of the hedgerow. Two, three, four of them, all wearing sacks over their heads with holes cut out for eyes.

Cameron screamed.

The man in the red shirt grabbed the team's harness, and the spotted mare reared in fright. The small carriage tilted precariously, and Cameron grasped the side to keep from tumbling out. When the horse landed on its front hooves again, she slapped the reins as hard as she could. "Ha!" she called, trying to force the terrified horses forward.

But men blocked the horses' path. The animals were well trained; they would never hurt a human on purpose. Another man grabbed the second horse, and Cameron snapped up the buggy whip. She cracked it over the second man's head, trying to startle him. The second time she snapped it, she caught the top of his sack-covered head with the tip of the leather whip.

The man screeched in pain.

Another man, heavy, with cutoff trousers, climbed up the carriage wheel, reaching for her.

Cameron let go of the reins and stood up, trying to find her balance. She grabbed her skirts and leaped off the other side, but as she landed, the hoop of her crinoline caught on the wheel. She fell facedown in the dry grass.

Cameron landed hard, but the ground was soft. When she hit, the air was knocked out of her, but she quickly recovered. She was on her knees, scrambling up to run when a fourth man grabbed her by her chignon, preventing her escape.

"Got 'er," he hollered. "I got the bitch, Clyde!"

Another man came around the hedgerow, pulling one of the masks over his head. "Don't call me by name!" He leaned over Cameron who had been forced to her knees. "Looks like we got us a fine pickin', first night out boys, eh?" he chuckled. "Y'all dumb asses know who we got? Miss Cameron Campbell, the senator's daughter."

"Bet they got plenty of cash to buy 'er back," someone muttered.

Cameron could smell the liquor on Clyde's breath. Liquor and sour sweat and rotting teeth. She almost gagged, but she didn't look away. She glared with hatred right into the eyeholes cut in the sack.

Clyde smiled and backed up. "Tie 'er up. Unhitch them horses, and we'll take them. Leave the carriage with my note, so they won't miss it."

The one holding her pinned to the ground by a hank of her hair jerked her to her feet and pulled a section of crude rope from the back of his pants. "Ya gonna let us have a little fun with 'er, boss?"

"This here's practically Mississippi royalty," Clyde growled. "If anyone's gettin' 'er, it's gonna be me."

Cameron winced as her captor jerked her hands behind her back to tie them. As he did, she glared at the leader thinking to herself that if Clyde raped her, she'd be the last woman he ever raped, because she'd cut off his stem at the root.

Jackson lingered in the stable at Atkins' Way after he fed his mount. The stable was quiet and somehow reassuring in the darkness.

His mission in Memphis had been successful; it had been a stroke of luck intercepting the message that Thompson's mother had died. Thompson confessed to Jackson that he and his men had planned to march on Washington. They had planned to sneak into the city in the dead of night and burn the Capitol building. It was a daring plot that Thompson knew had little chance of success. But he sure as hell would have shaken up the government.

Jackson convinced the army officers with him to let most of the Southern soldiers go after interrogating them. Jackson felt they had been punished enough by the years of war. In the end, only Thompson and a handful of his senior men were transported to Washington to stand trial for treason.

And Jackson was released from his assignment, free to return to his wife.

Because it was so late at night, he had insisted Falcon spend the night at Atkins' Way. Bedded down in the loft above the stable where no one would see him, he would be able to ride out unnoticed at first light to the safe house ten miles from town. He would wait there for instructions telling him where Taye would meet him. Then they were going west, with Taye as his wife, if she would have him. Jackson hated the thought of his friend going so far away. He might not ever see the Cherokee again. But he couldn't help but be happy for him. Falcon truly did love Taye, and the life he had to offer her was one it seemed Taye would embrace with open arms.

Jackson crossed the yard in the darkness, listening to the night sounds of crickets chirping, frogs in the nearby pond croaking. He heard the flutter of wings of a large nocturnal bird. An owl, perhaps.

At the front door, he turned the knob quietly.

"Miss Cameron! We was scared to death—" Patsy flew up out of the chair just inside the door and stared at Jackson in surprise. "Capt'n?"

Jackson's brow furrowed as he stepped into the hall and closed the heavy paneled door behind him. "Why did you think I was Mrs. Logan? It's late. Isn't she here?"

Patsy shook her head in terror. "We can't find her."

"What do you mean, you can't *find* her?" Jackson bellowed.

Patsy burst into tears.

A door opened down the servants' hall, and Naomi came bustling out, her starched petticoats rustling. "Thank Noah's Jesus yer here," she said somberly.

"What's going on?" Jackson crossed the marbled front hall to Naomi. The candelabras were still burning, despite the late hour.

"Cameron is missing. Noah jest got back from town a minute ago. He was supposed to go back to The Magnolia at ten to get 'er. They was havin' a dinner to celebrate Miss Taye bein' set free from jail. Only Taye tole Noah, she done left hours ago."

"And no one has seen her since?"

Naomi shook her head. "Noah's gettin' set to ride the road again, but he said she wasn't on the road to town. Didn't see no carriage, either."

Jackson felt a quiver of fear deep in the pit of his stomach, a fear so unsettling that for a moment he couldn't think clearly. All he could do was imagine Cameron lying on the road somewhere, injured, perhaps dying. Jackson had faced many life-and-death situations in the last couple of years, and he had certainly known trepidation, but he had never truly been afraid. Not like this.

"Capt'n," Naomi said gently, brushing her hand against his coat sleeve. "Ya hear me? I said, Noah's gettin' men together now in the kitchen. Ya want to ride out with 'em, don't ya?"

Jackson lifted his gaze to Naomi's dark, beautiful face, and he saw fear in her eyes, too. He took a deep breath. "I'll ride with them. Falcon is here. He'll go, too."

Naomi lifted a brow at the mention of the "missing" Cherokee who had supposedly kidnapped Taye, but she didn't say anything.

"And Noah said Taye was certain Cameron intended to come straight home?" Jackson asked, feeling as if he had suddenly snapped out of some kind of fugue. He strode across the hall, headed for the kitchen.

Naomi had to trot to keep up with him. "Taye told my Noah that she left the hotel 'bout seven-thirty. Said her stomach was upset, and she was goin' home to Atkins' Way to sleep."

"Her stomach was still upset?" Jackson halted and grabbed Naomi by the forearm. "She's pregnant again, isn't she?" He stared into Naomi's black eyes that were said to be able to cast spells. He believed it. "Don't lie to me, Naomi. Not about this."

She offered the barest hint of a knowing smile. "She

didn't say nuthin' to me, but she got a little girl in her arms. I read it in the bones. An' them bones never lie.''

Jackson felt as if someone were squeezing his heart in a bare hand. He grabbed Naomi by the arm and started down the hall again. ''We've got to find her, Naomi, and we've got to find her quickly.''

Behind them, Jackson heard the front door open and the sound of voices. Patsy spoke and Taye replied. Then Thomas.

''Back here,'' Jackson shouted to them. ''In the kitchen!''

Taye rushed down the servants' hall, with Thomas bringing up the rear. He coughed and had to stop to catch his breath. Taye helped Thomas into the kitchen where Noah was already gathering a group of workmen, black and white. He was organizing them so that small groups could ride in different directions. They would all take the best horses Mrs. Logan's stable had to offer.

''I want these roads scoured,'' Jackson ordered tersely, his mind flying in a thousand different directions. He wanted to think that Cameron had just taken off on one of her jaunts, like when she had left Baltimore to come to Mississippi without him. Who knows what crazy idea might run through her hard head?

But in his gut, Jackson knew differently. He *knew* she was in mortal danger...if she wasn't already dead. ''And not just main roads,'' Jackson went on, forcing himself to concentrate on the task at hand. ''Every dirt path, every field. Even the river.'' He pulled his pocket watch from his coat and checked the time. It was after eleven. ''Noah will set up a place on the edge of town where you can check in. Two men ride together at a time. No one goes out alone.''

He studied the men's faces. He looked into their eyes and saw their concern, and it did his heart good. For all of

Cameron's trying ways, she had made a positive difference in these men's lives. She had given these men jobs, a roof over their heads, food in their bellies. He could see in their eyes that they all respected her. Cared for her.

"All right," Jackson said gruffly, fearing his emotion might seep into his voice. "Let's move out."

"Wait," Noah called. "First bow yer heads, boys."

Every head in the kitchen bent. Even Naomi closed her eyes in prayer, and she swore she wasn't a Christian.

Jackson wasn't a praying man, but he closed his own eyes. As he did, he felt Taye's small hand slip into his.

"Father above," Noah said in his deep, rich voice. "Please be with these men. They're good men, all of 'em. Carry 'em swift and sure. Lead them to Miss Cameron. Keep 'er safe 'til we can bring 'er home. An' if the worse done happened, you take her straight to heaven and send who hurt her to everlastin' hell. In Christ's name we pray."

"Amen," many of the men muttered in unison.

Jackson opened his eyes, watching the men file out. He turned to Taye. "You're sure she left at seven-thirty, and you're sure she was coming here?"

She nodded and looked to be sure no one could hear her. "But there's something else I need to tell you."

"What is it?" he demanded when she hesitated. "Taye, I have to go."

"Marie LeLaurie was here."

Jackson stared at her. "Here?"

"The hotel. I don't know where she came from. Thomas said she's already gone, but she—"

"She told Cameron," he finished flatly.

"She implied that you were having an affair with her and that it would continue."

"But it isn't true!"

"You need to tell Cameron that," she whispered.

He covered his face with his hand. "If I can find her in time."

36

Taye sat on the bottom step of the grand staircase and stared into the flickering candlelight of sconces left lit on the wall. The candles had burned down to sputtering nubs and would soon go out, leaving her in darkness if she didn't get up to replace them. She shivered despite the warmth of the night. Alone in the empty front hall, the room was eerie with its tall trembling shadows and hollow echo.

Jackson, Thomas and the workmen had ridden out only fifteen minutes before and she had spotted Falcon among them. She'd wanted to run to him, but knew he needed to ride with the others, and that he would return for her. All she could do now was wait.

"She ain't come home, is she?" Lacy asked, her footsteps light on the stairs behind Taye.

"Hasn't come home," Taye corrected as a matter of habit. "No, she hasn't."

Lacy came down the stairs, looking like a much younger version of Cameron, with her wild red hair and her chin jutted out in determination. Her bare feet peeked out from the hem of her soft yellow nightgown.

"Then why we sittin' here?" Lacy asked, dropping onto the step beside Taye.

"Why are we sitting here? Why, because the men are looking for her." Taye hesitated. "Because...I don't know. I suppose because Jackson *said* to stay here."

"He ain't the boss of me." Lacy rose. "No man is ever gonna tell me what to do." She turned on her bare feet and started up the stairs again.

"Where are you going, Lacy?"

"Upstairs to get dressed and get my ridin' boots."

"You are not going anywhere, young lady!"

"I am unless you plan to tie me to a bedpost. I'm goin' to hunt for Aunt Cammy. You comin'?"

Taye contemplated the outrageous idea for only a second and then grabbed her skirts and ran up the stairs after her charge.

Jackson stood beside Cameron's abandoned carriage, the crumpled note in his hand. He was so angry that he could not speak.

Falcon stood in silence beside his friend, knowing the black mood well.

Thomas paced back and forth in the weeds, coughing and wiping his mouth. "Perhaps we should do what they say, Jackson, go back and get the cash," Thomas suggested.

"Look at this note. The bastard can't spell *her!* How long do you think she'll be safe with a man—" Jackson glanced around, noting the weeds that had been trampled and the number of hoof prints. "*Men* like that?" he demanded.

Falcon squatted in the grass beside the hedgerow and pushed at the weeds, studying the many hoof and footprints in the moonlight. Picking a set, he followed them to the roadway and glanced up thoughtfully. "Men too foolish to

even cover their tracks,'' he mused aloud as he walked to
his horse and mounted. ''We'll follow them.''

Jackson leaped into his saddle, urging his horse forward
before his boots were in the stirrups, leaving Thomas to
catch up when he could.

Taye and Lacy rode quietly toward Elmwood, cutting
across a field to avoid Noah's checkpoint. Lacy knew the
area well and seemed amazingly comfortable in the saddle.

''What if she's not at Elmwood? What if the men have
already been there and she's not there?'' Taye asked.
''Then where do we go?''

''Don't know.'' Lacy stared out into the dark, overgrown
fields, studying every movement of the trees overhead with
a keen eye. The moon had risen full in the sky, and it lit
their way like a pale white beam of lamplight. ''Mama
always said ya got to go by instink. And I'm tellin' ya, my
gut says go this way.'' Lacy pulled back on the reins, settling in her saddle. ''Hey, you see that?'' she whispered.

''What?''

Lacy eased her horse back until she was right beside
Taye. ''Right there—that ole tree?''

Taye stared hard into the darkness. ''Yes?''

''You see that limb stickin' out kinda funny from the
trunk?'' Lacy looked at Taye. ''You know any tree limbs
stick straight out of a big ole oak tree like that?''

''No, but so? It's dark. In the darkness, your mind can
play tricks on you.''

Lacy eased out of her saddle and dropped to the ground
as she dropped her reins, leaving the horse ground tied.

''Where are you going?'' Taye whispered.

Lacy lifted her thin finger to her lips as she eased slowly
across a small ditch, heading toward the oak tree.

Taye watched as Lacy moved through the darkness,

seeming to glide on the night shadows. She was nearly to the base of the oak when Taye saw sudden movement, and Lacy set off at a dead run, chasing the shadow.

"Lacy!" Taye cried, sliding off the mare just as Lacy hit the running form full force with her body and they both fell hard in the fallow field.

Taye took off at a run. "Lacy, please!" She crossed the distance between them quickly and halted, letting her skirts fall from her hands.

Lacy straddled a woman, her fist cocked back threateningly. In the moonlight, Taye could see that it was Efia.

"Where is she?" Lacy demanded.

"Where's who?" Efia struggled.

"My aunt Cammy!" Lacy drew her fist back farther.

"I don' know what yer talkin' 'bout, crazy girl. Get offen me!" Efia looked up at Taye, wild-eyed. "I don' know what she's talkin' 'bout. I swear I don'."

Lacy sat back, crossing her arms over her stomach, still keeping the slight Efia pinned to the ground. "It's the middle of the night. Ain't nobody walking alone on this road in the dark except people up to no good."

Efia shook her head emphatically. "No. It ain't like that. I...I got nowhere to go's all. I was just walkin'. I swear it."

Taye noted Efia's bare feet and the fact that she was dressed in nothing but a thin, sleeveless dress. "Miss Cameron is missing, Efia. Have you seen her?"

"M-missing? What'cha mean?"

Lacy narrowed her green Campbell eyes. "What she means is, if ya don't tell us where my aunt Cammy is, I'm gonna pound ya into the dirt!"

Efia managed to free one hand, and she drew it up to protect herself. The fear in her eyes touched Taye, even after all that Efia had done to her.

"Lacy," Taye said gently. "Let her up."

"Not 'til I pound the truth out of her," Lacy muttered, raising her fist again. "I'll make her spill what all she knows."

Taye grabbed Lacy by the shoulders and dragged her off her captive. Instead of getting up and running, Efia just lay there, streaks of tears on her dark cheeks.

"Clyde put you out, didn't he?" Taye asked.

Efia sat up, wiping her damp, dirt-streaked cheeks, and nodded.

"And you've got nowhere to go?"

Efia shook her head.

Taye only hesitated for a moment. "Get up and we'll take you back to Atkins' Way. It's not safe for you to be out here alone at this time of night."

"Ya...ya mean that?" Efia stared at Taye as if they were not speaking the same language.

"Of course I mean it." Taye couldn't bring herself to smile at the pathetic woman, but she still felt sorry for her. "Maybe we can find some work for you, at least get you something to eat and some decent clothes."

Efia kept staring at Taye as if she were a specter or maybe an angel. "Ya would do that?"

Taye nodded.

Efia looked to Lacy and then back at Taye. After a moment, she spoke haltingly. "What she talkin' 'bout? What happen to Miss Cameron?"

"We don't know." Taye offered her hand to Efia and pulled her to her feet. "She left town around seven-thirty and she was supposed to be going to Atkins' Way, but she never reached there. No one knows where she is."

Efia turned her gaze on Taye, trembling in obvious fear. "I...I got an ide' where she might be."

* * *

"You should let me go now," Cameron said, eyeing Clyde in his sack mask. "You let me go now. Let me walk out of here. Better yet, let me take my horses with me." She raised her voice; just the thought of leaving her well cared for animals with this man was abhorrent. "You do that and you just might survive the night."

Clyde tilted a crock to his lips and drank deeply.

"If you don't let me go, my husband is not just going to kill you when he gets here," Cameron went on. Honestly, she had no idea where Jackson was. Still in Alabama, for all she knew, but Clyde didn't know that.

"He's going to torture you first before he kills you," Cameron warned. "He's going to pull down your trousers and—"

"God a' mighty, woman! Don't ya ever shut the hell up?" Clyde shouted, spraying her with spittle and alcohol.

Cameron closed her eyes against the onslaught. Most of the other men were asleep or passed out drunk. If she could only get loose, she thought she had a good chance of escaping. If she could get out of the chair, she might be able to wait until Clyde fell asleep, then walk out, taking the horses with her.

And then what? Cameron wondered. If she survived the night, what was she going to do with the rest of her life?

Earlier this evening, when she'd left the hotel, she'd made up her mind to divorce Jackson. As she drove the buggy, her anger, her pain, had eaten at her until all she wanted was revenge, even at the cost of her own happiness. But then a couple of hours ago, all that had changed, changed the moment Clyde wrapped his filthy hand around her wrist. She knew then that she wanted to survive. She wanted her baby to live. She wanted Jackson. The truth was, she still loved him. If Jackson was willing to try to recover the trust and love they'd once felt for each other, if he'd give up Marie and come back to her and stay faithful, she'd have him. She was willing to take him back because she'd loved him since she was seventeen and she knew she would never love as fiercely and deeply as she did with Jackson. No other man would ever come close to being what he was to her.

Cameron wiggled her hands behind her, determined to free herself. She would not die here.

Jackson, Thomas and Falcon followed the hoofprints. According to the Cherokee, there were eight horses in all, two riderless, one carrying double.

Several miles outside the town of Jackson, the tracks led off the main road. When the search party spotted what appeared to be an abandoned farmhouse in the distance, they dismounted.

Not ten yards from where they tied their animals in the trees, Thomas began to cough. Falcon halted, concerned that if the raiders were inside, they might hear the noise. "Maybe you should go back and stay with the horses," he ventured quietly.

Thomas lowered his head to the crook of his elbow, coughing into his coat. "No," he rasped. "I want to help. I want to do this for the senator."

Jackson reached out and slid his arm around Thomas's shoulder, stunned when he realized the man was nothing but skin and bone. "You have your pistol?"

Thomas nodded, handkerchief pressed to his lips.

"You guard the horses," Jackson said firmly. "Because we're going to need them to get the hell out of here. Anyone else comes down that road, you need to holler out. You've got our backs." He released Thomas, and the younger man turned away, shoulders hunched with disappointment.

Jackson swallowed the lump in his throat and fell into step behind Falcon again.

Taye and Lacy followed the road slowly by moonlight, Efia riding double behind Lacy. When they turned off the road, Lacy insisted they dismount and leave the horses.

"Ya have to be sneaky," she whispered as they slipped through the pine trees toward the spot where Efia said there would be an old house Clyde used to store stolen goods until he could smuggle them elsewhere.

When the women heard a horse nicker in the distance, Taye turned back to Lacy. "It sounds like someone is here," she whispered, fretting with her hands. "I wonder if one of us should go back to town. Find Noah."

"I ain't goin'—"

"Am not going," Taye corrected.

Lacy turned around, planting her hands on her hips. "I am not going back to town," she said, carefully enunciating each word. "I am going to find Aunt Cammy. And if those bastards have her—"

"Lacy! Young ladies do not use such foul words."

Lacy screwed up her face. "Ladies shouldn't be in the kind of predicaments that calls fer such talk, but we're here, ain't we?"

Taye almost laughed. It was precisely the kind of retort Cameron would have made.

"All right," Taye whispered, following Lacy and Efia. "We'll try to see if Cam's here. But I'm warning you, if we find her, we're going back for the men. We're going back for a whole blessed army."

As the three women moved farther through the woods, they spotted three horses and the figure of a man leaning against a tree. They circled quietly around and continued through the woods, toward the back of the house, passing more horses, all hobbled.

"Clyde's here, all right," Efia muttered bitterly. "I can smell his stench."

As they crept closer, all was quiet, but Taye spied candlelight glowing in one of the front windows. "We should go back," she whispered. "Get the men."

"Mean bastard," Efia muttered, creeping closer. "I cooked and cleaned and washed his drawers, and what did I get?"

"Efia, no." Taye reached out to stop the young woman, but the black girl seemed in a daze as she walked closer to the house.

Taye caught Lacy's hand. "Lacy, honey. We have to go back."

"My, my, my," Cameron's voice broke the stillness of the heavy night air.

Taye and Lacy froze. Efia kept walking toward the dilapidated structure.

"I would hate to be you, come morning," Cameron taunted from inside, her voice strong. "I can't imagine walking around without your necessary parts, or having them dangling all bloody between your legs. They say a man bleeds to death...eventually."

"Did you hear me?" a male voice came from inside. "I said shut the hell up, else I'll shut you up!"

Taye heard a loud slap and cringed, knowing the man must have hit her sister. "We have to go get help," she whispered desperately.

But Lacy and Efia didn't turn back. At the sound of the man obviously striking Cameron, both women dashed across the clearing, through the opening where a back door had once hung.

Jackson and Falcon had just edged into the bushes beside

the sagging front porch when they heard a woman shriek. They'd heard Cameron berating her captor nonstop for the last five minutes, but this wasn't Cameron's cry...it was someone else.

"What the hell?" Jackson muttered.

"Efia, no!" Cameron screamed.

Jackson and Falcon leaped onto the porch, then charged through the open front door. Jackson carried a pistol in each hand, Falcon a repeating rifle.

Jackson spotted a disheveled and dirt-streaked Cameron in a chair, her arms bound behind her. A few feet away, Efia held one of the kidnappers at bay with a rusty butcher knife. It appeared to Jackson that his wife was trying to maneuver her chair behind the black woman.

Movement to the left caught Jackson's eye. A pistol barrel flashed in the doorway. He turned sideways and fired. A man slumped to the rotten floor, dead before he hit. Jackson fired again and dropped a second man, then a third.

"Cameron, get down," he yelled. She couldn't have been four yards away, yet she might have been a mile. He couldn't reach her!

Falcon's rifle boomed. The thug reaching for Taye grabbed his belly, groaned and crumpled at her feet.

"Damn ya ta hell, Clyde!" Efia lashed out and cut a deep slice in her opponent's forearm, but he reached out and seized her thin wrist, wrestling the knife from her grasp. Sneering, he plunged it into her chest.

"No!" Cameron screamed, finally pulling free from the ropes that bound her to the chair. She lunged forward, trying to catch Efia as she slid to the floor, her tattered dress blossoming scarlet.

Jackson tried again to get to his wife, but three more armed raiders poured into the farmhouse. Falcon's rifle cut down two as a lantern shattered and hot, flaming oil raced across the table.

"Cameron!" Jackson could hardly breathe for the stench of smoke, gunpowder and spilled blood.

"Jackson!" Cameron cried. "They have Lacy."

He twisted to see the form of a hooded man dragging Lacy along the floor into a back hallway. Falcon's rifle spit flame and lead. Lacy's assailant hurtled backward, struck the wall and slid to the floorboards, lifeless. Lacy crawled across the floor, sobbing and whimpering Cameron's name.

In the midst of chaos, Clyde reached Cameron, knotting his thick fingers in her hair and dragging her to her feet in front of him. "I got a knife," he warned as he drew a Bowie knife from his belt and held the twelve-inch blade against her throat. "Anyone makes a move and I kill her." Holding her against him like a shield, he backed out through the front door.

"Cam—" Jackson stepped forward involuntarily and Clyde pulled the knife across Cameron's throat. She cried out in pain.

"Back I told ya, or she's dead. Ya can kill me, but she ain't gonna make it, neither."

Blood seeped down Cameron's pale, slender neck and her petrified eyes locked on Jackson's as Clyde dragged her into the darkness.

Falcon strode soundlessly across the room. "I will go out the back and follow them. He will not see me, Jackson. Your wife will live."

"No...no..." Cameron's screams pierced the night. "Jackson!"

"Cameron!" Jackson lunged through the door to just make out a flash of Cameron's dress in the darkness. She was on her knees, two figures struggling above her. One fell to the ground, and Jackson's pistol roared, knocking the other to the ground as he fled for the woods.

"Taye!" Cameron screamed, sobbing as Jackson raced across the clearing, falling to his knees beside her.

Cameron held Thomas in her arms, Clyde's hunting knife protruding from his blood-soaked chest.

Taye appeared out of the darkness to drop to her knees at Cameron's side. "Oh, Thomas, Thomas," she sobbed.

Cameron gently lowered Thomas's head to Taye's lap. The lawyer stared sightlessly into the blue eyes he would always love.

It was midafternoon when Cameron stirred and opened her eyes. "Hey, sleepyhead."

She lifted her lashes and smiled up at Jackson. "Hey, yourself," she said sleepily. And then she closed her eyes for a moment, thinking back on the night's tragic events. "Taye?" she whispered.

"With Falcon in the garden. And you had better start calling her Minette. A death certificate will be issued for Taye within a few days. Poor girl somehow got caught up with a gang of thieves and murderers and died among them last night."

She pressed her lips together. "What about a body?"

"No one to claim poor Efia. At least now she'll have a decent burial."

"And Lacy?"

"In the kitchen entertaining Naomi's little one."

Cameron opened her eyes again, tears stinging the backs of them. "I still can't believe Thomas is dead. I can't believe he sacrificed himself for Falcon. Did he know Taye loved him?" she murmured, still not quite understanding.

"Thomas was a good man. A good man who was dying. So instead of passing away in a bed somewhere, coughing out his lungs—" Jackson reached out and tenderly swept the hair off her cheek "—he died a hero's death."

Cameron's gaze met Jackson's and he cleared his throat. "Taye told me that Marie was here."

Suddenly afraid, her amber eyes filled with tears. "Do you love her?" The words were whispered.

He shook his head, taking her hand and kissing it. "Cameron, dearest, I love you, and I'm sorry I hurt you. You have to believe me when I tell you that only once did Marie and I—" He cut off his words, gazing into her eyes. "It was two years ago, a lifetime ago, and it was wrong and I'm so damned sorry."

"Oh, Jackson," Cameron sobbed. She wrapped her arms around him and buried her face in his neck. "I'm sorry, too, so sorry for everything. Everything I've said, everything I've done that's hurt you." Tears ran down her face as she drew back to gaze into those gray eyes she loved. "I could give you a million excuses, why I've done those things, but they would still just be excuses. Please give me another chance. Give us another chance."

"Cameron," Jackson groaned, his voice filled with emotion. "You were right about so many of the things you said. I did come home to Baltimore and order you around. Then I was jealous of Lacy, of Elmwood, even of your father's diary. I'm sorry. And I swear by all that's holy, my work with the government is done. I'm a civilian once again."

Cameron was laughing and crying at the same time. "I want to go home," she whispered, resting her head on his shoulder.

"Sweetheart, it will be months before Elmwood is livable."

She tipped back her head. "No, Jackson. Home. Home to Baltimore. I don't belong here anymore, I realize that now. Our children don't belong here."

"Our children?" He touched her chin with the tip of his finger.

She smiled as she caught his hand and drew it over her belly. "I didn't want to tell you yet because I didn't want you to be disappointed. If something happened, I guess I didn't want you to blame me again."

"Blame you again?" Jackson's forehead creased. He moved their joined hands to his chest so that she could feel his heart pounding. "I never blamed you, Cam. I blamed myself."

"You? How could you have made me miscarry?"

"The way I shouted at you that day at Elmwood. The cruel things I said."

"Oh, Jackson," she groaned. "How silly we both are. I thought you blamed me. I thought that was why you wouldn't come to my bed, why you were gone so long."

"And I thought you didn't want me," he confessed.

She laughed again at her own foolishness as well as his. "Promise me that in the future we will both speak up. Ordinarily, we seem to be rather good at that."

"I'll promise if you'll promise." He brought her hand to his lips and kissed it tenderly. "Do you really want to go back to Baltimore? Because if you don't—"

She silenced him with a kiss. "You said you bought that plantation on the Chesapeake." She smiled up at him, nestling her head on his shoulder. "That sounds like a nice place to raise our son."

"Or maybe our daughter." He tipped her chin with his fingertips and brushed his mouth against hers.

"I suppose we should rise," she said against his lips. "We should talk with Taye. They need to go quickly. I'm sure Captain Grey will be here again and will want to talk to all of us."

"I don't think they'll leave until after dark. And Captain Grey is already taken care of. I told him you would be indisposed today, but that we would see him first thing tomorrow morning. He's got custody of what's left of those men and that's what he cares about.''

"Well, then.'' Cameron slid over in the bed, making room for Jackson. "Would you care to join me?''

He lifted an eyebrow boyishly. "I'm sure that I've need of a nap right now.''

"A nap was not what I had in mind, Captain Logan,'' she murmured huskily, reaching out to pull him into her arms. And as their lips touched, as she tasted him, Cameron knew deep in her heart that some fences could be mended, while others could just be left behind.

"When is the train coming?'' Lacy asked, bouncing up and down in her new slippers. "I never rid—I have never ridden a train before,'' she corrected herself.

Cameron glanced up from the wooden bench in the train station and smiled. Seeing Lacy so excited about their trip north made her feel good inside.

Taye and Falcon had been gone almost a week. They left immediately after Thomas's private funeral at Elmwood. Taye's absence had left a soreness in Cameron's heart. But she knew that her sister was safe and truly happy.

"Is it coming yet?'' Lacy asked, bouncing toward Jackson, who stood to the side with their baggage.

Cameron clutched her father's diary to her chest and smiled as Jackson reached out to tug one of Lacy's braids. There was still going to be a period of adjustment, but they seemed to finding their way with each other.

Cameron's gaze shifted to Patsy, sitting on the bench across from her, who appeared as nervous about taking the train as Lacy did excited. The young woman was returning with them to Baltimore to serve Cameron as a personal maid.

Naomi, Noah and Ngosi would remain in Mississippi.

Naomi said her bones told her the land needed her. When Jackson had gently asked Cameron what they should do about Elmwood, place it up for sale or simply board it up, Cameron had decided then and there to give the plantation to Naomi and Noah. The house, the stables, every acre. They, in turn, would divide up the land into farming plots to be leased out to freed slaves. Black families would have the opportunity to buy the land at a reasonable price, and they would have Naomi and Noah available to advise them.

Jackson had declared she was insane, but he'd then gone straight into town to begin the necessary legal paperwork.

It was odd, Cameron remembered, how easy it had been to look Naomi in the eye and tell her the land was hers. It seemed small payment for what her brother had done to Naomi, what he had done to all of Elmwood's slaves.

Smiling to herself, Cameron opened her father's diary. There were only a few entries left. They were scattered now, and sometimes months passed, even years, before David Campbell wrote again.

November 29, 1855. Went to town today to see my grand-daughter, Cameron read. Her breath caught in her throat. *She is a most delightful child. Bright, inquisitive. I only wish that Grant would be willing to take a more active part in her life. He does not understand the joy children can bring. Even children born on the wrong side of the blanket, as my Taye was.*

Cameron scanned the words, barely reading them as she skipped forward. Then, at last, there it was. She glanced up.

"Jackson! Lacy! Come here." She slid over on the bench, making room for them, one on each side of her. "Listen to this." She read from the diary.

"While my precarious position will not allow me to bring the child home, I continue to provide for her and her

mother. Once this political unrest has passed and I can retire, it is my wish to bring her home. It is my wish that Lacy take the name that is rightfully hers—Campbell."

Cameron looked over at Lacy, tears filling her eyes. A month pregnant and she could do nothing but cry. "You are my niece," she murmured.

"'Course I am," Lacy said matter-of-factly. "I told you that before, Aunt Cammy." Then she got up and walked away.

"So go ahead and say it," Jackson said from beside her. "Say it in front of everyone." He gestured good-naturedly.

Cameron closed the heavy diary on her lap and turned to look at him. "Say what?"

"That you told me so."

A smile tugged at her lips. "I could be persuaded otherwise."

"How?" He leaned close, gazing down at her, his eyes filled with a love that seemed different to Cameron than before.

"A kiss."

"One kiss as payment?"

"Just one," she whispered.

He pressed his mouth to hers. "And I was thinking at least a thousand."

Epilogue

Five Years Later
Day's End Plantation, Maryland

"Jackson, have you gone deaf?" Cameron demanded good-naturedly as she walked through the apple orchard, ducking branches, Taye's latest letter from California in her hand. The fruit trees were just beginning to blossom, and she could smell the nectar of the tiny white flowers and hear the hum of honeybees.

Jackson looked up from where he sat on a wooden bench nestled among the trees. "We're coming."

"Are we? Are we?" Cameron teased, kneeling in front of the bench to put both hands out to tickle her daughters' bellies.

The twins, seated on each side of their father, burst in wild giggles, kicking their little leather riding boots beneath their matching green riding habits.

"Mama!" red-haired Abby cried with delight.

Katie, sporting tiny red pigtails from beneath her bonnet, reached out to touch Cameron's cheeks. "Mama! We rode the ponies!"

"You did? Well, my goodness. And I missed it. After supper, you will have to ride them again so that I can see you."

Cameron tucked the letter beneath her arm and held a small hand in each of hers. For a moment she feared she was too happy to live another hour on this earth. In the last five years, her childhood dreams had not just come true. Her life with Jackson and their girls was better than she could ever have imagined.

Cameron knew now that she'd had no idea what it was to love until Naomi, visiting from Mississippi, had placed her two daughters into her arms the day they were born. Cameron had not truly known what it meant to love a man until she glanced up to see the tears in Jackson's eyes as he kneeled at her bedside in thanks.

"What have you got there, my dear?" Jackson asked.

"A letter from—" She almost said Taye, but caught herself. "Minette." Cameron released the girls to flip through the pages. She missed her sister so much, and yet she couldn't help but be happy for her. Minette and Falcon had carved a life for themselves in the wilds of California, and were doing better than anyone could have hoped. "You can read it later. She and Falcon are well, and—" she looked up, nearly bursting with excitement "—she's expecting."

Jackson grinned. "Falcon's a lucky man."

She met his gaze and was lost in their gray depths for a moment.

"Mama." Katie tugged on her mother's hand. "Is Lacy done with her studies for the day? Can she see us ride the pony, too?"

"She *is* done, and we must all be on our way. Patsy will fuss with us if we're late to the table," Cameron said, rising to her feet.

Jackson got up off the bench, helping each girl down.

"I think we should race," Katie said. She tugged on Jackson's sleeve. "Think we should race, Papa?"

"I don't know." Jackson shook his head dramatically. "Mama always beats us."

"On your mark," Abby said, thrusting one little foot forward, her skirts bunched in her hands, almost up to her waist.

"Go!" Katie squealed.

And the little girls took off across the orchard.

Cameron turned to Jackson; she couldn't stop smiling. "So how was the riding lesson? Honestly?"

"Honestly?" He slipped his arm around her waist and they followed the girls at a leisurely pace. "Well, only three tumbles between the two of them." He glanced at her, his eyes dancing. "A good day, I would say."

Cameron laughed with him, halting to turn and face him. "If your teaching skills are that fine, perhaps I should take some riding lessons from you myself?"

He wrapped his arms around her waist and pulled her against him. "Oh, I could teach you a few things, Mrs. Logan, but it wasn't the same *riding* skills I had in mind."

Cameron laughed huskily and closed her eyes as he lowered his mouth to hers.

"Mama! Papa!"

"Mama! Papa Bear!"

Suddenly they were surrounded by little red-haired girls tugging on their clothes.

"You said we was going to race!"

Jackson sighed as he let go of Cameron. "Girls, I don't think your mother wants to—"

Cameron lifted her skirts and took off, running through the orchard. "Last one to supper is an old toad!" she shouted over her shoulder.

The girls squealed with a mixture of horror and delight and trotted after her.

"Wait for me!" Jackson hollered, breaking into a run.

"You have to catch us!" Cameron cried, laughing. And the four of them raced through the orchard, headed for home and the happiness they had made there.